BY ORDER OF THE SLAVE LORD

Lord Tantos looked down at the book that listed the name, home city, and description of each captured slave. He stuck one red finger on a name, read off Tull's description, height, and weight. "This Tull Genet—Lord Atherkula informs me that this big Tcho-Pwi killed two of his sorcerers, along with one of our Crimson Knights. He suggests that we make an example of him, let him die in the cage of bones. Has he been put to death yet?"

"No," Mahkawn said, controlling his anger. "The death sentence is just, but the young slave is good, strong fighting stock. I wish him to fight in the arena, to earn the privilege of becoming Blade Kin."

"A raw slave, fresh from capture?" Tantos asked. "Dubious. I doubt you could break him. If he fights as well in the arena as he does in the wild, he will certainly win his life back. Yet I suspect that he'll remain Pwi at heart and run off the first chance he gets. I think we should execute him outright."

"No one who has read much of Wolverton's work doubts that this is a major talent."
—*The Magazine of F*
& *Scie*

Don't miss these other exciting Bantam Spectra titles:

Path of the Hero

Dave Wolverton

BANTAM BOOKS
NEW YORK • TORONTO • LONDON • SYDNEY • AUCKLAND

PATH OF THE HERO

A Bantam Spectra Book / April 1993

*SPECTRA and the portrayal of a boxed "s" are trademarks of
Bantam Books,
a division of Bantam Doubleday Dell Publishing Group, Inc.*

*All rights reserved.
Copyright © 1993 by Dave Wolverton.
Cover art copyright © 1993 by Paul Youll.
No part of this book may be reproduced or transmitted in any form
or by any means, electronic or mechanical, including photocopying,
recording, or by any information storage and retrieval system, without
permission in writing from the publisher.
For information address: Bantam Books.*

*If you purchased this book without a cover you should be aware that
this book is stolen property. It was reported as "unsold and
destroyed" to the publisher and neither the author nor the publisher
has received any payment for this "stripped book."*

ISBN 0-553-56129-4

Published simultaneously in the United States and Canada

Bantam Books are published by Bantam Books, a division of Bantam
Doubleday Dell Publishing Group, Inc. Its trademark, consisting of the
words "Bantam Books" and the portrayal of a rooster, is Registered in
U.S. Patent and Trademark Office and in other countries. Marca
Registrada. Bantam Books, 666 Fifth Avenue, New York, New York
10103.

PRINTED IN THE UNITED STATES OF AMERICA

RAD   0 9 8 7 6 5 4 3 2 1

*To Sergey Poyarkov for sharing his dream of freedom,
with special thanks to Laurel and Jonathan Langford,
and Cheryl for their thoughtful suggestions.*

Foreword

In 2866, a group of genetic paleontologists began a great work while orbiting a large moon named Anee, some 1,950 light years from their home world of Earth. Their goal was to build the galaxy's greatest terrestrial zoo by recreating extinct plants and animals from Earth.

The terraformers divided Anee into three great continents and populated each with plants and animals of a distinct period: the Jurassic, the Miocene, the Pliocene. They collected gene samples from many places: stinging insects encased in amber supplied samples of blood and tissues necessary to clone many of Earth's larger animals, such as the dinosaurs and the dire wolf; the same amber supplied pollen spores and samples of vegetation to help recreate ancient floras. The paleontologists took tissue specimens from woolly mammoths trapped in Siberian ice, and found marrow in the hip joint of a Neanderthal who had died in a peat bog 38,000 years before. Blood samples on an ancient hand ax supplied the genes necessary to recreate *Homo rex*—giant carnivorous ape men. And when the paleontologists lacked actual tissue specimens, they rebuilt ancient plants and animals protein by protein, gene by gene, basing their work on dyed samples taken from fossilized DNA, bridging the gap between predecessors and descendants.

The paleontologists set creatures born in the same

era each upon their own continent. To ensure this separation, the paleontologists created biological walls called *eco-barriers*. They gave form to great sea serpents that patrolled the oceans, eating any animal that sought to swim from one continent to the next. They filled the skies with genetically engineered dragons that hunted the pterodactyls which soared long and far over the oceans.

For 212 years the paleontologists worked above Anee in their orbiting space station—until the alien Eridani sent their Red Drones to destroy every Earth vessel that flew among the stars and forced the starfaring paleontologists to descend to their wild planet. Some paleontologists took the native Neanderthals to be their friends, and together they formed an easy alliance in exile.

Other paleontologists took the Neanderthals to be their slaves, hoping to use them to build weapons of war so that they could strike a blow against the Red Drones of the Eridani, and they became known as the Slave Lords. The Slave Lords repeatedly failed in their attempts to escape Anee, and just as a caged lion turns its thoughts from escape and begins to make itself cozy in its cage, over generations the mighty Slave Lords turned their faces from the stars and consoled themselves with physical gratification, and they turned their military might toward the pursuit of conquest, enslaving both the wild Neanderthals and all their human rivals. In the slave pens of Craal and Bashevgo men dreamed of freedom and spoke with conviction of the Okansharai, the Redeemer, who would someday break their every bond.

As the ancient starfaring humans dwindled in numbers, the technology that allowed travel between stars was forgotten by all but a few. In a last-ditch effort to maintain the ecological balance of their world, the remaining paleontologists formed the Creators—a race of sentient wormlike beings designed to synthesize DNA according to plans stored in their crystalline brains—and as Anee declined into its own Dark Ages, the Creators continued the paleontologists' work, recreating extinct life forms and trying to balance Anee's plant and animal populations.

Generations prospered and multiplied. The Slave Lords' dominion spread from sea to sea until only a few free men were left to eke out an existence in the wild. The Creators watched the humans and their captives breed and fill their land to overflowing, destroying the fragile ecosystems. In turn the Creators prepared mankind's destruction, until upon a certain night . . .

Chapter 1
The Replacement Wife

The night before Fava married Tull, she lay in the hogan beside her little sisters and could not sleep. The embers in the fireplace glowed a soft orange, and overhead she could hear wind stirring the redwoods, a sound almost as constant in Smilodon Bay as the beating of her own heart. A horned owl hooted in the distance, and Fava's father, Chaa, crept in and lay on the furs beside her.

"Oharaza ne-pila shar-e. I greatly hoped your eyes would not be tired," Chaa ventured in the soft nasal language of the Neanderthals, or Pwi, as they called themselves. He draped one strong arm over her shoulder, and Fava snuggled into him. Deep under his brows Chaa's eyes reflected the gleam of the fire, as did his orange hair and delicate lashes. As Spirit Walker for the Pwi, Chaa had a look of ageless wisdom, though he was only in his mid-thirties. He said, "You feel happy to be marrying Tull?"

"Yes," Fava said. "But, I'm restless too, like the mink. Something about Tull isn't right since he returned from Craal. . . ."

"He speaks too little?" Fava nodded, and Chaa added, "So you wish me to tell you his travails among the slavers?"

"You have Spirit Walked his life. You know what happened."

"Yet if he wishes to stay silent," Chaa said, "that is his right. When Phylomon and Scandal return from Craal, perhaps they will tell you more. Still, you've seen the scars on Tull's back from the lashes of the whip. You know some of the pain the slavers caused. Can you imagine the scars he bears on his heart? He left friends behind on that journey."

Fava frowned at the euphemism, "left friends behind." The Pwi seldom spoke of the dead, and Fava still grieved her brothers Ayuvah and Little Chaa, two of the "friends" Tull had left behind along with his first wife, the human girl Wisteria. Yet, Fava looked into her father's eyes and wondered if he could not have saved them. As a Spirit Walker, Chaa could leave his body and walk the paths of the future. Chaa could have warned Tull to take some other path into Craal.

Fava's eyes filled with tears of grief. She tried not to let Chaa see her pain, but it was too powerful, too pervasive. Chaa held her, and in the glowing firelight she saw tears in his eyes, too. "It is all right," Chaa said, "to hurt—even to hurt badly. If you were too stern to cry, I would worry about you."

"Father—you sent my brothers to die. You sacrificed them. Perhaps for mother and for everyone else in town, it is enough to know that you had reasons. But I have to know why."

"When I sent them, I saw the future truly," Chaa said. "I sent Tull to Craal to bring back sea serpents, for only he could have caught them. Without the serpents, dinosaurs would have swum over from Hotland. Thousands would have died."

"That is only a piece of truth!" Fava said. "You could have gone to Craal. You could have guided Tull, made his journey soft. You did not have to sacrifice Ayuvah and Little Chaa."

"A strong man does not become strong without bearing heavy burdens," Chaa answered.

"Then it's true!" Fava said. "You could have saved them!"

Chaa closed his eyes for a long moment, frowning. "Yes, I could have saved them for a time—a few years. But not in the end. I am a Spirit Walker, and because you are little more than a child, you think I am very powerful. 'Ah, to see the future,' you say. But I have limits. In this matter I can only witness. The trails people follow in life help make them what they are. If Tull is to walk the path of the hero, I cannot lighten his load. To do so would weaken him, and in the end he might fail because of me."

Fava said, "If you sent Tull to Craal to become strong, then do you hope that he can perform a task that you cannot?"

In the firelight Chaa's eyes gleamed wetly, and he seemed to be staring far away. In those eyes Fava saw—hope? "Yes," he whispered, "if he can free himself!"

Fava thought it an odd thing to say, for living here in the wilderness called "The Rough," Tull was already free, unlike the millions held captive by the Slave Lords of Craal and Bashevgo.

On the day that Fava married Tull, even nature cooperated. Though it was midwinter in Smilodon Bay, the sun rose above the whispering tops of the redwoods and quickly burned the night's frost from the ground in thin white vapors that rose like the pale smoke from the barbecue pits under the golden wedding tent. The Neanderthal women came from town in droves to Chaa's hogan to help dress Fava and carry all her possessions out to her wedding circle.

Fava was almost oblivious to the bustle around her. The women dressed her in cream-colored silk from South Bay, with a beautiful belt woven from the same silk, and her mother decorated Fava's shoulders with a pale green shawl that held dangling silver bells and teardrops of rose quartz. Fava's long strong legs were deco-

rated with thin black leather garters, each with a single
blue jay's feather to signify she was not yet married. The
women of town brushed out Fava's red hair, then
braided it and looped it around her forehead like a
crown. Through it all, Fava just sat basking in the
moment, overwhelmed. The Pwi had words for her feelings: *tana-zheh-amma,* joy above the mountains; *tana-
iipali-tchavsen,* joy more refreshing than spring water;
ozha-pwanda-ti, the meadow's peace. All those words
described it, and none could describe it alone. It was a
feeling so singularly beautiful that Fava did not know
whether to revel in it or to worry that it might someday
end.

Suddenly the Pwi women finished dressing Fava.
Her mother, Zhopilla, stepped back near the fireplace
to look, and the other Pwi women did the same. The
shadowed room smelled of wood smoke, and the Pwi
women circled her in their dark cotton tunics. Fava felt
intensely conscious of her own bright silks, as if she
were a clear agate on a beach covered with duller
stones. Fava folded her arms over her stomach, suddenly nervous, wishing to hide.

"*Tcho-varan, Itsa.* Don't be afraid, Little Mouse,"
Zhopilla teased in Pwi, and she smiled. "Today when
Tull sees you dressed like this, he will wonder in dismay
how he could ever have married that human girl he left
behind in Craal."

Zhopilla had mentioned the land where her children died almost casually, hiding her grief, and Fava
knew that speaking this seemingly small compliment
had cost Zhopilla much. Fava savored the words, trea-
suring them.

At noon the music of drums and pipes filled the air
outside, the drums beating in a steady sedate manner,
the reed pipes shrilling like bird calls while wooden
flutes moaned like the wind.

As the music rang, the Pwi women escorted Fava
out to sit on a dais of lion hides on a wedding pallet
whose runners were carved from two long mastodon

tusks. Along the length of the ivory, a Pwi artist had clumsily carved images of young men and women dancing. At Fava's feet were her prized possessions: a jade sculpture of a cave bear, that her dead brother had given her, combs made of silver inlaid with azurite, soft leather to make clothing for the child she hoped someday to bear. Across her lap she carried a handsomely carved short spear with a thin, wickedly curved tip. All these items seemed to Fava to radiate strong emotions, or *kwea*. When she touched the sculpture of the cave bear, she could sense the love that her brother had felt for her as he carved the thing. With her spear she had once killed a scimitar cat, and to her Neanderthal mind the spear seemed almost to whisper reassuringly of its deadly power.

As the young women carried Fava's pallet from her father's hogan, she glimpsed the wedding company down in the field by the pavilion. It seemed everyone in town was there: the humans dressed in pants and tunics and long woolen coats, while the stocky, chinless Pwi were dressed in their traditional winter tunics and furs. Uphill the men came from Tull's, carrying him upon an identical ivory pallet.

Fava tried not to stare at Tull, for his eyes shone when she looked at him, eyes the color of sunlight beating on flecks of green dying grass. With his broad shoulders and deep-red hair, he looked wild, strong—like some forest creature never meant to be held. Tull was taller than any of the Pwi in the crowd, for he had inherited height from his starfaring human ancestors. Yet from his Pwi mother he had inherited the great strength of the Neanderthals, which showed in his broad chest and thick arms. Beyond the height and a certain emotional detachment, Tull's human ancestry did not show at all. He still had the sloping forehead, the chinless face, short arms, and massive hands of a Pwi. He wore a cape of sabertooth lion hides and his bright clamshell necklaces and bracelets. He held his long spear in his right hand, and his left held a shield covered with iguanodon hide, newly painted with the emblem of the sea serpent. At his feet Tull had his own prized possessions —scattered iron coins, a gun captured from slavers in Craal, an ancient weather globe made by the Starfarers, and a box of tiny clamps and pliers that let him—even with his clumsy Neanderthal hands—contrive clocks and other delicate things. At the center of the pile sat Tull's little three-year-old brother Wayan, whom Tull had adopted as his own son, and Wayan held Tull's sword made of rare Benbow glass, a carbon-and-cesium alloy laid down in a matrix tougher than diamond.

As the Pwi sang, the young men and women sedately carried Tull and Fava to the wedding field, where white stones were arranged in a huge figure eight. Fava's possessions rested within one circle, Tull's within the other. The bearers marched around the figure eight twice, then set Fava among her possessions.

Fava's father Chaa came to begin the ceremony, and he looked pleased. He stood in the figure eight, one foot in each circle, and held out his hands as a signal for Tull and Fava to come forward.

"Our people have always feared slavery more than the lion's tooth," Chaa said. "Tull has known chains on his feet"—he nodded down at Tull's ankles where high moccasins hid the scars—"and he has felt the pain of living in bondage." Chaa's eyes looked out accusingly toward the crowd, and locked with someone. Fava did not have to look to know whom he stared at: Jenks, Tull's human father who had kept Tull chained as a child. "To keep another in bondage can be a great evil," Chaa said, "yet we Pwi seek our own bondage. It is a good thing to bind yourself to someone you care for, someone who matters. Gladly we seek *thrallzho,* the love that enslaves. Today, Tull and Fava feel this love, and have come to give themselves to one another. We shall witness this miracle."

Chaa motioned for Tull and Fava. Tull stepped forward and knelt at the edge of his circle on the figure eight. He held his palms out and up, in a beggar's ges-

ture, and Fava knelt before him. They clasped one another's wrists.

Tull spoke the words of the wedding ritual without
quavering so that his voice sounded calm and assured.
"I invite all my friends here to witness this day," he said,
looking around the group, "that I come before you
seeking shelter from loneliness. I bring all that you see
within this circle. But mostly, I bring my heart."

Fava stared into his eyes and had to concentrate to
remember the words she'd practiced a thousand times
in her imagination. "My circle, my house, is empty without you, just as I am empty without you. I offer you
shelter, until hand in hand we go to live in the House of
Dust."

Then Tull kissed her, a long slow kiss that seemed
to last days, and Fava felt peace flowing into her, flood-
ing her, so that as if in a silent place she listened to the
beating of her own heart and wished that she could hold
him forever.

Fava pulled Tull's hands, and he stepped into her
circle, and around them the Neanderthals cheered and
the children beat their drums and blew their whistles
and began dancing. The young men ran to the pavilion
and opened the barrels of green beer, unearthed the
hogs in their barbecue pit along with a great heap of
baked apples in curry. Tull and Fava took their place by
the hogs and passed out food to all comers, with Wayan
clinging to Tull's leg. As each person took a wedding
plate, they dropped a few coins in a bucket for the bride
and groom, or laid a present nearby. Tull and Fava kept
busy thanking those who wished them happiness.

Many women hugged Fava, and the afternoon became a haze—people smiling, congratulating her—moving past. One old Pwi woman who was married to a
widower hugged Fava and whispered, "Don't worry,
there is no shame in being a replacement wife." Fava
smiled, thanked her, and continued on with the next
guest.

When the guests had eaten, Tull took Fava's hand

and whispered, "It's time. Let's go." He hugged little Wayan good-bye, leaving the child in the care of Fava's parents.

Fava's mother gave her a hug and cried. Fava pulled up her dress and untied her black leather garters one by one, leaving the blue jay feathers on them, and passed the garters out to the young unmarried women. When she finished, they hurried down to the docks where a single-masted sailboat waited.

The sky was clear and the breeze light as they set sail up the narrow fjord of Smilodon Bay between the towering redwoods. White gulls and black cormorants wheeled like confetti in a whirlwind above. For years the Pwi of Smilodon Bay had honeymooned a few miles south, on a deserted atoll among the Haystack Islands. They sailed toward the island, and as the salt spray misted Fava's face while the boat leapt over waves, she thought about the wedding and the old woman calling her a "replacement wife."

Is that how Tull sees me, Fava wondered, *as a replacement for Wisteria?* Tull had not talked much about his first wife since returning from Craal, except to say that she had died in an accident when the wagon she drove rolled down a hill. Fava had thought it fortunate that Tull had managed to live without the woman. The Pwi mated for life, and if a woman died, then, unless the husband had children to care for, he would give in to his grief, refuse to eat, starve himself until he could join his wife in the House of Dust. But now Fava wondered. She did not know if Tull had refused to join his wife in death simply because he was part human, and the humans did not feel passion as deeply as the Pwi, or if he had stayed alive because perhaps he did not love Wisteria strongly. They had been married only a few weeks, and it was possible that Tull had not learned to love the girl deeply. The Pwi named many types of love—among them were *thimanozho,* "sweaty love," the desire to protect; *pwirandizho,* "love that makes people crazy," the compulsion to mate; *hechazho,* "cattle love," the herd instinct. But the strongest love was *thrallzho,* "the love that enslaves," love that bonds two people so tightly, they willingly seek the House of Dust together.

Fava's love for Tull was strong. The goddess Zhofwa had blown her kisses upon Fava, and she felt the love that enslaves for Tull, and the love that makes people crazy, and even the easy talking love.

But what did he feel for her? Would she be only a "replacement wife" for Tull, as if she were a worn coat or battered tool that was purchased out of a sense of necessity?

Fava went and lay beside Tull in the boat, setting her head in his lap, and her Neanderthal mind registered more than the heat of his body. To her, it seemed that love flowed out of him, touching her, caressing her. Yet when she looked up into his face, he seemed distant, preoccupied. Though his green eyes were set deep under his brows like those of a Pwi, Tull was half-human. *Father says that Tull needs to free himself,* Fava thought, *but from what?*

Fava often found it easy to read the thoughts of a Pwi. The furtive movements of a frightened Pwi could speak whole sentences about fear. A slight hunch of a Pwi field hand's shoulder would tell eloquently of his resignation to a task. But she found Tull to be enigmatic, often difficult to read. Fava could not imagine what ideas circled within his head, so she asked, "What do you think about?"

Tull opened his mouth as if to speak, then seemed to change the subject. "I've been thinking about building another room to the hogan," he said, "digging back into the hill the way that your father did, but now I'm not so sure. I think I would like to build a bigger house, perhaps north of town."

For a moment Fava was at a loss for words. Among her Pwi ancestors, it had always been the woman who built the hogan, and it was therefore the woman's job to decide whether it should be enlarged, what it should contain. But the Pwi of Smilodon Bay had lived near the humans for over a century, and among the humans, the home was considered the property of both husband and wife. "The hogan will be big enough for us," she said.

"It's fine for one, even two, but I never meant it for three. With Wayan there, we will always be stepping on each other's toes. We'll hardly have room to turn around, and the land I'm on doesn't offer much space to enlarge."

Fava supposed he would see the hogan as small. Tull was a big man. "We can wait until summer to build," Fava said. "If we have to squeeze tight until then, we will just have to suffer." She hugged him, leaning into him with her weight, and he turned his attention from the rudder, kissed her passionately.

Tull laughed. "I think we'll have children soon. We'll need a big house, and you should have the best. You should have a house bigger than the mayor's, more elegant than the Troutmaster's old mansion."

"We don't need a big house," Fava said. "I just want to be cozy."

Tull touched her lips with his finger. He pulled her hand to his mouth, kissed her knuckles. Fava slid a leg over him, pushed Tull back down into the boat. He held the rudder loosely and laughed. After a long slow kiss she crouched over him on her palms so that her breasts filled her dress as they dangled above his chest. "Tonight, you will sleep between my legs," Fava whispered. "Ah, *Tell-zhoka, faan!* Ah, *zhoka-pwichazai!* Tull, give me love that will give me peace! Give me the love that makes people wild!" Tull was trembling slightly. She could feel him, warm between her legs, quivering. She whispered in Pwi, "Ah, poor little mouse, to shake so badly." She grabbed his sable-red hair, a handful on each side of his temples, and pulled him up to kiss him.

He hugged her, body and soul, so that she was sure that for the moment he could think of nothing but her. Fava silently cursed the woman who had spoken the words "replacement wife," causing the worms of fear to lodge in her head.

A cool wind swept from the north that afternoon as they reached the atoll. The cabin, among fir trees on a hill, was not built for chill weather, for most Pwi couples married in late spring. So Fava set the fire while Tull made trips down to the boat to get food, clothing, and warm furs. Fava laid a bearskin out before the roaring fire, and on Tull's last trip, she stripped and wrapped herself in a new blanket.

The kwea—the sum of the emotions—of the time was strong, as if the goddess Zhofwa herself were in the room, yet Fava still felt unsure. She whispered a prayer softly, "Zhofwa, bringer of love, blow your kisses on Tull. Make him love me. Make him love me."

Outside in the bushes, she could hear little sparrows twitting and jumping, and overhead the gravitational wind sighed through the trees as Anee's largest moon, Thor, began to rise. Perspiration dotted her forehead, and Fava wiped it away. Outside, Tull was grunting and struggling with the last load. He swung the door open and stood staring, admiring, as if awed at her beauty. For one moment the look on his face was that of a little boy, then he dropped his packs and closed the door.

He came to her then, he came, as if the evening breeze carried him, trembling and uncertain, a small flame-red bird in a towering dark-green forest. Fires coursed through him, flickered in his flesh, consuming, so that he sighed dry air. *"Fava-zhoka-thrall. Fava-zhoka-Pwirandi,"* Tull said. "Fava, give me the love that enslaves. Fava, give me the love that makes people crazy."

She gazed into his eyes. "I will not be just a replacement wife for you?"

Wrapping his arms around her, Tull smiled, leaned his forehead against hers, and Fava wished intensely that she were a Spirit Walker, wished she could see into Tull's soul and know exactly what measure of love he felt for her.

"When we were children," Tull said, "I thought of

you as if you were a sister. Now I see that you will be more than a wife—you are my other self—not someone who could be replaced."

Fava stood, letting her blanket fall away, naked but for a white comb above her ear. Tull struggled out of his own clothes and let his eyes wander over her pure form, then he leaned into her, and her soft nipples brushed the hair below his chest. Tull laid his bearded cheek on her forehead, tasted her beaded perspiration. "You are the generous fruit of my long search, the only companion fit for my devotion."

Fava huddled next to him. Her fingers trembled as her hands hesitantly, inexpertly, molded around his naked waist—yet she held back. She wanted him to be the aggressor, she wanted him to place the first caress. A wise woman had once told her that "of all the body parts, the tongue is most sensual—not for the physical delights it may confer, but for the words it may speak." Fava wanted him to speak those words now, to trumpet an avowal of passion. She wanted to perfect their communion.

Fava shifted her weight, leaned into him, her light bones softly whispering in anticipation. *What need have we of words, when the whole body sings?* she wondered. *What need have we of vows, whispered to the darkness?* A touch, a sigh. Two lovers clutching on the floor can grasp far more than probing flesh, moist lips, a tumultuous wonder or a ravaging ecstasy.

His loins shivered, and Fava's shivered in answer. She licked the sweat at the hollow beneath his throat, and groaned, her voice a whisper. "You taste of passion."

He bent low, embraced her, one kiss cradled between the mounds of her breasts, one kiss placed on her heart. She could hear it beating, the stirring of a crazed animal. Tull's perspiration glistened like nectar on his bronze skin. She kissed his forehead, and it seemed to burn her lips, hotter than mulled wine, sweeter than any memory.

He carried her to the bear hide then and laid her in the writhing light next to the fire. In the dancing heat, their bodies sang in harmony.

As they lay huddled together on the bearskin the next morning, drained and yet full, a cold wind blew through the chinks in the cabin. Tull held her and yet stared away, lost in thought, his muscles clenched. Fava almost felt as if something were drawing him away, and he whispered, "I want to go where spring is. I've had too much of winter."

"South?" Fava asked. "To Hotland?"

Tull smiled. "That sounds good."

Hotland, where the ancient Starfarers had placed the dinosaurs. Both Fava and Tull had made the journey many times—young Pwi often sailed across the ocean to Hotland in the spring to hunt dinosaurs—but they had never gone alone together. It would be dangerous without a large hunting party, without the war horns and weaponry and guards. Yet the journey would be thrilling. If they sailed south for a few days, spring would be there. She imagined the lush forests of fern. The orchids would be in bloom—flame-orange, freshly minted gold. And the pteradons would be nesting in the cliffs along the beach. "Yes," she agreed, "that sounds good."

They sailed south and east to Hotland, stopping at each main river for the night, making love in Pwi hunting lodges along the way. The weather was much warmer than they expected, for thermal winds blew out of Hotland's great central desert. After four nights, they had gone farther south than either of them had ever traveled before, and if the Pwi of Fish Haven or South Bay had built hunting lodges, Tull and Fava did not find them. The weather became warmer at each successive stop, and after five days Fava felt they had gone far enough. They reached a fertile land where orchids bloomed and the air smelled rich, sweet. Gray-and-green-striped stegosaurs roamed the fields in a loose herd, and among them Fava felt safe from larger predators. It seemed a good place to play.

But the next morning Tull insisted that they go farther, and as they sailed that day, his face became taut, and he stared ahead as if driven, compelled by some force she did not understand. If Tull had been a full-blooded Pwi, Fava would have thought kwea drove him, some memory of being happy and fulfilled here in the south. Yet he was sailing into the unknown, and now Fava wondered if it were some evil kwea, perhaps a mad need to prove his courage, or perhaps he was fleeing some ugly memory from Smilodon Bay. *He must free himself,* she thought. *Perhaps that is what he struggles for.*

On the ninth day, they skirted a great herd of plesiosaurs fishing near the surface at the mouth of a wide river of blue-gray water. They sailed upstream. If it had seemed spring farther north, then here it seemed summer, for the fern trees had grown tall and thick in their foliage. Hadrosaurs with honey-yellow stripes and bright crests of plum, lemon, and robin's egg, loped along the marshy banks and dug for plants with their wide bills in the shallows, muddying the water.

The sun was just dying out on the sea when they sailed around a bend and came to the ruins of an ancient city made of huge granite blocks, stained crimson by the setting sun. The city rose up the side of a mountain in neat steps, and atop the mountain was a circle of standing statues of Neanderthals raising round shields and ancient *kutows,* double-headed war axes. Most of the statues were damaged—broken axes, missing arms or heads. Fronds of giant ferns and flowering vines obscured much of the stonework. For a long time Tull and Fava sat in the evening silence, listening to the whistling songs of frogs, the croaking of pteradons as they hunted insects above the river.

"What is this place?" Tull asked.

"I don't know." Fava studied the buildings. The stones used to build the walls were huge and rounded so that many men would have had to carry them. The roofs of the buildings had been made of logs and had rotted away. Obviously, no one had lived here for decades. The buildings were constructed in simple designs. Some doorposts had bas-relief representations of Pwi in ancient garb fighting dinosaurs or weaving baskets from palm fronds. The craftsmanship lacked the detail that humans would make with their small hands, yet it was flawless—the kind of work done by Pwi who enjoyed the kwea of their work.

Tull guided the boat to ancient stone docks, green with algae, and together they climbed up to the city. Once again Fava looked into Tull's face, and he seemed distant, driven. He'd look into one building, reject it, then look farther on, as if searching. The grass was a green carpet beneath them, covered with morning glory, and Tull nearly ran. From the river the city had looked large, but now Fava saw that it was small—twenty buildings that seemed impressive only because they were made from massive stones and all sat on the same side of the hill. As they neared the top, Fava saw that the river forked around the hill completely, so that the town was built on an island. When they reached the crest of the hill, Tull stood to catch his breath outside the circle of statues. The totem warriors were mostly broken, with lichen-splotched arms or torsos lying near the feet. Each statue would have stood thirty feet tall and measured six feet at the base. All the statues were blockish, identical, as if depicting the same warrior again and again.

Within the circle was a bed of stone with six legs carved like trees. Upper branches held the bed, while globes, as if they were worlds, also hung from the branches.

On the plain below, a hadrosaur bellowed in fear, and shortly thereafter a tyrannosaur roared to announce its kill. Fava stood for a moment, panting, then looked into Tull's eyes. His face was pale with fear.

"What frightens you? What?"

"This place," Tull said. "It feels . . . strange."

Fava shivered. She folded her arms as if to ward off

a chill, but realized that the breeze was warm. "Do you want to sleep here tonight, or should we go on?"

Tull nodded. "Let's sleep here. I'll go down and get the supplies." He sounded . . . almost eager to stay.

Fava wandered around the table, but would not touch it. "Wait," she said before he could leave. "My father told me that there are places of power for the Spirit Walker where it is easier for him to move from our world into the Land of Shapes." Fava did not doubt that this was such a place. The hair on her arms stood on end, and even the animals were silent and avoided this hilltop. "Why else would the ancient Pwi have built this temple, except as a sanctuary to take Spirit Walks?"

"I don't know," Tull answered.

"I'm afraid. My father says there are creatures in the Land of Shapes—dangerous things. I don't think we should stay."

"It's almost dark," Tull objected. "I don't think creatures from the Land of Shapes could get us. This will be good enough for one night." Fava shook and hugged herself, unsure what to answer. Tull went down to the boat, and Fava stood for a moment, studying the canary and crimson blotches of lichen on the standing statues.

When Tull reappeared carrying up the bundles moments later, they set a fire and cooked a small dinner, yet Tull would not eat. He stared into the night, up at blazing stars. As if he were a million miles away. He hardly spoke at all, and as they lay upon the stone table, cuddling, Fava realized that somehow he was farther away than ever before.

Fava rested, the granite cool against her back. The waxing moon, Thor, rose huge in its winter colors of mauve and cinnabar. Woden rose beneath it like a pale blue eye, and one of the Red Drones, the ancient warships of the Eridani, glided among the pinprick stars of heaven like a flaming comet. The shadows of the statues ringed Fava, many with *kutows* raised high in the air, as if ready to defend the ancient ruins. Down at the river the frogs whistled in the night, while Tull slept softly in her arms.

Fava closed her eyes, slowed her breathing to match Tull's. Now was a time for sleep, time for the whole world to sleep.

She dreamed that she was in a ship, lying in musty-smelling water among bundles of cloth that had somehow become tightly wound about her chest. A low groan issued through the bottom of the ship, something barely audible, easily mistaken for the creaking of timbers. But it was not the creaking of timbers. It was the call of a sea serpent—one of the great predators that the ancient starfaring humans had placed in the oceans to keep the dinosaurs from swimming over from Hotland. Yet the serpent's call was distant, so distant. In the dream Fava climbed up to the deck of the ship and looked out over an endless blue sea. Far away a great black serpent leapt into the air, its head and neck coming a hundred feet out of the water, its dorsal fins swaying like a huge fan as its bloody red gills flashed in the sunlight. Fava wondered why it was bleeding, and the serpent roared. Even from a great distance, its fishy yellow eye pierced her, as if the creature stared right into her soul.

Fava opened her eyes and bolted upright, her heart pounding, the serpent's roar still ringing her ears. In the valley below she heard a second roar, a dinosaur crying out in pain. Somehow in the dream, she realized, the two sounds had mingled. Perhaps the roar of the dinosaur had caused the dream.

Yet Tull lay beside her, tossing and moaning, talking in his sleep. "We are walls, you and I," he slurred, "meant to protect the small things of the world." He stopped speaking a moment, as if listening to a distant voice. In Craal, Tull had said, he discovered that the sea serpent was his animal guide. According to Pwi beliefs, Tull would now become like the serpent. Fava had not considered what that might mean. The serpent was restless, vigilant, fierce. Tull shared those traits. Tull spoke in his sleep, "Come to me. I can heal you."

Fava lay back and closed her eyes, listened to the sound of her heart beating, to the sound of Tull's heart, the air drawing in and out of their lungs, the whistling of frogs—now grown quite rare—and the roaring and bellows of dinosaurs among the ferns down on the plains below. The sounds all seemed unnaturally clear, and she felt almost as if she could move out of her body, draw closer to each sound. She listened to the faraway dinosaurs—the grunting and cracking of bones as a pack of allosaurs fed upon some large beast, the distant call of a giant quetzalcoatlus as it glided through the sky hunting for carrion under the moonlight, the buzz of cicadas. And there, in the distance, very faint, she could hear a man running—crashing through the brush, panting, groaning in weariness. By the sounds of it, three men chased him, and the man lunged ahead heedlessly. One of the pursuers cried out in Pwi—"Get him! Stop him!" And Fava bolted upright.

Everything was quiet, and she realized she had had another bad dream. Yet even waking, she could hear the faint echoing of pursuit in her head. And Fava could not put off the feeling that a stranger was fleeing toward her. Not since childhood had Fava been bothered by such dreams.

The night air had cooled the stone table. Tull had pulled their furs up to cover his face, leaving Fava's feet exposed. She wiggled her toes, decided to put more wood on the fire. She got out from under the furs and tiptoed about, placed the wood on the fire, then sat on a stone with her feet next to the flames. The night air seemed to close about her. A high, thin haze obscured the stars, and the shadows of the totem warriors hovered above her.

Closing her eyes, Fava hung her head to rest. The bad dreams had come so thick and fast, she felt as if she had not slept at all. She got a fur from the pack and wrapped it around her and dozed the night away. When she woke in the morning, she recalled only one more dream: An old Pwi woman in black robes was putting moccasins on Tull in the darkness, and the moccasins glowed like the sun, brighter and brighter, until finally she had to close her eyes against them. When she woke, Fava looked for the moccasins by Tull's feet, half-expecting to see them. The dream filled Fava with foreboding, for the moccasins were the symbol of the Spirit Walker.

As they ate a breakfast of boiled oats with cinnamon, Fava asked, "Did you dream last night? All night I was troubled by dreams."

Tull hesitated. "No."

"Are you sure? I heard you talking in your sleep. You said you could heal someone."

Tull stopped eating, gave her a queer look, and considered. "I don't remember dreaming anything."

The trip home seemed hurried to Fava. Tull sailed north early in the morning and stopped at sunset six days in a row, so that on the sixth night they slept in the cabin at the Haystack Islands. Tull seemed to want to go farther that night, all the way to town, but a bank of clouds came in and their light failed. They slept soundly, for the thick clouds kept the night warm.

At dawn as they lay in the cabin, Fava heard a guttural cry, and her eyes sprang open. She ran to the door and looked down into the forest. The clouds above had dissipated, showing a pale blue sky, but the ocean was covered in fog, as was most of the forest. She heard the cry again, and the sound of branches cracking among the firs downhill.

"Tull! Hurry!" Fava shouted. Tull leapt up, grabbed his gun, and came to the door.

A Neanderthal was running toward them uphill in the deep ferns, his legs pumping mightily, weighed down by a heavy pack and thick winter furs that flapped as he moved. He was gasping for breath, his head rolling as he struggled uphill, and he carried a longspear wrapped with dull red cloth, feathers tied around it. Fava could see that he was an old man with graying hair, fatigued, ready to drop. He shouted incoherently and fell in a bed of ferns.

They watched where he lay, saw him struggle, then drop, resting his head on his forearm and panting.

Through the silver mist downhill, from between the black trees, they saw the pursuers, two men all in crimson, startling red body armor of leather, brilliant red capes—yet their faces were black, hidden behind iron masks. The men ran uphill in step, as if they were a single entity.

"Blade Kin!" Tull whispered, and there was a look on Tull's face that Fava had never seen on a person before: a look of such feral hatred, it left no doubt that he would attack, yet Tull restrained himself, like a hunting dog awaiting its master's orders before treeing a bear.

The fallen Neanderthal raised on his hands, looked back, gave a wordless cry, lunged toward the cabin.

At first Fava thought that the Neanderthal had seen them and was calling for help, but then she realized that he was running blindly up a game trail, that his eyes did not focus on them, for the cabin was concealed between standing stones and had blackberry bushes trailing up the sides of it. The old man rushed past the cabin, sweat pouring from his forehead, terror in his face, blue eyes wide with fear, his long red hair in tight braids wrapped with green cloth. He stumbled past, clipping the branches of a tree. Tattoos of ownership were on his left hand, and he clutched a long circular map case made of stained wood.

He rushed to a fallen tree, turned, and leveled his spear.

The armored Blade Kin charged uphill, seemingly unfatigued, fluid in their movements. Tull stepped forward, pulled up his gun and fired. One Blade Kin was lifted from his feet, blood spraying from his face mask, and slid backward in the ferns.

The other warrior hesitated only a moment before

reaching into his belt for a long-barreled pistol. Tull dropped his rifle, unable to reload, then pulled his sword of Benbow glass and leapt downhill, gambling that he could attack before the slaver drew. He shouted, and the Blade Kin fumbled the pistol, misfiring as he yanked it from the holster.

For one crazy moment Tull was leaping toward the man, his sword gleaming in the morning sunlight as it flashed, and the Blade Kin put his hands up to ward the blow, and then Fava blinked and looked away as the sword chopped through the armor with a whack. Tull ran downhill to the body of the warrior he had shot, and Fava dared look up.

Tull stood, bloody sword still in hand, pulling the warrior's pistol. He grabbed the gun and lunged downhill, and Fava shouted, "Where are you going?"

"There's one more!" Tull yelled over his shoulder. Fava ran to follow him, and Tull rushed down through deep fern beds. The Blade Kin's trail was not hard to follow—they had knocked the morning dew from ferns, and while the wet ferns gleamed, these seemed dull and lifeless. Tull ran as fast as he could given the limp in his right leg from wearing shackles as a child, and Fava was hard-pressed to keep up.

When they reached the bay, through the fog Fava saw two sailboats in the harbor. In one sat a Blade Kin in red armor, fingering a pistol. He looked up at Tull, pulled off a shot as Tull ran downhill. Tull seemed not to notice. He raced to the water's edge, and the Blade Kin fumbled to load a second bullet in the gun.

Tull leveled his pistol at the Blade Kin, and the warrior tossed the gun and pulled his sword. Tull fired into the Blade Kin's unprotected throat, blowing the man backward into the water. He began to sink slowly as the water filled his leather armor.

Fava stood, stunned at how swiftly Tull had killed the warriors, yet knowing the slavers would have done the same to them. Tull stood with the gun in hand, looking in the water. The fog around Tull and the boats dimmed the scene, making it seem surreal.

"Who were they?" Fava asked.

"Judging by their armor, palace guards to the Slave Lords in Bashevgo—a thousand miles from home," Tull said with wonder in his voice. He looked back uphill, and Fava followed his eyes. The old Neanderthal had come down to the ridge above them and now sat in the ferns, gasping, resting on his spear. The feathers on his spear fluttered in a slight wind. Fava saw now that what she'd taken for furs were really ratty old woolen rags, the kind of clothes many another would throw away. The old man tried to speak, grunting and making urgent gestures, but the slavers had removed his tongue, a practice common in the houses of the Slave Lords, where secrecy was a way of life. Fava's eyes rested on the map case. The old Neanderthal held it protectively, as if to guard it even from Tull and Fava.

"I think he is a slave of some importance," Tull said.

Fava nodded. The whole incident seemed unreal, and she found herself shaking. "How did you know there was a third Blade Kin?" Fava asked.

"I heard him running," Tull answered.

"No you didn't—he was sitting quietly in the boat. How did you know he was here? You couldn't have seen him through the fog."

Tull started to say something, and his eyes widened as he sought an explanation. "I just . . . I heard . . ."

"Ayaah, you heard him," Fava said, "just as I heard him a week ago, in my dreams while sleeping on the bed of stone."

Chapter 2
From out of the Wilderness

The night Tull and Fava returned from their wedding journey, the young Pwi of the village gathered to celebrate three miles south of town at the edge of a small lake that the Pwi called "Perfect Mirror for a Blue Sky." They sat beside a bonfire singing and drinking beer all evening and told stories about Tull and Fava in the same way that humans will when someone dies. In a way, Tull and Fava would be leaving their single friends forever as they clung to one another in their new life.

Beside Tull the old Neanderthal sat, looking suspiciously at the group in his coat of rags. He still clutched his map case and spear, as if fearing that someone would attack him at any moment. Since he could not tell his name, Tull called him *Etanai*—the Pwi word for "cripple." The old slave seemed not to mind.

Tull's little brother, Wayan, was combing Tull's hair, and as one boy finished telling a story, Wayan asked Tull in Pwi, "You feel buttery. What makes you feel buttery? Is it because the moon is shining on you?"

"The word is *sweaty*. I feel sweaty because I am too near the fire and I'm dressed in hot furs." The smoke from the crackling fire crept low over the lake; two of

Anorath's dogs yapped as they hunted mice beneath a tangle of mossy logs. Thor hung overhead, yet enormous redwoods blocked the moon and starlight, deepened the night.

On the other side of the fire was a human girl, Darrissea Frolic, a dreamy-eyed young artist who eked out a dubious existence by crafting fine-scented paper by hand, then inscribing love poems on it. The love poems were sold to men who were too clumsy or too illiterate to create a poem themselves, and seldom did a ship leave Smilodon Bay without a sheaf of Darrissea's poems. Tull felt honored to have her present this night.

Darrissea pulled her wool cloak tight around her throat to keep out the crisp air, stirred the yellow-hot coals at the edge of the fire with the toe of her fine otter-skin boots. She looked out of place, the only human at the celebration. Her awkward features contrasted sharply with the blunt, chinless faces of the swarthy Neanderthal boys with their deep-set eyes. Her long wavy hair was nearly black as her eyes—far from the hues of the pale blonds and redheads among the Pwi. Darrissea was thin, with a slender artist's hands, not the knobby fists of a Neanderthal. She wore a brilliant blue cloak embroidered with golden geese flying around the edges, a white silk shirt with a lace collar, cream-colored leather pants. Many Pwi boys were wearing only moccasins and long black cotton breechcloths, as if to prove to each other that the chill air did not bother them.

Among the Pwi, Darrissea appeared almost alien. But even among the humans of town, she'd always been a misfit. Her father had been a freedom fighter—a stern man who hunted slavers and openly fought pirate bands —until he'd died of poisoning right here in town five years back. Darrissea lived alone in his house now, never making close friends with her own kind, somehow more comfortable among the Pwi.

Darrissea sipped cautiously from a mug of warm green beer, the kind the Neanderthals liked, and scowled at the taste, then looked around nervously to see if anyone would notice her scowl.

"Would you prefer wine?" Tull asked. "We can have one of the boys go back to town to fetch it for you."

Darrissea looked up, and her dark eyes glittered in the firelight. "No. You're a Pwi, now that you've turned your back on the human half of your heritage. This should be a Pwi celebration—even if it means drinking beer that tastes like . . . this."

Fava cut in. "It would not be a bother—"

"No bother, I'm sure," Darrissea said. "But you Pwi are taking on too many human customs. A hundred years ago every Pwi on this coast lived in a hogan, but now a stranger can wander the street in Smilodon Bay and not tell where the human part of town ends and Pwi-town begins. You work the farms and mills, but your grandfathers hunted with spears, trailing the mammoth herds." Darrissea nodded at some of the boys and girls who had painted their faces blue and decorated their hair with swordtail ferns and strips of cloth—not the kind of garb they would wear while working in Feremon Strong's fishery. No, tomorrow they would come to work with their hair combed down, many wearing pants and tunics like any human. But tonight the young would party the night away in celebration of the wedding just as their ancestors had done on Anee for a thousand years, perhaps as their ancestors had even done on Earth a hundred thousand years before. Though Darrissea and Tull had been speaking English, the universal trading language used by her starfaring ancestors, Darrissea raised her mug and spoke in the soft nasal language of the Pwi. *"Hezae, anath zhevet-pwasha palazh.* Friends, let us reverently continue to give life to the past."

Tull and Fava drank to the toast, and Tull asked, "Will you give us a poem for our wedding present, something I can read to Fava?"

Darrissea looked into the fire, dancing flames reflected from her black eyes. "I think your life should be a poem to the person you love. You just live the poem— each act, each carefully measured step, designed to convey your love, so that as your lives unfold the catalog of your deeds reveals the depth of your passion." Darrissea smiled and looked up at Tull and Fava. "But if you want words on paper, I will give you those, too."

Anorath, a young Pwi of nineteen got up and walked to the beer barrel; his bracelet of painted clamshells rattled as he scooped out a mugful of beer. "I gladly remember a time," he said, "when Tull first moved here. That old human, Dennoth Teal, had a big peach tree, and every year he hid all the peaches away like a packrat and would not sell any, so Tull and I decided to steal some peaches.

"We went at night, when Freya and Woden gave just enough moonlight to pick the peaches, and we each carried three bags. No wind blew; the only sound was the mayor's dogs howling as we picked, when we suddenly heard humans sneaking toward us." Anorath laughed and stomped on the ground, imitating a human trying to sneak in his clumsy boots. "So Tull and I climbed and hid in the thickest branches.

"When we were at the top, I heard a human whisper, 'Here it is! This is the tree where I saw them!' and I was so scared I thought I would pee, because I knew old Dennoth would club us.

"But two men climbed till they were so close, I could smell the human's stinking breath. I was sure I could smell a gun in Dennoth's hands, and I hoped only that he would beat me instead of shoot me. I got all dizzy from fright, and thought I'd fall until Tull grabbed my arm and pulled me higher."

Anorath stopped for a long drink of beer. A boy pushed another mug full of beer into Tull's hands, and Tull downed it quickly.

Anorath continued. "The humans began picking peaches. They were only humans who had come to steal the same peaches. They worked several minutes, filling some large baskets—and friends let me say: It's wrong for us Pwi to always pick the fruit; with their tiny, clever hands, the humans worked faster than Tull or I.

"They began at the bottom and picked the tree as they climbed. When they were almost on us, Tull grabbed one human by the neck and shouted in English, 'Now I've caught your ass, you thief!'

"The human squealed like a pig and dropped his peaches. He fell from the tree, and they fled so fast that when we got down, we found a shoe left on the ground. Tull and I took all the peaches and ran home."

The Pwi laughed, and Tull smiled. "I'd forgotten stealing those peaches," Tull said. "That was eight years ago. A good time."

"Ayaah, I had almost forgotten, too," Darrissea said from across the fire. "I'm the human *girl* who fell from the tree—though I'd say that rather than squeal like a pig, I squeaked like a rat!" Anorath nearly dropped his cup in surprise.

Fava and the other Pwi laughed. Tull had never told anyone about stealing those peaches. He felt a great sense of peace and realized that he had been drinking too much and now he was drunk; yet he was drunk on more than beer. He was drunk with kwea, a deep sense of satisfaction, of merriment, at being with old friends.

Tull sighed. "It will never be like this again," he said, "with all of us here. All of us drunk and laughing."

Fava hugged Tull. "Just because we're married, it doesn't mean the world will end. We'll still get together with our friends." Fava turned to Darrissea. "You must come and visit us, soon."

Tull looked across the fire smiling a melancholy smile. The slow gravitational wind hissed through the tops of the redwoods, signifying that Thor would set shortly. Tull said, "I hope you're right, Fava. May we all get together with our friends and laugh often." Darrissea nodded her head solemnly, looked at the ground, mist in her dark eyes.

"The peaches were good," Tull said, "if that consoles you. They tasted sweeter for having been stolen twice."

"I'm glad you enjoyed the fruits of my labor," Darrissea said. "I forgive you."

In Darrissea's eyes Tull saw only sincerity. "You always speak the truth. I like that in you."

"It's a bad habit. One that I'm trying to break."

"Don't break the habit," Tull said. "I find it entertaining."

Darrissea cocked her head, questioningly.

"I remember when we were young," Tull said. "Your father was still alive, working with freedom fighters up at Storm Hold. He had come home for a summer, and you were mad at him. You stood in front of Moon Dance Inn, yelled at him, 'You know, if you stick your ear up to your ass, you can hear the ocean.' Everyone laughed, but your father slapped you. Now that I think about it, I've always enjoyed watching you. You can say the most amazing things."

Darrissea raised an eyebrow. "Which entertained more, the remark or the beating?"

"The fight was fun at the time, but I still laugh at your joke all these years later."

"I remember getting hit, but I'd forgotten why my father hit me. You know, you remember those words simply because it is something you wanted to say to your own father. You were always a quiet rebel, full of anger. I could see it in your eyes. I was always a noisy rebel, a dumb one with a bloody nose."

"You had the courage to speak the truth," Tull said.

"And you had the wisdom to keep your mouth shut."

A log broke in the fire, and a shower of cinders spiraled upward. Tull raised his mug. "To rebellion, and truth, and martyrdom."

Darrissea raised her mug in return, shook her head, "To all but the last."

The old Neanderthal, Etanai, suddenly stirred in his coat of rags. He grunted softly, got up, and went to the keg of beer where a lantern lay, then set the lantern next to the fire and grunted, gesturing for everyone to come near.

Etanai carefully unscrewed the lid to his map case, and all around the fire, people drew close. He pulled out a thin piece of cloth, gently began to unroll it on the ground. Tull wondered what would be on the map, but as the crowd of Neanderthals drew in close, he could see little over their backs except a flash of color, while those nearby gasped.

Tull pushed his way forward and saw that the cloth did not have a map drawn on it, but a painting, and something in it took his breath. It was a large painting—a landscape of a bleak plain: In a junkyard littered with broken guns and swords was a pale green swathe of land with some tired daisies where a young Pwi man and a Pwi woman made love. But above them mountains towered, and carved in the purple-gray stone were the greedy faces of the Slave Lords of Bashevgo: ruined old men, slavering and leering, as if they would eat the young lovers, or as if they pondered something more evil. An ingenious use of contrasting colors, a grandeur in design, made the portrait stunning. Tull could feel the kwea of the art, as if the painting itself were vibrating and causing movements throughout the crowd. He seldom got that feeling from mere objects—yet some pieces of art carried it, held more power than they should. Etanai's painting was that way—an icon of power.

The crowd around Etanai quieted, and the Pwi became solemn. Tull realized that there was really little beauty in the picture. Only horror. Pain and suffering. And the beauty that existed in the lovers upon the green swathe of lawn was all overshadowed by the horror of the Slave Lords. The picture itself was a story Tull did not want to hear, yet he could not take his eyes from the painting.

Etanai pulled out a second canvas, spread it before them, and once again the Neanderthals breathed in

awe: The young Pwi woman lay tied to a beautiful bed
carved of ivory, gazing out of the picture, and tiny crows
flew from her mouth. A handsome human straddled her
voluptuous naked body, smiling curiously. The human
seemed intent on the pain and terror etched in his victim's face. He wore a shirt of golden butterfly wings, and
golden rings adorned his ears, and everything about him
spoke of wealth and grace. Behind him a string of other
beds lay, each holding a dead woman. In his right hand
he tenderly fingered the Pwi woman's throat, but everywhere there were crows flying in the background, so that
the background became only a mass of black crows, and
on a distant hill, Etanai sat by a wall of stone while a
crow perched above him, speaking into his ear.

Tull wondered if the picture represented a real
rape, or if it represented the rape of Etanai's people in
Bashevgo. He listened to the murmurs of the Neanderthals, heard their unspoken outrage. Etanai was a
master artist, playing his audience carefully, a man of
wit and passion and skill, and his works stunned the Pwi.

A third picture showed Etanai running down a city
street, a small and insignificant creature charging full tilt
between tall buildings of stone that opened like a dark
throat, a bloody knife in one hand, a child's doll made
of reeds in another. From every window, from every
darkened passageway, eyes looked out, and from above,
one could see that the world was a maze of dark passages with no escape. Tull knew then that this was
Etanai's story, his personal story, and not a symbolic
retelling of the horrors of all the slaves in Bashevgo.
Some of the Neanderthals looked at the bloody knife,
grunted, "Well done!" for they were happy to see that
Etanai had killed a Slave Lord.

Etanai reached into his case and pulled out a final
painting, and the crowd moved forward. Before Tull
could see it, he heard snarls of those in close. The picture was done in blacks and purples, and showed
Etanai, broken, bruised and frightened, sitting on a hill
of skulls clutching the child's doll; above him was a cage

of bones, without a key or lock. Dancing through the sky, ghouls with grave clothes leered down, and dancing in the sky among them were men in red armor, men without faces, and two of them stooped, as if having just set Etanai in the cage.

The hill, the ghouls, the cage of bones, Etanai's vacant and hopeless eyes staring out. Anorath drew the lantern nearer, so that everyone could see, and all the young Neanderthals frowned. Tull had heard rumors of the Cage of Bones, where Neanderthals sentenced to death for murdering a Slave Lord were sent. Rumor said there was no escape, no exit. Tull's heart pounded, and all his world narrowed to those eyes, staring out.

Etanai pointed at the man in the cage and groaned tonguelessly, pointed to himself. "That is me in that cage," he was saying, and pointed helplessly at the men in red armor.

"Those are Palace Guards of the Blade Kin," Fava said, pointing at the men dancing through the sky in red. "Like the men who were chasing Etanai."

The dark-purple nighttime, the yellow bones, the flying Slave Lords and their demonic servants. Yet the pain in Etanai's eyes is what captivated Tull. The painting was beautiful, yet it horrified Tull to the very depth of his soul. Here was a man who had lived in a chasm so fast and deep that Tull could not fathom it, while Tull and his friends stayed here in the relative freedom and safety of the Rough. Tull thought idly, *For every one of us Pwi living here in the wild, a thousand live in slavery in Craal or Bashevgo. All my life,* Tull thought, *I've enjoyed my freedom, never considering how the vast hordes live.* It shamed him.

Darrissea leaned in among the crowd and touched the last canvas, caressed a corner as if judging the worth of it, and she looked up at Tull, rage in her dark eyes.

She held it up for all to see, then whistled for attention. "This is Bashevgo! This is our future. All our lives we've been hiding out here in the Rough, living here in this wilderness of sleep. We all know that someday the slavers will come, and some of you talk of escaping to Hotland before then. But I don't see many places left to hide!" She pulled a knife from the sheath on her hip, drew it across her wrist. "I swear to God by my blood that I shall free Bashevgo before I die!"

She raised her bleeding wrist for all to see. Tull thought, *She must be drunk.* Old Etanai grabbed the knife from Darrissea, drew it across his own wrist, silently held it up.

Tull's heart was pounding, blood was thundering in his ears. He had never heard talk like this, open talk of war, and he marveled that an old man with a handful of paintings could hold such power over them. Yet the rage was in him, the pent anger over what the Slave Lords had done. Tull grabbed the knife, drew it across his own wrist, and shouted, "I swear to God by my blood, that I shall free Bashevgo before I die!"

The young Pwi of town watched as if they were three madmen. Fava said, "You can't expect a hundred Pwi to take on the Slave Lords of Bashevgo!" Tull looked in her eyes and saw not fear, but rage. She was angry at him.

"Are you sure?" a soft voice asked from behind them. Tull turned to see Chaa at the edge of the clearing, in the shadows. Chaa stepped forward so that moonlight fell on him. "Are you sure we cannot win— sixty thousand Pwi of the Rough against sixty million slaves and their lords? I've walked the paths of the future and know what I have seen."

Chaa strode purposefully toward the fire, stood next to Tull, raised his own ceremonial dagger, and slit his wrist. He held it up for all to see. "I swear to God, I shall free Bashevgo!"

Around the fire at Lake Perfect Mirror for a Blue Sky, a hundred half-drunk Pwi screamed in unison, cutting their wrists, so that their first war cry became a roar that echoed for miles above the trees.

Amid the excitement Tull looked for Fava. She

walked quietly to a tree, hugging Wayan, without joy in her face. He went to her and asked, "What's wrong?"

"We've been married only for a few days, and already you talk of leaving me?"

"I . . . I didn't think," Tull said.

All around them the young Pwi shouted and beat their chests, their eyes shining in the light of the fires. Old Etanai stood among them grinning. Little Wayan clung to Fava and looked around wildly. Tull hugged them both and found that Fava was sniffling.

"I won't go for a while," Tull promised. "Not until summer at the earliest."

"You won't go at all," Fava said, and Tull started to protest. *"We'll* go together. We'll fight as man and wife." Fava sat with her back against a redwood, holding Wayan and singing softly. Tull wanted to argue, but knew this was not the time. He sat with them for an hour, resting a hand on Fava's knee. The camp began to quiet as the Pwi broke into small groups. Some of the young Pwi boys stripped and jumped into the cold lake, swimming in the darkness. Someone banged on a log, using it as a drum, and others played their shrill flutes. They sang an old Pwi love song:

> *"When I was young and hollow,*
> *I hunted in wheat fields under starlight,*
> *and my feet left shadows in the white fields,*
> *and I was as empty as those shadows.*

> *"When I was young and hollow,*
> *the girl I married had no beauty.*
> *She was breastless and lacked front teeth,*
> *and with her mother she ground bread dough.*

> *"Now I am no longer hollow,*
> *For this woman fills me with beauty,*
> *In her smile I see white fields and starlight,*
> *And she gives me her breast as a pillow."*

Chaa came, sat on his heels. "Come with me, Tull. We have things to discuss," he said, grabbing Tull's forearm.

Tull tried to stand and found his right ankle numb, as often happened on cold nights. He limped off under a canopy of trees, into a deep grotto filled with trumpet-shaped mushrooms. The two men sat facing each other on a carpet of musty redwood needles. The Spirit Walker leaned his head back, breathed deep, his nostrils flaring to taste the night air.

"You are nervous tonight," Chaa said. "Why?"

Tull considered. As Spirit Walker for the village, Chaa had traveled to the gates of death so that he could leave his body and connect his consciousness with Tull's in a realm beyond time, and thus walk both Tull's past and future. Nothing was hidden from Chaa. "You know what troubles me."

Chaa laughed. "You test my skills? You hoped to wait until Phylomon and Theron Scandal return from Craal before warning people of the dangers they face. You fear the slavers, for they gather on our borders to the west. But you fear the Creators far more."

In the distance a young Pwi laughed on the lake and splashed water. Tull wrapped his arms around his knees. In his mind he returned to Craal, to the rocky coast at the Straits of Zerai where he, Theron Scandal, and Phylomon the Starfarer had separated. At the spawning ground of the great sea serpents they'd found serpents dead from parasites—pale lampreys with venomous mouths that fastened to the serpents' gills. The stinging lampreys drove the serpents mad, till they scratched out their own gills by rubbing against submerged rocks. Only the Creators, ancient breeding machines formed by the Starfarers, could have made the parasites. Yet long ago the human Starfarers had formed the Creators to protect the environment. The idea that the Creators would purposely sabotage such a vital species did not make sense.

But on the plains near the straits, Tull and Phylomon had also found some wild humans—half the size of normal humans—that could not speak, could not hunt or dress or fend for themselves. Instead they were animals, and it was obvious that the Creators had formed them. Yet the Creators also sent gray birds with lampreys in their gullets to attack the children. Only then had Phylomon guessed the truth: The Creators had formed the humans so they could practice their plans for genocide. Mankind had overextended, so the Creators intended to destroy mankind, wipe them from the planet. Phylomon and Scandal had stayed at Zerai to protect the small humans, move them to safety.

"I know how to fight men," Tull offered, "but I do not know how to fight the Creators. Phylomon says he will raise an army when he returns. But I cannot imagine that it will be easy."

"Then it is good that we began building our army tonight," Chaa said. "Still, I do not know how to fight the Creators either."

Tull drew a breath in surprise. He'd always imagined that a Spirit Walker would know everything.

"On my Spirit Walks, I have not seen the Creators, but I've connected to men who know of them. They are secretive, like great worms, and live deep in caves far to the north, but—they remain invisible to me. The Starfarers gave them bodies of flesh, but their brains are made of crystal. The Creators are machines. I can't Spirit Walk their future. I can only guess their intent."

"Phylomon believes they will destroy us if we don't kill them," Tull said. "What do you think?"

"They have little choice. The Creators were made to protect the land and its animals, but now the entire west is filled with people. The mammoth and woolly rhino have been hunted to oblivion beyond the White Mountains, as have other animals. For the Creators to obey the commands given by the Starfarers, they must reduce our numbers. But we have guns. If the Creators strike only to thin our numbers, we would retaliate. They know that.

"No, the Creators must wash us like dirt from a

bowl and start over, replace us with humans and Pwi grown from their wombs—men so ignorant that they cannot build weapons to challenge them."

Tull sighed. "I was afraid that if I warned our people, it would cause a panic."

"Phylomon and Scandal will return soon," Chaa said. "Let Phylomon bear the bad news." He looked ahead, as if staring at something others could not see. "You are young, with many concerns. You fear the Creators and the Slave Lords of Craal—but if you think, you will see that you fear only one thing: the future.

"At your wedding you received many gifts, but I can offer you one more. I offer you knowledge of the future."

Chaa shuffled his feet, and Tull thought that he would now reveal a plan to destroy the Creators. It took Tull a moment to realize that the Spirit Walker was slipping off his moccasins. Chaa extended the moccasins to Tull. They were so black, they seemed to swallow the darkness, except for small crows sewn from silver thread that gleamed in the moonlight.

Tull lurched back, as if the moccasins were rattlesnakes. "No!" he said.

"I want you to wear the moccasins of a Spirit Walker," Chaa said. "The power of the shamans runs in your blood. Yet old laws require me to tell you this: Once you take a Spirit Walk, you can never go home." Chaa held out the moccasins, but Tull would not touch them.

"I wouldn't make a good Spirit Walker." Tull tried to sound calm. "I've seen your eyes after you Spirit Walk. When you walk, you taste the grief and rage and fears of other men, and your eyes become vacant, lost. I . . . I don't think I could eat the pain of a thousand men. I don't think I could."

Chaa sat for a time, letting Tull consider. "When you joined the tribe of the Pwi, I gave you your true name, *Lachish Chamepar,* Path of the Crushed Heart.

Your heart will be crushed whether you become a Spirit Walker or not."

You could save me, Tull thought. *You could keep my heart from being crushed.*

"I cannot save you," Chaa said, answering the unspoken thought. "If you run from this pain, it will simply overwhelm you."

Tull didn't want to hear these words. "How do I know you are right? You play games with people's lives! You look into their future, then trade their hopes and dreams like coins to buy . . . to buy, I don't know what."

"To buy peace, for as many people as possible," Chaa said. "Just as I can give you peace. I do what I must. I traded my sons' lives for yours; now I ask you to give a life back to me. Bringing the sea serpents back was a worthy goal. But I want more from you. I want you to become a Spirit Walker. If you do not fulfill your potential, then the sacrifice will have been for nothing."

Tull looked at Chaa and wondered how Zhopilla could still love him, still sleep with him at nights, knowing that Chaa had sent her sons to die in Tull's behalf. Tull held his arms around his legs, curled almost in a fetal position. "You talk as if becoming a Spirit Walker is a big thing—yet look at the armies of Craal, look at the Creators plotting our destruction. What have your powers gained?"

Chaa stared into Tull's eyes. "Now we talk of mysteries, things I would not openly reveal. You cannot guess what we have gained, Tull. You could not imagine this world without us. Ayaah, we've strong enemies—sorcerors among the Blade Kin, even enemies left from the dream-time in the Land of Shapes. They've brought our world to the edge of ruin. But we withstand them."

Tull put his hands over his eyes. Like a dog circling its bed, he returned to the previous argument. "Once I take a Spirit Walk, I can never go home. I would be lost to myself!"

"Or perhaps you would be found," Chaa said. "I

am not the same young man I was before my father took me on my first Spirit Walk, just as the oak is no longer an acorn. I've walked the lives of ten thousand men. Does that make me less a man, or am I now a man ten thousand times over? Sometimes I walk a man's future and see that he will be destroyed by pain, and I know that when I wake, I will feel his worms in my head. It is inevitable. But I can teach you to bear such pain. As a Spirit Walker, you will learn the flavors of men. For every person whose life is vinegar, you can find a person whose life is honey. Tull, wear the moccasins of a Spirit Walker!"

Tull closed his eyes, rubbed his face.

"You are right to be afraid, Tull. If you were not afraid of the gift, you would be too stupid to be worthy of it. You are right: I've sacrificed children to bring about a better future. You know that you would be required to do the same, and you ask yourself: What if I failed to bring my dream of heaven? How much guilt would I bear?"

Guilt. That was the crux of it, Tull realized. To know the future was to become responsible for it, just as Chaa had become responsible for it.

For a moment Chaa took a pinecone, absently wrote with it on the ground. "You are a good man. I think you will follow the laws written in your heart. I have given two lives for you, and in time you will see that now that a gift has been given, a gift must be returned. This is a natural thing. When the earth gives you water to drink, you must return it. You may hold it in your bladder for a long time, still you must give it up. So I can wait for you, until you decide to give yourself."

The young Pwi in camp started to sing and abruptly stopped. A commotion began, people shouted. Darrissea Frolic came rushing to the grotto. She stood at the top of the small ridge for a moment, her blue cloak flapping in the moonlight as she peered into the shadows.

"What?" Chaa asked.

"You had better get up here, Chaa," Darrissea said. "There's a big gray bird out here, like nothing I've ever seen, and it is asking for the town of Smilodon Bay."

The Spirit Walker rose to his feet, nervously dusted the redwood needles from his pants. Chaa said to Tull, "It seems that the future is thrust upon us, whether we have seen it or not."

Tull rushed from the grotto to the campfire, and there he found the young people of the village standing next to a huge gray bird as large as the great-horned dragons. The beast stood six feet at the shoulders, yet it was no ordinary bird. It had the face of a woman, young and beautiful, with wide-set gray eyes and strong lips. Fine downy feathers covered her cheeks.

The Pwi boys stood close, almost daring to touch her, and Tull's heart pounded. "Back!" Tull shouted. Some boys turned to look at him, and Tull shouted again, "Run! Get back!"

The boys stepped back tentatively. Chaa followed Tull. "Get back or she'll kill you!" Chaa said menacingly, and the boys leapt away at the Spirit Walker's warning.

Anorath had a gun propped against a tree, a pump-action smooth bore that fired a slug large enough to rip open a woolly rhino; he grabbed it, covered the bird. Other boys pulled their swords and *kutows*. The bird sat on the ground, wings folded, feathers unruffled. Her huge gray eyes were empty, staring ahead as if dazed.

"What happened to her?" Tull asked, wondering why the bird was so still.

Anorath said, "She asked where Smilodon Bay is, and asked for Phylomon the Starfarer. We told her that Smilodon Bay is near, but that the Starfarer is gone. She stopped moving and now just sits. What should we do?"

Chaa shrugged, looked at Tull. "You tell them."

Tull studied the bird. Her face, her wings. She was far larger than the deadly gray birds he'd seen up north, and she had a human face rather than a beak. He didn't know if she was dangerous. Perhaps the Creators had given her lips and a voice so she could deliver a message? Her head was smaller than a human's. He wondered how much intelligence lurked behind those eyes and decided to test her. He whispered to Anorath, "Ready your gun. If she moves, shoot her." He grabbed a *kutow* from a boy, stepped close to the bird. *This is foolish,* he told himself. *If you flirt with death, she will cleave to you.* He looked back at Chaa for advice, but the Spirit Walker just shrugged.

"What do you want?" Tull asked, his mouth dry. She didn't answer. "What town do you seek?"

The messenger's eyes suddenly focused on Tull, and he cringed. She dug her great talons into the ground and said, "Smilodon Bay. I seek Smilodon Bay."

"This town that you see is Smilodon Bay," Tull said, gesturing expansively at the redwoods. The gray bird studied the trees quizzically, as if inspecting them.

"And who do you seek here?" Tull asked.

The bird sank her talons into the thick humus, readjusted her wings. "Phylomon the Starfarer."

"I am Phylomon the Starfarer," Tull said.

The gray bird tensed, like a hawk ready to pounce, but studied his feet, ran her eyes up over his body from toe to head, obviously mystified. "Phylomon the Starfarer has blue skin," the bird said.

"I am blue," Tull answered.

"You are not blue!" the bird screeched, flapping her wings in anger, glaring out over the crowd of young men that circled her.

Tull gestured to one young Pwi boy who had painted his face blue. "You are right! I am not blue, and I am not Phylomon. That man is Phylomon."

The bird batted her wings. Her eyes fixed on the young man. She screeched and leapt into the air, making gagging sounds as if she would vomit.

"Kill it! Kill it now!" Tull shouted, and Anorath fired, catching the bird's right wing. The bird spun to the ground, tilted her head up to see, and Tull leapt forward and slammed the *kutow* into her head, splitting her skull.

Yet something swelled the dead bird's throat, crawling up. Tull slammed his *kutow* into its neck. A terrific jolt of electricity arced up from the wound, blinding him, hurling him back. He lay on the ground, dazed, the wooden shaft of the *kutow* smoldering in his hand, the soles of his moccasins smoking.

Chaa rushed forward wielding a brand from the fire, and a wormlike creature wriggled from the dead bird's throat, ripping out her esophagus. The worm was huge, at least four feet long and a foot tall at the back. Its eyes were the same pale blue as its skin.

Chaa held the flame in front of the worm's nose, and the creature stopped, as if blinded. "You young men get back! Get back! There is more danger here than you can imagine!" Chaa shouted to the boys. He eased toward the fire. The worm followed the flaming brand, sliding like a snake. It twisted its head from side to side, but its pale blue eyes seemed not to see the boys. It followed the flame.

When Chaa reached the bonfire, he tossed the brand into its heart. The great worm rushed forward to strike. It wriggled into the flames and began to writhe, circling within the fire, seemingly unable to leave. A small bolt of lightning arced out of the worm, split a log by the fire, and yet the beast continued to race in circles through the flames.

Behind Chaa, the Pwi gasped. The beast whipped about, muscles in its back straining like cords, scattering coals across the ground, plunging its long rasping tongue into flaming coals at the heart of the fire. Tull watched that tongue, recalled how other worms in the north had attacked—flicking their tongues into the brain stems of their human victims, taking control of their bodies.

Chaa went to Anorath, took the gun, and began shooting into the great worm. Holes ripped into its side, holes large enough to put a fist through, yet the wounds healed even as they watched. He shot off all rounds, reloaded, shot, and reloaded until he ran out of bullets.

The worm spun in the fire in a frenzy, looking for an enemy to strike, blind to anything but flames. Tull's head cleared. He sat up dizzily. Even with fifteen bullets in it, the worm did not slow.

Chaa shouted, "Use your spears to push the logs back into a circle. Throw sticks into the fire to keep it hot—or the creature will see you! Do not let the beast touch your sticks!" The boys moved forward cautiously.

Tull swallowed, listened to the sizzle and pop of the beast in the fire as the boys worked.

Chaa came and whispered to Tull. "The worm has a skin like Phylomon the Starfarer's. The Creators made this one especially for him. You could not have killed it. Phylomon himself would have died here." Tull saw that Chaa's hands were shaking even though his voice sounded calm.

Fava walked up beside Tull, holding Wayan, who slept in spite of all the noise. Tull asked Chaa, "Did you know the bird would come?"

"No. I suspected an attack, but sometimes it rains even on a Spirit Walker. I saw worms like these in my Spirit Walk, and I've touched their minds. Fire is their weakness. It draws them, yet blinds them."

Chaa supervised the boys until the blue worm rolled to its back and lay twitching. And finally Chaa told the Pwi about the Creators' treachery, how they'd killed the sea serpents with their lampreys, and how they planned to do more. He made the Creators' plans sound like a small thing, the schemes of children, and none of the Pwi doubted that Chaa had seen how to foil the Creators' plot. Tull had already brought the sea serpents back from Craal, defeating part of the Creators' plans. Now, when Phylomon the Starfarer returned, he would lead them north to destroy the Creators.

Tull stood with Fava and listened not to the Spirit Walker, but to a fox barking in the distance and the wind rushing through the redwoods. He looked up through the black branches at the sky, and Fava nudged him.

She said, "Now I know why your eyes have seemed to gaze a thousand miles away. You have been keeping many secrets from me."

"I did not want to ruin the kwea of our wedding," Tull said. "I wanted you to always be able to look back and think of it as a happy time, not mingled with fear."

Fava got up on her tiptoes and kissed him. Tull took Wayan from her. They began ambling home, and when Tull glanced back, Chaa leaned over the fire, ringed by Pwi. He was squatting over the carcass of the worm with a knife, skinning it. Chaa had many hunting trophies in his house—teeth of dinosaurs and lions, hides from bears—but Tull imagined the pale blue worm skin as a rug on the Spirit Walker's floor, and thought it an odd trophy.

Tull carried Wayan back to the cabin. All through his walk, Tull held the small boy and wondered what the future would bring for Wayan. Perhaps he would someday be carried away as a slave to Bashevgo, or perhaps the boy would die at the hands of the Creators. Maybe he would live here in town and be happy, marry well, grow old and die among friends. Yet that seemed too much to hope.

It had been only three weeks since Tull had taken Wayan from their father, rescued the child so that he would not be abused as Tull had. And in Tull's mind a little voice whispered, *When you took Wayan to raise as your own son, you took him because you wanted to promise him a future.*

When Tull reached the cabin, he laid Wayan in bed with Fava, set the fire, then went outside to think. He looked out over the waters at Smilodon Bay. The town below swept around him in a bowl shape, the gray stone houses hidden among the shadows of the redwoods. Pale lights from fires shone through some windows, and the light of Freya—one of the two smaller moons—

made the smoke hanging over the chimneys gleam as if pale white ribbons floated above the town.

Overhead the stars seemed to want to burn a hole in the darkness. A Red Drone warship flamed like a comet overhead, and Tull stood, tasting the cool night air on his tongue, and he decided. *Tomorrow I will become a Spirit Walker.*

Garamon Goodstick, the mayor of Smilodon Bay, slept fitfully the night of Tull's return. He kept tossing in his blankets so they wound around him and pulled off his wife. At four in the morning someone knocked at his door, softly, three times. Then he heard a faint scratching. Eyes of Bashevgo, he realized—a member of the secret arm of the Blade Kin, who worked here in the Rough.

He hurried to open the door. "What do you want?" At the door stood Kelvin Bywater, a local glassmaker. Garamon had known Kelvin for thirty years, but had never known him to be Blade Kin.

"I thought you should know," Kelvin said, "Chaa and some of your local boys have just sworn to overthrow Bashevgo."

Garamon stood in the doorway, confused. "Bashevgo? They can't be serious!"

Kelvin whispered, "They're serious, friend."

"But the Pwi—certainly they wouldn't be so naive as to try!"

"The mute that Tull brought back today has managed to be quite an agitator. Your Pwi would march tonight if Chaa asked them."

"Well then," Garamon whispered. He wrung his hands in the darkness. "We can't have that, can we? We must keep the merchandise pacified. So we shall have to agitate the agitator."

Chapter 3
The Attraction of Small Predators

Mahkawn lay in bed in a stone shack on the isle of Bashevgo and listened: Outside, roosters crowed down the street, and a few blocks farther a pig squealed as it died in the market, the sounds muted by a rain that fell to a street so cold that the droplets gave an odd tinkling when they impacted, then skittered across the frozen cobblestones. Mahkawn closed his eyes and tried to soak in that sound. Learning sounds, tuning himself to sounds, was an old habit he'd acquired when he'd lost his right eye.

Beside him, Pirazha stirred in bed, throwing her naked leg over him. She opened her eyes, raised on one elbow, and looked out the window. "I must get up. My master will need bread."

"No," Mahkawn said. "Don't go to work. Tell him that you were breeding with a Blade Kin. It is your privilege." As a general among the Blade Kin, it was indeed Mahkawn's right to select any slave he wanted to sleep with. Her master would not begrudge the time that Mahkawn spent between her legs.

"You don't want me to have to explain this, do you? What if he sends someone to look for me? I told him last week that I slept with a Blade Kin, and he asked your name. He suspects that you have been coming around again."

"No," Mahkawn said. "I don't want you to tell." He did not need to ask if she'd given his name. She would have kept silent, lied, done anything. She could not let it be known that she was sleeping regularly with the same man.

Pirazha rubbed her face into the thick hair of Mahkawn's chest and sighed. She ground her hips into him. "I can stay for a few more minutes." She bit his shoulder hard enough to bruise it.

Mahkawn petted her sagging breast, ran his finger under the curves, playing with the dark nipples. *Three of my sons have suckled from these nipples,* he thought, and the kwea he felt from them, the beauty of his own times lying with this aging Thrall, smote him. Breathing in, he could smell the yeast from the bakery upon her, as if she herself were bread, a staple. Pirazha's hips were wide from giving birth, and Mahkawn pushed her to her back, slid into her easily, then just lay atop her, staring at her face, her thin orange hair, eyes that glowed a deep gold. Like all Neanderthals, her skin was pulled tight over the smooth bones of her skull. Her only wrinkles were thin traces, as if cobwebs lay on her skin. She was growing old, and Mahkawn felt pain in his own bones, the ache of his own knotted muscles, knew he was growing old, too. One did not quickly rise from slave, to arena fighter, to Omnipotent among the Blade Kin. One of Mahkawn's old masters, a human general, had said it could not be done in a lifetime, certainly not by a Neanderthal. Mahkawn had thought it an odd statement, but now believed it true: Mahkawn felt as if he'd lived more than one lifetime, as if the fire that had driven him in his youth had somehow burned up many lifetimes in propelling him.

Pirazha reached up and played with his hair, ran one finger down to the nub where his right ear had been before Mahkawn cut it off and gave it to his first sergeant. She smiled. "Someday, when you are old and no longer Blade Kin, you will look at me like that, and maybe then you will tell me you love me."

Mahkawn narrowed his eyes in sudden disgust. He grabbed her throat and squeezed, pushing his thumb up under her esophagus so that she could not scream, and he hissed. "You fool! No matter how old I become, no matter how senile, I would never say that!" Her eyes were wide, frightened. "One cannot love without becoming ruled by love! And no matter what happens, I will never be ruled. I will not become a Thrall like you! I will not be chained to a wall. I will not be chained!" He held her throat, choking her.

Pirazha tried to wriggle under his grasp, tried to shove him away with her left hand and slugged at him with her right. Her face began to purple, and Mahkawn held tight. *I should kill her, strangle her now,* he thought. Tears streamed from the corners of her eyes, and he resisted the impulse to bend over, kiss those tears away. She was a Thrall, and though they shared Neanderthal ancestry, she was inferior, an animal, a creature that reveled in kwea and stupidly sought his love. Breeding with her was a shameful thing. *I should have saved my seed for an equal,* he thought. *Not this beast. Captain Itena or one of the other warriors.*

"The body is a tool of the mind," Mahkawn hissed, "not something to be enjoyed as an end to itself!"

Pirazha's eyes began to roll back in her head, like the eyes of a dumb cow under the slaughterer's knife. He saw her sense of betrayal, saw her stupidity, and realized that his concepts were above her. To teach her the mind and soul of the Blade Kin would be impossible. Mahkawn let her go.

Pirazha gasped, her naked chest heaving, and tried to push him away, to roll over onto her stomach. He slapped her face and realized he was still inside her, that he was hard, and he pinned her shoulders to the bed.

"Get off me!" she shouted, and began crying. "Get off!" But he held her in place, thrusting in deeper and harder between her wide hips, and she crossed her arms over her face and sobbed. He rammed in rhythmically, like a machine, like the pistons that shattered iron ore in the mines above Bashevgo, and though his face was near hers, he watched as if she were miles away. *This is how a warrior should breed,* he thought. *Shove the sweet potato in for only one purpose.*

From the back bedroom, Mahkawn heard his sons rouse, come stumbling out of bed. He pulled out of the woman, wrapped a sheet around his waist.

Only one of the boys opened the leather flap to the doorway, Uffin, the eight-year-old. He stood, not fully awake, watching his father. A dire wolf pup followed behind the child, jumping on great clumsy feet. Pirazha told the boy, "Go away!"

Mahkawn rolled off the bed, stood naked. "No, stay."

Uffin hesitated. "My mother told me to leave."

"You will obey me," Mahkawn said softly in a tone that did not invite rebuttal. "You sleep with that wolf?"

The boy nodded.

"How long have you had it?"

The boy shrugged. "A long time." Mahkawn realized that the boy did not know how to count. Eight weeks. It had been eight weeks since Mahkawn sent the pup. For a moment Mahkawn sat thinking, wondering about the attraction of small predators. Why did humans and Pwi like them so? Dogs, cats—among the Slave Lords, small vicious dinosaurs were popular.

Outside, someone banged Pirazha's door, and the pup began barking. Mahkawn heard the distinct sound of a ring scratch the doorpost—a signal identifying the intruder as Blade Kin. "Open the door," Mahkawn said, and the boy opened the door as Mahkawn pulled on his black tunic.

The bright yellow sunlight hurt Mahkawn's eye, and in the doorway stood a tall man, a narrow-faced human, gangling arms. He wore the black leather cuirass and black cape of all Mahkawn's officers. "Jaffrey," Mahkawn greeted.

"Omnipotent, last night I received your summons for six o'clock this morning," Jaffrey said. "Pardon me if I have disturbed you while you bred."

"That is quite all right. I was going to bring you here anyway. How did you know where to find me?" Mahkawn had not told anyone of his liaison with Pirazha, had in fact come to her on a whim, and he was sure no one had followed.

"It is known that you frequent this place," Jaffrey said. "You must take more care."

Mahkawn gauged the younger man. He found it difficult to tell if humans were lying. Still, the news did not bode well, for if some rival suspected that Pirazha was Mahkawn's favorite, she'd be murdered. It was a game among the Blade Kin. If a Neanderthal took a lover, rivals within his ranks, perhaps a junior officer like Jaffrey, would slit the lover's throat to see their senior officer react. Even among the Blade Kin, Neanderthals sometimes starved themselves with grief when a lover died, like common Thralls, leaving an open position for some more heartless junior officer to fill.

"The sex has been quite good with this one in the past," Mahkawn said, pulling the cover from Pirazha, exposing her body, the flaccid breasts, the wide hips. "You really should try her."

"I do not doubt it," Jaffrey said, reaching down to stroke her face, "but I like them younger." His tone was that of a man who was declining some small pastry at a banquet. He was a man without great ambition. Mahkawn did not think Jaffrey would kill Pirazha himself, but Jaffrey might sell her name to another.

"How may I serve you?" Jaffrey asked.

Mahkawn pulled on his sword belt and pistol, put his cape over all. He ordered Pirazha to comb and plait his hair, then sat pensively. "The boy here, Uffin"—he nodded toward Uffin, who still stood gaping—"has a pet wolf cub, and he is eight years old today. He sleeps with the pup."

Jaffrey looked at the child knowingly. "A wolf pup?" he said, then walked over before the boy. He reached down, patted the pup. "Tell me, does it have a name?"

Uffin nodded.

"Good dog," Jaffrey said, patting it on the head. The dark-gray wolf licked his hand. "Do you love your pup?"

"Ayaah," Uffin whispered.

Mahkawn pulled his knife from its sheath, tossed it to the floor. It spun lazily, glinting in the early-morning light, and landed, cutting deeply into the wood. "Then kill it."

The boy stood momentarily, watching the knife. Mahkawn pulled on his boots. Into his belt he tucked a golden scourge, a solid-gold bar with eight golden chains, and upon each chain was a tiny ball with a hook. He displayed it proudly, for it marked him as Favored Omnipotent and possible replacement to Lord Tantos, Minister of Retribution. No other Neanderthal had ever earned the right of succession to a human Slave Lord. "I am Mahkawn, Omnipotent among the Brotherhood of the Black Cyclops. You will do as I order."

"No, don't ask him to do that!" Pirazha whispered at Mahkawn's back, and she grasped his cape. Mahkawn pushed her hand away.

Uffin looked up, licked his lips. He shivered and tried to look away. He knelt to the floor and buried his head in the dog's gray fur.

Mahkawn watched. It was a ritual as old as the Blade Kin, and by law Mahkawn could say nothing more. Uffin was mature enough to understand: He could be a Thrall, remain a slave for life, or he could free himself now by killing the thing he loved.

If I have bred true . . . , Mahkawn thought, and he watched the boy's hand, willing him to take the knife. *A dog is nothing. You are worth more than a dog. We ask so little of you. Come now, better that I ask the life of a dog than the life of a friend.*

Mahkawn glared at his son, stood with his back straight, muscles rigid. Under that glare, the boy inched across the floor to the knife. He pulled it out, hefted its weight. His hands were shaking and his lower lip trembled. He looked up at Mahkawn, and his eyes were full of tears. The tears did not matter—he could cry, he could curse, he could run away afterward. It only mattered that he do the deed, that he subjugate his animal feelings and show that he could harden himself, become a Blade Kin.

The boy set the knife on the floor, shoved it toward Mahkawn's foot. "My pup didn't do anything wrong."

"It is not a punishment," Mahkawn explained. "I know it has been a good pup. Just kill it." By convention, even these few words were too much. Yet he could not give up on the boy so easily.

"No," Uffin said, then he sobbed and picked up the wolf pup. "When the Okansharai comes, he will kill you!" Uffin shouted, and he ran into the back room.

Mahkawn hissed through his teeth to show his displeasure and stormed out the door, into the bright red sunrise. The freezing rain had quit falling, and the red sun shone on the frozen road, making it gleam like a river of blood. *I whelped a Thrall! He's a Thrall, just like his mother!* Mahkawn dared not speak the thought, for it was bitter. Jaffrey hurried after him.

"Omnipotent! Omnipotent!" Jaffrey called. Mahkawn stood with his back to the human. "I am sorry the boy did not pass the test."

"No matter," Mahkawn answered, resigned. "He has a strong back. He will make a good slave."

"I know we leave for the Rough soon," Jaffrey continued. "I would like permission to go to Mole Hill for two days."

Mahkawn considered. Their mission in the Rough was to last for twelve weeks, and he estimated that it would take at least that long to sweep through the wilderness, capture what was left of the wild Pwi. If they

met any organized resistance, it could take much longer.
"All right," Mahkawn said, "you have two days."

All that morning Tull felt the urge to move, to walk.
The young men of the village got together in the afternoon, and Chaa began teaching them how to use
swords. Tull and Fava attended the practice, and Tull
spoke with Chaa briefly, made an appointment to see
him that night. Tull did not tell Fava of his plans.

That night while Fava slept with little Wayan, Tull
slipped out into the cool night air, listened to the sigh of
breakers pounding the rocks, the howls of a cat in heat.
He walked down the path to Chaa's cabin, and in the
manner of the Pwi, called softly at the door, "I am
here." Chaa opened the door. Tull could smell curry and
beer on his breath.

"I'm ready," Tull answered.

"Then come with me." Chaa escorted him through
the front door, holding Tull's elbow, guiding him down
the corridors in the darkness to his Spirit Room, a circular chamber with a dome-shaped mud wattle roof. A
circle of stones at the center of the room was used as a
fireplace, and a large water jug sat by the ashes of a fire.
The fire had burned out hours ago, and the only light
came from a small hole that let in moonlight. The room
smelled thickly of smoke. A mat of woven reeds lay on
the floor next to the fire.

Around the room the walls were decorated with
hunting trophies—the serrated teeth of a carnosaur
gleamed whitely even in the diluted light. The shadowed
shape of a bear hide hung on the wall. Tull could not see
much beyond that.

"Would you like me to light a candle?" Tull asked,
but Chaa shook his head.

"We have more than enough light to see by," Chaa
said, and he motioned for Tull to sit on the mat. Chaa
sat beside the fire, and the thin moonlight coming in
from the smoke hole illuminated his features. He spoke

softly. "Before you were born, your spirit roamed in the Land of Shapes, and your spirit did not comprehend some of the things you understand now—lust, greed, fear. But it understood something. Mostly it understood intense curiosity. Shortly after conception, your mother summoned those in the Land of Shapes, and enticed you to enter the fetus." Tull listened intently, for he had heard of the Pwi custom of "summoning" spirits, and it was said that among the Pwi, a mother who was adept could choose the spirit of her child rather than leave it to chance. Yet all of this was woman's magic, and the men were not allowed to know the mysteries of how the summons was accomplished. "So your spirit entered your body in order to sate its appetite for curiosity—to learn to see with physical eyes, to move and taste joy. The Land of Shapes is behind you, and it is ahead of you.

"For now, your life is like a bridge, a narrow trail connecting two vast worlds. But the new sensations that you feel, they overwhelm you, so that you have been blinded to your previous life in the Land of Shapes. Your physical eyes cannot see it. Your tongue cannot taste it. In a sense you have fallen asleep, but your heart knows the terrain, the geography of the Land of Shapes."

"You mean I am asleep now?"

"Yes, a fitful sleep. You are asleep to your own beauty, your own potential, like all the other people in the world. Most of them can never be wakened. Their spirit eyes are firmly closed. But I have seen that you are different. You seek places of power for your spirit. You can feel your enemies even in the dark or behind stone walls. It is only because your sleep is uneasy that I can wake you."

Chaa motioned to the water jug. "Tonight I will begin to teach you to see in the Land of Shapes. It will be a great task for you just to open your spirit eyes, and that alone may take many weeks. Do not worry if it seems difficult at first." He picked up the water jug. "I have made seer's tea. It has mushrooms to open the eyes, roots to open the ears, seeds to open the mind."

"Like the drugs the Okanjara take?" Tull asked. The wild Neanderthals of the plains took many drugs, often to excess, and Tull did not want to be like them.

"Yes," Chaa said. "But the drugs will not harm you. They will not take you close to death."

"But won't such tea make me crazy?"

"With the Okanjara, fear makes them crazy. They gaze into the Land of Shapes but do not comprehend what they see, and so it makes them crazy. With the tea you will see a land where time can stop, or exist all at once. You can see the holiness of stones and men. Once you drink the tea, I will speak with you, guide your journey. You will not become lost." Chaa opened the small clay jar. It was rounded on the bottom like a gourd, with a long neck, and it had been painted with dancing birds in bright whites and yellows, yet when Chaa handed the jar to Tull, Tull was surprised to find it nearly empty.

Tull swirled the jug, drank a sip. The water felt greasy in his mouth, gritty with seeds and bitter roots. Chaa took the jug, poured it all down Tull's throat.

"Here, lie upon my pallet," Chaa said, and Tull lay on the mattress of woven reeds. He suddenly felt dizzy and wanted to vomit, but realized he was dizzy with fear and that he wanted to vomit only because his stomach was knotting.

"This will not take as long as you think," Chaa said, and he waited, holding Tull's hand. After several minutes he said, "In our world, we imagine that everything is separate, that I am separate from you, and you are separate from your friends, but in the Land of Shapes there are fewer boundaries.

"When I play a song on my pipe, and you sing, and another taps his foot, and another man dances, we all see ourselves as separate entities. But in the Land of Shapes, we see that the music and the dancer, the singer and the drum, all are one thing connected, blurring into each other. The music is shared, and we all become part of it.

"In the same way, you are not a single person, but part of your mother and father, all blurred into one, and they are each parts of other mothers and fathers, all blurred outward over time, so that all people are really just different manifestations of a single person, manifestations that expand outward with time.

"But in the Land of Shapes, there is no time, and all the connections are more easily found. Once you learn to see and maneuver in the Land of Shapes, you can touch another person on the far side of the world, or share the life of someone long dead, or glimpse the future of people who may yet live. You will learn to see the beauty in every man and understand that your enemies are no less glorious than the sunrise. Doors will open to you. Yet it will not all come tonight. It will not happen in a moment.

"Tell me, how do you feel?"

Tull considered. Chaa's voice was loud, yet Tull suddenly realized that Chaa had been whispering. Below the dirt floor Tull could hear the soggy noise of earthworms gushing through their holes. He had not been aware of the change coming over him. He'd felt only a peculiar lightness, as if he were floating. "I don't know. I feel strange. Everything is so loud."

"But it is not an unpleasant loudness?" Chaa asked.

Tull considered. He could hear Chaa's intestines squeaking and rumbling as they digested. "No."

"You are just more open to sound," Chaa said. "Tell me if I speak too loud. Now I want you to relax. Stare at the hole in the ceiling," Chaa said, nodding at the hole where moonlight streamed in. "It is like the hole above your navel, which we Spirit Walkers call 'the hollow of your soul,' where your dark desires and fears are kept, only there is no light streaming from the hollow of your soul. Darkness streams from it sometimes, when it can. That is the nature of souls."

Tull tried to relax and watched the hole. He was very aware of the stars shining through the hole in the ceiling, so distant, so distant, yet he could almost make out the planets that circled them, he thought, if only he could lean a little closer.

Tull realized that Chaa was touching him above the navel, but below the sternum, stroking him gently in an arc only two inches wide. He found the sensation very soothing, the way a cat must be lulled when you scratch between its ears, and Tull closed his eyes, relished the sensation of touch.

"I will tell you a story," Chaa said, stroking Tull above the stomach, "about a man who lived long ago, and even though you close your eyes, I want you to watch the ceiling, the hole in the ceiling, where only darkness streams through."

Chaa's voice seemed to have become muted, as if he were in a forest. Tull's tongue was thick in his mouth, and he idly wished that he could pull it out, lay it beside him in the dirt until they were done, and then put it back.

"Long ago," Chaa said, "before the wind learned how to breathe or before the sun learned how to laugh, or before the first human was trained at the hands of a Neanderthal how to throw a spear, there was a vast plain where bison roamed beneath blue skies, and a man lived upon this plain." Tull had to force himself to concentrate as Chaa spoke, and he found that his eyelids had grown heavy. He tried to open them, but they were so heavy, and he wondered if Chaa had set stones upon his eyes to keep them closed. Tull could not rouse the strength to open his eyes, but he looked to the darkness streaming in from the ceiling. He saw it now, a hole with darkness streaming through, only it had moved to the side. He let his head flop to his right, and he stared at the hole.

"The man who lived on this plain found a bear's den one day, a den so large that he could not walk around it to guard it, and he feared any bear that could dig such a hole—he feared that the bear would come running out at any moment, and he decided to guard that hole, the hollow of his soul, and slay any bear that tried to leave. The man's name was Man of Peace, and he had twenty-one children, and all of them were like him, made of lightning, and they danced around the great hole, keeping the bear inside."

Tull could hear something in his head trudging about. He opened his mouth, and lights came streaming out in ribbons of canary and vermilion.

Chaa kept stroking Tull's stomach, and he said roughly, "These twenty-one children are called the Lightnings of the Soul, and they dance over the surface of the hollow of your soul and keep the darkness from streaming out."

Tull looked at the dark hole. Lightning danced across the surface on tiny feet. The threads of lightning were blue and thin as a willow switch, but incredibly long. They did a slow melodic dance, waving, weaving patterns over the darkness.

"One day, Man of Peace had a dream." Chaa said, "He dreamed that he needed help, he dreamed that he wanted something desperately, and do you know what it was?"

"Help," Tull said. He could feel his body sinking, sinking into the dirt floor. *I am only made of mud,* he thought, *and that is why I must sink down into the mud of the earth.*

Chaa kept stroking above Tull's navel, digging his fingernails into the hollow just beneath his ribs, and Tull suddenly understood that he had not been stroking at all, but that Chaa had really wanted to dig something out of there. Something stuck under the flesh, and Chaa was digging a hole with his fingernail.

"Yes, Man of Peace wanted help," Chaa whispered. "For Man of Peace feared the Slave Lords of Craal. He had gone into their country to hunt for sea serpents, and while he was there, he had killed some soldiers and a sorcerer. So what do you think he did?"

Tull wondered for a moment before he answered, "Gah."

"Man of Peace planted the seed of a tree on a black hill, and in only moments the tree began to grow."

Tull felt something enter him, a sharp pain in his abdomen. He looked down, and just above his abdomen on the black hill, blood flowed like a stream. Tull realized that Chaa had been scratching and picking at that dark place, and now he had pushed a seed into it, and he could feel the seed swell and grow, rumbling in its power.

"The tree grew fast, faster than Man of Peace could imagine, and it filled the sky so that the stars hung in its midnight-blue limbs like ornaments, and it became the World Tree, where the future hung heavy on the branches like globes of fruit. It is above you even now, and Man of Peace knew that if he climbed that tree, it would take him into the future, where he could explore its many branches, but Man of Peace did not want to climb among the tall branches; he only wanted to climb the trunk, then look up at the leaves to find where the slavers hid."

Tull studied the World Tree bursting from his belly. Its bark was rough and dark, rough like the bark of an oak, and it was tall with many branches. He could no longer see his feet. The trunk of the tree was enormous —filling the room, and the tree itself filled the sky. Stars blazed among its branches, moons hid in its leaves, and the tree was dark blue, the hue of the dark between the stars.

A flame leapt at the tree's trunk right before Tull's eyes—a single streak of pink lightning, and it tentatively wavered at the bole of the tree.

"That is right, let Man of Peace climb," Chaa urged. "There is so much to see in that tree. Its roots stretch deep into the past, and its branches flare wide into the future, twisting endlessly. Only here do the two halves join in a single moment. Let Man of Peace climb.

Do not try to stop him. Don't even try to help him. Man of Peace has climbed many trees and needs no help."

Tull watched the lightning waver at his belly, pinker than the sunrise, then begin to climb. Tull asked, "Why is Man of Peace pink?"

"He only looks pink today," Chaa answered. "Turn your eyes toward me. Look at the lightning of my soul."

Tull turned, saw blue lightning dancing over the black hollow of Chaa's soul. The Spirit Walker's body was but a pale shadow, like the flesh of a jellyfish. Within the gelatin lightning played, and the black sphere seemed small, a tiny black hole like the iris of an eye. The gelatin, the sack of flesh, was tinted slightly blue, coloring the lightning.

Tull gazed at his own navel, saw the hollow of his soul—large, like a huge ball, and the pink lightnings flashed over it, and the gelatin of his body colored the lightning pink.

Man of Peace had nearly climbed the tree, and Tull wondered what would happen if he fell. He became very concerned. The lightning snapped back into him.

Chaa swore mildly. "You were almost there! Here, Tull, close your eyes. If you must look anywhere, look at me. Let the Man of Peace go where he will. Think only of one thing, think of the slaver he wants to see. Imagine the slaver—the color of his hair, the shape of his nose, the strong arms."

Tull lay for a long time, and a calm dizziness entered him. He imagined a slaver in the forest, a slaver of the Blade Kin—a tall man, human with a strong nose and single eyebrow. He hid in the woods above Smilodon Bay, at night. Tull had never seen the man, but in his heart he recognized that this was how the slaver would look. The slaver stood on the hill above Smilodon Bay and crept quietly, all dressed in black. The man's heart pounded, afraid. Down in Smilodon Bay, lights shone in the streets.

Man of Peace watched the slaver, watched him and wanted something badly. Man of Peace went to the slaver, beheld pale green fronds of lightning dancing over a dark orb. Man of Peace entwined himself around a single rod of green light, and then with his tip, he danced across the dark hollow of the slaver's soul.

A strange sensation passed through Tull, as if a breeze were blowing through him, and Tull realized he was touching this human—that in some way, Tull's spirit was communicating with the slaver.

Suddenly Tull felt as if a blade of ice had pierced him, and he broke contact. He sensed something behind him, turned to see two huge black orbs floating through the redwoods. An inner voice shouted, "Spirit eaters!" and Tull fled.

Sound faded. The vision fragmented. Tull's head ached as if struck with a mallet, and he crawled to his knees, vomited seer's tea into the ashes of the empty fire. The room spun, and he lay a moment, trying to regain consciousness, and then found himself walking with Chaa through the dark, stumbling on a narrow trail. A light rain fell, and Tull suddenly remembered that he had wakened earlier to find Chaa urging him to his feet.

"Where are we?" Tull asked.

"We are on the way back to your house," Chaa answered.

"Oh," Tull said, and he stopped. He realized he had blacked out and didn't know for how long. "What time is it?"

"Still early. Your endeavors lasted only for a couple of hours."

"Did I connect with the slaver?"

"No," Chaa said, laughing mildly. "You did not connect. To connect takes very long. You only saw him and touched him, then you were frightened away."

"What are spirit eaters?" Tull asked, and he stopped, waiting for his head to clear. He suddenly realized that Chaa had sent him to seek the slaver for some purpose.

Chaa helped hold Tull upright a moment. "Spirit

eaters . . . in the Land of Shapes are creatures you cannot comprehend. Spirit eaters are . . . sometimes living people, who have hidden the lightning in their souls, concealed their own *effan*—their own holiness, or divinity. Instead they are dark, and they feed on the souls of others. Sometimes spirit eaters are incorporeal, like the ones that came to you. That is all I can say about them."

"Why did you have me seek a slaver?"

"I was testing to see how much control you had in the Land of Shapes. I hoped you would work harder if I gave you a warrior's task. You did very well for a first try."

Tull wanted to ask more, but his thoughts came slowly. He let Chaa usher him to the door, help him through. The fire was burning low in the fireplace, and on the mat in the corner Fava and Wayan lay huddled together asleep.

"Good night," Chaa whispered. "Get some sleep." He left.

Tull stood and stared stupidly for a moment, watching Fava. He squinted, realized that the drugs had not left him, for he could see into her, see the pink tendrils of light at her navel. There was almost no hollow to her soul—just the smallest of beads—and because of that he realized that she was a special woman, very precious. He went and lay beside her, wrapped his arms and legs around her, and clung to her.

Etanai worked hard after Tull's party, showing his pictures, trying to tell the people of Smilodon Bay the terrors of Bashevgo. The following morning he went with the Pwi boys out to a field and began learning the basics of swordsmanship.

Etanai had never touched a sword. The Blade Kin did not permit it of Thralls. Yet he marveled how naturally the sword fit his hand, how clean his blows could be. He suffered through hours of practice, wishing he were young. He felt shamed to be an old Thrall with no children, nothing but desire for vengeance keeping him alive. Often, when the grim despair struck and he thought of his sweet woman, he wanted only to die as she had died. But rage made him live.

Yes, it had been a good day. In all his years as a slave in Bashevgo, he'd never imagined anything so beautiful as this, watching the seeds of an army sprout.

When the sun set over Smilodon Bay, he went to Moon Dance Inn, which quickly filled with young Pwi from Finger Mountain and Muskrat Creek and Song of Glee—all young men who had heard rumors of strange happenings in town. Etanai showed them his paintings, and his heart leapt when he saw their rage, the fanatic gleam in their eyes. For a man with no tongue, Etanai had become persuasive, even eloquent. But after nearly two days without sleep, he finally signaled to the townsmen that he needed rest, even though the hour was early.

"Please, I would be honored if you would sleep at my house!" one young boy said, the beginnings of a yellow beard under his chinless face. Etanai remembered the boy's name, Farranon. Farranon's eyes held awe, as if Etanai were some great Lord instead of an old cripple.

Etanai grunted, carefully rolled his canvasses and placed them in their wooden map box, clutched the package under his tired arm.

Farranon wanted to carry them, but Etanai held tight. So many months of work had gone into the paintings. He could not bear the thought that some clumsy youth might stumble and crush them.

The boy opened the door, nearly dancing forward, and grabbed a taper by the doorway and set it alight. "This way, this way, just down the bridge and over the river to Pwi-town!"

The night was chill, and a thick fog had risen from the bay. Up in the sky Woden gleamed pale and milky blue, like a blind eye, half-closed. An evening drizzle muddied the streets, and Etanai hurried in the cold, just behind Farranon, who walked in his circle of light.

Etanai smelled the humans before he saw them—the musky human scent of vegetables, like broccoli or molding corn. But the boy must not have smelled them, for a man in black robes rushed forward, swung a club down, and knocked Farranon aside.

The torch fell in the mud, sputtered, and Etanai saw men around him, at least six, all in black robes. Two stuck a sack over Farranon's head, silently dragged him away.

"You should have stayed in Bashevgo," a deep-voiced human said, stepping forward. He was huge in girth, if not in height, and he had a great dark beard. Two men groped for Etanai from behind. He dropped his pictures, yelled "Ahh," and tried to pull away. Something hit Etanai hard in the back of the head, staggering him, and the attackers managed to grab Etanai's arms. Pain lanced through his arthritic shoulders, searing hot. His legs wobbled, and he nearly fell, but the men kept him on his feet.

Etanai looked at his shoulders where the pain lanced through; his captors held him upright with meat hooks. They did not intend to ship him back to Bashevgo. They wouldn't ship such torn merchandise, so Etanai screamed for help.

The man in front of him laughed. "Go ahead and scream, you tongueless bastard. Come on, let's hear it!"

Etanai screamed, leaning his head back, trying to project his croaking voice toward the inn. He sounded like a hound.

"Gah, gah, gah," his captor barked, mocking. "Right, right. Enough of that," he laughed. "Behold your executioner." He pulled back the hood to his robe, exposing his face. The mayor smiled down at Etanai, pulled a long knife from a wrist sheath.

"Go ahead! Scream once more. You can't wake anyone in this town," Garamon said. He plunged the knife into Etanai's stomach and twisted, and Etanai screamed from deep in his belly, screamed for release, his ruined voice no louder than the croak of a gull soaring over a vast and empty sea.

Fava and Tull were sleeping when the alarm rose, a cry of "Murder! Murder!" The sound came distantly to his little hogan from across the bay. Tull staggered up. "What's happening?"

"I don't know," Fava said. "Someone got killed. Go see who!" She handed him his sword, and Tull ran out, strapping it on. He could see dozens of people in the human part of town on the far side of the bay, gathered in a circle. He ran to the place.

Old Etanai lay in a pool of blood, a burnt taper near his elbow, still smoldering. Nearly fifty people had gathered in the street, shock apparent in their pale faces. Whatever tracks might have been in the mud were hopelessly erased.

At first Tull thought Etanai dead, but the old man panted in short gasps. Someone had bandaged the wound, but the pool of blood beneath Etanai was fresh, and Tull realized that the attackers had not gotten far. All around him he listened to comments. "Just got here . . . heard him scream . . . someone get some light . . ."

He looked up and down the road. The mayor's house sat on the corner two doors down, the windows lighted within, and the mayor's dogs were not barking. They were locked in their shed behind the house. *Garamon must have heard the shouts,* Tull thought. *An honest man would not hesitate to find out what was going on, even if it meant he had to run half-naked into the night.*

Tull glanced behind him. "Anorath, come with me," he said sprinting for the mayor's house. He watched the windows as he ran, saw a shadow within— the mayor at the fireplace. Tull decided not to call at the door, and when he looked behind, nearly everyone was with him. Tull hit the door full tilt, smashed it.

The mayor stood, stoking the fire in his night-clothes. Garamon turned to Tull and shouted, "What's the meaning of this?"

Tull grabbed the candlestick from the table, waved it near Garamon, saw dark splotches on the carpet, and said, "You've tracked blood on the floor!"

Garamon's eyes grew wide. "That's only mud!"

Anorath bent to inspect the floor. Garamon reached into his robe, pulling out something that flashed in the candlelight. Tull only guessed that it was a pistol when the muzzle flash went off, and someone cried out behind him. Anorath fell, grabbing Tull for support, tackling him.

"He's got a gun!" someone shouted too late, and the mayor spun, heading through a maroon curtain back toward the kitchens. Tull grabbed Anorath, and a moment later the Pwi rushed through the house, went back to the bedrooms, shouting, apparently unable to find the man. Some boys brought out Garamon's wife along with his twelve-year-old daughter. The women stood huddled in a corner, their faces pale. Garamon's wife had dark red hair and an aging face, but his daughter was all Garamon, the same black hair, the flabby cheeks. One of the Pwi rushed to the fire, pulled out a half-burned map-case filled with Etanai's smoldering paintings.

Tull sat on the floor, watching Anorath bleed from the ribs. The wound was small and clean, and Tull decided his friend would live. Yet Tull felt impotent, helpless. He could do nothing but sit and hold his friend. The mayor's house was large, the furniture rough-hewn, rustic. On the mantel above the fireplace were odd-shaped decorative glass bottles—midnight-blue, lime-green, amber, and scarlet.

As the crowd grew, the young men began running from house to house, shed to shed, looking for the mayor. Zealous young Pwi shattered the windows to human shops, then ran in to search. They herded some humans into the streets for questioning.

Chaa himself strode from room to room in Garamon's house, checking the walls. At last he settled before Garamon's wife and asked plainly, "Did you know your husband was a slaver?"

She looked at the pitiless faces of the Neanderthals and shook. "I didn't know!"

"Did you ever guess that he might be a slaver?"

"Never!" she said, but her eyes showed that she lied.

Chaa turned to the daughter. "And you, did you guess your father was a slaver?"

"Maybe," the child said.

"Do you know what we do to slavers?" Chaa asked the child. "Do you know the penalty?"

"You chop off their heads."

"That's right," Chaa said. "Behind the wall in your kitchen, I hear muffled cries. There is a passage behind it where your father takes his slaves. He has one there now. Can you show it to me?"

The girl only stood, unmoving. Chaa put his arm around her. "I will not harm you. Please, show us the passage."

The girl led them to the kitchen, pulled back a cupboard to reveal a secret tunnel. A dozen Pwi boys rushed into the hole and soon returned with Farranon, chained hand and foot. "The passage comes out at one of the warehouses by the docks!" one boy reported. "But Garamon has already left!"

Tull looked down the passage in the darkness; rage filled him. For an hour the Pwi searched the docks, until it became evident to all of them that the mayor was gone.

When Chaa returned from the hunt, Tull took his arm and snarled, "Help me find Garamon."

Chapter 4
Friendly Knives

T he morning after the attack against Etanai, the men of the village hunted for Garamon. Tull drew guard duty on the north end of town and took Wayan with him, while Fava sat at her father's house and painted a figurine for Wayan—a sabertooth she had carved. She'd already daubed a coat of soft tan over it, and now she painted its teeth and underbelly white, using a piece of wild cotton. Her clumsy Neanderthal hands were not designed to perform such detailed work, so it took great patience.

As she invested care into painting the sabertooth, she could feel the kwea of the figurine becoming stronger. The figurine itself was becoming a thing of power, and it emanated beauty in the same way that a fire emanates heat, until Fava felt suffused.

When Tull and Wayan came to the door, Tull clapped his hands and said, "I am here." Fava hurried to hide the figurine. Wayan ran into the house, down the dark passageways, looking for Itzha, the youngest of Fava's three sisters.

"Did you find Garamon?" Fava asked as Tull stepped through the door.

He hugged her and held her for a long moment before answering. "Not yet. Some boys took the mayor's own hounds and set them to tracking him. They went southwest of town for about a mile, then circled back to the north part of town. They lost his scent just inside the mayor's cloth shop. We're fairly sure he went there to get something—money, clothing. After that, I don't think he could have left town. We've set the Pwi guarding every entrance and patch of bushes. I think he's hiding in someone's house."

"In the house of a human?"

"Probably," Tull said. "It would have to be another slaver. Etanai is doing better. He drew stick figures to show that at least seven others were with Garamon."

Fava felt uneasy, shifted on her feet. Eight slavers in town. So many. "Are the Pwi searching the humans' houses?"

"Not yet," Tull answered. "I don't think it would be a good idea. It would frighten them. Besides, all those houses were built a hundred years ago, when the slavers still used to try to sail into the bay. They all have escape hatches and secret passageways. I suspect we could hunt for weeks and never find him."

Fava nodded, changing the subject. "Are you ready for lunch?"

"If you want," Tull answered, and they went to the kitchen and made small talk while Fava mixed cornmeal, dried pumpkin, salt, soda, and cream together to make thin cakes. As Fava worked, Tull seemed nervous. He paced the room, looking out the windows. She asked him to go to the icehouse out back and cut some moose steaks.

Tull got an old rusted blade from the knife shelf. "Don't use that knife!" Fava warned. *"Tcho-kwezhet!* It isn't friendly."

"It's the only one here," Tull explained.

She looked at the knife, feeling the kwea, the residue of her accumulated emotions, black and seething. The knife did not like them at all. "That knife has a bad heart," she said. "My father must have taken the others to the smith's to sharpen. You had better go there and get one."

"This knife is all right," Tull said, heading out the back door.

"No!" Fava shrieked, imagining Tull with that evil knife, falling and gutting himself in one motion. "Please, get another knife."

"I'm not going across town to get another knife. This one is fine." Tull hurried out the door. Fava ran and looked after him. He crossed the yard to the ice-house, which was dug into the back of the hill behind the main house. Tull unbarred the heavy door and went in. Fava kept expecting Tull to fall, kept expecting to see him come out covered with blood, but he returned safely with the steaks. Still she watched each step, afraid he'd stumble, slit himself open. It seemed that he made it to the door only by some great fortune. She could feel the malevolence from that knife, hissing and steaming like soup boiling over into a fire.

When he reached the door, she took the knife, carefully with both hands, and set it back on the shelf. "Please," she said, "don't ever touch that evil thing again."

"It isn't evil," Tull said. "It's just a knife."

"It isn't just a knife!" Fava shouted. "It's an angry knife!" Tull looked at her oddly, and Fava asked, "What's wrong?"

"You don't understand? Do you?" Tull said, and he paced the room. "How does the sky feel today?" It was a common greeting among the Pwi, meaning "How do you feel?"

Fava took his hand, placed it between her breasts, just holding it. "The sky feels good today, because you are with me."

Tull shook his head, led her to the hall. "Look at this room. What do you feel? What do you feel when you look at that skull?"

Fava looked up. Above the hallway that led to her father's Spirit Room was a mastodon's skull, and its long tusks curled down to the floor on either side of the hall. The kwea that issued from it was one of enjoyment; she had climbed and slid down those tusks many times as a child, so that the tusks were still ivory-colored on top, but had yellowed underneath. "I feel happy," Fava said.

"Aren't you afraid of those tusks?" Tull asked. "One of your sisters could fall on them, could even get hurt, couldn't she?"

"Yes, but it has never happened before."

"Still it could happen," Tull said. "So why don't you take the skull down?"

"But it has never happened. The skull likes it there. It has always treated us well."

"And what of the knife?" Tull said, waving toward the kitchen. Icy fear washed through her. It was a knife she would never touch. Tull was being cruel to keep referring to it, to have displayed it. He knew that it held vile kwea.

"That knife is very dangerous," Fava said. "It does not like me."

"How do you know? Because it cut you?"

"Yes. It also cut Zhopilla once and almost took off her finger! You should not trust it. It is very dangerous!"

"It's sharp," Tull corrected. "You have other knives in the house that are just as sharp, just as deadly, yet you feel no evil kwea emanate from them."

Fava simply stared at him. She could not see his point. That one knife might like you while another would not was well-known.

"I don't see the world like you do," Tull said. "I'm trying, but you Pwi all live in the past. You see the world and everything is shrouded with kwea—an alley scares you because a dog jumped out of it once, but the alley next to it makes you feel secure because you found shelter from the dog there. Phylomon the Starfarer explained it to me. He says that part of your brain, called the hypothalamus, is too large. It makes the Pwi feel everything more deeply than humans do—fear, love, despair, loneliness, joy. And all these emotions color your world. When you touch my hand, I don't really radiate love, do I?" Fava touched him, felt the invisible waves of joy radiating, tangible as a lover's cry issuing from his mouth. She knew that humans claimed not to feel kwea, but that seemed hard to understand. *Humans claim there is no kwea only because they feel none,* she thought. *They are all like blind men who teach that there is no light only because they cannot see it.*

"Yes, you radiate love for me," Fava said.

"Yet I haven't always loved you," Tull said. "I loved Wisteria."

"Even then your spirit radiated passion for me," Fava countered. "Always. Even if you only felt *hechazho,* cattle love, for me, you always enjoyed my presence."

Tull shrugged as if at his wit's end. "Who rules Bashevgo?"

"Adjonai, Him We All Fear." It was a question any child could answer.

"And can you feel his kwea? Can you feel him reaching out to snatch you?"

"The redwoods hide us," Fava said uncertainly. She did not like thinking about Adjonai. It made perspiration rise on her forehead.

"But the redwoods can't always hide you, can they? The slavers find us sometimes and take us to Craal."

Fava began trembling. She could feel the dark god beyond the mountains, searching for her, stretching his long hands across wilderness like a cloud. She choked back a sob.

Tull stepped close and held her. "Adjonai is not really here," Tull said. "He's an illusion, created by your fear. I've been to Craal. The sun shines just as brightly on Denai and Bashevgo as it does here. People laugh and fall in love there. But their fear is strong. They fear the Blade Kin and the Slave Lords. They are so frightened that their feet would not carry them if they tried to run away. There is no Adjonai. He is only the embodiment of your fears.

"Yet," Tull said, "you don't fear the Blade Kin enough. That is not your fault; it is the fault of kwea.

You don't believe they will come in force, only because they have never done it before. They are a knife that has never cut you deeply. They've never attacked a town this large. Yet the humans here fear such an attack."

Outside, the gulls wheeled over the ocean and cried. The sound came through the windows distantly, almost like the startled cries of children, and Fava could feel the blood pounding in her veins. "You are saying the humans are smarter than us. I don't think they are smarter. They just have clever little hands. They are just lucky that their ancestors lived among the stars. Now they rot down here on the ground, just like us."

"No," Tull said. "I think that our ancestors on Earth could never have gone to the stars. We Pwi, because of kwea, because our thoughts are so strongly tied to our emotions, we always live in the past. We surround ourselves with the people we love, with the things we enjoy, and we live off the accumulated kwea. As long as we had our huts and our families and our favorite meat on the fire, we would have been overwhelmed by pleasant kwea, and we would have been content."

Fava looked at him, and everything he said seemed so obvious. Who could want more than that? It should be enough for anyone.

"We cannot think like the humans do," Tull said. "We don't look to the same source for happiness. The humans, because they are seldom aware of kwea, they live only in the future. They look ahead and plan to be happy somewhere in the future, at some distant time, when they have accumulated all the wealth and power they think they will need. For them, a family and a hut and good food on the table is not always enough."

Tull squeezed her hand, and Fava looked down. Tull had huge hands, big paws like a Pwi, with robust joints on fat fingers and a thumb that was not tilted like a human's.

"If they can never be happy, then we should pity them," Fava said. Then she looked up at him, and realized what he was saying. "You mean to say, you are Pwi, but your heart is human? You find it hard to be happy today because you live for tomorrow?" She saw it was true. Tull was like her father, like a Spirit Walker, always scheming and thinking about tomorrow. The similarity had never occurred to her. She had married someone like her own father.

"I am neither human, nor Pwi," Tull said. "I am Tcho-Pwi, No People, the Un-family. I can wear your clothes, even look like a Pwi, but I cannot be Pwi at heart, just as I can never be completely human. I don't feel kwea as strongly as you do. I feel no animosity emanating from this knife as you do. To me, it is just a piece of wood and metal. Yet in some things I do feel kwea. I feel love emanating from you. I feel the kwea of our time together, and even though I love you, I fear that perhaps the human part of me will never let me crave you the way that you crave me. I am not a Pwi. Even if I were, you know how I have lived. You know how my father beat me and kept me chained to the wall as if I were one of his dogs. My past is so dark, I cannot find much pleasure in it. And when I look at the future—I cannot see much reason to hope for happiness.

"Maybe that is why, when I'm with you, I wish time would stop, so every moment would become endless. I guess that what I want most of all is for just a few days to forget about the world, all of its past and all of its future, so that I can enjoy you."

Fava stood for a long moment. "I understand . . . I think. If I could give you those days, I would. But I don't know how to do it."

"Fava," Tull said, "your father has asked me to become his student, to learn to Spirit Walk." Tull touched her shoulder. For a moment Fava felt a foreboding. Chaa would take Tull from her as certainly as if he were a slaver dragging Tull to a distant land. By the tone of his voice, Tull was asking permission to go.

Fava nodded thoughtfully, considering whether to give that permisson. "He asked you this two nights ago, when he took you aside at the lake. Didn't he?"

"Yes," Tull answered softly.

Fava watched him standing there, a little too far away by Pwi standards, and his face was closed, secretive. Tull still hid something from her. She could read him for the moment, read him as easily as if he were a Pwi, and something in her craved to be able to read him always, hungered to grow so knowledgeable about him that his body would become like a paper with words written on it.

"You are hiding something from me," Fava said. "You keep doing this to me. You keep secrets, and the secrets keep us apart."

Tull sighed deeply. "I didn't wait for your permission," Tull said. "I didn't ask for your advice. Last night, I crept out of the house and met your father. He gave me seer's tea to help open my spirit eyes."

Fava's nostrils flared, and the blood ran hot and angry in her veins. She tried to control her words, to keep from saying angry things, but the words seemed to fly from her mouth. "Am I even a wife to you? Do you pretend to give yourself to me in the wedding circle, and then sneak out of our bed?"

Tull stepped back, his face a mask of surprise, as if he had never imagined that Fava was even *capable* of becoming angry. "I'm sorry," Tull said. "I just wanted to protect you!"

He stepped close as if to hug her, and a strangled cry escaped from deep in Fava's throat. "You don't need to protect me!" Fava shouted. She slapped him in the chest, hard. Fava knew her Pwi strength. If Tull had been a full-blooded human, the blow might have broken some ribs. As it was, he stepped back, obviously stung.

"Can't you see? Can't you see what you are doing?" she said, and she stood, gasping, struggling for words. If Tull had been a Pwi, he'd have known. He'd have seen the hurt and hopelessness in her eyes when she learned that he had kept a secret of such magnitude. If he had been a Pwi, he would never have picked up an unfriendly knife and showed it to her. If he had been

Pwi, Tull would have felt the kwea of her love radiating to him, across space, across any distance, and he would never dare to violate her trust.

But he wasn't Pwi. He was an emotional cripple, blind to kwea. If Tull were a legless beggar sitting outside the inn, his injuries could not have been more horrifying to Fava.

She turned, ran out the back door and stood, wondering what to do, almost choking on despair. The air seemed cold with the evening chill, and Fava sat on a chopping log and stared down at the cream-colored chips of alder by the woodpile. She could see no way to make Tull understand what she felt for him. She'd always known that his human ancestry made him different, made him somehow difficult to communicate with, but she'd always hoped he would overcome it. Now Fava saw the truth: Tull could never love her as deeply as if he were a Pwi. They would always have a chasm separating them.

Tull walked out and stood behind her, his shadow making a cool spot on her back. Fava cried uncontrollably for a while, and Tull did not try to touch her. The kwea of love seemed to radiate from him, as if his warm fingers stroked her hair, played down her shoulders.

"I love you," Tull whispered.

Fava remembered something her father once said when she was a child. "Humans must explain their emotions so much, because they feel so little." He had said it as a joke, but now Fava saw the bitter truth hidden beneath the words. Words. They seemed such an inadequate vehicle.

Fava wiped the tears from her eyes, and realized that Tull could not read her. If he was ever to understand her love for him, she would have to speak it, instead of relying on him to read her emotions. "I know you love me, and I know you are different from me." Tull came and stood behind her, wrapped his arms around her. She took his big hands and just held them.

"If you hunt for happiness in the future, like some

human, then you will need my father's training. I wish
you peace like a meadow, joy above the mountains."

Tull slept throughout the day while the Pwi guarded the
mayor's exit. Chaa did not come home until late afternoon, and by then his eyes were red, with dark circles
beneath.

After a quick dinner, Tull went to Chaa's Spirit
Room and asked, "As a Spirit Walker, can you use your
power to find the mayor?"

Chaa was sitting cross-legged on the mat on the
floor. He looked up. "I could try, but it is hard," Chaa
answered. "If Garamon wants to remain hidden, his
spirit will make itself invisible to me."

"Do you know where he is now? Have you seen
where he would hide during one of your Spirit Walks?"

Chaa hesitated. "No," Chaa said. "His spirit is
dark, completely without light. On my Spirit Walks, I
avoid touching the souls of corrupted men, as you must.
Long ago Terrazin Dragontamer showed us the folly of
that path."

"So you have never walked Garamon's future?"

"No."

"Then how shall I find him?"

"Look inside yourself. Perhaps you already know
part of the answer," Chaa said. "Last night you began to
open your spirit eyes, and you saw a slaver of the Blade
Kin. He may be the answer. If you find him, you will find
the mayor nearby."

Tull sat down next to Chaa, looked him in the eyes.
"How do you know?"

"I am not certain," Chaa said. "But you touched
the Land of Shapes, and there you saw something from
the future. Your spirit eyes knew that you would be
hunting Garamon soon, and so they showed you something."

"They showed me the answer to a problem before I
knew of the problem?"

"I think so," Chaa said.

"I know where I saw him," Tull said eagerly. "He was on the hill above my cabin."

"Yet do you know *when* he will be there?" Chaa asked. He became silent a moment, and hung his shoulders as if tired. Through the smoke hole in the roof, Tull could hear some children laughing on the street outside. Among the Pwi, if a man seemed too eager to purchase something, the Pwi had the habit of growing silent for an extended period of time, making the offender wait. Chaa adopted such a silence now, letting Tull know that his eagerness was not appreciated. After three minutes, Chaa continued, "In the Land of Shapes, there are no boundaries of time. You must *connect* with the slaver from your vision. Connecting is much harder than simply viewing, for you must take on the person's thoughts and memories. Still, it is not so complex as taking a Spirit Walk." Chaa put his hand to Tull's head. "Your spirit eyes are still struggling to open. Rest now. You must be patient. We can try in a few days."

"I am ready now," Tull said.

"It is too soon for you to take another journey in the Land of Shapes. You don't know the dangers," Chaa countered. "Your spirit eyes are just beginning to open, and for the first few times that you journey in the Land of Shapes, each time you see it, it will change again. Rest for a few more days before such a journey."

"Are you afraid of the spirit eaters? Could Garamon himself attack me in the Land of Shapes?"

"No, I am not afraid of him. But there are worse things than spirit eaters," Chaa said. "Things . . . I cannot explain."

"Tell me about my enemies," Tull said, hoping to learn just a little more.

Chaa struggled for words. "When you drank the seers' tea, part of you was opened. I showed you the Land of Shapes, and there you saw the hollow of your soul—the place where your dark urges reside, and you saw darkness streaming out, trying to escape. Dancing over that, you saw the flames of your spirit, the pale fronds of lightning that eat the darkness as it tries to escape, and all of these reside in a jelly, the thing we call 'the clot' of the soul."

"Yes, the colored jelly."

"The lightning of your soul does continual battle with the hollow of your soul," Chaa said, "eating the darkness before it can escape. The lightning of your soul is your inner beauty struggling to break down that darkness."

"And the clot?" Tull asked.

"Is only the way your spirit eyes see the body that it wears. The colors in your clot are emotions, and they form a cloud over both the hollow of your soul and the lightning of your soul."

Chaa poured himself a drink from a nearby pitcher. For a moment, Tull feared that Chaa would get the seer's tea out, but this pitcher was small and blunt, with pictures of frogs painted on it. Chaa drank long and deep, and clear water spilled down his lips. "For most people, the hollow of the soul and the lightning of the soul seek some kind of balance. The pale lightning does not overwhelm the dark, and the hollow of the soul never outgrows itself. But for some, the dark hollow streams out constantly and smothers the lightning. Men who are thus afflicted lose consciousness of their own inner beauty, their own divinity, and they will send their darkness outward, struggling to overshadow the lightning in the souls of others. Seldom does even a small frond of lightning take root in them again. Such creatures become spirit eaters."

"How do I kill them?" Tull asked.

Chaa pondered a moment. "You can't. You can only resist them. Rather than kill them, I would have you remember their beauty. The divine fire that is in you also burns in them, though it is hidden."

Tull let his eyes wander across the tiny room to the cabinets where Chaa kept his drugs. "You said that sometimes these spirit eaters are men," Tull said. "Do I know any of them?"

"You do not have to be a Spirit Walker to know their names."

"Garamon was one," Tull said. "And my father?" Chaa nodded. "But what of Fava? She has almost no hollow to her soul."

"That is why I named her *Fava*, after the pear tree, most generous of trees. She will only give light to others."

Tull sat thinking for a moment. He had been surprised at the size of the hollow of his own soul, so large in comparison to Fava's. "What of the birds and animals, what of time and the future?" Tull asked. "I saw nothing of them. I saw so little."

"This is true," Chaa said. "The spirit eyes open slowly, and you caught only a glimpse of the Land of Shapes. It is incredibly much larger than what you saw, and it will change each time you enter for the first few times. As your eyes open, you will see more clearly. There are beings there, neither hollow nor lightning nor clot, which can influence you, yet I cannot name them. Some would harm you, and some would help. Most do neither.

"Time there is a river, which you can stop at will.

"Animals and plants and even stones exist there, much in the same form as humans. In time you will learn to see them. You must learn to value them, for the divine light shines in them also.

"I will send you back to the Land of Shapes soon, and you will see more, begin learning how to *connect*— to perceive the thoughts and hearts of others. Yet even connecting is only a small art. Connecting is to Spirit Walking what a child's crawl is to dance. Until you have learned to connect to others, I cannot begin to teach you how to walk the future. Until then, rest."

Tull asked, "But when you Spirit Walk, do you need rest? I've seen the sorcerers of the Blade Kin lying near death, just as you do when you take your Spirit Walks."

"Taking a Spirit Walk requires concentration, focus," Chaa said. "The past is immutable, a straight line to what has been. We can relive it, but we cannot change it, and so viewing the past is easy. However, when we come to the future, we see that it is vast and complex. The great tree branches in so many places, that exploring it takes profound concentration. It is only when we leave our bodies, become tied to the past and the present by only the tiniest thread, that we focus enough to create the future."

"Create?"

Chaa frowned. "Yes, *create* is the right word. The future exists without us, yet each moment offers us the potential for change, and so we must organize, *create* the future." He stretched, looked up.

"Tell me more," Tull said.

Chaa sighed, rubbed his eyes. The silence stretched out, and Tull realized Chaa was punishing him again for his eagerness. At last, Chaa said, "I am disappointed in you. You keep speaking of hunting, and killing, and enemies. A Spirit Walker is not a hunter. A Spirit Walker is not a killer. He has no enemies. It is time for you to leave. But I want you to do something for me. I want you to walk home now, in the dark. Take thirty seconds between each step, and consider where best to place your foot—remembering that each blade of grass represents a life as vigorous as your own, each insect or worm you crush has a life that it regards as equal in value to your own. I want you to walk home," Chaa said, "cautiously. Be considerate of every step you take. Let the peace that is within you guide the tiniest footfall, so that you pass gently."

"You want me to walk home without crushing any grass or killing any worms?"

Chaa nodded solemnly. "A Spirit Walker gains great power and can crush a man as easily as a worm. Restraint and good intent—these two lie at the heart of the art of Spirit Walking. Until you practice these two traits, I will teach you no more."

Tull got up wearily. Fava and Wayan had already eaten and gone home so Tull set off alone. The walk should have taken only five minutes, yet when Tull left Chaa's hogan, Tull removed his moccasins and walked carefully in the full moonlight, staying to the most worn parts of the trail, using his toes to move aside blades of grass and probe for the limp bodies of nightcrawlers. The cold ground numbed Tull's feet, making the task all but impossible. The journey home took most of the night.

In the early afternoon Phylomon the Starfarer tacked into the long fjord at the mouth of Smilodon Bay and began the journey upriver to the town itself; the sails sagged once they escaped the open sea, as did his shoulders. Even in the cold wind, the ancient Starfarer wore little, relying on the pale-blue symbiote that he wore as a skin to protect him.

On the hills beside him, huge redwoods overshadowed the river so that it felt as calm as a lagoon. Woodpeckers tapped the trees about him, and gray squirrels and jays chattered to announce his presence. Scandal the innkeeper lay in back of the boat under a tarp, snoring. Phylomon recalled other trips he'd made to Smilodon Bay, hundreds of years ago. He'd been taking seritactates then, and the drugs had let him record memories flawlessly.

Eight hundred years ago, Smilodon Bay had been nothing. On his first visit he had come to see how the woodland mastodons that his father had introduced were faring. The redwoods had been younger, hardier. Two hundred years later, he'd sailed here again, bringing a load of cloth to a Neanderthal fishing village. The natives painted themselves blue when they saw Phylomon and worshiped him as a god. On that warm spring day the Pwi were smoking fish, slowly roasting them on twigs along an embankment. Oily smoke swirled among the trees and hung heavy near the ground. A shaman

had complained bitterly to Phylomon that battles with
slavers had killed all the old men, so now there were not
enough old men to teach the young boys. It was a bla-
tant attempt to get Phylomon to stay, to share his
knowledge, but Phylomon had left anyway.

Two hundred years later, when he returned, the village had crumbled, hogans rotted into the ground. Not
even a circle of stones showed where campfires had
been, and Phylomon had wondered if he had stayed for
a season to help the old shaman, teach the young how to
protect themselves from the slavers, if perhaps the village would have remained.

At that time Phylomon had been a warrior with his
wife and sons, leading a band of Pwi, hoping someday to
attack Bashevgo. Among the ranks was a promising Pwi,
only a child really, with rippling cords for muscles, anger
in his eyes. Terrazin Dragontamer. It had been in this
camp that Terrazin first called a dragon from its nest—a
young brown tyrant bird that dived into camp, beady
purple eyes staring from a blood-red serpentine head,
waving its venomous horn as it glared at the Pwi. The
psychic link between Terrazin and his animal guide had
been frightening to behold. Phylomon had looked into
the small dragon's eyes even then and recognized that
they were familiar. They were Terrazin's eyes. The similarity, the bond between the two creatures, had shocked
Phylomon. *It should not have surprised me,* Phylomon
thought, *that Terrazin would become so ruthless. It should
not have surprised me that the psychic warrior went mad,
killed so many.*

Phylomon's blue skin tightened, as if preparing for
attack. The ancient symbiote felt his distress. *I am not
afraid,* Phylomon told the symbiote, *I am only old. I feel
older than my thousand years.*

When Phylomon came within sight of the city, gulls
spun in lazy circles by the shore while cormorants shot
past. The watchmen at the inn above town spotted Phylomon, waved, and fired one of the nine-inch cannons.
A colossal waste of gunpowder here in the wilderness.

In the back of the boat, Scandal woke, gazed at the city through the soft haze of the sea wind, grinning to be home again. "Hah," Scandal laughed, "they've shot a cannon for us, a fine welcome!"

Phylomon watched the black stones of the houses and inns. A deep unease settled on him, something he could feel but not explain. "How well do you know Tull?" Phylomon asked. As he said the words, he realized the source of the unease. Tull was from this town, and Terrazin had gained his power here. Tull had taken the sea serpent as his animal guide, Terrazin the dragon. Both creatures formed from scratch by the Starfarers. An odd coincidence, but one Phylomon found hard to shake.

"Why, I've known him for eight years," Scandal said.

"Do you trust him?"

"Of course," Scandal answered. "He's honest. I sent him south to White Rock with a shipment of beer when he was fifteen, and he never so much as cracked a keg."

Phylomon looked back at him. "How easily can he harm others?"

Scandal sat, taken aback, and Phylomon could tell that Scandal feared to answer. He did not speak because he wanted to know the right answer in advance. Scandal sighed. "He scares me a bit, I suppose. You know, you can live next to someone all your life and never really know him. I love that boy, but when we were in Craal, after the Blade Kin whipped him, Tull could have walked away quietly. Yet he had to grab a sword and kill them. He has a strong sense of justice."

"When you looked in his eyes as he killed, what did you see?"

Scandal squirmed in his seat. Phylomon stared, forced him to answer. "I guess I saw him butchering those slavers. They weren't his equal in a fight. He wanted more than blood, more than justice. He was so relaxed, like a man who has just made love. My wife used to say that Tull had 'Revolution in his eyes,' but I pitied anyone who met him while he held that naked sword. I'll be honest. His blood lust scares me."

"You love him, but he scares you?" Phylomon said. "Me too." Phylomon pondered a moment, considered the similarities, tried to put the thought from his mind.

The cannon shot brought people running, and as the little sailboat swept into town, Phylomon searched the banks, but did not see Tull. The mayor's house had burned to the ground, and the ashes still smoldered. A crowd of Pwi ran north to cross the redwood bridge, shouting that Phylomon had come to town.

At Moon Dance Inn that evening the beer flowed freely and a crowd gathered around Phylomon. Scandal sat on a table next to a cage that carried a sour-smelling "bird" from Hotland, and began telling his and Phylomon's story. The bird was more than half lizard and hung from the top of its cage by its feet, the claws on the end of its scaly fingers gripping the bars. Scandal fed it sweetmeats from his tray as he talked.

Nothing Scandal said seemed to astonish the crowd, though the innkeeper worked hard at it. News of Craal armies a thousand miles away did not impress them—no matter how large the armies. The villagers had already heard from Chaa about how the Creators had formed small humans and were experimenting in genocide. Yet the Pwi did not fear it, and Phylomon realized he should have known: The Pwi could not generate much fear of the Creators, for the Creators had never attacked before. No evil kwea had been established in the Pwi's minds.

"So we got down to Storm Hold," Scandal said, describing the last leg of their trip, "hoping to get a little rest, and the snow was falling a foot deep in places. You would think that under such conditions, folks would be happy to see us, honest folks escaping Craal, but no. Phylomon and I got no welcome there, and I swear that half the men in the room were pirate slavers, wintering out of Bashevgo."

Storm Hold, being on the edge of the Rough bordering Craal, had always been rife with shady dealing. But Scandal said, "I'm telling you boys, the town was filled with greedy bastards—not just pirates, but merchants who were just as bad as pirates, men that couldn't be slimier if they bathed in snot. You wouldn't catch me dead trying to walk into that town alone. Ayaah, things have changed. When I was a kid, Storm Hold was a fast ally, and a strong one. Now it's an outpost of Craal in all but name."

Suddenly Phylomon could feel an electricity in the room, a tension that had not been there before. Though stories of distant armies could not faze the Pwi, this small betrayal close to home caused considerable dismay. Tull entered the front door of the inn with Fava and a human girl. Phylomon motioned for them to come sit, and they pressed through the crowd.

"It's good to see you," Tull said to Phylomon, clasping his arm.

Phylomon looked deeply into Tull's eyes. "Good to see you," he said mechanically. He saw no dragons in the boy's eyes, but something had changed. "I understand congratulations are in order. You married since last I saw you?"

"Yes," Fava answered, and as the three seated, Scandal began telling the crowd how he and Phylomon had stolen a boat to escape Storm Hold.

The two girls, Fava and a dark-haired human, sat with straight backs, muscles tensed. Phylomon could tell that they were uneasy around him. As last of the Starfarers, he was more legend to them than man. Yet Tull remained open, familiar.

Phylomon said, "I've been gathering news from your townsfolk. It seems you made it here with the serpent eggs intact. I'm glad. I suppose I should be glad that the Creators thought highly enough of me to send one of their messengers to kill me—though you and Chaa made short work of the beast. Still, it established

some bad kwea among the Pwi. Perhaps they will see
the Creators as a threat now."

"Ayaah," Tull said, "the Pwi will march when
you're ready. I've had the boys practicing with swords
for the past few days. But what news have you? Were
you able to save the tiny humans?"

Phylomon leaned back in his chair. "Gray birds attacked us twice in as many weeks. They watched us from
a safe height and followed until we got to a valley of fog
and escaped in the night. We managed to get ninety
small humans to an Okanjara village. I paid the Okanjara well to care for our charges." The blue man leaned
forward, folded his hands. "You saw the lamprey that
the Creators sent for me. Did it look exactly like the
lampreys they tested on the small humans?"

"Yes," Tull answered, "except that it was larger and
had a blue symbiote, like the one you wear."

"That concerns me," Phylomon admitted. "Are you
sure the lamprey is dead?"

Fava said, "The Pwi were afraid, so they burned the
body down to ashes."

"And Chaa skinned it," Tull said.

Phylomon looked up, suddenly cautious. "He took
the symbiote? Where is the hide now?"

"He is tanning it, in the shed behind the house,"
Fava answered.

The Starfarer glanced quickly around the room,
stood. "I must go look at it." *For the first time,* Phylomon
thought, *I am sure. Chaa is playing with me, like a cat
with a mouse.*

Phylomon realized he must have betrayed a look of
nervousness, for Tull apologized, "He meant no harm.
He only took it as a hunting trophy."

"You are far too naive a pup to understand what he
means," Phylomon countered, and he excused himself
from the table, walked out the front door of the inn into
the afternoon air. A crisp wind had blown in, carrying
the smell of salt spray, and Phylomon hurried down the
street, walking loose in the joints. After a week in the

boat, he hadn't got his land legs back. Tull, Fava, and the dark-eyed girl followed.

They rushed downhill through the human part of town with its buildings of leaning gray stone. Phylomon did not want to show his concern about the worm's symbiote. It was a powerful weapon, and he did not want those around him to know how easy it would be to acquire the thing. He decided to try to divert the group's attention. As they passed the smoking ruins of the mayor's house, Phylomon said, "This artist you rescued, I trust he is still doing well after the attack?"

"Ayaah," Tull said. "He's recovering a bit."

Phylomon crossed the redwood bridge, hurried past the log hogans of the Pwi with their sod roofs. When he got to Chaa's house, he walked around the outside to the back, found the worm skin stretched round like a beaver's pelt. The skin was light blue, the symbiote still alive and healthy. Phylomon touched the thing, could almost feel its desire as it sought another host.

"You see," Fava said. "It's here, as I said."

Leaning close, Phylomon tried to study the knife cuts. He took one knife from his leg sheath, pried off the nails that held the hide to the board, and matched the left and right halves of the symbiote. They fit perfectly—knife stroke for knife stroke. Chaa had apparently not removed any of the skin. And yet, Phylomon reasoned, Chaa was a Spirit Walker with a great deal of knowledge. He could not be so stupid as to leave the symbiote here, waiting for a host, while near-immortality stood within his grasp. "What is Chaa up to? What is he thinking?" Phylomon whispered more to himself than to the others.

"He's been busy the past couple of days," Tull offered. "Chaa has taken me as his pupil, training me to become a Spirit Walker."

Phylomon whirled and grabbed Tull's arm, holding it, and he looked deeply at Tull. "What have you learned so far?"

"Nothing," Tull answered defensively. "I received

my first lesson. He began . . . by trying to open my eyes." Phylomon's grip tightened, and Tull tried to pull away.

"What are you afraid of?" Tull asked.

Phylomon looked deep into Tull's pale green eyes, searching for . . . something. Tull seemed hurt, confused, and Phylomon realized that the boy deserved better treatment. They had traveled together for months during the summer, worked and sweated and despaired together as they first hunted for young serpents to bring back to Smilodon Bay, then hunted for serpent eggs as a last resort. If not for Tull, their quest would have failed. The boy deserved to be treated as a friend.

"I'm sorry. I didn't mean to hurt you. I . . . do not want you to train as a Spirit Walker," Phylomon measured his words. "To do so is to turn your back on the future. There is a college opening at South Bay where men are beginning to unravel the technology of my ancestors. In fifty years radio waves will begin to reach us from Earth, and we can rediscover how our ancestors entered the atomic age. You could help build the antennae to catch those radio signals. You could learn of their medicines, their machines, their spaceships. All the ancient knowledge of the Starfarers could be yours. You do not need to become a Spirit Walker."

"Fifty years?" Tull asked. "Perhaps it seems like nothing to you, but I'll be an old man when those signals reach us. Besides, our ancestors sent radio signals for generations before they made any real discoveries."

"I know my path sounds difficult," Phylomon offered. "You would need to be patient."

"And watch our people die? You have seen the Blade Kin on our border. Do you believe we have fifty years to wait or study?" Tull ripped free of Phylomon's grasp and shouted desperately, "I need some way to fight them now! I need a weapon!"

Phylomon looked deep into Tull's eyes. His words were blasphemy. No Spirit Walker in his right mind would knowingly train a pupil who saw the power as a weapon.

Suddenly Phylomon recalled a memory over three hundred years old: He had been on a battlefield, burned black with cinders, littered with twisted corpses, and on a hill he saw an oak, blackened like the bodies. Under the oak rested a dragon, a simple horned dragon like all the ones that the Starfarers had formed to protect Calla from the pteradons and pterodactyls that would otherwise fly over from Hotland. But this dragon was blackened and its feathers singed, as if it too had been burned in the fire. As Phylomon walked to it, the dragon lifted its wing: Cradled beneath the wing was a young boy, a Neanderthal with piercing blue eyes set deep beneath his brows, eyes aflame with rage, hair so blond, it almost gleamed white: Terrazin Dragontamer. The memory came so clear, so frightening, that Phylomon drew a breath. The final battle of the Talent War flashed before Phylomon's eyes, the battlements of Bashevgo cracking from the blast, laser canons warping in on themselves while legions died, clawing their battle armor from their faces, clawing their own eyes from their sockets, clawing the air.

Phylomon began to breathe heavily. The memory frightened him more than he could say for reasons he could not begin to fathom. *I taste your fear,* his symbiote whispered.

"Are you all right?" Tull said, and Phylomon looked into Tull's eyes; they were Terrazin's—hinting at rage, despair, and madness.

The Starfarer closed his tired eyes, whispered to his symbiote, "I've executed many men for what they have done. In that I was just. But I've never executed a man for what he might do."

What he might do.

Circles, Phylomon told himself, *I've been walking in circles all these years. Here I am, at Smilodon Bay, and it is all starting again.*

Things Chaa had said after his last spirit walk suddenly made sense to Phylomon. After Chaa had looked into the future, trying to learn why the sea serpents had died, he spoke to Phylomon, saying, "Tull can end the war in two years. He alone can destroy the nations of Craal and Bashevgo, defeat the Slave Lords. You will die within two years." Phylomon had hoped Tull would be a great warlord, but now he began to see. If Tull were another Terrazin, of course he would defeat the Slave Lords. If Tull were another Terrazin, Phylomon would not escape him alive. What hope could Craal and Bashevgo have against such a monster? Their six million Blade Kin against Tull—their resistance would matter less than that of grass against a scythe.

I taste fear, the symbiote whispered, and Phylomon's skin tightened involuntarily, preparing for attack.

Chaa, Phylomon told himself, *you foolish young Spirit Walker, to harbor such hopes. I managed to destroy Terrazin once, at great price! At great price!* As if doors had opened in Phylomon's mind, he saw the truth: *Do you think to train Tull, to keep your monster on a leash, then kill him once he has won your war for you? Do you think to sacrifice him as you did your own sons?*

Phylomon took the pale-blue symbiote, carried it across the street, and hurled it into the bay.

For the rest of the afternoon Phylomon hunted for Chaa, but the Spirit Walker eluded him till dusk. Phylomon found Chaa down at the redwood bridge, fishing pole in hand, like some human. He had a wooden bait pail at his side. The Spirit Walker looked up at Phylomon, smiled.

"So, you have had a good day?" Chaa asked. Chaa didn't have his line in the water. Instead, the bait—a ball of chicken guts—rested inches from the surface.

"I've been searching for you," Phylomon said.

"I know," Chaa answered. He squinted off toward Tull's cabin. "You know, I think Tull and Fava will make a good pair. Everyone in town has given them wedding gifts. What will you offer them? Gold? A jewel? An old man's loyalty?"

"I know what you are thinking," Phylomon said. "Your plan is dangerous."

Chaa nodded thoughtfully. Waves rolled beneath them, and suddenly Chaa dropped the line, let it sink. Almost as soon as his line touched the water, a huge fish lunged upward, grabbed the bait. Chaa fought it for a moment, then swung it up onto the bridge. It looked like a lingcod, with sharp teeth, but it had a blue skin like Phylomon's. Chaa looked up at the blue man. "You think evil of me, but I know what I'm doing," Chaa said, and he wrapped the fish in a blanket.

Phylomon stood, dazed by the Spirit Walker's nerve. "Throw it back!" he warned. He looked in Chaa's eyes.

Chaa asked evenly, "Do you think I am a stupid man? a wicked man?"

Phylomon moved forward, and Chaa grabbed the bait pail, splashed the contents over Phylomon, and the blue man's skin burned where it splashed—puckering and steaming. *Ammonia,* Phylomon realized too late. His symbiote convulsed, throwing him to the ground, and in his mind Phylomon could hear the symbiote, shrieking in pain. Acid could not mar the thing, fire could not burn it. But pure ammonia shredded the Starfarer's symbiote like paper.

Chaa stepped up, put a foot on Phylomon's chest, and held the bucket over him, threatening. The Starfarer could only lay panting, his symbiote shocked into unconsciousness. He looked around, embarrassed to have been taken down so easily, afraid that other townsmen might see, learn his secret weakness.

"I am neither stupid nor wicked," Chaa said. "I've Spirit Walked the lives of ten thousand men, and though my body is young, I have lived far longer than you. I am not stupid. I know how you Starfarers removed your symbiotes. And if I were a wicked man, I would kill you now! But I do not need your skin. For the first time in

three hundred years, a living symbiote has fallen into
our hands. Do you think you are the only one on this
world who desires or deserves immortality?"

"No," Phylomon admitted.

Chaa stepped back. "I am a man of peace, but I
know what you are thinking. For a thousand years you
have fought the Slave Lords and failed. You fear to
leave a symbiote where your enemies could get it. But
now it's my turn to fight, and Tull's. I warn you: Leave
me and my family alone!"

Chapter 5
A Crimson Night

Over the next four days the people of Smilodon Bay settled into a routine. Tull spent mornings and afternoons in a field outside town with Fava, Phylomon, and the Pwi. They sparred with swords, longspears, shields, and the Neanderthal's *kutow*—a double-headed ax as heavy as a mace. The practice field became crowded as Pwi and an occasional human poured in from nearby towns and back country. Often more than six hundred would practice at once, young men and women like Tull and Fava, children from the age of twelve on up, old men who should have fought their last battle ages ago.

Fava exulted at the sight. "Have you ever seen so many people!" she cried over the thump of maces on shields, the clack of wooden practice swords, the laughs and yelps of pain. "Surely we are a great army! The Lords of Bashevgo will never expect our attack!"

Tull did not have the heart to tell her that in Craal he had watched an army pass him on a mountain road taking over six hours just to move the ten thousand warriors with their armored mammoths. "Yes, we are growing strong," he offered.

In the Rough guns had long been rare, the supply of gunpowder unpredictable. Human Slave Lords who depended on armies of Neanderthals to protect them controlled the dispersal of personal armaments in order to keep them from the wrong hands. Even in the Rough, men who sold guns and ammunition had a curious way of dying young—blown apart with their own gunpowder. The Pwi feared such weapons. But Phylomon taught them the ancient arts, and in the back of the blacksmith shop they learned to combine sulfur with potassium nitrate and crushed charcoal from the ashes of the forge to form a weak gunpowder. They smelted brass and copper for bullet casings, tin for bullets, and with six men working at the forge at six shifts per day, they were able to make crude long-barreled guns like those that the Blade Kin of Craal had begun to use, yet their output was less than two a day.

During the nights Tull and the others kept a tight watch over the town, still hunting the mayor. For nearly a week there had been no sign of him, and Tull was becoming more and more certain that Garamon had escaped the net. But on the morning of the fifth day after Phylomon had returned, Tull was still keeping watch on the north end of town, at a communal fountain where the human women washed their clothing.

Darrissea Frolic came that morning, wearing her long black cape. Her face was flushed and sweaty from practicing on the sword field with the Pwi. The gangling human girl was obviously far outclassed by the Pwi with the sword, yet she had been working hard during the week. She broke the thin crust of morning ice from the washing rocks, went to work scrubbing a heavy wool tunic. As she scrubbed the clothes, Darrissea talked endlessly about weapons and sword strokes and parries until Tull wearied of her chatter; then she turned to him and changed subjects. "You know Phylomon better than anyone. Do you think he likes me?"

An intensity hung in the girl's voice, and Tull felt unsure how to answer. "I don't know. Have you ever even spoken to him so that you can ask him?"

"I've thought about it," Darrissea admitted, "but

every time I try, I feel stupid. I want to know how he feels about women."

"He has married once or twice," Tull said, "hundreds of years ago. The kwea of those marriages weighs on him. He loved his wives very much. But he is so old now, so different from us, I do not think he will ever marry again."

"Oh," Darrissea said, and she looked dreamily into the sky.

Tull laughed. "Do you like him?"

Darrissea scowled. "Go ahead and laugh. He's a good man. The first good man I've seen around here in a long time. I'm going to marry him someday."

Tull laughed harder, and Darrissea pulled her tunic from the water and splashed it at him. Suddenly there was a shout from behind the houses west of town, and they both looked up: On the hill a Pwi boy was pointing into town. "Garamon! Garamon—behind the cloth shop!"

Everywhere Pwi took up the shout and began running for the jumbled buildings behind the cloth shop. Tull stood firm, knowing that with so many guards deserting their posts, the mayor might try to slip through the net. For the rest of the morning, the Pwi rushed through the business district, but found no sign of the mayor.

When another Pwi came to stand guard, Tull hunted. The mayor had owned the cloth shop, but as a criminal his goods had been confiscated, distributed around town. Tull went to the empty shop, which still had bolts of cheap fabric strewn on the floor. The day was overcast with feathery clouds, and thin sunlight fell cold on the floor. In the silent room Tull stood, stretched out with his mind. What had Chaa said? "You can feel your enemies even in the dark or behind stone walls." The walls were stone, the room barren, yet Tull could feel Garamon nearby. He recalled the stone walls in Garamon's home—the hidden passage behind a cupboard, and Tull went to work pulling shelves from the walls. He felt like a dog yapping at mice in a woodpile, frenzied, panting with excitement. He could taste the scent. Garamon was near, the murderous bastard, and Tull could feel him.

Tull pulled the fixtures from the walls, but found no passage. When he was done, he stood, panting, exhausted. He looked up into the rafters of the building, the strong beams crisscrossing under the roof. There was no place to hide. He looked at the planks of the floor, began pulling them up at random. By afternoon Tull had exhausted himself, and the sensation that Garamon was near had vanished. Either Garamon had left, or Tull had become so numbed to the sensation that it no longer mattered.

Garamon has come out today, Tull thought. *Perhaps he has run out of food or water. He will come out again.*

Walking home, Tull tried to think of some other place the mayor could hide. The rafters? Could there be a false ceiling above them? He planned to check in the morning. Tull had left a cloak at Chaa's house the day before, so he stopped to get it. Zhopilla and Chaa were gone with the children. Probably visiting old Vi or some other friend. Tull went inside, found the cloak in Chaa's Spirit Room.

Being thirsty, Tull got the water pitcher, then opened the drawer where Chaa kept his herbs and looked at them. There were three bowls—powdered roots to make him hear, seeds to open his eyes. Even now Tull could almost feel Garamon. The murderer was near, so near. Tull took a pinch from each bowl, chewed it, and lay down on the floor.

I must open my spirit eyes, he told himself, *learn to see. Garamon is near.* Tull felt abruptly dizzy, realized that he could hear the ocean outside across the street, the waves lapping, as if he were outside. *I must open my spirit eyes.*

Tull dozed, then wakened in a dark pit filled with rubble, bits of broken red brick, some of them whole, all of them covered with lichen in metallic green or flecks of gold. The sky was the muted ocher of brass before it is burnished, and distant stars burned in it, dull, like flecks of mica beneath molasses. Tull rose, looked out, and found himself in a tower overlooking a barren plain of red rocks—no wind rushed through trees, no lark peeped at the sunset. The day seemed bitter cold.

Around him Tull glimpsed a landscape pocked with similar haphazard towers in the distance, and he glimpsed other spirits, brilliant in hues of purple and silver and fiery red and black, each guarding its little crater of rubble. The empty land between them looked like the scarred battlefield of some horrible apocalyptic war, a place where plants and life could never be again, a place of age-old broken stones. Somehow, lifting himself above the rock wall caused Tull discomfort, left him feeling vulnerable. He did not understand what kinds of creatures the other glowing beings might be. Some would pop up above their walls momentarily, only to float down, reminding him by their actions of marmots in an alpine meadow, sticking their furry noses from their burrows to test the air.

The hollow of his soul hovered above ground, a solid dark mass. Tendrils of shadow, like tiny hairs, kept erupting, seeking to escape, but the white lightning flared over the hollow, twisting in a crazy dance, erasing the darkness. Tull could see his body dimly: translucent hands, fingers, torso. Only the barest of substance, almost a distortion of space. His line of vision emanated from a position roughly where his head should be, but he could spin and view the world in a 360-degree circle without regard for appendages, as if this translucent body were meaningless in this world.

Tull explored the hole better—pieces of brick and blasted stones had been clumsily piled to form a wall of sorts, a wall that encircled him, leaving scant room for movement. Dark shadows filled his crater, and Tull sank in the darkness.

The ground was muddy and trampled—no clean paving stones for the floor—and beneath the ground a rugged tunnel wound down into blackness, branching here and there. In the tunnel below Tull could see a human skeleton, hand outstretched, carrying a bit of broken stone as if ready to place it.

Tull sank into the cave, observed the skeleton, picked clean by ants and beetles, reddened by dust. The room was similar to his cratered tower above, ramshackle and haphazardly created, barely able to support the weight of the stones above. Tull hovered over the skeleton, peered into the dark of its eye sockets. Just beneath the bones the tunnel branched again, leading to lower chambers, where the white glint of bones hinted at more skeletons in each little chamber.

The silence of the chambers made him nervous, and Tull floated back upward. Stones were strewn in the dirt, and Tull surveyed the wall around him. A gap on one end showed a place where the stones had fallen, in need of support. A stone the right size and shape would do much to repair the wall, and Tull hovered upward, looked at the wall, tried to remember the shape of stone he needed, and then floated out of his crater.

Everywhere were stones, broken and twisted, cracked by sun and rain. As Tull floated downhill, he was amazed to see that there were far more craters than he had imagined, each with glowing spirit creatures inside. Around him he heard popping noises. He wondered what they were, until he saw one large stone crack in half. A moment later he saw two other stones silently join together.

Among the craters spirits hovered, and all of them seemed to be trying to build houses, as if piling cracked rock were the only occupation in this land. Yet most of them failed—they had not built houses or walls at all— instead the creatures sat on the barren plain with only a few scattered rocks standing about them in obtuse piles, contemplating their shelter. Tull was intrigued by their witless performance, their inability to form even the most ludicrous of pits. They seemed mindless as sal bugs.

Tull floated down the valley, crossed a small hill, and in the distance saw a great structure, a twisted tower with vast rooms and open courtyards climbing into the sky. Dozens of buttresses ran up against it in odd places. Some buttresses seemed to turn into long running walls that stretched away from the tower for miles in all directions, all lending it support. The tower stood, convoluted almost beyond recognition, as if it had been pulled from potter's clay as alien in design as if it had been the handiwork of termites or crabs. At the top of the tower a green ball of flame bustled up and down, busily at work.

A strange compulsion overtook Tull, and he moved toward the tower, floating like thistledown. He looked down at his legs, found that they were running faster than he would have thought possible, jumping from stone to stone, trying to maintain balance. Tendrils of light leapt around the hollow of his soul, pushing him forward. On some level he understood that legs were irrelevant in this stony land.

Along his way Tull began to look at the edifices he passed, and in one of them—a tiny hovel upon a near-empty field—a yellow ball of flame worked, trying to hold a pile of stones upright so that his single wall would not collapse. Tull moved in closer, saw the shape of the jellied clot. It was Byron Saman, an old gentleman from town, and Tull suddenly realized that these hovels and fields of stone were Smilodon Bay seen through his spirit eyes.

Tull passed beyond Byron, saw Caree Tech wandering outside a carefully tended little garden of stones set in mounds, one at each corner of the compass.

Tull moved uphill and realized that this great edifice, this towering monument to oddity, could only be Theron Scandal's inn. It was true that Scandal had, in one sense, the largest house in town, and that Scandal was a man of grand ambitions, but Tull wondered at the towers' proportions, and glided up a buttress, crawled into an open window. The grand ballrooms had winding staircases and were enormous and solid, large enough so that everyone in town could have fit in one of them. Not like the pitiful structures in the valley below, yet the rooms were empty of furnishings, littered only with bones, human skeletons reddened with dust. Tull floated up the staircases, through room after room, until he came to a small tunnel at the top of a minaret.

The passage above was blocked by the emerald glowing beast, the hollow of a soul massive and magnificent. Green tendrils of flame shot around from it crazily, and the beast toiled and fretted around the tower, building as fast as it could, straightening and re-arranging. Tull wondered at this, wondered what Theron Scandal was building. Yet as he floated in closer, he saw that the jellied emerald clot was not Theron Scandal, but Phylomon the Starfarer.

Tull hovered upward, eased around Phylomon, and sat upon a stone wall, looking from the tower, gazing down upon the city of Smilodon Bay: Tull could see better from here, stretches of barren plain where rock had been cleared, sweeping fields punctuated by the grubby dens and hovels of the town's witless citizens. Yet something about the shape of the town bothered him. All across town, where ignorant spirits built as mindlessly as ants, piling one block against another, Tull saw that it had all been brought into harmony, the sweeping fields, the hovels.

It reminded him of the endless stair above Sanctum where an ancient mathematician had placed stones and bits of twisted metal on the ground so that the rising sun cast ever-changing shadow pictures on the land. Only on this cracked plain, these piles of stone were not meant to cast shadows. Each structure, each pile of stones was part of a mosaic, a single shape in a grand portrait that covered the countryside.

Tull let himself rise higher and higher, above the top of the minaret, until the pattern came into focus: Chaa, the great magic crow, was flying across the face of the land. Tull's house had been the eye of the bird, and the exotic castle of Phylomon was the ruffled feathers at its neck.

On the high winds Tull let himself sink as he pondered what he saw. Tull had imagined that he was seeing shelters, perhaps the houses people someday dreamed to live in, or perhaps the shelters people thought they lived in.

Yet over it all, binding the construction together in ways that were invisible to others, was Chaa.

Tull sat, uncomprehending. He went back to his own little hovel, crawled back into his own little hole, and floated down into the tunnel beneath. He observed the skeleton lying there still, and recognized that its skull was human, the shoulders broad, about the same size as his father, Jenks. *Though Jenks is still alive,* Tull realized, *my spirit eyes see him as dead, because I have rejected him and he is dead to me.* In an antechamber that Tull had not noticed before, he found a Pwi skeleton, the skeleton of his mother.

Yet still nothing made sense. Tull could see things missing from his hovel. Where were Fava and Wayan? Why could he not envision them in his crater? Why were the walls of his hovel so broken and haphazard? Tull rose to his wall, saw where it had crumbled. *Somewhere there must be a stone to fill this gap,* he considered, and suddenly he was shooting forward, blurring over the landscape faster than a ruby-throated hummingbird, faster than a falling star, until he came at last to an open field.

He stood in town, behind the spice shop. There before him was a stone to fit the breach. He manipulated the clot of his soul, so that the ghostly appendages hefted the stone. It looked right, felt the right size. He brushed off the red dust.

The stone glowed in his hand, came to life like a hot coal. He looked into it and saw another world, a world of darkness with a tiny man in it: not a painting, not even figures drawn by the most expert hand, for the place had breadth and depth. He bent forward, looking closer and closer. Garamon was there, in a dark place, shivering and hungry. He fumbled for a latch, opened a door—and looked out to the back of the cloth shop. The scene faded.

Tull shook the stone. It seemed solid, rough with splotches of lichens. Only a broken stone, of an odd size that would fit the wall of his shelter.

Chaa had warned him that as his spirit eyes opened, things would change with each progressive vision, but Tull was not prepared for so many changes.

Before I sought this vision, Tull thought, *I had hoped to see the world more clearly, and this is how my spirit eyes perceive the world: people in hovels, recklessly stacking stones, some creating shelters, some . . . people in hovels, building on the bones of the past, the sagging ruins of previous generations.* And then he understood. The stones on the plain were incidents, possibilities ripening in time, waiting to happen, waiting to be organized. And the shelters, the hovels that others sought to build, were the futures that they constructed for themselves.

Some of the townspeople were witless, people without vision, taking no thought for the future, and those sat openly on barren mounds; others, like Phylomon, built exotic castles, stretching for miles across the countryside, large enough to fill the whole earth, but often habitable only by eccentrics like themselves.

There was no ultimate shaper of things. If left to themselves, the stones would have continued to propagate, the future would continue, disorganized. A flat barren plain with stones being made and destroyed. But he could make something of it, build any type of shelter he wanted. His vision of the world tree only days before had dimmed, to be replaced by this.

Suddenly shamed by his own little hovel, Tull decided to take the stone back, mend the wall, and begin considering what type of future to build. The copper sky above suddenly darkened, blotted out, and a whining hum rose all around. Tull nearly dropped the stone.

Above him hovered an immense black orb that

blocked out the sky for miles. It was dark, like the hollow of a sinister soul, and Tull imagined that it was as large as a moon. It hovered in place, and Tull realized it observed him dispassionately, just watching. Balls of light floated up into it and were consumed, hapless souls that seemed unable to resist. The orb pulled at Tull, inviting him forward, inviting him to float up like the others, to be absorbed.

"What are you?" Tull shouted.

The great ball of darkness closed half the distance, stopped again and waited.

"Who are you?" Tull asked.

The earth filled with the sound of thunder. The answer struck him with horrible force, like a great fist, the words compressed into a single thought: "Beast/ God/Adjonai," and a river of darkness burst from the sky, stretching out to touch him.

Clutching the stone, Tull pulled it close. The lightning of his soul flashed out as if to do battle, and Tull fluttered and fled.

Shortly after dark Fava took Wayan down the trail to town, looking for Tull. Where the trail met the road, she heard Tull screaming, the cry of a victim being hacked to death, a scream that shook her very soul.

She followed the sound to Chaa's house, passed Zhopilla and her little sisters huddling just inside the front door, and ran to the Spirit Room. An icy cold wind seemed to be blowing, spinning lazily through the house. She stopped. The air was oddly clouded and felt as thick as milk.

Chaa was already in the doorway to the room, his eyes wide, his face pale. He backed away slowly, saying, "Fool! What have you done?"

Fava tried to push past Chaa, but as she touched him, she ran into a wall of ice, a rush of air so cold that it threatened to snap her fingers. She put her hand forward gingerly, felt the cushion of cold, as if she had stuck her hand into a river of freezing ice water, and her fingers disappeared. She could see the walls, the room, she could see Tull lying on a woven reed mat within the fog, his eyes open and fixed in terror. Chaa grabbed her, pulled her back to the doorway, and she realized the air was thickening.

"You can't go in there!" Chaa shouted. "It will eat you!"

The Spirit Room began to tremble, and its walls shook. The dagger made from a carnosaur's tooth rattled from its peg on the wall, dropped to the floor, and lay there spinning. The shelves with Chaa's medicines rumbled, and suddenly the wood ruptured, exploding into a thousand shards, and splinters flew against the wall and embedded themselves like a forest of toothpicks into the shape of a crow, then as quickly pulled out and blew around the room in a maelstrom, as if caught in the center of a whirlwind.

"What is it?" Fava shouted, recognizing that something invisible was in the room.

"The beast!" Chaa croaked in horror. Fava heard water dribbling, saw that a pitcher was hovering in front of them, pouring water onto the ground. "You can't save him!" Chaa staggered backward, pulled Wayan from Fava's arms, and yelled for Zhopilla to take the children out of the house.

"Tull?" Fava called, looking into the darkening room. She pushed against the wall of cold, tried to step into it.

Tull's head twisted. "No! Stay back, Fava!" he cried, and the splinters of wood whirled past her face. The bearskin suddenly pulled from the wall and dropped onto all fours, the bear's claws scratching on the floor as the rug scrabbled forward.

Pots of herbs splattered against the ceiling, and suddenly the bearskin reared up, filling out as if it were a living creature, and the hide wandered around the Spirit Room, huge and brown, sniffing at the walls.

From the front of the house, Chaa shouted for Fava

to run, and Fava heard Zhopilla crying, the children running from the house.

The bearskin ambled to Fava, sniffed her crotch, watched her from empty eye sockets. It reared on its hind legs and pawed the air, then dropped to the floor like a rag.

Tull floated up into the air at waist height, rotated so that he faced the floor, and screamed.

Chaa came back in the hallway. He grabbed Fava's arm, began pulling at her. She pushed him away, and Chaa slugged her, hard, knocking her against the wall.

"Please! Please! He's dead! You can't save him!" Chaa shouted, and he began pulling Fava from the house.

As Fava backed away, Tull's arms spread wide, and he floated up until he lay splayed against the ceiling. *The beast toys with us,* Fava realized. Tull began to spin like a pinwheel, arms and legs flailing while his back remained flat against the ceiling, and whatever force held him, whatever kept her from entering the room, was so powerful, Fava could not hope to fight it. She backed off slowly, as she would from a bear—hoping not to attract its attention. She reached the front door.

Outside, Zhopilla and Chaa held each other, sobbing, and Wayan and Fava's little sisters all stood in the street. Fava was numb, mindless.

"What can we do?" she said, and Chaa shook his head.

Inside the house Tull screamed one last time, a long plaintive note. There was a tearing sound, like the shredding of cloth, and then the back part of Chaa's house caved in. A huge wind rushed across the field behind the house, bowled through the forest, snapping two giant redwoods.

Chaa stood frozen in place, and Fava did not move. From the tearing sounds she knew that she did not want to go back in there, she didn't want to see Tull's mangled corpse shredded on the floor.

She felt weak, and an evil kwea hit her, a feeling of

grief so profound, she could not voice it. She fell to the
ground and wished only for her own destruction.

"You could not have saved him," Chaa whispered.
"The beast saw him, knew what Tull was, and I was not
there to protect him. The beast knows its enemies.
None of us could have done anything."

Fava lay on the ground. The words were no comfort
for the empty place in her heart. She shouted, hoping to
voice her pain, and Tull opened the front door, stepped
out, his face a pale mask.

"It let you live?" Chaa hissed, and Tull nodded,
staggered to Fava, knelt, and put his arms around her.
"The beast tasted your soul, and let you live?"

Tull nodded dumbly. "I—I don't know what happened. I walked the Land of Shapes, found the mayor,
then it came. The beast swallowed me. And spit me
out."

Chaa reached for Tull's hand, but then would not
touch it. He looked deep into Tull's eyes, as if viewing a
stranger, and Chaa seemed sad, more grieved to see Tull
alive than dead. He stood for a long moment, just holding Tull's shoulders. "The beast knows its enemies—as
well as its allies," Chaa said at last, turning away, his
voice husky with revulsion.

A crowd grew outside Chaa's house, and Tull turned
away from Chaa, so numbed by Chaa's rejection, so
shocked by what had happened, that Tull didn't know
what else to do. Fava held Tull, her hands brushing
against him, as if to reassure herself that Tull was alive.
Yet no one else would come near them. Wayan huddled
against Zhopilla's legs, and the street began to fill with
Pwi who had heard the screaming. Some people went to
the woods, stood staring at the massive redwoods that
lay snapped, sprawling across the barren field where old
Vi kept her cows and pigs. Others looked with dismay at
the back of Chaa's house, where the wattle roof to the
Spirit Room hung close to the ground like the mouth of

a cave, yet they would not approach the opening, as if they feared that something else might exit.

Tull stood, panting, and when the crowd grew thick, he told some younger Pwi, "I know where Garamon is hiding. Who will come with me?" Several boys shifted nervously, then stepped forward. He took six Pwi boys into town, and went behind the mayor's old cloth shop to a doorway hidden behind an old stump on the ground. Behind it they found mayor Garamon Good-stick, asleep, huddling in the cold, a loaded pistol in his hand.

They grabbed him before he woke, and some of the boys set to beating him mercilessly before Tull ordered them to take Garamon to Phylomon for questioning and execution.

The Starfarer had learned many tortures in his thousand years, and it took him less than an hour to extract the names of those who had attacked Etanai. The Pwi went to each house, brought the slaver out, then opened the homes for looting. When the slavers had been rounded up, Phylomon beheaded all seven on the cobblestones along Merchant Street.

Afterward Tull was shaking, and Fava helped him home to his bedroom, then set the fire. He lay across the room from the fire, gazing into the flames.

"I hear a serpent's voice," Tull said. "A big one, swimming over from Hotland. He's very sick. Tired."

"Are you sure?" Fava asked, realizing that whatever had just happened, Tull did not want to talk about it.

"Yes," Tull said. "Can you hear him? Listen . . ."

Fava listened for several moments. A gust of wind buffeted the house, and waves whispered down in the bay. Other than that, nothing. "I'll be back soon," she said. "I'm going to get Wayan. Will you be all right alone?"

"I'm fine," Tull answered.

Fava went out, walked down the dark trail to her parents' house. Several dozen Pwi stood outside. Fava walked back down the long hallway toward her father's Spirit Room, thinking to speak to her father some more, ask questions.

Phylomon was talking loudly, and Fava stopped to listen, peeked around the corner.

Phylomon asked "Where is Tull now?"

Chaa said, "He went home. I must consider carefully. I do not know if I should keep him as a pupil."

Phylomon grabbed Chaa's shoulder, turned the Spirit Walker around. "Tull is a talent warrior, isn't he?"

Chaa nodded. "Yes. Very powerful."

"A warrior like Terrazin?" The Starfarer's voice betrayed genuine fear, as if it were an accusation. His tone confused Fava: She knew the names of ancient talent warriors—Thunatra Dream Woman, who battled men in their dreams; Kwitcha the healer, who raised men from the dead; Uth, who called poisonous snakes from their holes to protect him. But Fava had never heard of Terrazin.

"Much like the Dragontamer," Chaa said. "Perhaps too much. I thought I could control this one, bend him to my will. But tonight Adjonai beheld Tull, and it approved of him!"

For a moment Phylomon held silent. "For these past months, I've trusted your judgment. You said that Tull could destroy the Slave Lords, even though it may cost my life. What is your judgment now?"

"Last spring," Chaa said, "when I took my Spirit Walk, I viewed a possible future. I saw Tull return with the eggs of the sea serpents from Craal, and everything has happened nearly as I foresaw, until tonight. Tull tried to take a Spirit Walk contrary to my orders, something I had not foreseen. And I had not seen that Adjonai would approve of him. I had hoped that Tull would go to Bashevgo, throw it down, and reign as king. I had seen a future where Craal toppled within a few years. Now, I wonder . . ."

Phylomon laughed with a note of worry in his voice. "Sometimes it rains even on Spirit Walkers. You were able to see six months into the future—that is better than many Spirit Walkers could do. If you have misjudged, what harm have you done?" He tried to make light of the situation, but fear still carried in his voice.

"Who knows?" Chaa said. "Everything has changed. Perhaps nothing will happen as I saw it—your death, Tull's reign. Now Tull's spirit eyes are opening. If nothing else, I've wakened him. That is very dangerous. Terrazin woke to his power when he first stared into the pit of death, as you well know. It may be dangerous to try to kill Tull now."

"It could be dangerous to wait," Phylomon said. "If Tull wakens to his power, we may not be able to kill him."

Chaa stood, looking down at the ground, as if lost in vision. "Tull has not begun waking to his power. He is trying to learn the art of Spirit Walking. He has not even guessed his potential."

Phylomon shook his head in confusion, crossed his long blue arms and stood, head leaned back, eyes closed in concentration. "Have you discounted the prophecies of Pwichutwi? He said the Okansharai would be born to the Mother of Evil. If you look for someone to free the Pwi, then look for him in the city of Bashevgo."

"I know the prophecy," Chaa sighed, "and I have no faith in it. I can see six months into the future, perhaps a year or two. My great grandfather—one of the best—could look only five years into the future. I do not believe Pwichutwi could have seen five hundred years. He only dreamed. Still, I hope for an Okansharai. I hoped Tull would be the one." Phylomon still stood with his head leaning back, eyes closed.

"What if Tull disobeys you again? What if he tries to continue training as a Spirit Walker?"

Chaa took a breath, voice ragged. "If he succeeded in taking a Spirit Walk, he would learn his own potential. Still, Tull does not have enough training to do that. He has not made any allies in the Land of Shapes. I think that path would be closed to him."

"Terrazin trained himself to Spirit Walk. Tull could do it. But you have allies in the Land of Shapes," Phylomon hinted dangerously. "You could warn them, make sure Tull does not learn how to Spirit Walk."

"You are asking me to murder Tull because you do not want the blood on your own hands," Chaa said. "But he is innocent. He has not committed any crime—yet."

"Do you have any doubts that he will?" Phylomon asked. "If Tull learns how to kill a man with a thought, how long will the armies of Craal last?"

"For less than the length of a heartbeat," Chaa answered. "Tull would wipe them out down to the last man." He hesitated. "And he would kill you, if he suspected that you would try to stop him. Still, he is not Terrazin. He has not been corrupted."

"Are you so sure? Adjonai touched Tull's mind, and then let him live! Adjonai approved of him. . . ."

Fava shuddered. Even now, as Phylomon spoke the name of the dark god, Fava could feel Adjonai's evil kwea, as if he were listening, drawing close to hear what others said of him.

"Then there is only one thing to do," Chaa said. "Now I must take another Spirit Walk. My last."

"Your last?"

"I must walk the future of the Slave Lords," Chaa said. "They play too important a part in the affairs of men for me to ignore them in such a matter. And the Creators are making weapons—the gray worms, perhaps others. I may be able to connect with them and learn what the Creators plan for us. But if I look into the minds of those evil things, my allies in the Land of Shapes will renounce me. I won't be able to go back. Ever."

"And if you erred in waking Tull?"

Chaa said bitterly, "Then we must kill him in his sleep, before it is too late."

"I must leave for Sanctum in the morning," Phylomon said. "I won't be here for a few weeks. If Tull needs to die, I expect you to take care of it."

"Ayaah," Chaa said with reluctance. "I'll take care of it."

Fava turned and ran blindly down the hall.

Throughout the following day, Tull spoke infrequently. He went to see Phylomon off at dawn. The blue man left Smilodon Bay without much fanfare, heading inland toward Sanctum.

Tull spent the rest of the morning playing with Wayan. Fava envied the child, so innocent and easy to please. Tull gave Wayan pig-a-back rides around the floor, then threw him down and tickled him, then taught him to count to five. Tull put the boy down for an afternoon nap, and after a while Tull looked into the back room. Wayan was lying in bed, the covers pulled tight against his chin, obviously frightened.

"What are you afraid of?" Fava asked.

"Bad dreams," Wayan answered.

"Then you're in luck," Tull said. "When I built this house, I made sure that no bad dreams could get in."

"I know," Wayan said. "The ghosts keep scaring them all away." Tull laughed, lay down beside Wayan. When the boy finally fell asleep, Tull went to his workbench in the back room and, using tools stolen from Craal, took apart a small golden watch shaped like a daisy, then reassembled it.

Tull kept getting up, walking around. When he spoke, he spoke of inconsequential things.

"The worm of fear gnaws you," Fava said. "That is why you cannot stop moving."

"I suppose," Tull admitted, and he came and stood next to Fava, holding her hand.

"If you think we must," she said, "we can sail to Hotland."

"No," Tull said. "We can't hide in Hotland. The Creators would come there someday. And even if they didn't find us—what would we come back to? Once the Creators begin to cleanse the land, they may not let our descendants come back for two hundred years! And what of the Thralls? Millions of children would die in Craal. It is bad enough that they are slaves! Must they die in horror simply because we don't want to act?"

Fava watched his face. She could see anger in his eyes, in the way his nose flared in fear, as if he were a trapped bobcat. "I was not thinking about the Creators —or the slavers. I was thinking about this other thing. Oh, why can't you have simple problems—like bears pawing through your garbage or a leaky roof?"

"What are you talking about?"

"I heard my father and Phylomon talking. They're afraid of you. My father plans to take another Spirit Walk to look into your future."

"And if he doesn't like what he sees, what then? They plan to kill me?" Tull's voice was remarkably calm, Fava thought, remarkably controlled, and she realized that it was only because Tull understood and accepted such behavior. If Chaa found it necessary to kill Tull, Tull would understand.

"That was their first thought. But I have another plan: If Chaa finds that he does not trust you, then you must promise not to become a Spirit Walker. Maybe you could become a carpenter or a fisherman. I was thinking that if Chaa is afraid that you will hurt other people, then we will go someplace where there aren't any other people. We could go to the south of Hotland and make a home, and I would still love you, and I would be happy forever. This town is just a place. We don't have to stay here!"

"That wouldn't be enough for me," Tull said. "I would not be able to stop thinking of all the other peo-ple in the world. I would have to help free them."

His animal guide is the sea serpent, Fava thought, and she could perceive the serpent in Tull—restless, vig-ilant, ferocious in its attacks. She looked at his ankles, at the ugly scars where his father had shackled Tull to the bed. All those years Tull had pulled against the shackles, trying to break them, and even though he had freed himself years ago, his heart was still captive. He would have to keep breaking those chains, over and over again, until there were no more chains left in the world to break, and Fava knew that such a day could never come. Fava said, "You won't rest. I think my father will find only honey in your soul, as I have. But you'll never be happy. You can't, and I feel sad for you."

"I'll rest," Tull said.

Fava shook her head. "Between battles? Just as a sea serpent rests between feedings? You've been home from Craal for less than a month, and already in your heart you are out fighting other battles, already you are frenzied."

"Maybe you're right," Tull said. "Fighting battles is what I do." He let go of her hand. "I am going down to the blacksmith's shop, to work on a gun." Tull wrapped his cape around his broad shoulders and stepped outside.

Fava stayed in the house and fumed, found herself shaking while tears poured down her face. She could understand Tull, even sympathize with him, but she could not protect him, could not persuade him to turn away from his self-destructive path. Like a lone sea serpent battling plesiosaurs in the open sea, Tull would keep attacking, preferring to die rather than succumb or retreat.

Later that afternoon a cry rose from town that a serpent had entered the bay. For years it had been a cry of terror, a warning to stay back from the water, but since the serpents had died off, this was a cry of rejoicing. Fava ran down to the redwood bridge, and saw the serpent there, lying on the shore with its head out of the water. Its great dorsal fins rose forty feet in the air, and its head was wide as a house, while its huge teeth were each longer than a man. The coloring of the serpent's body changed with its environment, and this one was a sandy brown with black speckles, the color of the ocean floor in the bay. All in all, the serpent was at least two hundred feet long, with golden eyes as large as war shields, and everyone stood looking at it in awe: a serpent to guard the bay, a serpent to stand between the town and the dinosaurs that otherwise would swim over from Hotland.

Fava was so enthralled with the creature that it took her a moment to notice its odd behavior, the way it lay with its head on the beach. Blood flowed from its gills, and the gill flaps were so mangled, it looked as if the serpent had barely survived a great battle. Fava wondered if the serpent had come here to die; then she saw Tull: He was in the monster's mouth, working among the gills, slitting open the bodies of long gray lampreys that clung to the serpent's gills, then tossing the bodies of the lampreys back to shore.

And Fava recalled the serpent she'd seen in her dreams in the south of Hotland, the blood pouring from its gills, and how she had wakened to hear Tull promise: "I can heal you." The promise seemed to wash through her now, as if Tull had spoken the words just for her hearing. The act of cutting the lampreys away, of stripping them, was gruesome. Yet Tull carried it out tenderly, almost lovingly.

He seemed absorbed in his work, single-minded, eager to please the serpent. The beast widened its gill flaps almost as if at Tull's command, and Fava looked into the serpent's huge golden eyes, saw rage and pain there. She saw something of Tull.

Life became an uneasy game of waiting for Tull after that—waiting for the snow to clear in the north, waiting for Phylomon to return from Sanctum, for Chaa to return from his Spirit Walk.

By setting a target dummy behind the house and dressing it in a shirt of Craal armor, Tull found that his powder was not very effective. His bullets could barely pierce the thick lacquered mastodon-hide armor worn by Blade Kin. So on the forty-seventh day of the month of White, he made new bullets, pointed bullets with steel tips that could pierce a Blade Kin's leather armor.

As Tull worked, Chaa finally starved himself to the point that he passed out. On the verge of death, he took his Spirit Walk.

No one needed to tell Tull. He learned of it on his own. During the night it had rained so that the sodden practice field was unusable, and all that morning the rain splattered down. Late in the afternoon, while Tull poured tin into his bullet molds, he felt the icy touch of a Spirit Walker, a shock of cold that pierced him. A blue haze in the shape of a man formed in the darkened smithy beside a workbench, then slid into him.

Tull imagined he could feel the Spirit Walker moving—an icy stab in his left kidney, a cold trail crawling up his stomach, as if the organs of his body were chambers and Chaa were a lizard slithering from room to room.

He tried to imagine it from the Spirit Walker's view: Chaa's lightning would dance over the hollow of Tull's soul, Chaa's lightning would entwine with his own until Chaa learned Tull's ways.

Long ago, Tull thought, *this is how the Spirit Walkers began, as Truthsayers, shamans who touched the past of suspected criminals, assigning guilt when found.* But Chaa's deliberation would be something more, a meditation on the worth of Tull's potential, a judgment of what he might become. For years Tull had known he was different from other men. He found it hard to love, hard to relax, easy to kill. Tull feared what Chaa might find. "Chaa," Tull whispered. "If you find me to be vile, I will not resist what you must do."

That following night, on the forty-eighth day of White, the Pwi of the Rough normally celebrated, for it was on that day, three hundred and sixty-seven years earlier, that Phylomon had overthrown Bashevgo during the Talent Wars.

By custom each family held a great feast, and in the evening Scandal put on the play of *The Pirates' Hand* at Moon Dance Inn, where beer and rum flowed freely.

Fava and Tull had helped with the play for years. Fava tended the footlights, and Tull moved scenery and props. The night of the play came with scattered clouds and cool skies. The play told of greedy men who discovered pirate treasures guarded by the animated hands of dead pirates—hands whose magical attacks were fearsome to behold. One hero, struggling to overcome his own greed, eventually found a great chest containing a fortune, but it also held the corpse of the evil pirate king himself along with one hand from each of his crewmen.

At that point, the evil pirate king, played by Scandal, came to life and uttered curses, slithered from the grave, while the hands of his long-dead crewmen fluttered around him.

Tull worked the marionettes to make the hands dance as Scandal rose from the dead, sporting a flaming sword, while thunder crashed behind him. Tull looked at the crowd, saw fear etched in the faces of children. He smiled, wondering if they'd be as terrified by a real pirate.

"By all that is unholy, unsightly, untrue," Scandal roared, "I'll wield a cursed cutlass to disembowel you!" In trying to project his voice, he spat out over the crowd.

Poor old Byron Saman, who sat in the front row because his hearing was going and he could hardly see, stood up and said loudly, "We best get out of this storm, before lightning strikes us all dead!"

Everyone in the crowd laughed, and at that point the story's spell broke, and Tull's special effects could do nothing to instill terror in the audience. The play continued to its happy conclusion, when the penitent grave robber donated his treasure to aid the poor of the city, breaking the pirates' curse, and everyone laughed and clapped.

After the play Tull and Fava talked with friends, had a few drinks, then Tull carried Wayan home asleep in his arms. He felt more lighthearted than he had in weeks. Fava walked at his side, smiling up at him and laughing.

On the outskirts of town, a mere quarter mile from Tull's little cabin, they stepped off the road, walking the narrow trail along the hillside to Tull's house.

Down at the bay someone fired the cannon. Tull smiled at Fava, imagining someone had fired it to celebrate his drunkenness. Then a second cannon fired, and from the woods around town a shout rose, a long ululation like nothing Tull had ever heard, the sound of ten thousand Blade Kin voices raised in a war cry.

Wayan leapt awake in Tull's arms, cried, "What's that?" and Fava and Tull ran up the trail toward home. They were well off the main road that led to town, but they could hear Blade Kin on the hill above, running toward them through the woods. They ducked into the cabin. Tull grabbed his gun, strapped on his leather cuirass and his sword of pure Benbow glass, sharper than any steel.

Fava grabbed her short spear, and Wayan stood on the floor crying, grasping Fava's legs. A small fire in the hearth shed light, red coals glowing, and down in town gunshots peppered the night. Tull said, "Go out the back door! Hide!" and pushed Fava and Wayan toward a small door that led up a seldom-used path.

The town only had twenty-five guns—too few to ward off a full-scale attack by slavers. Tull rushed out the front door, heard hoots as Blade Kin ran for town. Uphill, off the road, others were making their way through the woods toward the cabin, snapping twigs and swishing brush. In town a warehouse burst into flames, casting an eerie light. Tull could see townsmen like ants rush from building to building, and Blade Kin in black armor and capes rushed among them.

And Tull recalled his first visit to the Land of Shapes, the Blade Kin he had seen dressed in black above the house, and realized his mistake. Tull had never gone back to learn if the man posed a threat.

The Blade Kin wore some sort of masks, and they shot at people with strange guns, large pipes that issued smoke, and Tull's people silently fell.

Some Pwi had guns, yet fewer and fewer were shooting, and all across town Tull could hear the Pwi shouting, crying for help. Tull watched dozens of Blade Kin swarm to Moon Dance Inn, then suddenly Tull heard someone close.

He turned. A Blade Kin rushed up the trail toward him. By his size, the man appeared human, too narrow in the chest and shoulders to be a Pwi, and he wore a strange mask with a short trunk like a mastodon's, and glass windows over the eyes. The man raised a long dark tube, pressed a button, and Tull raised his gun and shot him in the chest.

The Blade Kin warrior was thrown backward, and Tull rushed forward to dispatch him with his sword. A geyser of steam hissed from the tube, shooting through the air. The smell of it numbed Tull's nose.

It is a weapon, Tull realized, *a weapon that shoots poison air,* only the mask kept the Blade Kin from breathing the poison. Tull pulled the mask from the man, found that it was a black hood made of leather and wood that fit snugly over his head. Tull put it on himself. Up by the road, a commander shouted for someone to go toward Tull's house. They had heard his shot.

He put another bullet in his gun, rushed back into the cabin. Fava was trying to coax Wayan through the stickers at the back door, but the boy shrieked and would not go. Tull took off the mask for only a moment, pushed Fava out the door, slammed it closed, and moved a cabinet to hide the exit. Someone rushed into the cabin, and Tull spun and fired, hit the Blade Kin in the abdomen. The Blade Kin just stood, looking down at his gut. Tull loaded another bullet into his gun, leapt up, and decapitated the soldier.

Fava banged at the door, and Tull shouted, "Leave!

Hurry! I'll meet you up the hill!" but he lied. Far too many Blade Kin were closing in. He could hear them in the brush down the trail. Neither of the two men he had met so far were armed with anything other than the poison gas sticks and swords.

Tull swore to himself. *Chaa must have seen this. Chaa must have known the Blade Kin would attack tonight.* Yet he had warned no one. Tull leapt out the door, and in the bay a huge iron ship five times longer than any wooden ship Tull had ever seen sailed into the harbor. None of the town's cannons fired on it.

All over Smilodon Bay, Blade Kin scurried, picking up fallen townspeople. Across the harbor Tull saw flames leap from a building in a great arc, like a fiery rainbow racing toward a man who was shooting with his rod of gas, and then his container of gas erupted in a ball of pure white. Around the inn the gas was so thick that for a moment the superheated gases glowed like plasma, and then every nearby rod of poison gas suddenly exploded. The whole inn erupted in a flaming ball, and a great mushroom cloud flowed from the inn up into the sky, lighting the hills as if the sun had just shone from behind a cloud.

Until that moment Tull had hoped to escape in the dark, but in the low brush around him, dozens, perhaps hundreds of Blade Kin stood gazing at the ball of flame. Tull couldn't sneak through that crowd.

He ducked back into the house, to the fallen Blade Kin who lay on the floor. He thought about rushing out back, sneaking behind Fava and Wayan, but realized he would not get away in time. His only hope rested in disguising himself as a Blade Kin.

He wrestled with a body, pulled off the man's cape, and started to untie the man's cuirass. Someone stood in the door above him. Tull swung his gun up, fired, and saw two more men outside. He didn't have time to reload, so he rushed forward, met the Blade Kin in the dark.

Tull swung hard with his sword of Benbow glass,

and the man tried to parry. Tull's blow broke through the parry, sliced cleanly into the Blade Kin's shoulder.

I am a wall, Tull thought, *protecting the small things of the world,* and the thought calmed him. The second Blade Kin called for help and jabbed with a spear. Tull was grateful that Smilodon Bay was afire, for the towering flames gave him enough light to fight by, and he grabbed the shaft of the spear, turned it aside with one hand, slashed the Blade Kin. But two more sprang up behind him, spraying a cloud of smoke from their tubes. The whole hillside was filled with smoke, which rose from the ground like a fog.

Tull began to feel light-headed, realized his helmet did not fit snugly. Suddenly there were men behind Tull, men jumping from Tull's rooftop, men who had just come downhill. Tull shouted, turned to face them, found himself surrounded.

A woman jabbed with her spear, and Tull judged the blow to be inexpert. He'd heard rumors of how the Blade Kin trained, yet this woman couldn't even match Fava. Tull jabbed and she leapt away, tossing her spear. Tull barely had time to dodge, realized he should not let himself be taken in by such an easy ploy.

He leapt forward, swung his shield, knocked one man down, brought his sword up beneath a second man's guard and gutted him, slammed his sword into the fallen Blade Kin, and spun just in time to forestall an attack from behind. The fog was thicker, too thick, and Tull played with the helmet, tried to push it snug to his face, but it was little use. The helmet was not made for him.

With six dead men on the ground so near the doorway, Tull felt that he was running out of room to maneuver. From up the trail by the house someone shouted, "Halt!"

Out of the darkness came a man taller than the others, a man whose legs and arms were not naked like those of a simple Blade Kin. He wore gleaming red armor that covered his body—not the cured leather of other Blade Kin, but something that shone like dull metal. He wore a black mask of the same metal, a long red cape. A Crimson Knight, Tull realized. One of the twelve who wore the ancient armor and guarded Bashevgo. Tull's legs felt weak, for it was said that even a bullet could not penetrate that armor.

"Surrender," the knight whispered. His voice was not human. Instead it seemed as if a thought sprang into Tull's head, and Tull felt compelled to drop his weapon, to set it on the ground. The feeling was so strong that many Blade Kin leaned forward, dropped their weapons, as if to surrender to their leader.

Tull felt his head spin, held his sword to prop himself up, then stepped back. "No," he said, and whispered to himself, *I am a wall. I am a wall. Fava and Wayan may not have escaped yet. They may only be just behind the door.*

The Crimson Knight strode forward. "You are tired, you've run so far," he said, and a great weariness rushed over Tull, a profound fatigue. "You're weary of fighting, so weary, it avails you nothing. In your heart you know I am your friend."

"Go back to Bashevgo!" Tull shouted, swinging his sword in defiance. He almost tripped over a dead body.

The flaming lights of the city danced on the hillside, bathing everything in red, and the Crimson Knight moved closer. "I don't wish to harm you. You must come back to Bashevgo with me—" and Tull knew he could stand no longer, he was about to fall.

He leapt, swung with all his might. The Crimson Knight pulled his sword, parried Tull's blow in one swift move, pushed Tull back with one hand. The man was unbelievably quick. Tull found himself jarred awake, his senses screaming that he was in jeopardy.

Tull feinted a clumsy blow, and the Crimson Knight moved to block. Tull came alive, twisted his sword over the parry, and slashed the man's neck. Even with all the force he could muster, the blow seemed barely to pierce the armor, slicing an inch in depth, but blood gushed from the wound. Tull's head reeled.

The Crimson Knight reached up, touched his neck, then staggered. He dropped to his knees, panting, and Tull leapt forward and smashed his sword into the knight's head, slicing the helmet open.

Tull planted his sword in the ground, tried to hold himself upright, but then felt himself falling. When Tull hit the dirt, his mask jarred loose, but in the blackness he no longer cared.

Mahkawn came to Tull's cabin at daybreak, escorted by four men. "Are you certain this is the same Tull who escaped from Denai last fall?" he asked.

"Quite certain," Atherkula the sorcerer said. "I have felt him ever since we passed Storm Hold. The beast confirmed this."

"I require tangible proof," Mahkawn said, and the sorcerer ducked into the house a moment. The sorcerer disturbed Mahkawn. People said that Atherkula lived more in the Land of Shapes than in the present world, and the sorcerer had earned a reputation for cruelty.

Mahkawn looked across the gray water. Smilodon Bay had burned to the ground overnight. On the main street the Brotherhood of the Black Cyclops had gathered their captives. Mahkawn could hear screams as his men went through the slaves, preparing to cull the oldest and the infirm, those not worth transporting back to Bashevgo. Other than that, small boats were already porting the youngest and strongest of the newly captured slaves to the ship.

The smell of burning buildings, the bodies of his warriors here at Tull's doorstep, all were a grim reminder that taking this small town had cost more than it was worth. Over a hundred Blade Kin lost, taking only a thousand slaves. A poor trade. And this man, Tull Genet, had killed a Crimson Knight.

Mahkawn looked at the squat little hut that served as Tull's home. "Amazing, amazing," he clucked.

"That a warrior could live like this," one of his men finished the thought.

Atherkula returned outside, threw a blood-red cape to the ground. It bore the insignia of the city guard of Denai, the cape of a Dragon Captain. "This Tull is the one who escaped Denai. He killed my sorcerer, and your Blade Kin. I can feel his power. He is dangerous."

Mahkawn nodded. *Sorcerer, warrior, barbarian.* Mahkawn walked into the hovel where Tull had lived. A bed stood against a wall. On the floor were some woman's dresses and robes, a carved sabertooth toy, a gun. All Tull's life, his loves, all within these walls. Mahkawn felt like a voyeur.

"Did we catch the woman and child?" Mahkawn asked.

"Many women and children were captured," Atherkula said. "We haven't cataloged all their names yet."

Mahkawn kicked at the bed, went to the kitchen, poured a drink from a pitcher. In a small back room he found tools and dozens of little watches that had been torn apart and reassembled, all in various stages of completion. Sketches on the table showed how to do it. Mahkawn bent near the watches: The watches were intricate, amazing things that only a human would be able to assemble, full of tiny gears and clasps. Silver watches with gold petals opening from them so that when you folded the petals out, you saw the faces of the clocks as if they were daisies. Marvelous things no larger than a Pwi's thumbnail. Yet Tull had clamped their pieces onto boards, and with the aid of strange implements made from bent pieces of metal, he was taking them apart and learning to reassemble them.

A man with an eye for detail, and appreciation for intricacies, Mahkawn thought. *A warrior who does not fear our sorcerers. A man who has killed fourteen Blade*

Kin, including a Crimson Knight. A good warrior. As a Blade Kin, Mahkawn valued such aggressiveness.

On the bench, between two leather-bound books, sat a ball made of brass. Mahkawn recognized it as an artifact, some strange creation of the ancient Starfarers, a likeness of Anee. He gingerly lifted it, put it in a sack, wondering how Tull had come by such a valuable piece.

Mahkawn walked back into the living quarters, surveyed the room, amazed: Here was a man who lived in a tiny house, a poor man, yet Mahkawn felt something odd stirring in him. Envy. Here was food, warmth, sex, a mind alive with interests. Here was a Pwi who read and worked. Mahkawn envied this barbarian's simple life, his hobbies, the fact that he could openly breed with the same woman throughout his lifetime without worrying that some competitor would slay her. Mahkawn lifted one of Fava's dresses, smelled it. Vanilla water, the musky scent of a woman.

"Clean out the contents of the hut," Mahkawn ordered. "I want to study them more closely on the ship."

Atherkula looked up. "What are you thinking?"

"I'd like to learn more about this Tull Genet."

"There is nothing more you need to know, Omnipotent," Atherkula said. "Tull is a murderer and has been sentenced to death. We've sought him for months. That is all you need to know."

I must fence gingerly, Mahkawn thought. As an Omnipotent of the Brotherhood of the Carnadine Sorcerers, Atherkula was Mahkawn's equal in rank, even if he was not the favorite of Lord Tantos. "Yet Tull was unjustly convicted. Since he was not a slave, his 'crimes' were only the actions of a warrior in battle."

"I doubt Lord Tantos will see it that way," Atherkula warned. "This Pwi slew a Crimson Knight. Tantos will demand retribution."

"I obey all my lord's commands," Mahkawn whispered. "But I see here only a man who defended himself, as is a warrior's right. Even if he is sentenced to death, he must be given the opportunity to choose the arena."

Atherkula studied Mahkawn. "So he can win entrance into the Blade Kin? I think not! He has slain members of my order!"

"And he has slain a dozen of my brotherhood. I have a greater claim." Mahkawn stood tall, moved in close to old Atherkula. Mahkawn's size, the grim cast of his face, cowed most men. But Atherkula was a Neanderthal of the old blood. Mahkawn said at last, "I will *civilize* him."

Atherkula closed his eyes. A cold wind whipped through the room, picked up a blanket, and tossed it against the wall. The wind felt bitterly cold, more bitter than any wind Mahkawn could remember, and he realized it blew from the Land of Shapes.

"Yes," Atherkula said. "Civilize this creature. The beast approves. *We* approve." Mahkawn shuddered, turned, and walked down the path as his men began packing Tull's things, his life, into any handy sack.

Mahkawn wondered, *Why am I doing this? Certainly Tull will never need any of this again. Even if he were to become Blade Kin, what use would it be?* Yet something in the back of Mahkawn's mind whispered guiltily, *You are stealing a man's life. Perhaps you hope that someday he will steal it back.*

Chapter 6
Tears of Blood

In Tull's dream the lightning of his soul swept through the forests like a wind, rushing over icy mountains, skipping across clear blue lakes. The beast came behind, a nebulous darkness, swallowing all light.

At last he found Fava in a mountain glen where the knocking of woodpeckers was the only sound. She sat on the ground, on her knees, studying paintings of Bashevgo. Yet somehow Fava had changed. Her skin was as soft and tender as that of a Dryad, and she had small blue-white teeth like those of a fox. Fava knelt close to the paintings and watched Etanai suffering in his cage. Only it was more than a painting, it was a window into Etanai's world, and Tull could hear the old Thrall shrieking in agony.

Fava touched the painting, reached her hand deep inside it, and her pale finger came away stained with blood. "You know," she said, her voice soft, "I don't think he caught what it really feels like, the cruelty of the cage." Then Tull heard the spirit beast behind, and darkness overtook them.

Tull woke with a dark cotton bag over his head. He lay face down in the street, hands and feet shackled behind his back. All around him people coughed and wept. Some cried out, and the smell and minute shuffling sounds told him that he was surrounded by many, many bodies.

The air carried the cool scent of dawn beneath the dry reek of ashes. He could hear water lapping nearby, and he guessed that he was at the docks. He lay for a long moment, numbed, and realized dumbly that he should try to escape. He tested his irons, pulling at the feet and legs. They clanked softly but didn't give. He tried letting his hands go limp so he could pull them through the irons. He pulled his left hand softly and steadily until his wrists bled, then used the blood as a lubricant. All to no avail. His huge Neanderthal hands would not come through.

Tull lay gasping for air. The sweat on his arms cooled quickly, and Tull cursed himself for his lack of foresight. In the back of his mind, he'd always known that the slavers would come someday. Though slavers had not openly attacked Smilodon Bay in over a century, everyone had known the town's luck would not last. Even as a child Tull had dreamed of the elaborate mechanisms he would someday prepare for his escape. Yet here he lay, among the people of town, trussed up and ready to be sold on the blocks at Bashevgo or Denai.

Tull's hatred for the slavers burned hot in him, and he wondered which of the seven lords had taken the city.

He twisted his head in the dirt, trying to look for an escape route. He could see, barely, through the cotton bag. Warehouses were burning, and he could discern shapes of people around him, some sitting up, gazing in fright. They didn't seem to be hooded, like him. He rolled onto his back, sat up, and looked around.

"Tull," Jenks grunted, "is that you?"

"Here," Tull answered, and he turned his head. His father sat only a few feet away, chained.

"What are you doing with that bag over your head?" Jenks asked.

"I don't know," Tull answered, but he feared that he might know. Once, long ago, a neighbor had told a story of a young man named Soren who was caught by slavers and set on the beach with his friends, and the slavers had placed a bag on Soren's head. When the slavers took the young men away, they took the bag— with Soren's head still inside. Tull swallowed hard, and his heart began to pound. Tull knew he would be lucky to make it out alive. "Have you seen Fava or Wayan?"

"No," Jenks whispered. "Maybe they got away." He waited a long moment and added, "But don't get your hopes up. The Blade Kin are searching the woods even as we speak, bringing in more every minute. They got your mother, too. She's already on the ship. The bastards burned our house."

"You're lucky you weren't in it," Tull said.

"Ayaah," Jenks said. "Uh, I'm a fat old man. You don't think they'd cull me, do you?"

Tull had no idea. His mind raced. "No," he said at last. "If they were going to cull you, why bring you down to the docks?"

"Right," Jenks said. "I'm a big man. Why, I work harder than any five men, and I've got plenty of years left in me. If they have sense, they'll see that, put me to work in one of the lord's estates. You'll tell them, won't you, who I am? You'll stick up for me?"

"Ayaah," Tull said, though he doubted that the Blade Kin would come asking him for references. "Is there any way to make a run for it that you can see?"

"No," Jenks hissed. "We're surrounded, guarded tight."

"Is there any cover? Even a bush I could hide under?"

Jenks waited a moment to answer. "No. Nothing. They've already taken some folks from the hills to the ship—all the folks from Finger Mountain and Harvest, and I'd say they've taken half the folks from town.

They've got a circle of guards down by the water, all the way up the hill. You can't get out."

Tull sat and listened for a while. His stomach began to growl. In the distance his mother-in-law, Zhopilla, wept as the Blade Kin dragged her to the boat, and Tull sat amazed, wondering how Chaa could have let this happen, let his wife and children be captured by slavers. The sun was rising, and Tull could make out only the thinnest of human outlines through the cloth.

Several times over the next hour, Tull heard boats come up to the docks, and one by one the people of town were led away.

With each departing boatload Tull knew his chances of living would be less and less. Few people sat around him now. Old Caree Tech lay weeping a dozen yards from his feet. Byron Saman was behind him. A few others. The old and infirm. Culls.

Just before sunrise several men came and stood above him.

"This is the one who killed a Crimson Knight?"

"Yes, Omnipotent," the men answered, and Tull cringed. The title *Omnipotent* was saved only for a man with the rank of Cyclops, the generals among the Blade Kin. Someone stepped forward, pulled the bag from Tull's face, taking a handful of Tull's hair with it.

A man dressed in immaculate black leather armor stood before Tull, a short Neanderthal with threads of gray running through his rusty beard, a black patch over his right eye. The Omnipotent had a weathered face, blank, emotionless, yet when he stared at Tull, it was as if he more than gazed. Tull felt consumed. The Cyclops wore a gold scourge in his belt—ancient symbol of the Slave Lords—signifying that he was favored and would someday become a lord himself. Tull wondered that this Neanderthal could hold such rank.

Behind his captors Tull could see the great iron ship in the harbor, dark brown with a huge smokestack. The ship was taller than any building Tull had ever seen —at least four stories.

"What is your name?" the man in black asked. He stepped back, rested his hand on the pommel of his sheathed sword.

"Tull Genet."

"The same Tull Genet who killed eight of my Blade Kin at Denai?"

"No," Tull answered.

The Blade Kin looked closely at Tull, chuckled. "You lie? That is wise, I suppose. I would hope for as much from any of my men. You see, I know all about you. You gave your name to a slave in Denai, and he told it to many people. I am Mahkawn, commander of the Brotherhood of the Black Cyclops, and the Blade Kin you've had the pleasure of killing belong to my Lord Tantos, the Minister of Retribution. Do you know what penalty he has set for your crimes?"

"By your law, I have committed no crimes," Tull said. "I fought in my own defense, as a free man of the Rough. I have heard that even Lord Tantos does not exact revenge from warriors who kill in battle."

Mahkawn said, "You argue with me? I think I will kill you anyway, Thrall." He looked down at Tull's feet, at the black leather moccasins with a crow sewn into them. He paused for a moment, tugged off the moccasins, held them up for inspection.

"He is one of us, as I said," an old man whispered behind Mahkawn. Tull looked at the fellow for the first time, an ancient Neanderthal only slightly bent with age, a man with sagging pale skin, a blank emotionless face, like Mahkawn's, yet somehow more cruel. He wore a black robe with crimson trim, and he wore no armor.

The old man stared at Tull, then closed his eyes. A lance of ice pierced Tull, the touch of a Spirit Walker, and Tull realized it was some form of attack, even though he had never heard of a Spirit Walker who could use such power while still conscious. Tull imagined himself to be far away, thought of a field of daisies where he had played as a child, a place where many badgers had burrowed.

The icy touch dissipated, and the old man opened his eyes, glared at Tull. "Kill him, Omnipotent," the old man urged. "He turned me, easily."

Mahkawn whipped out his blade, a long straight blade unlike the curved scimitars that most of his kind wore. He swung it once, past Tull's neck, and Tull did not blink.

If I die, I will at least die with a little dignity, Tull thought. Tull held Mahkawn's one good eye with his own. Mahkawn stuck the blade in Tull's eye and pushed slightly, as if testing to see when the Blade would pierce the eyelid. The weight of the sword forced Tull's head back, and Mahkawn studied the movement. Tull's heart beat a little faster, but he did not sweat, and he resisted the impulse to lick his dry lips. Instead, he looked into Mahkawn's eye. Tull saw no cruelty there, no joy in torture, yet Mahkawn showed no guilt, no recognition that he was harming another man like himself. *No, the Omnipotent is studying me,* Tull realized, and he saw a glimmer of admiration in the soldier's eye.

"One of the men you killed, the Crimson Knight, he was like a son to me," Mahkawn said. "Did you know that? I feel a tremendous loss. I want you to apologize before you die. If you apologize, I will give you a clean death, a brisk one. Otherwise, I shall rend you."

Tull listened to the Omnipotent's voice. If Mahkawn felt tremendous loss, his voice denied it. Its tone was cold, heartless, only mimicking the passion he claimed. Because of their enlarged hypothalamus, the Pwi loved more strongly, their fear was keener. Yet the Omnipotent spoke like one empty of emotion, a liar. Tull thought, *He is only studying me; he is testing me,* and Tull had no idea how to pass the test.

He chose an answer that perhaps Mahkawn did not expect. "You will have to rend me," Tull said, keeping his voice neutral. Mahkawn pushed the sword deeper, splitting the skin under Tull's eye. "I'm proud to have killed your Crimson Knight. Perhaps if he had been a better fighter, I'd feel sorrow at wasting a good warrior. But he was nothing."

The Omnipotent pulled his sword back a bit, open admiration shining from his eye. He rested the sword tip above Tull's right ear, as if he would slice it off. Tull knew little of the Blade Kin's customs, but the right ear was the one a soldier gave to his first commander, and Tull's heart suddenly leapt. A moment ago he had been facing a death penalty, but now he realized that this Omnipotent wanted him. If he were made Blade Kin, it would be easy to escape.

Tull leaned his head to the side, exposing his ear. "Take it, if you want. I give it to you."

Mahkawn hesitated, studied Tull. "You talk like a Blade Kin, but how can I be sure you are not a Thrall?" He thoughtfully sheathed his sword. "Take him to the ship," Mahkawn said at last, then turned to his men, "and separate out the culls. We sail in half an hour."

Two men grabbed Tull, pulled him to his feet, and he took tiny steps with the leg irons as they ushered him to a small boat filled with forty other prisoners. He turned to look at Mahkawn, but the Omnipotent and his retinue were walking away, over the redwood bridge into Pwi-town. Tull considered the words, *Blade Kin* and *Thrall.* He had always considered the Blade Kin to be Thralls, just Thralls trained as soldiers, but he realized that Mahkawn saw them as being vastly different.

Tull knew little about them. The Blade Kin served their Lord, and a Cyclops like Mahkawn led each legion of warriors. The Cyclops organized his men into "Brotherhoods" with dozens of "arms," each of which performed its own function—spies made up the Invisible Arm, foot soldiers the Blood Arm, cavalry formed the Mammoth Arm, while the Carnadine Sorcerers somehow served all the arms.

Tull did not know specifics about the various arms. But he knew that Blade Kin received special privileges: As a sign of status they swore an oath of loyalty to their commander. In return, the lords paid them and granted the Blade Kin breeding rights with the Thralls of their choice. To Tull the privileges had always seemed minor, a small reward for those willing to be cruel. But he wondered if to the Thralls—to people who had been robbed of wealth and freedom and dignity—the benefits seemed enormous.

As he reached the boat, a young blond Pwi girl walked in front of Tull. She wore a red cotton dress with many-colored beads sewn into it, silver necklaces, and she carried an infant in her arms. Tull imagined that she had been trying to make herself beautiful for her husband when the slavers came. The girl was younger than Fava, perhaps only sixteen. She kept saying over and over again, *"Adja, adja, adja,"* I'm afraid, I'm afraid, I'm afraid. Her jaw trembled and her eyes were wild. She clutched her child roughly, and Tull worried that she would suffocate the baby.

She was no one he had ever seen, probably from the wilds beyond Finger Mountain. The Blade Kin were clearing the countryside, perhaps scouring the whole Rough. Tull had imagined someday fighting the Blade Kin in battles near here, but the slavers were sweeping them up before the men of the Rough could offer resistance.

The woman stopped at the boat, would not get in. She glanced at the water to either side as if she would leap. The boat had nearly filled, and forty mournful people, some human, some Pwi—all with pasty faces— looked up at this woman. Tull whispered, "Get in the boat. Get in. You must live for your child now."

The girl glanced back at him, staggered in dismay. "Tears of blood," she said.

Tull realized the cut under his eye was dripping, making it look as if he cried tears of blood. He nudged her forward. Her knees shook, but somehow she managed to work her legs, clumsily leap into the boat. Tull looked up for one last second, out over the town, hoping for any sign of Fava. The Blade Kin filled the shore, and they had begun packing their black robes, switching into robes of forest green and tan. Tull guessed that at least five thousand of them filled the streets, and as he took a seat in the boat, the Blade Kin began to leap away to the south. Twelve miles by land to Muskrat Bay, Tull mused. A small town, hardly defended. The people there would not have a chance.

Four strong oarsmen pushed the boat from the docks. They were all Neanderthals, but they had not cut off their right ears, and they didn't wear Blade Kin uniforms. Mere slaves, Thralls. As the oarsmen rowed toward the ship, several older women began whispering to the Thralls, "Friends, save us! Hide us! Let us jump over the side and swim away!"

The Thralls ignored their pleas, until at last one whispered, "Keep quiet! Your chains are too heavy. If you try to swim, you will drown!"

And they kept rowing. The rocking of the boat, the smell of ocean spray, the city of Smilodon Bay, the cry of the gulls above him, Tull had known these things all his life. He sat back, watched the burned town as they floated past. *Even if I return,* Tull thought, *in ten years this town will only be charred ruins, covered with blackberry vines. Perhaps it will be a good place to hunt pig or bear, not a place to live.* But in his mind's eye, he saw much further than ten years, saw that someday buildings might fill this shore again, but in the future it would be filled only with Thralls.

At the front of the boat some captives cried out, and they looked with horror at the shore behind. Tull turned his head. The Blade Kin were slitting the throats of the old and lame, killing the culls that they had no use for.

Tull looked around the boat at the frightened faces of those nearby. Jenks was on the far side, watching the old folks get culled, undisguised relief in his face. The young mother beside Tull was nearly mindless with fear, and Tull whispered to her, trying to soothe her. Two twin boys at the prow seemed as frightened. Their roving eyes did not focus on anything nearby, only upon the horrors of their imagination.

Tull resolved to be a good example, show no fear, but as they neared the great iron ship, they heard screams from those aboard. Tull looked up, saw that up on deck was a kettle filled with fire. The Blade Kin were branding the prisoners as they climbed aboard.

A Thrall oarsman said, "Do not worry, the brands stop burning after a few days. You are all the property of Lord Tantos now. If you work well, you will gain privileges."

Tull looked at the floor of the boat. He knew the privileges. Tonight, he was sure, some Blade Kin would take the woman beside him and rape her; tomorrow would be another, and another, an endless succession of rapes. The same might happen to the boys. *Perhaps the same will even happen to me,* Tull mused. The Blade Kin would want vengeance on Tull for those he'd killed. Some might try to take it in bed.

He recalled a song he learned as a child, a song that slaves sang as they rowed.

> *Threads of iron, bind me to this world,*
> *Threads of iron, bind me to this sea,*
> *Threads of iron, bind me to this boat . . .*

The words could change to fit the circumstances of the singer, but always they spiraled in, coming closer and closer to home, until the song ended:

> *Threads of iron, bind me to this oar.*
> *And threads of iron, bind me evermore.*

One of the twins gazed long at the white faces of those around him, then threw himself over the side. The boy hardly splashed as he hit the water, just made a burping sound. The closest oarsman dropped his oar, grabbed for the boy, but the child sank too fast, dragged down by the weight of his irons. None of the prisoners could try to rescue him, chained as they were.

Tull looked over the side of the boat, saw the boy wriggling in the clear water, sinking down, down into the darkness. The young woman next to Tull dropped her baby, just let it fall into the water at the bottom of the boat, and she leapt over too. The oarsman behind grabbed for her, pulled away part of her dress, but the mother kept sinking.

The oarsman grabbed the infant and set it on Tull's lap, grunted, "Hold that," and picked up his oar. Tull looked at the faces of the others, at the horror and shock and stark fear etched there, and he remembered Mahkawn and his sorcerer, so empty, so passionless, and Tull saw the difference between Thralls and Blade Kin: passion.

The Blade Kin have trained out their passion, and Mahkawn admires me because I do not fear, Tull realized. As a Pwi, training out emotions was nearly impossible. A comb once worn by a lover seemed to radiate love. If a dog nipped at a Pwi child, forever after, the dog would seem to radiate terror. At times when he was younger, when great fear came upon him, Tull had even imagined that Adjonai, the God of Fear, towered above him wielding his kutow of terror and his shield of despair. Training out such fear had been the crowning achievement of Tull's life.

Apparently the Blade Kin felt the same.

When the rowboat reached the ship, Tull did not have to climb out. A platform lowered from above, and several Blade Kin dragged Tull and twenty others onto the platform. Above them, sailors raised the platform with pulleys.

When they reached the top, they stood on a large deck covered with iron. Tull could not imagine such a ship ever being defeated in battle, did not even understand how such a monstrosity could float. He looked around topside, surprised to see very few Blade Kin. He imagined that they must have all gone onto the land to fight.

Tull let a calmness settle over him, tried to adopt the unfeeling aspect of the Blade Kin. He held the child loosely.

Though others screamed in pain, Tull didn't flinch as the Blade Kin branded him with irons, burning the letter *T* on both the top and bottom of his left wrist.

"The *T* is for Tantos," the Blade Kin explained. "You're his now. You'll follow any orders we give you."

Tull held the baby, and the Blade Kin did not try to brand it. As they formed a line and marched into the hold, Tull thought, *T also stands for Tull.*

Fava slid on her belly through the brush, wiped the spider webs from her face, and looked up carefully. She was in a patch of tall ferns near the hilltop, in a *V* formed by two fallen trees. She could not see uphill, but as long as she kept her head down, she would stay in the shadows. She heard a Blade Kin cough nearby—just over one of the trees—and dared not move. Instead, Fava held her hands over Wayan's mouth, hugged him in the deep ferns. In town there were screams and gunshots, and a house was burning. She could see some of it from here.

She heard a dull plop nearby, muffled gunfire coming from the cabin downhill. Blade Kin rushed past her toward the cabin, closed their line, and Fava waited twenty seconds, till she heard no more footsteps, then leapt over the logs and ran.

At the lip of the hill, she stopped beside a standing tree, fearing to cross into the valley beyond. She glanced back. On the hill on the far side of the bay, the Blade Kin were shouting, their voices a soft roar, and the city exploded in a cloud of fire.

Something in Fava's mind seemed to break. She scooped up Wayan and ran blindly down into the valley and over the next hill, and the hill beyond, heedless of whether Blade Kin might be chasing her, unsure of any destination, until minutes later she found herself tired and aching in the shadows of a great fallen redwood nearly two miles from town. She found a twisted root where she had once hidden while playing hide-and-seek as a child. The game had lasted for hours. She crawled back into the old crevice—trying to force herself into an opening that had fit her as a ten-year-old—and lay still, her heart beating so wildly, she feared she would die.

Then she heard the Blade Kin nearby cracking redwood needles under heavy boots, their sheathed swords softly clacking against their leather armor.

Fava held still and silently berated herself. When Fava had left the back door of the cabin, she'd planned to sneak away from town. She'd planned to move calmly, control her fear, and stay hidden among the deeper ferns. But instead, she had thrown out all her plans of stealth, lunged, running blind with fear, just as a stupid cornered rabbit will leap into the jaws of the hunting dogs. Now the Blade Kin were after her.

She waited an hour till the Blade Kin all seemed to be gone, and suddenly she realized she still had her hand locked over Wayan's mouth. He was rigid in her arms, so frightened, he would not move. She took her hand away, stroked his forehead.

A twig cracked nearby, and someone came to the log, placed a hand on it. For one wild moment Fava thought Tull had come, for suddenly she remembered that it was Tull who had found her here all those years ago, and she hoped deliriously that he had found her again.

He stood quietly not more than five feet away, panting. For a long moment Fava froze. *It could be a Blade Kin hunting me by scent,* she realized. Some of the Pwi could hunt that way. *Or someone from town trying to escape.* Whoever it was, the person moved off. Two minutes later she heard screams nearby and the sound of a scuffle as some woman was dragged back toward Smilodon Bay.

All through this Wayan lay clutching Fava, not daring to speak, hardly daring to breathe. The small boy just hugged her and quivered in fear.

Toward dawn Fava almost slept when she heard another scuffling sound nearby, someone walking on the log above her. She heard the snuffling of some Neanderthal Blade Kin with a strong nose, hunting by scent.

Fava remained still, stifled the urge to scream. The odor of mildewing redwood was strong, and she prayed that the turpines would be powerful enough to cover her scent.

The man paced up and down the length of the tree, testing the air and sniffing loudly, and then he sat, waiting.

Fava felt sure the Blade Kin had caught her scent, was waiting, hoping she would bolt from her hiding place. She heard him quietly unsheathe his sword. Wayan nuzzled close, burying his head between her breasts, and cleared his throat.

Someone shouted nearby, not more than a hundred yards away, and swords rang. The prowler bounded off through the woods, and Fava lay, sweat pouring from her.

An hour later the sun rose, and faint outlines of light shone through the woods. Fava had crushed some ferns while backing into her hiding place. She straightened them now, scooped detritus in front to conceal herself.

Thousands of Blade Kin passed by just after sunrise, heading south toward Muskrat Creek, running through the woods so softly that Fava hardly heard them and only saw them as shadows in green capes. It made her wonder, *Could it be that fifty had passed by during the night for every one that she heard in the darkness?*

Two hours later no one else had passed, and Wayan whimpered, "I have to pee."

She let him up. He walked a short distance, peed, and came back, then fell asleep in her arms. No one moved through the woods all day long. Near dusk she saw one lone person creeping through the woods toward town—Anorath's wife, Vo-olai.

Fava stood up, motioned for Vo-olai to come hide, but Vo-olai stopped, stared at Fava as if she were some strange animal. Vo-olai's eyes were rimmed with red, and her pants and tunic covered with mud. She looked like a wild creature, something that had spent the week crawling through brush.

"No," she said.

"Come, please!" Fava hissed, but Vo-olai kept walking. Then she turned and spoke as casually as if they had just met on the street. "Have you seen Anorath today? Or Tchula? I can't find them."

Fava knew then that Vo-olai had worms in her head. A night of running from the Blade Kin had ruined her mind. Fava hissed, "Why don't you come here and wait for them with me?"

"No, I really think, I really think, they need me," Vo-olai said. "I must find them."

"Where do you think they are?" Fava asked.

"I'm not sure," Vo-olai said, and she began ambling back to town.

Fava wanted to call her, but dared not raise her voice. She climbed back under the log, planning to wait, but little Wayan looked at her with such fear and accusation in his eyes that she said, "Should we go save her?"

Wayan nodded his head yes.

Fava got up, picked up Wayan, and shot out from under the log, running after Vo-olai.

When Vo-olai heard the pursuit, she took off running, blindly racing toward town, and Fava knew she could not catch her carrying Wayan. They fell behind.

Fava and Wayan crept up to town slowly, and the sun was setting in a bloody sky. Fava watched the road ahead warily. Everything was so open here—fields ran back to the trees, and you could see for half a mile. She stopped, warily, with the creeping sensation that she was being watched.

In many ways the town looked the same. Two cats ran across the road in front of her, twitching their tails. Pigs rooted in the field behind Oolan's house. Yet the houses were but smoking ashes, charred walls. Blackened brick chimneys pointed to the sky. Fava looked at the little squares of ash and debris where houses had been, amazed at how small the homes appeared. The height, the wooden cross-beams, all had given them a blocky solidity, a sense of permanence they now lacked. Down the street a quarter of a mile, an old sow cave bear dug among the ashes of a home, looking for fruit or vegetables or grain, and Fava decided that the bear would not have stayed if others were around. The Blade Kin must be gone for good. Tentatively, she walked the road.

As she passed her parents' home, Fava stopped. The hunting trophies that had sat for so many years in her father's house lay in the ashes, just bits of whitened bone and cracked teeth. The great mastodon tusks that Chaa kept in his hallway were split by heat. The blade of his sword lay in the ashes. She walked through the rooms, surprised to find that the ashes were cold already. In the kitchen, in a hole in the floor where vegetables were stored, she found some potatoes and apples and onions. She sat with Wayan and tried to eat a potato that had cooked on one side, but her stomach objected, and she could not force it down. She didn't know if she was too frightened to eat, or if the grief that kills had come upon her. She knew only that she could not eat.

So she fed Wayan a bit, pocketed some apples, then they headed up the trail to their own home.

Fava was surprised to find it still standing. Four dead Blade Kin were laid out on the front doorstep, the way that a cat will leave dead mice by the door as a present. Wayan turned away, buried his face in Fava's chest, afraid to look at them. All the dead Blade Kin wore the strange masked hoods with glass eyes, but their weapons had been taken. So Tull had killed at least four of them.

Fava looked into the house, found it ransacked. Few clothes, no weapons. But the bedding and blankets remained, along with dishes and cooking pots, the winter food. Wayan leapt down from her arms immediately, ran to the beds, and picked up a carved mammoth behind a mattress and began to play.

Fava wondered if Tull could still be near. Perhaps he was moving the items to a safer place? But no. Whoever had ransacked the house was not a person bent on survival. The blankets had been left, the food. No, the Blade Kin must have taken Tull, along with their valuables. Perhaps he had been caught while trying to empty the house. Yet even that made no sense.

Fava sat on the floor a moment, looked outside. She felt suddenly weak with grief, dizzy. She fingered two empty bullet casings on the floor. Tull had killed at least four Blade Kin, and he had been caught.

She went to search for Vo-olai. She didn't have to go far. Just where the road dipped, the redwood bridge spanned the Smilodon River. Vo-olai stood in the middle of the bridge, holding her hands over her face and weeping.

Fava stopped, stared down at the docks. The old people of town lay in the street by the docks, twisted in odd shapes, ragged bloody holes in their throats. At least thirty lay there. Vo-olai's grandparents lay there.

Fava's heart pounded. She picked up Wayan, ran down to the docks, searched for Tull among the dead. After several minutes Vo-olai came to sit and hold her grandmother's hand in the dusk.

Everything was so quiet, and the sun had set. Clouds were coming in, soft dark clouds that smelled like snow. Up the street, in the human part of town, another bear had come to feed on burned garbage. It paced back and forth up by the inn, between the bodies of dead Blade Kin, afraid to come any closer to Fava and Vo-olai.

"We better leave," Fava whispered, tugging at Vo-olai. "All this blood, it might bring wolves or sabertooths." She did not say it, but she was even more afraid that the Blade Kin might return.

"At least," Vo-olai said, "let's give my grandparents to the river." Fava helped drag the old people to the docks and gently laid them in the water, watched them drift to sea.

"Come," Fava said. "Let's go back to my house. It isn't burned."

Vo-olai turned and collapsed into Fava's arms and began to sob. Until that moment Fava had tried to be strong, knowing that if she showed her fear, her utter desolation, it would only hurt Wayan. But now darkness took her, and she cried for her husband and wailed for her family; grief filled the hollow of her chest. They wept together.

"I want to die! I want to die!" Vo-olai shouted, and Fava held her and said, "No! Don't say that!"

"What do I have to live for? My husband is gone! My family is gone! How can I ever find them? We don't even know where they went! The Blade Kin could have carried them off anywhere."

"I saw a ship in the harbor," Fava whimpered. "They were carried away in a ship. That means they've gone to Bashevgo. They aren't dead."

"But they're slaves."

Fava licked her lips, forced herself to stop crying, to sound hopeful. "Maybe they will escape. They might come looking for us."

Vo-olai nodded doubtfully, began scanning the streets of town as if at any moment a whole crowd of people would come rushing out of the forest. Fava looked at her, realized that this was good. At least if Vo-olai had some hope, the killing grief would not come upon her.

"For now, let's go back to my house. We can sleep there for the night." She took Vo-olai then, and the girl followed automatically, almost unaware of her surroundings. "When did you sleep last?"

Vo-olai watched the houses as she went by, as if still

stunned. "I don't know. I don't know. I can't remember."

"It's not important," Fava said.

When they got off the dirt road onto the trail that led to Fava's, her fear subsided. The short twisted coastal pines and wild rhododendron along the trail hid them somewhat, and Fava no longer had the prickly sensation that she was being watched.

She took Vo-olai into the house, set her on the bed, and fed her an apple. Vo-olai sat there and Wayan patted her back. "We should go hide somewhere," Vo-olai said. "The Blade Kin are sweeping through the Rough. We should go hide in the woods, wait until Anorath escapes."

"Or go down to White Rock," Fava said. "The Blade Kin would never find us down in the mines."

"Yes." Vo-olai said. Vo-olai did not eat her apple, only held it. She looked at the floor for a long time. Wayan found a brush on the floor, began combing the twigs from Vo-olai's hair. "Anorath and Tchula won't be coming back, will they?" Vo-olai said. "No one ever escapes from Bashevgo."

"No," Fava answered.

Vo-olai sighed deeply, staring at the floor, her brow furrowed. "No one ever comes back. . . ."

"We can make a home in the woods," Fava said, worried. If Vo-olai did not eat, then perhaps it meant that the killing grief had come on her. The girl's eyes weren't focusing properly. "We could live together and have fun, the way we did when we were children. And we could wait. Even in Bashevgo, they can't always watch the slaves."

"Fava, I'm going to go to Bashevgo," Vo-olai said, her voice panicky. "I'm going to go live with my husband and sons. If we can't live here, at least we can live together as Thralls."

"You wouldn't be the first to do that," Fava answered calmly, trying to soothe her.

Vo-olai nodded, set her apple on the floor. "Well, that's it. I'll go to Bashevgo."

Wayan looked at Fava. "Is Tull in Bashevgo?" he asked.

Fava sat beside him. "Yes, I think so."

"Are we going to go there?"

Fava pursed her lips. "I don't know."

"I don't want to go," Wayan said.

It was full dark now. Fava laid Wayan and Vo-olai on the mattress, put a blanket on them. She could not help hesitating, sitting beside the bed and just touching the mattress where Tull had lain his head. The kwea, the remembered pleasure she felt from this place, so filled her with longing. Outside, snow began to fall; she made a small fire, hoping its feeble light and smoke would not attract any Blade Kin. By the time she had finished setting the fire, Vo-olai and Wayan had fallen into an exhausted sleep.

Fava looked around the house. Much of what they owned had been taken—clothes and weapons—but they had food and bedding and pots for cooking. *I can get clothing,* Fava decided, *if I'm willing.*

She stepped out into the darkness by the doorstep and began scavenging from the dead Blade Kin. Their dark capes were thick and warm, as were the cotton tunics under their armor. Two of them wore packs containing food and heavy overcloaks that would blend into the forest and brush. In one pack Fava found a long knife, the kind humans sometimes used for fighting.

She stopped a moment, recognized the futility of what she was doing. *All my life,* she thought, *I've been afraid the slavers would come get me, and now I'm planning to give myself to them? The Gods are playing cruel jokes with me.*

She looked at the dead people at her feet. The Blade Kin would be hard on Tull for that. And he had killed more of their ilk at Denai. The Blade Kin would punish him.

The despair came heavier, darker, in deep waves. It

knotted her stomach, and Fava bent over and retched, spitting up the small bit of potato she had eaten. She'd known other women who grieved like this, women who starved themselves when their husbands died. Going to Tull might save her life.

Fava tried to think of Tull, tried to imagine living with him in Bashevgo. Perhaps they would have to work hard, but they would live side by side, and so the work would be easier. Fava knew that she was young and pretty, that the Blade Kin would rape her, and she tried to imagine what it would be like, both for her and for Tull. Tull would never be able to take it. He would kill any Blade Kin who touched her, and in the end they would execute him. She knew—Tull could never survive in slavery, and Fava realized that she wouldn't want to survive herself. Her stomach knotted again, and she wanted to vomit.

She untied the straps to the Blade Kin's body armor, took off their leather cuirasses. The snow was falling on them, had already become an inch deep. When she began stripping the undertunic from the second body, she was surprised to find that it had breasts. She felt to make sure, then pulled the headgear off the woman.

There was little light to see by, but this Blade Kin was indeed a woman, a Pwi woman with a kindly face. Fava turned the girl's head, saw that she had only one ear, a left ear with a long dangling ornament in it.

Fava grunted her surprise. She had heard of female Blade Kin, knew they were rare. She stared at the corpse for a long time, at the tall black boots, at the undertunic and body armor. She pulled on the boots, and they fit her fine. She held the stiff leather cuirass up to her own breast, found that it would have fit if Tull hadn't put a bullet through the woman's belly.

She sat for a long time, in the darkness, with the snow falling. This little house, this little bay, felt so peaceful and quiet with the snow falling, the muffled world. She closed her eyes, and the kwea of her house seemed to swell around her like a mist—the comfort she felt in Tull's arms, the beauty of their wedding night. The raw unsatisfied lust she felt for him—not a lust for his body, but a lust for his life, for his dreams of spending a life together. And from down the trail, even though her parents' house was in ashes, she could still feel the years of happiness built up by accretion, weighing heavily—playing tag with her older brother around the lilac bush, the smell of an elk roast, the thrill of the day when her father first returned from Hotland bringing her the tooth of a Tyrannosaurus Rex, and the funny stories he told of how her uncle had tried to ride a triceratops.

For Fava the kwea of peace and joy, and dreams of peace and joy, lay upon the hills like a wet blanket of snow, muffling the recent cries of war. She wanted joy for her children. Nothing less. To offer less would be impossible.

Fava looked down at the corpses of Blade Kin and thought, *If my husband is in Bashevgo, then I must go and free him, and to do that, I must look the part.* She pulled the long-knife from its sheath and sliced off her right ear, and then sat, surprised for a moment by the searing hot pain, holding the stump of her ear.

Among the Blade Kin, a soldier always gave his ear to his first commander. Fava thought briefly of saving the ear, giving it to Tull when she found him, and she laughed and tossed the ragged piece of flesh into the brush.

Then she cried again. She cried because there was no one to see her and she no longer needed to be strong for anyone. She cried because she felt desolate, and missed her family. She cried because thinking of this town would never again leave her with happy kwea. From now on, the accrued memories would be tainted.

She sat down, a blanket over her back to keep out the falling snow, until at last the tears would not come anymore, and she found her drifting thoughts turning toward Tull, wondering what path she should take to get to Bashevgo.

The sound of a scuffling footstep drew her attention. Fava looked up through the falling snow. Someone stood on the trail leading to the house, only a dozen paces away, a human Blade Kin dressed all in black.

The human bent close and said, "There's always someone stupid enough to return."

Chapter 7
A Passing Grief

"Shhh . . . ," one of the women in the cage hissed. "The Blade Kin are coming." She huddled on a mat, ratted her hair so that if the Blade Kin came for sex, they would not take her. Tull lay on his pallet. The ship vibrated from the workings of its great engines as it eased over giant swells in the ocean, a great steel behemoth. Tull lay in its belly as he had for days and nights. He could not tell the difference anymore. Sometimes the ship stopped, and cannon fire rolled like thunder over the decks; then prisoners would swell into her belly—dazed Pwi with mud on their hands from working fields, rich merchants dressed in finery and amazement—all of them shoved forward, down into the depths of the ship.

But this was not one of those times. Tull looked out over the cell. A hundred men, women, and children lay on their mats, unmoving, trying to feign sleep. Overhead, in the gloom, Blade Kin watched from their turrets.

Keys rattled outside the cell door, and it swung open on well-oiled hinges. Tull lay listening for the whimpers of the Pwi women and children.

Someone softly walked to the mat next to his. The girl there was named Ruwatta, a delicate child of eleven from the town of Fish Haven, as were most others in this cell. Tull closed his ears, closed his heart, as the Blade Kin took her.

There was no stopping the rape. Tull knew that. He could have jumped the warrior, managed even to break the man's neck, but the Blade Kin in the turrets above would shoot at Tull, perhaps killing the child in the process. He had seen it happen before.

Someone tapped Tull's foot. He pretended not to notice, hoping they would go away. They tapped his foot again. He turned over, thinking that they would take him, too, this time. It was a Neanderthal woman dressed in black robes with red trim, the uniform of a Carnadine Sorcerer. Four Blade Kin guards stood behind her.

She studied him in the gloom, her mouth a tight line, betraying no hint of emotion. She leaned over him, looking into his face, into his eyes, as if she were a sculptor who hoped someday to make an image by memory. "Tull Genet?" she said at last.

"Yes."

"You have a wife? Fava?"

"Yes," Tull said, hopefully.

"I'm sorry, she has been killed." The words slapped Tull like a whip, and the sorceress pressed one of Fava's tunics into his numb hands, a scrap of green cotton with yellow meadowlark feathers sewn around the collar. It was torn and spotted with blood, but he could smell Fava's vanilla water perfume on it. "The Blade Kin caught her near Smilodon Bay. She tried to fight them when they raped her. They had to kill her."

She touched Tull's hand, wrapped her fingers around his to give him comfort. Blackness threatened to swallow him, stark cold blackness, and he looked in her eyes, and saw . . . curiosity. The woman watched him the way a child would watch a hog being gutted. Curious, dispassionate. Totally empty. The woman had no real sorrow in her voice, no pity. In fact, Tull looked at the glint in her dark blue eyes and imagined a smile behind, as if she were amused.

Another test, he realized, to see if he were Blade Kin instead of a Thrall.

"What will you do now?" she asked. "I know the grief must hurt. I know you want to die."

Tull fingered the tunic, wondered if Fava was really dead. No, he decided. The Blade Kin were ruthless, but they captured slaves: they didn't kill them. He'd been amazed at the efficiency with which the slavers had captured Smilodon Bay, taking the town by surprise, putting the merchandise to sleep rather than fighting some drawn-out battle. No, they would not have killed her.

"I cared for her very much," Tull said, and he let some of his fear, some of his real sorrow, creep into his voice. "I suppose I shall need to get another woman."

The sorceress glanced at the four Blade Kin guards behind, dismissed them. When she turned back to Tull, her voice became husky, her movements wary. "My name is Chulata," she said. "I need a man, too, for the night. May I comfort you?" She slipped off her black robe. Her undertunic fit tightly, displaying the curves of her body. She was strong and shapely, seductive.

"I do not need comfort," he said. "Besides, you would not satisfy my tastes."

Chulata raised a brow in surprise. "Who is to your tastes?"

Tull put his hands behind his head, considered possible lies. He recalled last summer, sleeping in the mountains outside Denai with the Dryad Tirilee. The Creators had formed the Dryad to care for the trees, and Tull had stroked the girl's silver hair, whipped into a mating frenzy by the scent of the pheromones she exuded. No normal woman could arouse such ecstasy in a man. "I slept with a Dryad of the aspens last summer while on my way to Denai. Now the rest of you women seem . . . tiresome." It was a half truth, and the honesty carried in his voice.

Chulata frowned, took the tunic from Tull, and her hand trembled with nervousness or anger, he could not tell which. "I will dispose of this for you," she said, glancing at him over her back as she left. She would be wondering how he could have escaped the Dryad's spell. The Pwi always succumbed to Dryads, served them as slaves.

Tull lay on his mat and wondered if he had passed the test. He smiled at the way Chulata had lost her composure at the end, counted it a small victory.

An hour later Chulata returned, her composure intact. "You say you have slept with a Dryad. Can you prove it?"

Tull considered. If he had not been certain that they were testing him before, he was now. "Ask the innkeeper Theron Scandal from Smilodon Bay. He saw it."

"Yet you fought our Blade Kin at Smilodon Bay. You held off our men while your wife tried to escape? You did it because you wanted to save the woman you love, you wanted her to escape. Your love for her is what made you fight so fiercely!"

Chulata tried too hard to manipulate him into the wrong answers. Tull felt close—she almost accepted him as Blade Kin. He decided to tease her. "Perhaps you are right," he said, and her expression remained unchanged. "Perhaps I did care for her too much, and it clouded my judgment. In the dark I didn't know I was surrounded—still, I must think about it and decide." Tull hesitated, as if considering, then asked, "You have been ordered to have sex with me, haven't you?"

Chulata did not answer.

"I hope so," Tull said. "I want you to spread your legs for me. But we will do it at my convenience, when I command you for my own reasons. Do you understand?"

Chulata stepped back, stumbled on a mat where the Blade Kin lay sleeping with Ruwatta. Chulata's face went red, and she felt foolish, so she turned and marched back to Mahkawn with all the resolve and dignity she could muster.

The Omnipotent was in his private quarters, preparing for bed when she knocked. He called her in, and she found him dressed in only a black breechcloth, setting his knives out on the table by his bed.

"You are right, he talks like a Blade Kin!" she said.

Mahkawn nodded. "And when he saw the tunic of his wife?"

"Nothing! A passing moment of grief, nothing more. He suggested himself that he would need a new woman, but none have pleased him since he slept with a Dryad."

"Perhaps we should not be so surprised if he seems more human than Pwi," Mahkawn said. "His father is human. Tull is Tcho-Pwi." Neither Pwi nor human, a nonperson. "Perhaps Tull was born a Blade Kin."

Chulata gritted her teeth. "I do not trust him. You can't think to make him Blade Kin."

Mahkawn nodded. Perhaps Tull did require further testing. He went to his desk, pulled out the brass ball from Tull's home. He pushed the tiny button on top, watched the three-dimensional image of Anee expand out, nearly filling his small room. Mahkawn kept little in the room: weapons, a bit of clothing. He lived the ascetic life of a warrior. The holographic image showed a great white storm swirling out of the blue southern oceans toward the Rough, bringing warm rains. By the time they reached Bashevgo, the rains would turn to snow. Mahkawn waited a moment, and the image of the world faded. The brass ball became only an oddity again. Mahkawn stared at the ball, mystified.

He poured himself a small glass of rum, swallowed it. Chulata still waited by the door. Mahkawn watched her—a beautiful girl.

A passing moment of grief. Nothing more. Mahkawn wondered how he would feel when his own lover died. Would he be able to contain so much pain? A passing moment of grief. *Tull is more Blade Kin than I am,* Mahkawn thought, and he admired the big Tcho-Pwi, sleeping down in his cell.

"Stay. Mate with me tonight," Mahkawn said to

Chulata, "if you will." It had been many years since he'd asked a Blade Kin to sleep with him. Perhaps Chulata could sate his craving, turn his thoughts away from home and his Thrall lover.

"I would be honored," Chulata said, her voice betraying the excitement she felt at the prospect of sleeping with an Omnipotent, and she closed the door behind her.

Fava crouched on the ground in the snow, blood pouring from her ear. She whisked out her long knife, waving it to ward off the Blade Kin.

"Don't be afraid," a female voice said, and Darrissea Frolic pulled off her mask.

"Darrissea!" Fava shouted, throwing her arms around the girl. They held each other for a long moment, and Fava heard a sniffle, realized Darrissea was crying.

"Is Tull here?" Darrissea asked.

"No," Fava said. "Only me and Vo-olai and Wayan. How did you escape?"

"I was in the outhouse when they attacked," she said. "I hid till this morning."

"Didn't they search it?"

"Not the part I hid in," Darrissea apologized. "Do I smell all right?"

"You smell sweet," Fava said, and gazed into the human girl's dark eyes. "But the poison smoke, didn't it get you?"

"No," Darrissea said. "It must rise. Are you all right, and Wayan?" she asked, staring at Fava's ear.

"I'm fine. So is Wayan. But I fear Vo-olai is not. Since Anorath got captured, she acts as if she has *owe taxa,* worms in the head."

Darrissea pulled off her backpack, got out some bandages. "What happened to your ear?"

"I cut it off," Fava said weakly. "I'm going to Bashevgo to free Tull, so I am disguising myself as Blade

Kin." *Going to free Tull.* Fava heard her own words distantly as Darrissea bandaged her ear. What was it her father had said? Tull could become more powerful than Chaa, if he could get free? Fava suddenly realized that something more important than her love for Tull was at stake. She had to get Tull free.

"Lean your head to the side so it doesn't bleed," Darrissea said, pulling Fava's head down so that her cut faced the sky. The human girl's hands shook as she worked. "So you are going to Bashevgo? What of Wayan and Vo-olai? Are you taking them?"

"I . . . I don't know," Fava answered.

"How *crazy* is Vo-olai?" Darrissea asked. Though she was speaking Pwi, she used the human word for worms-in-head.

Fava shrugged. "I have a mountain of worry for her. Come in the cabin, get some food and rest." Fava urged her to the house, and Darrissea ate a little, then told Fava to sleep while she kept guard. Fava reluctantly gave the human girl the long knife. She'd seen Darrissea practice, and the human girl, with her gawky arms and long thin legs, had good speed and reach, but no strength. She would not be much of a guard.

Fava slept soundly through the night, and woke at dawn to find Darrissea sitting in the half dawn, looking out the window. Snow was falling. "I've been thinking," Darrissea said. "We should not go outside today. With the snow on the ground, any Blade Kin left out there would find it easy to track us. Also, we should not build a fire. We can use the blankets and the cloaks of Blade Kin for warmth. If we need to cook anything, we can light candles."

Darrissea seemed to be thinking very clearly. "All right," Fava said. "Do you think anyone else could help us? My father? Surely he can't be far. The Blade Kin couldn't have caught him."

"They caught him," Darrissea said. "I found a lot of dead Blade Kin up by the inn, so I didn't have much difficulty getting a disguise. I dressed in the dark, then kept guard around the prisoners. I could do nothing to help them. I saw your father. He was unconscious when they dragged him from the house, weak from taking his Spirit Walk. Perhaps he saw that the Blade Kin were coming, but couldn't rouse himself from his trance. Everyone from town got caught, along with a lot of people I haven't seen before—people from out in the Rough. The Blade Kin have been everywhere. I don't see how we can hope for anyone to rescue us."

"What about Tull?"

"They took him on the ship," Darrissea said. "They were angry with him for killing so many Blade Kin. They knew about the men he'd killed in Denai."

"What do you think will happen? Will they execute him?"

Darrissea stopped gazing out the window, turned her dark eyes to Fava. "I don't know."

They stayed in the house for the day, and Fava watched the others. Vo-olai sat for much of the morning, rocking back and forth or humming, and Fava feared that the girl's mind was broken. She tried speaking comforting words to the girl, but nothing helped.

Wayan kept trying to sneak out to play in the snow, so Darrissea sang and told him a cruel story about hungry children whose poor parents were forced to send them into the woods to starve. There they met a sorcerer who lived in a candy house and tried to eat them, and the children escaped only by shoving him in his own oven "until his guts boiled like soup." When they pulled the sorcerer out, he'd turned into a great meat pie, and the children took it home and fed their parents, and none of them ever hungered again. Wayan seemed to enjoy the tale, but Vo-olai frowned in horror as Darrissea told it.

Yet as Darrissea spoke, Fava noticed that Vo-olai quit rocking, and when the human was done, Vo-olai put Wayan on her lap and told him a Pwi story, one Fava had never heard before, and Vo-olai's voice seemed strong, almost normal, as if she were telling the story to her own son.

"Long ago," Vo-olai started, "there was a great hero among the Pwi, and he was so fierce that when he wanted to go somewhere, he would jump on the back of a wild woolly rhino and drive it just as a child would ride a pig. I forget the man's name," Vo-olai said.

"Ananoi!" Wayan shouted. "It must be Ananoi!"

"Oh, yes, Ananoi, the Rhino Rider," Vo-olai said. "That was his name. He lived with his beautiful wife Shape-Changing Woman in a place not far from here. Well, in those days the animals had many problems getting along, and often they would come to Ananoi seeking his wisdom and help.

"One day a huge pack of dire wolves came to him along with the Lord of the Sabertooths. The dire wolves all hid their tails between the legs, and they howled as if in pain. The great Lord of the Sabertooths was very old and huge. He'd grown as large as a hill, and the poor old cat's teeth had grown longer than a mammoth's tusks, and they dragged the ground. He was weeping so hard that his tears filled the channel he had left behind. That is how we got the Smilodon River.

"Anyway, Ananoi took one look at the poor old cat's red eyes and the river of tears, and he said, 'Great Lord, how can I help?' Ananoi thought at first that the Lord had wormy teeth, but could not understand why the wolves came with the cat, and why they too were so sad.

"The Lord of Sabertooths kept weeping, and he snarled, 'I have just come from the south, and none of my people can sleep in that land. All of the Mammoth People have climbed up into the clouds, and they run among the clouds so much that the sky thunders. The whole earth trembles, and whenever they step on a cloud, they press water from it so that it falls on us. We cannot sleep!' As soon as he said these words, the dire wolves howled in chorus, 'Save us! Save us!'

" 'What must I do to save you?' Ananoi asked, and a green light flashed in the sabertooth's eyes.

" 'It would help if you would climb up the rainbow and ride the mammoths down out of the clouds,' the sabertooth said, 'so that we could sleep,' and then he licked his lips.

" 'Perhaps you should climb the rainbow and chase the mammoths out of the sky yourselves,' Ananoi said.

" 'Ooooo, we can't climb,' the poor dire wolves howled, and the Lord of Sabertooths snarled, 'It's too high for me, and the rainbow is always so wet and slippery.'

" 'Ayaah,' Ananoi said. 'If I chase the mammoth people out of the sky, will you promise not to eat them?'

" 'Yes, we promise,' the wolves and the sabertooth all said in unison. And because Ananoi himself was an honest man, he believed them, and he went to chase the Mammoth People out of the sky."

"The wolves and sabertooths were lying!" Wayan said. "I know it!"

"Yes," Vo-olai said, "they were lying, but Ananoi did not know this, so he rubbed his body with pitch to make it sticky so he could climb the slippery rainbow, and he climbed up into the clouds to chase the mammoth people from the sky.

"Well, that evening, when he finally got to the top of a cloud, sure enough, he found hundreds of mammoths up there, grazing on the tall blue grass in the clouds, and flocks of meadowlarks flew across the sky like stars at night. There were no lions or sabertooths or wolves, and only the smallest of trees, and all the many lakes up there were filled with huge sturgeon. All in all, it was very beautiful, and Ananoi could see why the mammoth people liked it so well.

"Since it was almost dark, Ananoi looked around for some dry mammoth dung to build a fire with. Although mammoth dung is plentiful up there, it is almost always wet, and it took him a long time, but he finally found some and built himself a nice large fire. Then he went to the lake and caught a huge sturgeon in his hands and sat down to eat.

"It was a cold night, and soon Vozha, Lord of the Mammoth People, came to Ananoi's fire to warm himself. Vozha is as large as a mountain, and the hairs on his back grow huge as redwoods, and the fleas on his back are big as coyotes, and when he blows water from his trunk, it rains on the far side of the earth. Not even the great Ananoi would want to pick a fight with such a monster, so Ananoi sought to reason with the great lord.

" 'You must force your people down out of these clouds,' Ananoi told him. 'Every day you stomp around in the clouds and trumpet, and below you the earth rumbles. You smash water out of the sky onto the people down below.'

" 'We like it up here,' Vozha said. 'The grass is tall and sweet; the sun always shines. What do we care if we smash water out of the clouds and make it rain on the people below?'

" 'You are just like all rich people,' Ananoi said. 'You care nothing for the people beneath you. If you do not mend your ways, I will be forced to throw you off the clouds.'

" 'I'm sorry if our behavior has bothered you,' Vozha said. 'We did not mean to dampen your people. We've been here a long time, and you are the first to complain.'

"Ananoi thought long about his words. The mammoth king was right. Ananoi had never been bothered by the thunder before, and in fact he liked it when the summer rains watered his crops. None of the other animals had ever complained—only the wolves and the sabertooths, and Ananoi wondered if perhaps the complaints had all been a ruse. So he said to the mammoth king, 'Perhaps I have been tricked by the wolves and sabertooths who sent me to complain.'

"The mammoth lord became very angry, and he raised his great trunk up until it put the dent into the moon Freya, and he said, 'You should not need a nose as long as mine to smell out this plot! They want you to throw us down so that they can eat our children!'

"Ananoi agreed that this had all been an evil scheme. So together they gathered mammoth dung and sculpted it to look like a young mammoth. They hardened it by the fire, then wove a mat of long dry grass and covered the effigy so it looked as if it were covered with hair. The next morning as soon as the sun rose, Ananoi carried the effigy of mammoth dung and tossed it off the cloud, shouting, 'Stay off this cloud, you evil mammoth woman!' and he watched below.

"As soon as the effigy hit the ground, sabertooths and dire wolves boiled from their hiding places in the brush and pounced on the thing. They thought they were tearing into flesh, so all of them ripped away great mouthfuls of dung, and then the wolves and sabertooths all rolled in the grass and tried to spit the vile dung out of their jaws.

"But some of the dire wolves liked the taste of the dung, and that is why even today, though they like meat more, sometimes you will see them eat dung.

"Vozha and Ananoi watched the predators and laughed from above, and Vozha trumpeted and stomped the cloud, making water fall from it and making thunder roll across the heavens. Then the two heroes each grabbed pieces of dry dung and set it on fire and tossed it down on the dire wolves and sabertooths.

"Now, even today, when summer dries the mammoth dung in the clouds, the mammoth people celebrate by running through the clouds, causing thunder and rain. Then they hurl burning dung to earth, forming lightning, and that is why the sabertooths all hide in the bushes during a storm, and that is why the dire wolves all howl in outrage the night after a storm."

Vo-olai smiled down at Wayan, and his eyes shone. Listening to the story reminded Fava of times she had spent on her mother's lap as a child. It all seemed so long ago and far away, but it lightened her mood. That night Fava dreamed it was summer, and Wayan sat on her lap as she told stories and fed him blackberry tarts; another child also sat on her lap, a girl with hair the color that the Neanderthals call "maple-leaf" red. In the dream the girl was Fava's own daughter, a child with soft skin, and a sweet, carefree smile.

When she got up the next morning, Fava saw Darrissea's wisdom in keeping the door closed and forbidding fires. From their window they watched six Blade Kin march north up the street through town. Some had guns and others carried gas tubes. All of them wore masks and camouflaged robes in forest green and brown.

They had a slave with them. Fava recognized the boy, a human named Mylon Storm. The Blade Kin stopped halfway to the bridge, and their leader pointed back toward the house. Two Blade Kin broke off, followed the road to the trail, then disappeared into the brush.

Fava rushed everyone to Tull's workroom, then hid behind the door with only a knife in her hand. Vo-olai became wide-eyed and shouted that the Blade Kin were going to torch the house, and Darrissea kept speaking to her softly, trying to calm the girl.

But after what seemed an eternity, Fava peeked out the window again. Through a crack in the curtain she could see all six Blade Kin poking around the ruined houses on the far side of town.

"They only came to look for footprints outside the door," Darrissea said. "Look! You can see their tracks in the snow." Fava watched as the Blade Kin searched the ruins in the human part of town, then headed inland on the dirt road that led to Finger Mountain.

"What do you think they will do with Mylon?" Vo-olai asked.

"They must be expecting another ship," Darrissea answered, "to pick them up and take them back to Bashevgo."

Fava sighed, moved away from the curtains. "We don't want to be here when they come back."

"But," Vo-olai said, "what if we were? What if we went up to them and asked them to take us to Bashevgo so we could live with our husbands?"

"I'm sure they would be happy to give you a ride," Darrissea sneered, and Fava realized that the human was not talking about a ride in a boat.

"No, I mean it," Vo-olai answered. "I want to find Anorath and live with my sweet children." Vo-olai's whole body was trembling.

"Do you think that is what your husband would want?" Fava said calmly, and she moved close and put her arms around Vo-olai. "Friend, would Anorath be happy knowing that you and your children will live in slavery? Or would he want you to be free? I think we should go to Bashevgo, to free Tull and Anorath."

"You can't think that!" Vo-olai said, her voice carrying an edge of hysteria. "Adjonai guards Bashevgo. He will hear your thoughts, punish you! You won't ever get to the city. I can feel him—reaching for us!" The girl's eyes widened, her face paled.

Fava knew she could not reason with Vo-olai now. "Shhhh . . . ," Fava whispered. "Think of good things. Think of lying with Anorath in bed, or the summer when we were children and Scandal made ice cream for us." Fava held Vo-olai and soothed her for a long time. Darrissea went into the back room, began making dinner, and Fava followed.

"We can't let those Blade Kin keep Mylon Storm, can we?" Darrissea whispered.

"They have weapons!" Fava countered. "What do you want to do?"

"We have a knife," Darrissea pointed out. "We could cut spears. They will be easy to track in the snow, in the dark. They will have to sleep sometime."

Fava dared not speak aloud for fear that Vo-olai would hear, but she knew it was decided.

Darrissea immediately began sharpening a broom

handle to make a spear while Fava lit candles and boiled water in a small copper pan. Fava thought that Darrissea looked like a shadow, dressed in black cape, black armor, with her dark hair and eyes. The human girl talked casually as she worked. "Did you see those Blade Kin today?" Darrissea said. "I thought they were disappointing: just normal men in camouflage, carrying weapons. I always expected something more of them, something monstrous and predatory, something inhuman."

"Hmmm," Fava answered.

"Nothing ever lives up to my expectations. Once I saw a relic from Earth, one of the fossils that the Starfarers extracted DNA from to recreate some kind of sea snails. The fossil sat in a shed up on Finger Mountain, covered with moss. I don't know. Since it was from Earth, I guess I expected more. But it was just a rock, just a brown rock—until you looked into it and saw the fossils. I mean, we both came from the same planet, and it made me feel, I don't know, like we were sisters or something. It made me feel old. Those snails lived four hundred million years before the first human walked the earth, and I realized they were my ancestors.

"Sometimes I wonder if I'll have kin living hundreds of millions of years in the future. Maybe they'll be as different from me as I am from those snails. Still, we'll be sisters. Maybe they'll feel my presence stirring in their bones."

Darrissea finished the spear, set it aside, and went to Tull's crude stove. She fished some charcoal from it, then went to the wall by the cabinets, and wrote:

Stones

When a thumbnail flakes off moss,
it makes such a small sound.
A gentle tug of the finger
draws the roots from the rock
and sends the small ones scurrying:

Sal bugs and white lice
flee into the light.

Yet beneath the fragile moss
the stone barely holds its fossils.
The chalky white curve of shell,
the bones of scallop, clam, and snail,
hoard truant hues of sunrise orange,
thunderhead blue.
For many their motion is hardly suspended,
Trapped in the act of living
they struggle against the hardening clay.

Fava watched in fascination. Though she had read many of the girl's love poems over the years, she had never seen the girl write one. Darrissea worked as if in a trance, slowly, contemplating each line, then stepped back. "Now," she said, "if I die at Bashevgo, perhaps a few of my words will live—" She looked back at Fava and grinned wickedly. "Even if they don't, in a few million years, perhaps someone will find my bones and write a poem about them."

They worked quietly to prepare a dinner of cooked vegetables; just after dusk Wayan came in from the front room. "Why can't I go outside?" he said. "Vo-olai did."

Fava rushed to the window in fear, looked out. The snow had slowed, and rain was falling. She could see Vo-olai's tracks outside, but no sign of the girl. "How long ago did she leave?" Darrissea asked Wayan.

"A whole bunch of hours ago," Wayan answered. Though Wayan couldn't tell time, Fava felt certain that Vo-olai had been gone at least ten minutes. Fava couldn't see her anywhere along the bay front.

"Do you think she went to get herself captured?" Darrissea said.

Fava nodded yes. "The rain is so warm that the snow will melt by morning," Fava whispered, "and Thor will be up soon. She went to follow the tracks of those Blade Kin before the snow thaws."

"Damn her," Darrissea muttered. "It's getting dark, and she'll reach them long before we could. Let's get some dinner and wait for moonrise."

Fava agreed, and they ate quickly. Fava put on her own Blade Kin disguise, grabbed Wayan, and left the food and clothes for Darrissea to carry. They slipped out into the night just before moonrise, moving through the burned-out town like wraiths, silent and quick, floating through the foggy rain. They headed up into the hills, walking beside the swollen river through the ancient forest, until at last the town of Smilodon Bay became lost in the trees and darkness. "We enter our underworld," Darrissea whispered just out of town, "the appalling wood."

They did not have to go far to find the Blade Kin. They walked ten miles to High Pass relatively quickly. Just before dawn they spotted the Blade Kin's fire shining through a hide window. They had made a small camp in the shelter of a stable, and one guard sat in the shadows outside the door, a blanket over his head to keep out the rain.

"Someone will have to take out that guard," Darrissea said.

"I'll do it," Fava offered, afraid Darrissea would muck it up. Yet Fava found her own heart pounding, her breath coming short. "Those are experienced swordsmen down there. You've never fought in a real battle."

"Oh," Darrissea said thoughtfully. "And how many men have you killed lately?"

"None. But I'm stronger than you."

"And you're shaking like a half-drowned rat!" Darrissea countered.

"Still," Fava said, "I've seen you fight in practice. You are not very good."

"I don't plan to fight them if I can help it!" Darrissea whispered. "I plan to murder them—the way the Blade Kin murdered my father!"

Fava sat back, cowed by the vehemence in Darrissea's voice. Even in the darkness the girl's eyes shone with anger, and she was speaking too loudly. Fava feared that the guard down the hill would hear them. She glanced in his direction. The guard still sat, huddled under his cape. Fava was so frightened, she wanted to pee. Darrissea spun away in the darkness, and Fava let her go.

Fava shivered in the cold rain, feeling vulnerable, huddling with Wayan in the trees while Darrissea stalked the Blade Kin. If Darrissea got hurt, Fava would never forgive herself.

Darrissea circled through the woods to the building, crept up on it from behind, and Fava prayed silently that the Blade Kin would not suddenly get up or turn his head. The wet blanket that he huddled under restricted his peripheral vision. When Darrissea soundlessly ran from his left, she slammed the long knife into the man's neck, and only then did Fava realize the man must have been sleeping, for he did not react until he was stabbed. He lunged forward, tried to grab his sword, and Darrissea's knife flashed in the moonlight as she stabbed him again and again until he dropped. Then Darrissea grabbed the disjointed corpse of the guard, held a hand over his mouth as he died. All in all, it was a sloppy murder.

Darrissea took her knife and the Blade Kin's scimitar and slipped into the stable. Fava's heart pounded, and she realized she could not just stand by.

She set Wayan on the ground and whispered, "If I leave you here, could you stay put and be quiet?"

The boy nodded solemnly, but Fava did not trust him. "I'm serious," she said. "If you cry, or if you call out for me, or if you try to come to me, we could all get killed."

Wayan nodded, his eyes wide in the moonlight. Fava hugged him. "Good. Stay here." She ran down to the stable, took the dead Blade Kin's gun, and listened by the door. Fava's heart pounded, and the stock of the gun felt slippery in her cold hands.

All was quiet inside except for occasional rustling

sounds from the hayloft. Fava waited for ten minutes, fifteen, and realized she was sweating. The beads of moisture on her forehead were as much a product of her own body as they were of the rain. Wayan crept down the hill, walking in the snow. When he reached Fava, he grabbed her leg, held on as if for dear life. Fava realized she had asked too much of the child, so she put her hand over his mouth and waited. After nearly half an hour Darrissea opened the door. The human girl's face was pale, and her sword red with blood.

"Watch yourself," Darrissea said. "A strange illness seems to be going around. People are dying all over." She smiled wickedly, opened the door.

Fava crept inside, and Darrissea climbed to the loft, began unshackling confused prisoners, who all asked questions. There were no Blade Kin dead on the floor, and Fava was grateful not to be up in the loft. *I've seen too many dead lately,* she told herself. Three prisoners climbed down from the loft. Mylon, Vo-olai, and an older woman named Tchavs—a dear friend of Fava's mother.

Tchavs hugged Fava, grabbed Wayan, and swung the child around. Mylon came up close behind, followed by Vo-olai. Vo-olai's clothes were ripped, and her eyes rimmed with tears. The Blade Kin had obviously raped her. For a few moments they all stood, touching.

Tchavs held them, and her eyes glowed. "We're all that's left of Smilodon Bay. What do you plan? Shall we head south for White Rock?"

"I'm not going south," Fava said. "I'm heading north to Bashevgo, to free Tull and my family."

Tchavs looked at her in dismay. "That's not possible."

"I think it is," Fava answered, because she *had* to believe.

"Tull's a friend, and I would like to see him free as much as any other man," Tchavs said. "But this plan doesn't make sense!"

"Perhaps," Darrissea said. "But I will accompany Fava anyway. You should find a place to hide."

"Where?" Tchavs asked. "The Blade Kin are everywhere."

"There must be a deserted cabin they won't check, someplace in the woods."

"I know a place," Mylon said, eagerly, "a hut where my father used to hunt birds, on an island at Lake Easy Swim. It's well hidden."

"Can you take Tchavs there?" Darrissea asked.

"Yes," the boy said, disappointed. He'd have preferred to come with Fava.

"Then you should leave before sunrise," Fava said, "and stay with her. She needs someone to hunt for her, someone who can help till spring."

Tchavs looked at Fava. "You can't take Wayan," she said forcefully. "You either have to stay with him or leave him in the care of someone else."

Fava held the boy tight a moment. After the past few days, hiding from the Blade Kin, caring for Wayan, she felt as if he were her own son. The thought of being separated cut her to the bone.

Tchavs put an arm around Fava. "I'll take the boy. He is Pwi. I would care for him as if he were mine." Tchavs did not have to add the words "if you die"; Fava could hear them in her tone of voice.

Wayan clung to Fava's neck and cried, "I want you! Where are you going?"

"To Bashevgo," Fava said, her lips trembling, "to bring Tull home."

"Are the slavers there?"

"Yes," Fava said. "I will have to try to find him, then run away from the slavers. I can run faster than you, and that is why I want you to stay here."

Wayan pouted, looked around the room, trapped in indecision. *It isn't fair, dumping him off like this,* Fava thought. Wayan had never had much of a life with his own father, and only in the past few weeks, after Tull forcefully took the child from his own parents, had the boy begun to learn to smile.

"Don't you like me?" Wayan asked. "You wouldn't have to carry me. I could run real fast. Watch—" He tried to squirm from her arms to show how fast he could run.

"We love you," Fava said. "I would carry you if I could. You've never been a burden to me, only a joy." She struggled vainly, looking for another solution. "I know you want to stay with me, but you want to live with your brother Tull, too, don't you?"

"I don't care about him. I want you," Wayan said.

Fava held him close. "I know that's not true," she said. "Someday soon I will bring Tull back, and he will build us a bigger house, like he promised. And we will get you a kitten or a puppy. But for now, you will have to go with Tchavs."

The boy took the words as if they were a physical blow, a blow that shocked and dismayed him, a blow he would take silently, just as he had taken beatings from Jenks in silence. He stared up at Fava, and she saw the wounds in the child's eyes.

Fava held him while the others prepared to leave. Mylon climbed to the loft, brought down the Blade Kin's gas guns and firearms, split them between the two groups.

Vo-olai would not meet Fava's eyes. Instead she just stared at the ground. Fava desperately wanted Vo-olai to come, but saw she would be a detriment to the group. "I'll find Anorath for you," Fava promised. "I'll bring him back, too. You stay here, help take care of Wayan and Tchavs."

Vo-olai nodded mutely. Fava closed her eyes. She could feel the evil kwea of Bashevgo, the long arms of the dark god reaching for her. She was frightened. She watched Darrissea, suddenly afraid that the evil kwea would frighten the human girl away. Darrissea had no family in Bashevgo, no kin. She really didn't have any compelling reasons to go except to avenge her father. It made more sense that the human girl would abandon Fava, leave her in the woods. Fava struggled to calm herself, and they made camp in the building, slept a few hours.

When the sun began to rise, a silver mist raised from the ground. The group ate in silence, then went outside. The morning air smelled sweet after the dry manure and moldy hay of the stable. They walked out to the road, and Fava found herself beside Darrissea, watching the girl's "soul cloud," the steam coming from her mouth.

"You won't leave me on the road to Bashevgo, will you?" Fava said, almost ashamed to ask. "You won't run away?"

Darrissea glanced at her, and Fava saw a new toughness in the wiry human. "No, I won't leave you," she answered calmly. "I swore to god to free Bashevgo before I die. I always keep my promises." Darrissea laughed, high and sweet.

Fava nodded, touched Darrissea's hand.

The two groups said their good-byes and separated. Fava felt saddened to see Tchavs and the children preparing to go south, but she looked at them and realized, *They really can't come with us to Bashevgo. None of us should be going to Bashevgo.*

Mylon dragged the body of the Blade Kin guard into the barn to hide it, and Darrissea pointed at the dead man—an aging Neanderthal with silvering hair and a fierce face. The Pwi called themselves "the Smiling People," but this man's face was a mask of cruelty—a harsh beak of a nose, a wide scowling mouth, a forehead marred by creases of worry. Even in death, the face could not relax. "Ah," Darrissea said, "there is the inhumanity of the Blade Kin. That is the monstrosity I was searching for yesterday." Fava looked at the face of the warrior, happy to see him dead.

Fava held Wayan till the last possible moment, then gave the boy to Tchavs. She stood on the road while Tchavs took the children and crept into the forest.

Wayan waved over her shoulder. Fava waved back, wiped a tear from her eye. Darrissea rested a hand on Fava's back. Fava smiled.

"How can you smile like that?" Darrissea asked.

Between gritted teeth Fava said, "I want Wayan to see me smiling. I want him to remember me smiling, in case he never sees me again. It will leave him with good kwea."

Tull lay among the sweat and stench of the slave pens, and the great steel behemoth of the ship beat a path between the waves. A tap to his heel woke him from a deep sleep. For a moment he realized he'd been dreaming of Fava, dreaming of her beside him on the bed, and he wanted only to hold that image in his mind.

He opened his eyes. Chulata stood before him.

"I need a body servant for the evening," she said. "You will come service me." The sorceress stood alone in the shadows without body guards. In her black robes she seemed almost an apparition hovering over him.

"I don't want to," Tull answered.

"You are a Thrall, and I am Blade Kin," Chulata said. "You will obey."

Tull looked up to the turrets. He had no choice. She led him from the cage, up the dark corridors. He passed several cells filled with his townspeople, and at one point his mother cried out to him, "Tull! Tull!"

Tull stopped briefly, and in the cell he saw Chaa and Zhopilla, circled by townsmen from Smilodon Bay. It took a moment longer to spot his own mother. Chulata stood waiting. He saw the disapproval in her eyes, and he stepped in line immediately.

"Good," Chulata said, as they got out of earshot. "Those who value father or mother or brother or sister more than the Blade Kin, are not worthy of the Blade Kin."

Tull had hoped that Chulata would take him to the ship's deck, and she escorted him past guard rooms with their barred doors, but just below the top deck she halted. A Blade Kin with a sword guarded a door, and Chulata winked at the guard, then took Tull into a cabin that was several times larger than his own small home in Smilodon Bay, sparsely but opulently furnished: a large bed with silk sheets, a sunken pool to bathe in, electric lights somehow built into pale green gems that glittered from the ceiling. Smilodon Bay had no electricity, though Tull had seen such lights before, down at Fish Haven, and in Craal. There were several windows, and Tull looked out one: he could see only the ocean, a slate-gray sea under billowing clouds. Night was falling.

"Do you like my room?" Chulata asked, and Tull wondered at the furnishings.

"It is very nice," Tull said. "Do you come here often?"

"This is my room. I live here."

"It does not look like a soldier's room."

Chulata smiled at him, and Tull looked into her eyes. She did not seem to be wearing her mask, hiding her feelings. Instead, he saw that he amused her. "I am highly paid. All those who achieve the rank of sorcerer in the Brotherhood of Carnadine Sorcerers receive a salary equal to that of a Dragon Captain."

Tull nodded. A Dragon Captain stood just below the Cyclops in rank, but Tull could not guess how much money someone of that rank might make.

Chulata smiled at him. "You will undress me and give me my bath," she said, her voice cold, commanding. "You will do it gently, as if I were your lover."

Tull stepped forward, struggled with the thought. He pulled off her black robe, and beneath she wore a tunic of some glittering cloth. The cloth was all of one piece, like a drape, held together on her right shoulder by a platinum broach shaped like a swan. She wore a fine leather belt wrapped around her waist. He carefully untied it, then removed the broach. Her tunic slipped off, revealing her full breasts, the generous curve of her hips.

The triangle of hair between her legs was a color the Pwi called oak-leaf red, dull red with a touch of brown, a color that normally showed only in those of mixed human and Neanderthal ancestry. This surprised Tull, for it was a much darker shade than the hair of her head.

Tull wore only his black cotton breechcloth, and Chulata leaned forward, put her hands on his shoulders, and sniffed at his neck. "You smell like the slave pens. Take off your dirty cloth. I do not want it to foul my bath water."

The breechcloth dangled between his legs, and Tull pulled off the dragon clasp that kept it tight. He looked for someplace to set it, and Chulata took it from his hand, dropped it to the floor, pulled off his cloth.

Tull felt relieved that he had enough control to keep his organ from stiffening. She took his hand, led him into the bath. Ivory tiles were inlaid around the tub, and the hot water swirled up to his chest.

"The water is too hot," Tull said. "Are you sure it won't scald us?"

"It only feels hot because you have never taken a warm bath, have you?"

"No," Tull said. "At home, I always bathed in the river."

"Give yourself a moment. You will get used to it."

Chulata grabbed a bar of soap from a dish, handed it to Tull. "Lather your hair and wash yourself."

Tull obliged, washed his hair and chest, gave the bar of soap back to her.

"You are not all clean," Chulata said. She moved forward, her head bobbing just above the water, grabbed his penis, applied the soap, and gently began to wash. "How old are you?"

"Nineteen." Tull wanted to push her away, but dared not.

"Four years younger than I," Chulata said. "Men your age are usually such animals. One woman is never enough for them."

"As I said, you are not to my tastes."

"Pecans yesterday, strawberries today. What would it hurt?" She kept massaging firmly, and leaned into him so that her nipples brushed his chest. She whispered in his ear. "I think you want to be faithful to the memory of your dead wife. No one is that strong. . . ." Chulata kissed him under the ear, and Tull's penis began to swell.

He fought back the urge and said, "I want to go back to my cell."

Chulata laughed. "You must wash me first," she said, turning her back to him. "We aren't even close to being finished."

The perfumed soap smelled of lilacs, and Tull felt grateful that she turned away, for it allowed him time to regain his composure. He washed her hair and shoulders, her back and buttocks, her breasts and arms, her thighs and legs, all as a body servant should. When he finished, Chulata wrapped her arms around him and laid her head on his chest.

"How does a Spirit Walker practice his art?" she asked. Her hands wandered down below his waist again. "Do you use Guides?"

"I don't know," Tull said truthfully. "I'm only an apprentice. How does a Carnadine Sorcerer practice her art?" He wrapped his arms around her.

Chulata looked up at him and her eyes glittered. They were eyes like Tull's, pale green with flecks of honey, and her nose was dainty. "Come to bed with me, and I will tell you."

"Yes," Tull said, and he got out of the tub and dried Chulata with a cotton towel. As he did so, he wondered how far he should go with this woman. Should he give sex to her, perhaps buy himself enough freedom to escape? In many ways it seemed a small price to pay. Tull did not believe that in her heart Chulata really wanted him; he told himself that she was only testing him, trying to learn the strength of his devotion to Fava.

Still, he could not do it and retain his peace of

mind. To sell himself to a woman as contemptible as Chulata seemed . . . a form of defilement.

When he finished toweling her, she grabbed his organ, pulled him to the bed. He lay beside her.

She looked in his face and smiled. "What was your wife like?"

"Fava is nothing like you," Tull said. "She is taller, and her hair softer orange. She has never slept on a bed of silk, nor bathed in warm water. I don't think she has ever harmed anyone, either on purpose or by accident. She would never lie or sleep with someone for gain. I think . . . she loves me as purely as anyone could. I suspect she is stronger than you. As I said, she is nothing like you."

Chulata's face hardened, all the humor and desire in her eyes turning to white-hot flame. "What do you want?" she asked bitterly. "To live in a cage like a Thrall, or to free yourself and become Blade Kin? Those are your only choices!"

The ship lurched as it suddenly slowed, and in the distance Tull heard the rumble of cannon fire. He slapped a hand over Chulata's mouth. "Listen, we are coming to port!" he said. He looked up at the windows. Full darkness. Chulata struggled, tried to scream, kneed him in the groin, but the ship's cannons fired in the night, growling above him like a beast. The bed rocked from the vibrations. He held her a moment, realized she was right. If he stayed in her world, he would be forced to become either a Thrall or a Blade Kin, with no other options.

"I'm sorry," Tull said, slapping her in the temple. Her eyes rolled back and she collapsed. He gagged her with a pillowcase, tied her hand and foot to the bed with strips of silk. Then he threw the covers over her so that no casual observer would notice. He rolled from bed, and his wits seemed to have left him. Licking his dry lips, he grabbed his breechcloth from the floor, wrapped it about him. He ran through the room looking for something to disguise himself. Chulata's robes were all he could find. Though they had looked bulky on Chulata, they were far too tight for Tull, and the red trim of the Carnadine Sorcerers would only attract attention. Still, he reasoned that in the darkness he might escape notice.

He ripped the red ropy tassels from the edges of the robe, drew the hood tight over his head. He searched the drawers of the dressers, thinking Chulata must have kept a sword since she was Blade Kin—but he found none. He knew the guard would still be at the door.

Tull went to the wall, touched it, reached out with his mind, trying to learn where the guard would be. Yet he was nervous and felt nothing.

Tull leapt out the door, hoping to catch the guard by surprise. But the guard was gone, and Tull wondered at his fortune. Perhaps he had gone above deck to watch the fireworks. Tull glanced down the hallways. The corridor behind him was empty, and he hurried up the stairwell to the deck. The fresh air that smote him was warm, as warm as summer air, and Tull realized that they must have sailed far south. The deck was relatively quiet—a few Blade Kin at each cannon—and Tull hid in a crack between two great pipes that served some unknown function in running the iron ship.

He looked out over the water for sight of land, and it seemed to be all about him, a huge sprawling city a hundred times larger than Smilodon Bay. The lights from it looked like ten thousand stars scattered across a black sky, and even at this great distance the war cry of Blade Kin carried over the water along with shouts of dismay. Cannon fire rolled like thunder, and balls exploded near the ship.

South Bay, Tull realized. This could only be the city of South Bay, largest in the Rough. That meant that the Blade Kin had captured every port from Storm Hold in the north on down. The free cities were taken.

The thought of it nearly stopped his heart, and he stood for one long moment, wondering what he would do if he escaped, and then he ran with all his might and leapt over the side of the ship, far out into the dark water.

Chapter 8
A Humbling Darkness

The acolytes and guards and body servants cowered aside as Atherkula stepped through the cabin door, gasping in the warm night air, and drew back his crimson hood, exposing long cords of twisted hair the silvered color of dry leaves. From deep-set eyes he looked upon the corpse of Chulata, who lay sprawled upon her bed, now covered with a ceremonial death skin, the tanned hide of a black dire wolf. The room was dark and moist, and the ivory walls held the odor of perfumes. Beside the bed, a candle lay at both her head and her feet to guide her on her path into the Land of Shapes.

Behind Atherkula the servants and guards and acolytes stared up at the aging shaman in horror. "Omnipotent," one of them called out, trying to appease him, begging Atherkula to speak if only to break the silence. Atherkula ignored him. The acolytes were terrified of Atherkula, and he could feel them, all working together to shield their thoughts, to shield their terror from him. *They fear me,* he thought, *because I feel no love, because it is said I am heartless and almost human.* Yet Atherkula's heart pounded inside him, wild with grief, wild with a desire to escape this room. *Ah that I were a mere human.*

Atherkula pulled the dire wolf skin off the dead

woman. Chulata was naked and lay atop her silk sheets. He could see stains on a silk pillowcase where she had vomited into her gag, suffocating. Fortunately, the guards had already cleaned her somewhat. Atherkula lightly touched her chin and was surprised to find the body so cold. "I thought you said she had just died?" Atherkula asked a young man.

"Yes, Omnipotent!" the guard cried falling to one knee. "I mean—I just learned she was dead."

"Are you not her personal guard?" Atherkula asked.

"Yes, Lord!" the young man shouted, his voice loud. "But she released me for the night so that she could spend time with the slave Tull!"

Atherkula closed Chulata's staring eyes, let his hands linger on her face. "She was a powerful sorceress for one so young. Perhaps in all Bashevgo, not more than three can equal her. We shall greatly mourn the loss," he said, as if speaking to himself. He turned to the young guard. "Where is Tull?"

The guard seemed almost to wither into the floor, yet Atherkula could not feel his thoughts, could not read his aura. The man had learned to shield himself. *He has listened well to Chulata's lessons. Wither, little would-be sorcerer,* Atherkula thought, *hide your thoughts from me if you can.*

"We could not find him. He must have jumped ship last night when we took South Bay. We are checking the other carriers now to see if he was picked up during the battle."

"Tull," Atherkula said. "Now he has claimed another sorcerer."

Outside, a gust of wind buffeted the ship. Atherkula stopped, listened to the wind with more than his ears. Out on the ocean he heard a spirit walking on the water, the spirit of a man who had drowned there years before. Atherkula could tell that the man was aware of him, could feel Atherkula's presence and was disturbed. "Leave me with the body," Atherkula commanded, nodding toward Chulata. "Wait outside."

The acolytes and guards and servants ran into the night, scattering like rooks from a loft, leaving the door ajar. Atherkula shut the door and locked it, then returned to Chulata sprawled upon her luxurious bed.

For a long moment Atherkula stood gazing at Chulata, and tears began to moisten the old man's eyes. *Almost human, almost human they call me, for they believe I am cruel and dead inside.* Atherkula felt a cavernous emptiness, a breathtaking sting in his heart. He stroked the dead girl's arm, let his hand caress Chulata's flat, hard belly, finally to settle comfortably in her thin hand. He knelt and kissed her lips, as he had wanted to a thousand times in life, and found them to be more than cold—they were dry and cracked, like paper. The smell of vomit clung to them.

Twenty-three years, Atherkula thought. *For twenty-three years I've known you were my daughter. I loved you and could not tell you.* Among the Blade Kin, no man acknowledged his children, lest rivals use his offspring as targets.

Atherkula stood, arms stretched wide as if to encompass the girl, and the sleeves of his red robe draped over her corpse so that Atherkula looked like some great red crab staking claim to its prey; then he stretched out on the cot beside her, hugging her gently. He held his breath.

Where many another sorcerer would have needed to pour out his life's blood until he stood at the gates of death in order to unleash his spirit and walk free in the Land of Shapes, Atherkula could feel something of it at all times. Unlike other men, he was not much bound to concepts of near and far, past or future, life or death. In a small vial chained to his neck, he kept a mild poison, the Wine of Dreams, a liquid often used by his Neanderthal ancestors. Atherkula uncorked the crystal bottle, sipped. The dark green liquid left only a musty aftertaste, yet the room immediately began to spin.

Atherkula cleared his mind. The Land of Shapes opened to him, a world where the steel walls of the ship seemed but thin vapors. A world where six dolphins leaping through the ship's wake glowed like fiery coals in a blacksmith's forge, their spirits vibrant, while corals and starfish and anemones on the ocean floor below shone with a flickering light. The black ocean waters became invisible, colorless as the air, yet the ocean's surface showed as a dark plain. Upon this plain he felt Chulata. The shadow of her soul yawned dark; the pale fronds of the lightning of her soul danced in dismay. One of those fronds appeared as a rope that seemed woven of starlight, and it formed a noose. She cast this spirit weapon far and wide, hoping to snare something. Atherkula waited for his poison to take full effect, until his body seemed to drop away, then sent a thought to young Chulata. "Do you search for Tull?"

Chulata was not surprised by Atherkula's voice. Having been cut off from her body, she no longer felt surprise. "He eludes me. Perhaps he is dead. He has disappeared."

"That is impossible," Atherkula said. "His spirit exists beyond death. Even if he were dead, you would find him." He considered a moment. "Let's hunt together."

Atherkula imagined a hook like the ones that slaves at the docks in Bashevgo used for gaffing large halibut as they unloaded them from ships. Atherkula concentrated until one pale tendril of lightning emerged from the shadow of his soul, curved into a hook, and glowed like an ember. His spirit weapon. He swung it through the air, once, twice, listening to it whistle, then began entwining his own power with Chulata's.

"Imagine Tull for me, since you know him best," Atherkula whispered, and he found himself standing in a world of twilight looking over an alpine meadow. Yellow buttercups dotted a field that extended to the forest. Chulata envisioned Tull—and Atherkula saw in his mind's eye the young man with long dark-red hair and angry eyes. Chulata cast her silver rope, and Atherkula swung his fiery hook, and for a brief moment they hurtled through the twilight toward the apparition, and then they seemed to slow. Young Tull raised a fist, pushing them back, and Atherkula swung his gaff and caught Tull in the ribs.

Briefly Atherkula saw from Tull's eyes, felt the young man fleeing through a green countryside of gum trees and orange orchards. But at that moment the world seemed to twist, and Atherkula found himself hurled back into the valley of buttercups. Chulata landed beside him.

Atherkula looked at the valley. The grass was lush, the buttercups in bloom. They were viewing a scene from the past, an illusion dredged from Tull's memories. Atherkula whispered, "He felt us hunting him, and he cast us here."

"You see," Chulata said. "He is powerful. Should we attack again?"

Atherkula considered. "I've hunted other sorcerers, renegades who tried to elude the Brotherhood. None turned me as he did. Yet I know the country Tull is in. I know where to hunt. Gather our dead comrades. I will call you again, and we shall hunt him in force."

Atherkula withdrew from Chulata and breathed slowly, moved back into his body. For a long moment he lay, envisioning his arms, connecting himself to his arms. Imagining that he had fingers and toes, connecting himself to his toes. The walls around him solidified, becoming metal once again. The electric lights glared, casting emerald shadows. Atherkula shivered. While separated from his body, he had felt no emotions. But now that he was reconnected, he felt a gnawing fear. Tull had thrown him off so easily. And he felt a yawning emptiness at the loss of Chulata. Atherkula separated himself from his daughter's corpse for the last time.

He unbarred the cabin door, weak and dizzy from the Wine of Dreams, and struggled to the deck. The body servants, guards, and acolytes waited on their knees, the cowls of their robes pulled low. It was near dawn, and from the deck Atherkula could see the gleaming lights of Bashevgo's fleet out over the ocean. Over sixty thousand slaves taken in the Rough, a whole new country opened, and it all belonged to Tantos. It made Atherkula proud to be Blade Kin. It was a sacred trust. He looked at the young guard who had found Chulata's body. The guard struggled to keep his thoughts veiled.

"No more secrets," Atherkula said. "I won't let you hide. You did not know that she had died and grown cold, for you were not watching her as you should have!" Guilt was etched on the young guard's face. Though he had been blocking his thoughts, his concentration snapped, and he could shield himself no more. Atherkula felt the man's guilt.

"You were not even near the door! You were sleeping with someone else! A lover!" The other guards and acolytes separated from the young man. The accused stood in shock, not knowing how to defend himself. "You are not worthy to be Blade Kin! You are not worthy to be even a slave! You are not worthy to live!"

The young man fell to the deck, whining like some animal, begging forgiveness. A rage took Atherkula, and he felt his power, raw and unyielding. The Wine of Dreams still flowed in his blood. He was still half in the Land of Shapes, lightly clinging to his body. The ghost out on the water felt Atherkula's wrath and fled. The dolphins leapt away from the ship, and a wind began swirling in long lazy circles around Atherkula, picking up salt rime and debris. "I shall rend you body and spirit," Atherkula said. "When you die, you shall not dwell in peace in the House of Dust! In the Land of Shapes are many terrors."

Atherkula reached out with his mind till he felt the shape of the beast, a massive dark creature that appeared to Atherkula as if made only from shadows. He could not see the beast, wrapped in night, only feel the force of its malevolence. *Strengthen me, Adjonai,* the old sorcerer demanded, and he felt the beast take notice. A wave of despair struck Atherkula, for he could not withstand the beast's gaze, and Atherkula begged again, *Strengthen me.* The dark beast divined Atherkula's intent, and a powerful wind rose from the creature, blowing tatters of night to circle Atherkula. The old sorcerer stood in the maelstrom, and the beast's power rose like a flood around him, surging through him. Atherkula reached out with the shadow of his soul, grasped the lightning of his victim. Atherkula was a Neanderthal of the old blood. Like some Talent Warrior of old he felt the power unleash and shouted, "Stand!"

With the snapping of bones the guard jerked into the air, where he hanged upright as if skewered on an invisible pole. The others on deck shrieked and tried to cower away, but Atherkula shouted, "Stay, all of you!" using his power to wrench their heads forward and open their eyes, forcing them to watch. The guard screamed and tried to twist away. He could not protect himself. "Body and spirit, body and spirit," Atherkula hissed, and he channeled his rage. The guard twisted in the air and began to gag. His chest heaved and his eyes bulged as a horrible ripping sound rose from deep within. Blood trickled from his nose and sweat streamed down his face. Suddenly his whole body quivered as something inside tore free, and his eyes went vacant. "Body and spirit," Atherkula hissed, and he held his hand in front of the guard's chin in a beggar's gesture.

Though dead, the guard continued to twist, and his feet did a little dance as they kicked, running, running from death. The guard's throat swelled huge, and his own bloody heart wriggled from his mouth like some animal and fell, plopping to Atherkula's open palm.

Atherkula raised the warm, dripping heart, waved it over his head. He felt a rage unlike anything before at losing his daughter. He felt a power like never before stirring within. Killing the guard had not satisfied him. Chulata was dead, his only child. The peons on the ground backed off, ran to hide. He let them go, but Atherkula was not finished. The guard's body was dead, but only the body. The others could not see the spirit, still fluttering in Atherkula's grasp in the Land of Shapes, a globe of lightning, green with fear. "Body and spirit," Atherkula hissed, calling the beast. Darkness swirled around Atherkula, around the boy in his hand, and he heard a snarling as if jackals lurked in these tatters of darkness. The beast moved in to feed. Across the Land of Shapes a cry of horror went out, the piercing shriek of a spirit being ripped to pieces.

Atherkula listened to the lonesome cry of the spirit dying, amused. He watched the green fearful light flutter in his hand as the darkness circled, watched the light falter and fade.

For one brief moment Atherkula imagined Tull smirking somewhere out in the Rough, thinking himself secure. *Ah, but you will not hide from me.* Atherkula bundled his energy as if it were a great fist and sent the image of the bloody heart hurtling through space toward Tull, and with the image, he sent the words, "Tull, I will crush your heart also!"

For most of the day Fava and Darrissea hurried through the forest, gaining altitude. The snow here was deeper, and no rains had come to melt it, but new snow was falling, covering their tracks. Twice they came upon the tracks of Blade Kin, parties of half a dozen each, heading south. Both women feared walking the road after a few hours, so they set off through the forest, slogging through the deep redwoods. They set camp in early afternoon, in a thicket of chest-high swordtail ferns. A redwood had fallen, leaving its torn roots standing fifty feet in the air. The roots provided shelter.

Fava woke in the morning to the sound of Darrissea snoring in her ear. It was an odd sound, one she'd seldom heard so close before, having been raised in a household of Pwi. She thought it odd that humans snorted like pigs in their sleep. But then humans were strange. They got rich, while the Pwi remained poor.

They had clever little hands that could sew and build machines, while the Pwi had big paws that could dig holes and swing an ax. Their ancestors had lived among the stars, and even if they were a fallen people and could not battle the Red Drones that orbited above, they had achieved far more than the Neanderthals. But how much had they really achieved? They still snorted like pigs in their sleep.

Fava studied a movement uphill, snow dropping from a vine maple. The world consisted of dark stripes of redwood boles against the stark white of snow. Where the undergrowth was thick, snow lay everywhere, yet it was melting even as she watched. The kwea of the day reminded her of times frolicking in the snow with her father and brothers during the winter moose hunt.

Darrissea came and sat next to Fava, and Darrissea had decided to comb her hair.

Uphill a jay flew from its maple leaf squawking. "Don't move," Fava said. A bull elk whistled someplace nearby, the frantic call of the rut. Then Fava heard men —creeping through the thick brush. She lowered her head slowly, to keep from arousing attention, and watched six Blade Kin pass fifty yards to the west. They were all searching the ground, looking for footprints. Fava waited for them to pass. Half an hour after they were gone, Fava whispered, "While we are in the woods, don't brush your hair. If anyone comes near, they will spot your movements instantly. If you want to care for your hair, do so at night. Make sure to tie a green cloth around your hair when you are done." Darrissea nodded. "We have seen so many Blade Kin. Do you think those men were hunting for us?" Fava asked.

"No," Darrissea said after a moment. "I think they were just hunting refugees. At the loft I covered the Blade Kin I killed with hay. I suspect that the bodies won't be found for a few days."

Fava moved only her eyes as she watched. When she had to turn her head, she did so slowly. No sudden moves, nothing to attract attention. Fava had studied deer in the forest, the way they flicked their tails or ears to communicate. When she had hunted with her brothers, such movements gave them away. Darrissea mimicked Fava, moved slowly.

"Those Blade Kin may have come from the Gate of the Gods," Darrissea said. "I suspect that they have the gate well guarded. We will have to go over the wall."

"Hmmm . . . ," Fava said, without nodding.

"I have to say, I admire the way you are handling this," Darrissea offered. "By the time we get to Bashevgo, your ear will be healed. You will look the part of a Blade Kin, though that will not be enough to pass among them. Though you know more about the woods, I know something about the Blade Kin. I can teach you some of their ways.

"Blade Kin use the same tactics, over and over. I suspected they would pass through town again a couple days after the attack, just as I suspect that they will come through about two weeks from now, and then again near the end of summer.

"As for these woods, they will scour them for another day, always following a north-south pattern. The men we saw will come back this evening, following the same path, searching for footprints of travelers going east or west—any such tracks will not be from Blade Kin."

"How do you know all this?" Fava said.

Darrissea answered, "My father hunted the Blade Kin for years before they killed him. He used to tell me these things on his trips home. I thought they were just stories as a kid, but when I grew older, I recognized the value of what he told me. I've been thinking all day, trying to remember. I guess—perhaps he was preparing me. I think he knew this day would come." Darrissea wrinkled her brow.

"In their camps at night, a Blade Kin party of sixteen or more men will always post four guards, one at each corner, about a hundred yards out. Smaller parties, if they camp in the open, will post two guards. If they camp in a building, they will post only one watchman at the open door. They will always bar any extra doors from inside rather than post a second guard."

"That seems stupid," Fava said. "They are so predictable."

"No more or less predictable than we are," Darrissea said. "They come back to towns after an attack because they know refugees will congregate there. Even if a whole town is wiped out down to the last man, any escapee will return. First he will grab a few necessities, cart them off, and try to survive in the hills. Then he will come back a few weeks later to slaughter farm animals left behind, and he will think he is safe because the town seems empty. Eventually he will plant a garden back in town where the land has been cleared and tilled, where the soil is proven, someplace where a comfortable house has been left standing after the attack."

Fava raised her eyebrows. "Like our house?"

"Yes, yours was the trap house. The Blade Kin knew that any refugees from town would want it because it is out of the way, because it offers a good view of the bay.

"In the same way, the Blade Kin know that a scared Pwi will usually not run on the road. He will sneak through the brush on one side of the road, perhaps a hundred yards out, the way a deer or a bear skirts a road. So the Blade Kin march north and south, paying particular attention to tracks just off the roadside. Now that the Blade Kin have passed us heading south, we should leave soon, walk parallel to their trail and head north. They may not see our tracks."

Darrissea fell silent, and Fava wished that she would continue speaking. Fava felt safe with the girl. Yet there was tension in Darrissea's voice, the sound of words unsaid. "What more should I know of the Blade Kin?"

A crow called in the distance, and Darrissea said, "You may look like the Blade Kin, and you can learn to follow their tactics, but in order to pass for one, you must act like them. Among their own, they strut and hold their heads up. The Blade Kin flaunt their sexual prowess and sleep with each other or with Thralls, raping Thralls if they must. But because they will think you are one of them, they must ask for your service. To refuse to mate or to pretend you are not interested is a breach of manners. I know that the idea of mating with them is abominable, but you must never let them see the disgust in your eyes or hear it in your voice."

"Your father told you about this?" Fava said, shocked.

"He told me a lot of unpleasant things," Darrissea answered. "As I said, I guess maybe he was trying to prepare me. Anyway, I have to tell you: Some Blade Kin work extra hard to impress their superiors in bed. To appear unwilling to do the same, I think, would be a mistake."

"I . . . I could never sleep with one of them."

"Then you had better prepare your excuses now," Darrissea said, and she fell silent.

Fava sat, trying to envision how she would excuse herself. She imagined looking at an officer's codpiece. If the man was small in size or average, she would pretend that he could not satisfy her. If the man was well hung, she would tell him, "Go mate with a cow!"

Fava stifled the urge to laugh. The woods had fallen silent again except for the occasional sound of melting snow dropping from branches.

Darrissea looked around cautiously and said, "Let's go."

They headed north alongside the Blade Kin's trail. By midafternoon they found the Blade Kin's camp by the great wall that encircled Smilodon Bay. The basalt wall seemed much taller than forty feet: Shaped by the power of the ancient Starfarers, the black stone appeared to be in one piece, without a single handhold. They were able to cross it only by finding a place where poplars grew beside the wall in some soggy ground. Beavers had chewed through a tree, and it had fallen so that it leaned against the wall. They climbed to the top of the wall, then walked along it west, looking for a place to get down the drop on the other side. The path was covered with detritus, the scattered redwood needles of a thousand years, layer upon layer of moss.

The woods were still and quiet, the unnatural silence one sometimes hears before a storm. Fava kept glancing at the sky. Last night's clouds had broken, but far away, to the north and west, she saw dragons circling, dozens of great-horned dragons. It set her teeth on edge, and she walked softly, cautiously, watching the forest on both sides of the wall.

The forest floor was a mess—great massive roots pulled in odd directions, the twisted remains of dead redwoods, a vast carpet laid down in layers—vine maples towering to forty feet, ferns and laurel below that, so that there were an endless number of obstructions to her view. Fava imagined that at any moment a Blade Kin scouting party would step out from behind a redwood, take aim, and fire. There would be practically no way for Fava to defend herself, yet nowhere that she looked could she seem to find a way down. If only they had a rope.

No jays called anywhere, no squirrels. Not even a sparrow chirped among the endless ferns and vine maples at the forest floor.

After nearly an hour they came to a glade where the carcass of a giant sloth lay, surrounded by a camp of giant Mastodon Men. The huge apelike men howled at them and tossed stones and branches up at the wall. The males formed a circle around their women and children, and a giant silverback male rushed to the wall grunting and baring his fangs, shaking his head in consternation when Fava and Darrissea would not answer his challenge.

Darrissea seemed unconcerned, for the Mastodon Men had fed on the giant sloth.

The women passed the camp of the Mastodon Men, left them a mile behind and nearly reached the

Gate of the Gods. Still the woods remained quiet, an unnatural stillness, and then they crested a small hill, and suddenly both of them heard it at once—a sound that made air tremble like distant thunder, that echoed through the black rock under their feet. A mile away, through a small clearing in the trees, they could discern a moving wall of green, an army of Blade Kin marching through the Gate of the Gods toward the lands to the south.

Darrissea motioned for Fava to stop, to kneel upon the turf. They waited for four hours, and still the army continued to march past; four columns of imperial mastodons went by, each followed by an army of men, more men than Fava had ever dreamed.

At nightfall the army stopped to camp, and as the river of campfires appeared, Darrissea whispered,

> *"Ah how the humbling darkness*
> *bends the knees of men*
> *and stifles the cries of mundane beasts.*
> *The pigeon whirls to its roost,*
> *I to my bed,*
> *The humbling darkness covers us all*
> *So that living men sleep with dead."*

"I have not heard that poem before," Fava said. "Whose is it?"

"Mine," Darrissea admitted. "I just made it up. It is a habit. I am beginning to think in poems."

"It's a strange sickness," Fava said. "I believe ten thousand men passed us this afternoon—more warriors than we have in all the Rough. I wouldn't think they need so many."

"They don't," Darrissea answered. "The Blade Kin in town were the warriors of the Black Cyclops—troops under the command of Lord Tantos of Bashevgo. You can tell by the black eye sewn on their chests. Of the seven houses of lords, Tantos's has long been most powerful, and it is the first legion of the Black Cyclops that has battled the Hukm and the Okanjara to the west for the past eighty years. None of these armies come from Craal.

"Under the forces of the Black Cyclops, I think that Lord Tantos hopes to tame the Rough in a summer, take control of the whole of it, and set up a third empire to vie with Craal and Bashevgo."

"Do you think he will go to war with the others?" Fava asked.

Darrissea cocked her head, and high and clear they heard the sound of a man laughing hysterically, the voice of a Blade Kin carried by a trick of acoustics. "I don't know. The Lords of Bashevgo fear Tantos. He owns a third of all the Blade Kin, two full legions. The other lords would enjoy seeing him scatter his forces by taking the Rough. It will make them feel secure. As for Craal? The five lords there have more land than they know what to do with. They are so concerned with balancing their forces that none would want to risk war with Tantos. My father used to warn me to never be fooled. He said it is not the Pwi's valiant efforts, nor those of the Hukm or Okanjara that have kept the Rough free for so many centuries. The Slave Lords have long been so concerned with fighting among themselves that none dared turn his face our way—till now."

Tull watched the small mud house and surrounding orchard from a thicket of tall marsh grass, almost like the cattails of his home. Behind him a wide brown river flowed lazily. The night was warm, almost as warm as summers in Smilodon Bay, and Tull had eaten little for days. Weariness wore him, and he could feel his nerves shredding. He didn't know how much longer he could take the hunger, the running. His stomach was so tight, he knew he'd have to risk going into the open orchard to pick from a tree. He had not seen a Blade Kin, not seen another person, for two nights now, yet in the past week of hiding near house after empty house, he'd come to realize that when he didn't see the Blade Kin, he was in the most danger. In the week since he had jumped ship, he had not gotten ten miles from South Port.

He climbed the muddy riverbank, resisted the urge to crawl, and made his way to an orange tree. There he blacked out for a moment. He woke to the sound of cicadas buzzing in the trees, and overhead a flock of geese honked, flying north in the moonlight. Thor was nearly full, and its cinnamon light basked the orchard, the empty mud house, the fields of sweet potatoes beyond.

Tull gathered some fallen oranges, ate one. It was soft, rotting, and he looked to the window of the house, seeking better food. The windows were of stretched hide, ample to let in light, but not to see from.

Somewhere in the distance a dog barked. *Probably waiting for its owner to return,* Tull thought. The area had been cleaned out. No one left. Just a few animals. Tull went to the door, walked through the rooms. There was a single cot with blankets thrown on it in a heap, yet otherwise the house was well kept, with worn furniture and the musky smell of an old woman—soured flesh, hair, dust. In a pantry he found food—wheat, dates, raisins, wine. He sat on the pantry floor to eat, yet even the act of sitting was too much for him and he fell in the attempt, rested for several moments, dazed.

"Hello?" an ancient voice crooned in Pwi, an old woman. "Is someone here?"

Tull sat for a moment, embarrassed. He had not thought to find anyone in this house, had imagined that the Blade Kin would have culled the owner.

"You there in the pantry, who do you think you're hiding from?"

"I . . . no one, Mother," Tull answered using the ancient Pwi term of respect.

"You should be hiding, Spirit Walker," the woman said. "Atherkula seeks you." A chill ran down Tull's spine, and he sat for a moment, dazed, wondering if this were some kind of trick. The door to the pantry opened, and an old woman stood in the faint moonlight. She was obviously Pwi, with a round face and deep, deep eyes. She walked carefully, as the frail will do. "Come out of there, and I will make you some dinner." She left the pantry door, went into the kitchen, and started a fire in the oven.

As she struck a match, silver gleamed from the tops of her black moccasins. "You are a Spirit Walker," Tull said. "What is your name, Mother?"

She lit a small twig in the fire, and it caught, burned brighter and brighter, and within a moment a small pile of twigs blazed. Tull saw that her black moccasins did not bear the image of the crow, but of a dagger in front of a moon. The image shocked him, so that he stepped back, suddenly afraid, but for reasons he could not immediately recall.

The old woman laughed and turned her head toward him, and Tull suddenly recognized her. "Yes, you have seen me before, in your dreams," she said.

"I saw you at the worm tower with Phylomon!"

"Yes, I rescued some women from their evil dreams."

Tull was staring at her, puzzling at her moccasins. He closed his eyes, and he felt her there before him, like a burning light, ravaging and powerful. "You are becoming wise, trying to see me with your spirit eyes. These moccasins on my feet are not those of a Spirit Walker—" the old woman said, "but of a Spirit Warrior."

The old woman set a white ceramic kettle by the fire, then put a loaf of bread on the table with butter and honey, cheese and wine. "The butter and cheese will go bad soon," she apologized.

He drank from the wine—weak, fruity, a hint of vinegar. He sat and looked at the house of mud, nothing like the cabins in Smilodon Bay. He imagined that the mud would stay cooler than wood, an advantage here in the hot south.

Hunching, he closed his eyes, dizzy. Hot, hot south.

Yet there was a cool night breeze stirring through the room, a breeze filled with freezing fingers. They stroked him, caressed his body, and the fingers were everywhere, tiny pinpricks of ice. They felt soothing.

"I know you are tired," the old woman said, "but look at me." The old woman pointed her finger, and Tull's head was wrenched toward her. "I must speak to your spirit. Have you heard of the Okansharai, The Freer of All?"

"I have heard that in Craal and Bashevgo, they dream of such a person and tell children tales. They hope he will free the slaves."

"Not just the slaves, but their masters also," the old woman said. "That is why he is called 'The Freer of All.'"

"But the masters are free," Tull argued.

"Not free of ignorance, or fear, or cruelty," the old woman said. "You've been bound by chains of fear. You know that chains that are invisible can be hardest to break. How could the Slave Lords be free when bound by such awesome chains?"

Tull did not answer. He sat remembering his father, Jenks. When Tull was a child, Jenks would go into a rage and so terrify Tull, he could not move. Jenks would then beat Tull or chain him at will. Those had been awesome bonds indeed.

"Yes," the old woman said. "You understand. Because the Okansharai himself is truly free, only he can free mankind."

"Where is this Okansharai?" Tull asked.

The old woman knelt down, slipped off her moccasins. "Perhaps if you open your spirit eyes," she said, "you will see him." She tossed the moccasins toward Tull, and they seemed to leap onto his feet, where they glowed like fire.

Tull knelt over, tried to pry them from his feet, staring into the symbols of moons and daggers.

He came awake with a start, still sitting in the pantry, food scattered around. He realized he had been dreaming, and he was so tired, he could not rouse. Tull closed his eyes, listened to his own labored breathing. His chest felt constricted. He forced himself to breathe deeply, slowly.

The room was becoming hotter, as if a wind blew from out of the desert, yet icy fingers fluttered at Tull's back, lightly tickling, hinting that he would feel better outside.

He began munching on some raisins, picked up the wine, wandered to the doorway and looked out. Moonlight drowned out most of the stars. A Red Drone had risen. The wind was blowing south, a strong and sudden gale, all blowing south.

South, Tull thought. *South is good.* The icy fingers nudged his back, and he began walking south, heedless of whether there might be any Blade Kin. He closed his eyes and saw the world even from behind his lids.

Tull raised his hand. It had turned to a pale gelatin the color of ivory, and within the ivory clot of his soul, lightning danced, yet otherwise the world seemed much the same. Only colors had changed—the orange trees and grass shone faintly purple, the night sky was deeper black.

Resisting the urge to walk south, Tull stopped. The wind whipped at him viciously, hissing through the orchard. Oranges plopped to the ground and rolled past, and Tull hunched down, put his hands over his face.

The howling wind carried words, "Come. Come!" A voice, strange and compelling, drew him south as the storm whistled in his hair. Tull tried to stop, but the wind blew fiercer, colder, and he grudgingly took one step south, then another, and another, only hoping to escape the cold.

With hands shielding his face, Tull stopped, concentrated on opening his spirit eyes. Suddenly the world turned to stone, cracking and breaking, an infinite number of possibilities. He stood in the shelter of his wall, a small fortress among the red sandstone, as if he were in

Smilodon Bay, while whipping tentacles of light tore at the wall, pulling it down stone by stone.

"My future," Tull thought, "they are demolishing my future."

He raised himself above the wall to see who would do this: and found that he was still in South Bay. He could see the faint purple shadows of the orange trees, and Tull marveled, for he'd never seen the spirits of trees before. The oranges themselves were white and glowing, nebulous orbs. A tentacle whipped out of the distance and snatched a stone from his shelter. A cat hunting among the fields shone like a blazing star, and Tull looked: Everywhere, everywhere, on the edge of his vision, the spirits of men shone like a river of stars.

Dozens of tentacles stretched forward across the miles, grabbing for the stones of his sanctuary, pulling them down. And at last Tull grasped a stone, tried to hold.

Across the fields and river, as if blown by the wind, hundreds of flaming spirits rushed toward him. They were blinding white, without color, as if they had no clots to their souls, and Tull knew they were not living beings. They circled so that he stood in the center of a blinding tornado, and all about him the lights whipped around madly, and the cold wind blew.

Tull wanted to run or hide, but his spirit stayed put. It knows its own powers, its own limitations, Chaa had told him. Tull realized he was trapped. Something in him cried out for Fava, and a single thread of the lightning of his soul whipped away far to the north, and he touched Fava, felt her. She was dreaming, and Tull knew she was coming to rescue him in Bashevgo.

Tull looked to the south, where colored lights glimmered on the horizon like smoldering gems. Tull would not have noticed them at all, but one among them was powerful, a brilliant black flame. It discerned his gaze and came striding through the air: Atherkula.

The dead gathered around Tull, whipping faster and faster. Tull tried to shield himself from Atherkula's probing tendrils of darkness, but it was hard. He had no strength, no will. He concentrated upon a distant time, a distant place, so Atherkula, free from the dimensions of time or space, would follow the false trail.

Tull closed his eyes and tried to recall the meadow where he had played as a child, alive with golden buttercups and wild garlic. Black-and-yellow bumblebees clumsily touched from flower to flower, and badgers snuffled in their dens.

Yet the overwhelming power behind Atherkula's attack made it difficult. A tendril of icy darkness shot from Atherkula as the sorcerer probed, and Tull watched in fascination as the black tendril grasped one squiggling light within him, held the lightning of his soul, and pulled straight.

Then dozens of Atherkula's dark tendrils streamed toward him, probing. Tull tried to flee, and the lightning of his soul danced madly, evading the tendrils that sought him, held him. The battle was long and gruesome, the light of his soul flickering far faster than he could see, yet each time Atherkula snagged a frond of lightning, Tull found that he could not pull it back, could not retrieve it, for the dead would grasp it too, so that hundreds of tentacles would take him. Tull viewed the whole scene with dispassion, knowing that he was watching some form of spiritual rape, that whatever happened, he would not escape this whole.

The air thrummed around him as the dead gathered, held him, and at last Atherkula pulled all twenty-two tendrils of light out straight, and matched them in pairs. They cinched tight, and Tull felt his feet rise from the ground, knew he hovered in the air, and then the dead fluttered around and beneath him, carrying him.

Tull concentrated on the smell of wild garlic, on a badger den where he had once lost a coin playing in the dirt, and cried out in his heart, "Please."

The lights that held him twisted, slamming him down toward the red sandstone, punishing him for his feeble attempts at escape. Tull's head bounced off the stones; still Atherkula held him. Tull imagined touching a flower, and still Atherkula held him.

Atherkula whispered, "I hold you by the fires of your soul. Sprout more fires if you like. I will take them, too."

Tull tried to do as he said, tried to sprout more tentacles. He thought perhaps he could escape somewhere, fight off Atherkula, but the tiny fires did not respond to his attempts. Instead, he floated slowly on the wind over the countryside, toward a sea of glimmering living souls that burned like gems—an army of Blade Kin.

Fava and Darrissea slept on the wall till Thor went down, then walked toward the Blade Kin camp in the dark. A half mile along the wall, they found a fallen redwood, a grand old tree nearly twenty-five feet in diameter. They leapt down from wall to tree, then climbed to the ground, cut over to the road beyond the Blade Kin camps, and marched north through the night in a light rain.

Dawn found them high in the coastal mountains on an old road beaten to mud by the feet of Blade Kin. The morning sun on the muddy road turned it silver, as if it were a river running through the trees. They followed that road for eight days, warily, and four times avoided caravans—Thralls carrying supplies to the Blade Kin.

They reached the Mammoth Run plateau one morning and stood on a hill gazing down at the brown plains free of snow. They were starved, worn from living on the run, in the open. They climbed down the hills, disturbing a tyrant bird that had killed a moose. They almost stepped on it by accident, deep in a bed of brambles. The small dragon was only four feet tall at the shoulder, with dirty-brown feathers and a small horn. It glared at them from ruby eyes and gnashed its teeth, then beat its wings and thundered overhead, landed in a tree and watched. They had not eaten warm food for two days, and Fava cut a back strap from the moose.

They set camp in a small thicket at the edge of the forest. Darrissea lit a single candle to cook the meat in a tin cup. Fava slept. A shout woke her from a deep slumber.

Fava raised her head in the darkness to see a pair of huge furry ankles, nearly a foot across. Her heart withered, realizing that it must be a Mastodon Man, and she was about to die. Fear smote her, so that Fava's arms and legs went limp, and she moaned.

"Don't shout!" Darrissea whispered, and Fava rolled weakly to her back, looked up at the giant hairy form in the darkness. The beast smelled of open fields and meadows, dry grass, a fragrance incongruent with the redwood forest. It stood a good nine feet in height, would have measured five feet across the shoulders, and the beast's white hair glowed a soft tangerine in the light of rising Thor. Moving silently, it bent over Darrissea and touched her breasts, then bent close in the moonlight, and the warm breath from its nostrils fanned Fava as it snuffled, tasting her scent.

Its breath smelled of hay and leaves, and Fava looked up into intelligent eyes. *A Hukm*, she realized. She trembled in relief. Over its right shoulder it wore a leather belt filled with pouches. The Hukm raised its head and sounded a long, plaintive howl—then took Fava's face in one hand and held her to the ground. Fava's heart began pounding again, for the creature could easily snap her neck. She held still.

Suddenly Fava became aware of movement all around her, and in the shadows she could see hundreds of the creatures, their massive white bodies whispering through the forest. Dozens of Hukm surrounded them in the darkness while others passed north, and Fava did not dare move. They circled, raising their huge war clubs, and some growled softly. In the distance Fava heard mammoths trumpeting.

The minutes stretched endlessly, and three more

times the Hukm stopped to howl in unison, until a huge mammoth thundered near, stopping overhead so that its shadow blotted out all light. Something heavy leapt from the mammoth, landed nearby.

"Move, and you both die," a soft, cracking voice said.

Both Fava and Darrissea cried out together: "Phylomon!"

Chapter 9
The Heron Woman

Tull woke in Chulata's bedroom to the sound of voices. The ship's engines growled steadily, and Tull could tell by the feel that they were far from the docks. A plate of food lay nearby, a breakfast of curry sausages and lightly baked squash with raisins and cinnamon. Tull ate greedily, though the fare was richer than what he was used to. He suspected Chulata would demand that he strip, ask him to perform the acts he'd refused. Perhaps her guards would whip him.

After Tull waited in the room for hours, Mahkawn entered. "I hope you are rested." The aging Blade Kin looked haggard. His braided hair had not been kept up, and stray threads escaped it. His black robes looked as if he'd slept in them.

"Yes, I am rested," Tull said.

"We stopped this ship to search for you," Mahkawn said. "Our ship is full of slaves, yet for seven days my men sought you when we should have been headed back to Bashevgo. Do you know why we spent so much effort?"

"No," Tull said, feeling unaccountably guilty, as if he had disappointed a friend.

"Why did you tie up Chulata," Mahkawn asked, "instead of killing her outright?"

Tull hesitated. "I wouldn't kill a slave unless it outlived its use. To do so would be a waste. Chulata had not outlived her use."

Mahkawn's single eye glittered like a hawk's. "Do you love her?"

The idea seemed ludicrous. Tull laughed. "No."

"Then you will not be saddened to learn that she died. She vomited into her bonds and strangled."

"I am saddened," Tull said truthfully. "I had not meant to waste her. I took care to keep her alive."

Mahkawn weighed Tull's words. "Well said. You speak like a Blade Kin, and I'd like your ear, but now that cannot happen. Atherkula seeks your death, and I suspect Lord Tantos will give you the full penalty. You are not a Pwi any longer. Even though you killed Chulata by accident, you killed her while making an attempt at escape. So you will be sentenced to death."

Tull was so stunned, he could not say anything.

"Did you ever consider what you want out of life?" Mahkawn asked.

"What is the point?" Tull said. "You say you plan to kill me."

"What do you want?"

Tull thought a long time before answering. Mahkawn seemed sincere, as if all the games were over. If Mahkawn planned to kill him, Tull had nothing to gain by lying.

"I have always wanted a large house," Tull said, "where I could live in peace with my wife and raise my children. I have wanted to be able to work for myself and keep the rewards of my labor. I have wanted to sleep soundly at nights in my woman's arms, without fear of the Slave Lords. I have wanted your nation to crumble, and for your masters to die, and for all your works to fall into the sea. I have wanted the Eridani to leave orbit, so that someday we could go to live among the stars."

Mahkawn thought a long time. "You often talk like a Blade Kin, but you still dream like a Pwi. I have most of the things you want. I have a big house in Bashevgo, though I do not have a wife. As a Blade Kin, I sleep with any woman I want, and I have spawned children. I suppose you could call them family. As a Blade Kin I sleep soundly, knowing I have nothing to fear so long as I obey my lord. And I've learned to live knowing that my masters will not all die by fire and that our cities will not crumble.

"There is no place in the world for men like you, Tull. I suspect there is no place for you on this world or any other. You are young, and I forgive your lack of wisdom and your idealism. I cannot let you go into the wilderness, and Tantos will not let you live as a slave. Still, I can arrange things so that you have a chance to become Blade Kin.

"So I ask you because I feel that you are a friend: Could you compromise? This *wife*"—Mahkawn said in disgust—"could you forfeit your dream of living with her? As a Blade Kin, that will never happen. A man who loves a woman can be controlled through that woman— and others would take advantage of your weakness. Still, you could sleep with women, father a thousand children if you wish, and if your woman is captured, you could sleep with her. Though we do not take wives, many Blade Kin have favorites. The sex is better with some than with others. It is the way of things."

"Do you have a favorite?" Tull asked, hoping Mahkawn would admit to a little compassion.

"Yes, but I would not marry the creature. She is a Thrall, in bondage to her emotions, and to marry a Thrall is to lower yourself to its level. You and I"— Mahkawn struck his chest—"are Blade Kin. We are above them; we are Blade Kin. Do you see? You could have affection for a dog, even marry a dog—but it would still walk on four legs."

"I don't understand," Tull said, trying to draw Mahkawn out. "You say we are different, but we look like them."

Mahkawn sighed. "Haven't you felt the difference

inside you? We are Blade Kin. We are not bound by kwea as they are. Have you not seen it? You have no fears as they do, and you do not love as they do. All the Pwi, they are already enslaved by love and fear, and since they were born slaves, we do no wrong when we put chains on them."

Tull sat a moment, said the words he knew Mahkawn wanted to hear. "I used to fear when I was a child, but broke free of it. When I was young, I did not know how to love, and I thought I would never be able to love a woman. I believed I was evil for feeling that way."

"No!" Mahkawn said, and excitement gleamed in his eye. "It's not a matter of good or evil. You were born Blade Kin. That is why you can control your fear. How many Pwi could do this? And because you are Blade Kin, you cannot love. You are one of the wolf people, and they are the rabbit people. You were meant to eat them, to digest them. Do you see?"

Tull nodded, felt uncomfortable. For years he'd considered his dispassion a handicap, as if he were born without legs or eyes, and he had expended great effort learning how to love. Yet Mahkawn valued Tull's weakness, his character defect, and this frightened Tull, for he saw that with very little effort he could have been a man like Mahkawn. If he had been born in Bashevgo, he would have become Blade Kin, and he would have excelled. "I see," Tull said.

Mahkawn clapped him on the shoulder. "Good. I must store you in a cell until the ship reaches Bashevgo, and there you will be sentenced to death. But since you are good warrior stock, I can have you put in the arena. There you can earn the right to become Blade Kin, as I did."

"How do I earn that right?" Tull asked.

Mahkawn smiled, a warm, genuine smile. "With a sword."

"Don't move," Phylomon said softly, and Darrissea dared not move beneath the weight of the Hukm.

The beast kept its paw on her face and growled softly. Phylomon raised one hand into the air and lowered it slowly, waggling his fingers and making a soft sighing sound as he did. The Hukm grunted, sniffed at Darrissea and Fava, and touched their breasts again. Then the creature displayed its own flabby breast, a great hairy sack, and backed away. She opened a pouch from her bandolier, pulled out a pinch of sweet-smelling leaves, and touched the leaves to Darrissea's lips.

"Eat them," Phylomon said. "She is a scout for the Hukm. She smells your fear and offers food. This is her promise that you do not need to fear her. Relax, but do not move. Especially do not smile—for the Hukm show their teeth only before they attack."

Darrissea took the leaves in her mouth, tried to choke them down. All around camp, hundreds of Hukm were loping north, moving like ghosts among the redwoods, swinging their long arms as they ran. A second Hukm came close, a crippled old dwarf of a male, not much taller than a huge man, and it sat down in the snow. The small male reached into a backpack and brought out a wooden flute, longer than Darrissea's leg. The flute was wrapped in cloth and decorated with blue dragon feathers. He sat under a redwood on a small pile of icy snow and played long low notes on the flute, a song of wind and thunder and clear rivers rolling slowly through the flatlands. As near as Darrissea could figure, the beasts were trying to entertain her.

She kept looking toward Phylomon for direction, but the blue man only gazed at the flutist, signaling with his posture that they should not try to speak. It was said that the Hukm did not trust humans, and Darrissea could see that Phylomon kept his silence in observance of some form of protocol.

After an hour a great white Hukm woman came on the back of a mammoth, and hundreds of mammoths followed. As she dismounted, her massive necklace of carved beads chattered like teeth in the clear night air. She hefted an immense club banded with iron rings and walked through camp, sniffing, fondled Fava's breast. The creature silently waggled her fingers, raising her hands and then letting them fall again.

"This is Ironwood Woman," Phylomon said, "leader of the Hukm." Phylomon translated, "She says she smells the scent of Tull upon Fava. She met Tull last summer when he traveled to Craal. She is honored to meet his new owner."

Ironwood Woman touched Fava's belly, then moved on to Darrissea, thumbed her shirt looking for breasts. She opened her mouth in joy when she discovered them. Many Hukm stopped to watch their leader. The smell of fur from the massed Hukm was somehow both subtle and overpowering, a scent Darrissea did not notice at first, but which permeated the woods like wild garlic.

The queen of the Hukm approached Phylomon and began waggling her fingers. The Starfarer spoke in kind, and for a long time Darrissea waited, sweating in the cold.

"The Blade Kin have been hunting the Hukm," Phylomon translated, "and have driven them from the south. Ironwood Woman's people are staying in the trees because of an army on Mammoth Run Plateau. So far the army has been content to stay there. The Blade Kin dare not come into the woods.

"The Hukm want the Pwi to join them in an attack upon Bashevgo. They've gathered nearly one hundred thousand for their attack—males, females, juveniles. Only their very old and very young will stay behind to stop the Blade Kin from pursuing the Hukm. They want humans and Pwi to help defeat Bashevgo's laser cannons. But they must hurry and get there soon, before the ice clears from the Straits of Zerai. She wants to know if you two women can lead your people in her behalf."

Darrissea answered shyly, "Tell Ironwood Woman

that the Blade Kin have attacked us, too. They've captured all the towns around Smilodon Bay, and we saw huge armies heading south along the coast."

The blue man said brusquely, "What of Chaa and Tull? Where are they?"

"Captured," Darrissea answered. "Chaa had hardly begun his Spirit Walk when the Blade Kin took the city."

"This is a great blow," Phylomon said. "The armies that attacked the Hukm came from the west. We hoped to draw new battle lines, take Bashevgo and cut off the Blade Kin's supply lines, force them back west of the White Mountains."

Phylomon spoke with Ironwood Woman for a moment, telling her of the capture of Smilodon Bay, and the great woman stopped and howled, a long ululating cry that was almost deafening. Darrissea did not have to speak Hukm to hear her distress. She made some violent gestures with her hands, then turned and grabbed her mammoth's ear, leapt upon its shoulders, and went galloping north. All the Hukm that had stopped to watch followed behind her.

Phylomon sighed deeply. "We may talk freely now. Have you eaten lately?"

"Not much for the past few days," Fava said.

Phylomon began setting a fire. "What happened?" Darrissea asked. "What did Ironwood Woman say?"

"She is continuing north, to attack Bashevgo."

Darrissea asked, "Just like that? She isn't even going to consult her people? How could the Hukm hope to defeat Bashevgo?"

"Hope is where you find it," Phylomon said. "Long ago, the ancients of Earth mastered the art of war. They learned that in order to destroy an enemy, you must first demoralize him—destroy his faith in himself. Often a small band of men has thrown off the shackles of a great nation, but only when they believe they can or must. Now, for the first time in their lives, the Hukm see that they must destroy Bashevgo.

"Still, I'm not sure Ironwood Woman believes she can win," Phylomon said. "For years the Hukm have battled Craal and lost. With armies marching from the south and east, Ironwood Woman's people are surrounded. The Hukm are creatures of the open plains. They fear enclosures, and as anyone who has ever fought Hukm knows, you never want to surround them. The Hukm will race to Bashevgo now before the ice thaws, to win their last battle or die in the attempt."

Fava asked, "Do you think they have a chance?"

"A chance?" Phylomon crouched in the snow, cracking twigs for kindling and setting them under the larger branches. "In the past Tantos has guarded Bashevgo with seven divisions. By sending men south, he must have siphoned off some of those—two divisions, possibly three. Even if Tantos has only four divisions still guarding Bashevgo, the Hukm will be outnumbered by four to one."

"But the Blade Kin have guns—Hukm fight only with clubs," Fava warned. "They can't win."

"Yet the Hukm fight in total darkness, when guns will not much avail the Blade Kin. And there is another possibility—Bashevgo's slaves could revolt, or they could flee into the wilderness where we could turn them into an army, given time."

Fava looked at the Starfarer, caught in his fantasy. "Will you lead their army?"

"That is for Ironwood Woman. They would not let a male lead them, much less a human. I may advise her, even fight beside her." He got the wood in place, opened his pack, and produced some long, thick matches. He struck one, set it under the kindling, and the fire began to blaze immediately. "So what are you two planning to do?"

"We're going to Bashevgo," Fava said, "to free Tull and my family." Fava's voice sounded small and frightened to Darrissea, and she looked around. They were surrounded by redwoods, and still on both sides of the camp, the giant Hukm passed like mist in the night, and they were sitting here speaking to Phylomon the Starfarer, more of a legend than a mere man, and Darrissea understood why Fava sounded so small and frightened. Two women, planning to sneak into Bashevgo, were insignificant.

Phylomon climbed his mammoth, pulled off a pack, and brought it to camp. He put a skillet on the fire, opened a sack of ground corn, and began making bread. He did not speak during all this. Instead, he furrowed his brow, and moonlight gleamed from his hairless head.

"So everyone wants to go to Bashevgo, but for different reasons. Ironwood Woman wants to make war. You want to rescue Tull. I find my loyalties divided. I don't know which of you to help."

"Perhaps you can help us both," Fava said.

"I am not sure I want to help you." Phylomon looked into Fava's eyes, and the Starfarer said softly, "Has your father told you what your husband is?"

Fava shook her head. "My father told me that Tull would become powerful someday, if he could free himself."

"I believe—your father believes—that Tull may become more than a Spirit Walker. He may be a talent warrior."

Darrissea cut in, "Like Thunatra the dream-giver, or Kwitcha the healer?"

"No. Like Terrazin the Dragontamer."

"Oh," Fava said slowly. "I have not heard much of him."

"What do you know of the Talent Wars?" Phylomon asked.

"I know you led the Pwi to battle against Bashevgo, and that with the help of Thunatra and Kwitcha and the faders, you threw down the Slave Lords. For a hundred years after, there was peace."

Phylomon smiled in the firelight, kindly, as if speaking to a child. "Three hundred and sixty years ago," Phylomon said, "I led a ragtag band of warriors to Bashevgo. In those days there were over four hundred

Starfarers in Bashevgo, and they wore symbiotes like mine that helped keep them young and strong and invincible, and their human children wielded weapons brought from the stars to enslave your ancestors.

"My friends and I were outcasts, for we objected to the practice of slavery, but we did not have the weapons we needed to fight.

"So we looked among your people, took their most talented psychics, and led them into battle. You know of Thunatra who could do battle in dreams, and Kwitcha the great healer, and you know of my brother who wore a fader, a device that let him walk almost invisibly into Bashevgo. But the warriors of Bashevgo also had faders, and they had Crimson Knights, and they outnumbered us."

"But we had Terrazin, and all the terrors of Bashevgo could not stop him. He was young, fifteen, a boy who wanted only to rescue a sister who had been captured by the Slave Lords. But he was a powerful warrior. Terrazin called dragons from the skies and ordered them to hunt the Slave Lords. He was a powerful Spirit Walker, and he confounded his enemies in every battle. He alone hunted the Starfarers to extinction, and the rest of us were but minor players in the great game. At the height of his power, Terrazin learned to do more than Spirit Walk the futures of other men. He used his power to manipulate people, so that the last of the Slave Lords slew themselves. Of all the Starfarers, only I and my brother survived."

"Why have we never heard of him?" Darrissea asked.

"Because he grew corrupt," Phylomon said. "In his long hunt for the Slave Lords, Terrazin often connected with them. He did more than learn their thoughts; he took on their nature. He became . . . deformed—as if he were the sum of all Slave Lords. Once he won the war, there was no hundred years of peace. That is a myth. Instead, Terrazin seized the world.

"Because I was his friend, Terrazin did not kill me.

Yet he suspected me, as he suspected all people. He grew paranoid, deadly. His allies were forced to turn on him. He killed my wife, my children—I couldn't stop him. Because I was his friend, I was able to kill Terrazin. No one ever spoke his name again. Thunatra and Kwitcha spent the rest of their lives trying to heal the hurt that Tull did."

"You mean Terrazin," Fava said.

"Uh, yes, I mean Terrazin," Phylomon corrected.

"You are afraid of Tull, aren't you?" Fava asked. "You are afraid he will become like the Dragontamer?"

"Yes, I'm afraid," Phylomon admitted. "Chaa has already begun to open Tull's spirit eyes. The sorcerers of the Blade Kin are sure to see him for what he is. The sorcerers of the Blade Kin do not walk the paths of the future—instead, they struggle to control men in the same way that Terrazin did. He was their first great teacher. He is still their ally in the Land of Shapes." Phylomon got a jug from his pack, poured a mug of beer, and passed it to Fava.

Darrissea said, "What do you mean, he is still their ally?"

"A hundred years ago," Phylomon said, "at the south gate of the city of Denai, the gate they call Oppression Gate, the sorcerers built a statue in honor of the god Adjonai, whom the sorcerers call 'The Beast.' The statue wears the face of Terrazin the Dragontamer, though I alone am the only man who would recognize it."

Fava covered her face with her hands. "The same beast that came to my father's house?" she asked. "The one that my father said 'approved' of Tull?"

"Yes," Phylomon answered. "The beast recognizes its twin here in this world."

Fava got up, paced beside the fire.

"Why did you tell her that?" Darrissea hissed. "She loves Tull. You'll scare her to death."

Phylomon looked into Darrissea's eyes. "She needs to know. She may love Tull, but other women loved Terrazin just as blindly. When I killed Terrazin, I was able to do it only because he loved and trusted me. Perhaps, if it becomes necessary, only Tull's love and trust for Fava will allow her to kill him."

Fava said loudly, her voice ragged, "You are wrong about Tull. He is nothing like this Terrazin. He . . . my father would not train him to be a Spirit Walker if he thought Tull would do anything bad. Who are you to judge him? You condemn Terrazin, yet was he any more ruthless than you? Everyone in town has seen how you behead slavers. You are a fanatic!"

Fava ran from the fire, stood out in the shadows among the trees, and cried. Darrissea looked between the two, not sure what to say. "Give her a moment," Phylomon said. "She has too much to worry about. I should not have added to her worries. I was thoughtless. Will you tell her I'm sorry?"

"She's terrified of what you might do," Darrissea said. "Your apologies won't alleviate her fears, and I doubt that you can gain her trust."

Phylomon looked at her sharply, narrowed his eyes, and Darrissea's heart leapt. For the first time Phylomon seemed to notice her. "You're very perceptive. I have seen you in Smilodon Bay, but I don't know your name."

"Darrissea. Darrissea Frolic."

"Was your father Dedemon Frolic?"

"Yes."

Phylomon nodded solemnly. "A good man. A good warrior. With ten thousand like him, I could free this land. You look nothing like him."

"Except in the eyes, I've been told," Darrissea said.

He looked into her eyes a long time and let his gaze drift down over the rest of her body. Darrissea lowered her head, embarrassed.

"You should not be so shy," Phylomon said. "Styles of beauty change over the years. By today's standards, you are too tall, too thin and long of limb. But among your ancestors, the ancient Starfarers, you would have been considered beautiful." He lowered his eyes and began cooking the corn cakes as if her beauty did not matter.

Darrissea's heart pounded, and she felt her face getting warm. She wanted him to say more. "Can we ride with you and the Hukm to Bashevgo?"

Phylomon nodded. "It would be a pleasure."

The sky was a soft cerulean blue out to the horizon, and the sun glinted on the waters. Mahkawn stood on the deck of the ship, squinted, looking off into the distance.

"See," Atherkula said, pointing out to sea. "There it is."

Mahkawn studied the white spray, finally saw it: a deep-red dorsal fin, rising above the water. A sea serpent, a large one. "Yes, there he is. What of it?"

"That serpent has been following us now for six days," Atherkula said ominously, "ever since we captured Tull."

"There are many serpents in these waters," Mahkawn said. "I've seen as many as twelve at a time."

"But none that follow ships," Atherkula said. "This serpent is following us. More than once it has come close, as if to attack the ship."

"I know," Mahkawn said. "I read the reports. The cannon fire drove it away."

"Still, it follows us. It follows Tull, to protect him. It is his animal guide, and the spirits of the two are connected. If we do not do something, it will attack."

"You can't be sure of that," Mahkawn said.

Atherkula nodded, his gray braids barely moving as he kept his eyes out to sea. "I'm sure. We should kill him. Now, before it is too late."

"You have been—overly eager for his blood," Mahkawn said.

"You hunted him too, after he killed your men in Denai. You were so eager to prove yourself to Tantos, you practically did not sleep."

"I thought he was only an escaped slave," Mahkawn answered. "Not a Pwi."

"Yet you hungered for his blood, and he has killed a Crimson Knight since. He has done you harm. And he has done me harm. He killed two of my sorcerers—one tenth of my forces."

"Calm yourself," Mahkawn said. "It is over. Even your ally in the Land of Shapes ordered you to let him live."

"It is not over," Atherkula warned. "I don't understand you anymore. You've killed hundreds of men for lesser crimes than Tull's."

Mahkawn turned, held Atherkula's piercing blue eyes. "You are becoming senile in your old age," Mahkawn said. "It shows in the way you rage. A Blade Kin should have more control. You embarrass yourself."

Atherkula spat at Mahkawn's feet. "I will kill him. You can't stop me!" He began to turn away, and suddenly there was a great splash, and water surged over the deck. A shadow fell on them, and Mahkawn turned. The serpent reared out of the water not forty feet behind the ship, its jaws gaping wide in the air, its huge yellow eyes glaring. The rear gunner fired his cannon, scoring a hit on the serpent's dorsal, and it submerged.

Mahkawn looked at Atherkula, and the sorcerer's face was pale. Mahkawn grabbed Atherkula's black robes, pulled him to the railing overlooking the water. The serpent was there, under the water, a great black mass trailing the ship.

"Think about it," Mahkawn shouted, holding Atherkula perilously close to the edge. "Think about killing Tull, and that serpent will attack. Kill Tull, and that serpent will take you. Do you believe you could stop it?" Atherkula struggled to free himself and lunged away from the water, stumbled. The old sorcerer sat on the deck, gasping from his exertions. "You see," Mahkawn added, "you cannot even consider killing Tull while we are still at sea. It is over."

"It is not over," Atherkula warned. "In Bashevgo

lives a Thrall woman named Pirazha, and three sons. The boys' father will be fortunate if he never has to feel the pain of losing a son." The old sorcerer got up from the deck, wiped the sea rime from his robes, and walked down below decks, his back bent as if he were a broken man. Mahkawn could only stand, staring blankly. *So Tull has killed one of Atherkula's sons,* Mahkawn thought, *and now Atherkula thinks to hold mine hostage.*

During the nights the Hukm traveled on mammoth back, and by day they camped in the shadowed woods, often standing or leaning against trees in a trancelike stupor. They had passed north of the redwood forests and had entered a forest of firs so old, they were only slightly less in stature than redwoods. Darrissea quickly learned to sleep while riding the mammoths, so that during the short days she could remain alert, walking the perimeter of the woods on guard duty with Phylomon.

Darrissea liked the soft humus of the deep forest under her feet; she liked to watch the white tail feathers of the flickers as they flapped in the shadows from ground to black limb, the startled leap of a deer. When composing her love poems, Darrissea had always used images from the woods: "Mine is the peeping cry of the sleek-bodied otter / whistling as it rises from the sensual water." Darrissea felt that her body was as long and sleek as an otter's, and often in the fall when the mountain water still held warmth but the days were cooling, she would strip bare and swim the Smilodon River, arcing her back, letting waves play over her skin. Oh, Darrissea knew why otters thrilled through life.

Then again, Darrissea could imagine herself a blue heron, poised on one leg in an emerald marsh, ready to gobble a bullfrog's tadpole, alert for predators, her wings spread like a hood as she hunted in her own shadow. The heron. No other forest animal sought as desperately to attune itself to its environment: sight, sound, touch, smell. A predator sandwiched in the food chain, always preying and being preyed upon. That's how Darrissea felt when gliding through the woods, searching for images for her poems, facing starvation if she did not come up with an exquisite line, a perfect word to fit the rhythm and balance of her poem.

Balance. A hard thing for a young poet to achieve, especially for one who was in love with a legend. Once, in the cold afternoon, Darrissea watched Phylomon napping on the ground, shivering from lack of warmth. Darrissea had been spending so much time with the Pwi that she acted like one. Darrissea went to lie beside him to keep him warm. She curled around his back and wrapped her arm around his shoulders, found his pale-blue skin cold to the touch. He held her hand for a moment in his sleep, and then his breathing caught as he awoke. Darrissea wanted nothing more than for him to continue holding her hand, but he turned, his pale blue eyes glittering in the shadows of the firs.

Phylomon whispered, "What's happening?" He did not pull away, and Darrissea wondered if it was all right, if he would give her permission to touch him. Darrissea caressed his cheek and she trembled and felt warm inside. She had never performed such a courageous act with a man. "Your skin is beautiful," she said, "so smooth, like the skin of a salamander."

Phylomon took her hand, pulled it away. "I'm too old for you, by about a thousand years." His voice was not as cold as his words, and his touch seemed to linger, giving Darrissea courage.

"You've loved other women, haven't you?" Darrissea asked. "Couldn't you learn to love one more?"

"It's not that easy," Phylomon said. "I took seritactates when I was young. I remember everything about my first wife—the way she held her head to the left when she was listening carefully to music, the time she cried after I gave her a haircut, the look of pain on her face when our second daughter died in childbirth.

When we were married for four years and twelve days, she sliced open her foot while trying to spear a salmon up on Fish Haven River, and I can still feel the texture of her fevered skin the day after. When we were married nine years and ninety-six days, she went into the woodshed and accidentally met a skunk that was hunting slugs. For months afterward, each time she washed her hair, the faint odor of skunk would keep me awake. I watched her hair turn silver, her skin loosen and sag, her bones soften and leave her hunched. I tried marrying once after that, and though the images are much more blurred, I still remember the pain, watching every moment of our lives together and knowing how it would all end. To lead you on would be unfair. I need someone to share my life with, someone I can love as an equal. And though you are lovely, you are only a temporary."

"You're afraid to feel," Darrissea said. "You're afraid of passion."

"Not the passion, only the pain that follows."

Darrissea took his face in her hands, kissed him firmly on the mouth, but he did not respond. The warmth in her chest, the hope, left her.

"You need to find someone else to love," Phylomon said.

She shook her head. "All these years of living, and you're afraid of life." She needed him to think about it, to wonder if he could give a part of himself to her. She found that she was crying, and Phylomon reached up with a finger, wiped the tear from her eye. Darrissea said, "I feel stupid for wanting you, for loving you."

"You should never feel stupid for loving," Phylomon said. "But perhaps you should consider what love is. If you think you love me, then perhaps you should think again. You lost your father when you were young, and he was a man very much like me, a warrior who hunted slavers. Someone that, as a child, you must have seen as strong. Perhaps you are only in love with my strength." He moved his hand away, turned from her, but he let her cuddle against him.

Darrissea could feel the muscular contours of his body. She kissed the back of his neck and could not sleep.

The following night the Hukm crossed paths with a large force of Blade Kin, a supply caravan with two thousand men and mammoths that pulled skids over the snow. The Hukm attacked with clubs in total darkness during a heavy snow squall. The Blade Kin were no match for the giant Hukm and were slaughtered down to the last man while the Hukm suffered only a few gunshot wounds. The Hukm seized the grain and food for their own use. In the morning Phylomon, Darrissea, and Fava went out to the site and walked through the bloody snow, looking for weapons and clothing and foods that the Hukm would not touch. The ground was a mess, covered with bodies of dead Blade Kin thrown from the wagons, barrels smashed open and tossed aside.

Phylomon came upon four wagons of gunpowder, and set the Hukm to unloading it. Fava spent her time peeking in wagons while Darrissea searched for food. The Blade Kin had been sleeping in their wagons when the Hukm attacked, and the Hukm gained such complete surprise that most of the Blade Kin were clubbed in their sleep. Darrissea could hardly bear to glance into the wagons. For most of the morning she hunted timidly, gun in hand, finding casks of frozen salted fish, barrels of rum, crates filled with manacles or shovels or nails or seeds. The Blade Kin looked as if they planned to build their cities and plant their gardens within weeks. In one wagon she saw several corpses strewn over boxes of hammers and tongs. One man was splattered against the back of the buckboard, and Darrissea started to leave, saw the man turn his head.

"Help," he whispered.

Darrissea raised her long-barreled gun up and nearly fired before she saw that the man was not splattered but chained to the wagon. "Don't shoot!" he whispered. "Help!"

She leapt into the wagon, made her way to the buckboard. The man lay almost unconscious, head hanging. He coughed, and Darrissea took his hand, tried to see how heavy the manacles were. His hand felt freezing. He wore a simple dark-red cotton tunic over leather britches with heavy rhino leather belts and moccasins—the sturdy garb of woodsmen who lived in the Rough. He exhaled softly, and his breath seemed—magical, sweet, so that Darrissea leaned close, breathed deeply.

She touched his face, caressed his cheek, and the stranger moaned, leaned his face close so that she could stroke him.

Darrissea's heart pounded with excitement. She took a hammer, beat the chains till the manacles popped, then pulled the man from the wagon. He was small, human, with hair a dark reddish brown and a handsome face. He looked up at her with yellow eyes and a golden complexion. Darrissea could not tell what it was, but somehow, when she looked into his eyes, he looked . . . miraculous, perfect. She set him down, and he grabbed some snow from the ground, thirstily stuffed it into his mouth.

"Don't eat that," Darrissea said, "you're already freezing. Wait a moment, and I'll get you something warm." She ran to a wagon where she had found barrels of rum, was surprised to feel how her blood thrilled so hot as it coursed through her, went to a campfire where pans from last night's dinner still sat covered with snow, and filled a pan. She carried it back to the prisoner, but he was nowhere in sight.

"Where are you?" she shouted, suddenly afraid he had run away. From within the shadows of the wagon, the man answered, "Here!"

Darrissea jumped, and the man softly said, "I'm sorry I frightened you. I came back for the key." He held up a key, unlocked the broken manacles from his wrist. Darrissea was surprised to see him looking so much better, as if in the past moments he had become invigorated.

He put on one of the Blade Kin's red cloaks and a sword. Darrissea just stared. "I'm Darrissea Frolic," she mumbled at last.

"Stavan," he answered, and he walked to the edge of the wagon, touched her hand clumsily. Darrissea looked into his eyes, nervous, and suddenly it seemed to her that the world just went away. She looked into his eyes, and it all went away.

"Stavan," she said, and began rubbing the manacle burns on his sore wrist. He smiled at her, and his teeth were even, perfect. "You have blood on your lip."

Stavan licked his lip, touched it, and winced slightly. "I bit it when I stumbled a couple of days ago, after the slavers caught me. It keeps breaking open."

Darrissea could not understand why, with all the pain and suffering in the world, this one man's sore lip mattered to her so. He stood beside Darrissea, shyly touched her shoulder. It was an odd gesture, the kind of thing that a Pwi would do if he liked you, but not a human, and Darrissea wondered about this strange man's upbringing. She checked to make sure that no Hukm were watching, then smiled at him, felt guilty for smiling when so much mayhem was going on in the world.

He sat down heavily, on the edge of the wagon, and Darrissea went into motion, setting a fire to cook him something. She had so many questions and didn't know where to begin, didn't know if she should ask while he was in such a condition.

"Where are you headed?" he asked at last, breaking the uneasy silence.

"To Bashevgo," Darrissea answered.

The man blinked. "Oh. Will a lot of people be there?"

Darrissea laughed. "Of course."

Stavan glanced around the battlefield. "Of course . . . ," he mouthed. "I'm sorry, I'm not making sense. I . . . the—they captured me three days ago, and I haven't slept." He wrapped his robe around his chest. Darrissea struck the match, and a light snow began to fall again. Stavan stared away at the wagon for a moment, then offered, "I would like to go with you to Bashevgo. We were going that way anyway."

"We?" Darrissea asked, taken aback.

"My sister and I. The slavers killed her."

"You were heading into slaver territory? What did you plan to do in Bashevgo?"

Stavan measured his words. "Hunting . . . hunting for my father. The slavers took him." And then he toppled to the side from exhaustion, and Darrissea grabbed him, let him rest on her shoulder for support.

"Forgive me," Stavan whispered. "I'm exhausted."

Darrissea laid him in the back of the wagon, made a bed up from the robes of his dead captors, and watched him sleep as if he were dead. She stood over him, just watching his deep breaths.

"Stavan . . ." She mouthed the name over and over, hoping she had finally found someone to love.

Chapter 10
Asking the World for Peace

In the lowest cell at the bottom of the ship, Tull could hear the dull rumble of the serpent's voice beneath the churning of the ship's engines. His animal guide followed and spoke incessantly of tearing open the ship, rending its belly in order to rescue Tull. Yet Tull refused to listen, imagining the carnage that would result, sending an image of all his friends and loved ones dying as a result. The serpent tailed the ship, enraged and helpless, while Tull searched for a way to free himself.

This deep, the air felt stale, humid; Tull waited in an iron cage among the cargo. Half a dozen Blade Kin worked in the hold at odd hours of the day and night, sorting crates of food and supplies in order to fill the orders that came down from above.

For the first nine days of their return voyage, the Blade Kin worked seldom and seemed to hurry above decks to the fresh air whenever they could. But on the ninth day, that changed. All twenty hands moved into the hull and would not go above decks. They filled their orders, then stayed in the sweltering hold, playing cards without their tunics, wearing only long breechcloths as if they were Pwi, and sometimes one would look up nervously as if fearing that a superior would come down to check on them.

Over the next few hours, the temperature climbed steadily, until all the men were sweating even as they sat. Tull lay, listening to the Blade Kin talk as they played cards. Deep in the night the men began to yawn, and one human said, "It's getting hard to breathe. When will they give us some more air?"

"When it's safe," another answered.

"Dathan, why don't you run up there and get a nice breath of fresh air, then bring it back down here for the lot of us."

The man who had complained looked up, frightened, and the others laughed at his expense. "Laugh, you asses," he said. "You didn't see those birds swoop down on the deck. You didn't have them chase you down below."

"When do you think they'll open the vents?" another asked. "They can't lock us down here forever."

Their sergeant, an old human with buck teeth, said, "As soon as they clear the eels from the shafts. We stay put till then."

"By God's bloated belly, I'd hate to be a Pwi, trying to clean out those shafts," one of the men laughed, and the others chuckled nervously. "I saw one fellow, they shoved him up a shaft, and they pulled him back with five big lampreys sucking on the back of his neck, sucking his brains out."

"Ayaah," one man said, "better him than me."

They spoke no more about it, but Tull understood. The Creators had sent gray birds to attack. The image flashed through his mind of the little humans he had seen in Craal, the eellike creatures attaching to their hosts at the base of the neck so that they could bore into the brain stem, take control. Once the eel attached, the two could not be separated. Tull pitied any poor Pwi used that way.

He could not sleep. For hours Tull breathed the

stale air, lay awake, until at last cooler air broke into the hold.

Tull dreamed that he hunted deep in the redwoods where wild raspberry grew leaves as large as plates and the vine maple grew tall and thin. Chaa's dead son, Ayuvah, and Tull ran, carrying their spears, and Tull's stomach growled.

The moss and brush before them was pitted and scarred—a giant mastodon had left its prints in the ground, had gouged the moss with tusks that dragged the ground. Tull could hear it ahead in the forest, crashing through trees, snapping branches.

"I fear the beast will not let us catch it, and I am hungry," Ayuvah said, and the young Neanderthal stopped and wiped the sweat from his brow with his forearm.

"I'm hungry, too," Tull said.

"Perhaps the beast will not give itself because we have not asked it," Ayuvah said. "We are not hunting as men of the Pwi should."

Tull stopped, and he suddenly felt guilty. It was a lesson Ayuvah had tried to teach Tull long ago, to ask the spirit of the animal to give itself before the hunt.

Ayuvah pointed forward to the shadows of the forest, and Tull saw a great shaggy brown back, like a small hill, moving ahead of them. "Perhaps we should not bother asking for this one," Ayuvah said. "It is more than we could eat anyway."

Is it greed that makes me hunt this beast? Tull wondered. His belly cramped in on itself.

Ayuvah studied Tull. "What do you hunger for?"

Tull looked in the distance as the mastodon crashed through the forest shadows. His stomach tightened. But instead of the mammoth, he thought of Bashevgo with its army of Blade Kin. He thought of gray birds sent by the Creators, dropping from above with their worms of destruction. He thought of Eridani warships streaking through the night, and his belly tightened. "I hunger for peace," Tull said.

Ayuvah nodded. "Then ask the spirit of the world for peace."

"How?"

Ayuvah pointed at the rich humus with his spear. "Take off your clothes, and lie naked on your belly, and beg the world for peace. Then listen to what it tells you."

In his dream Tull stripped and lay naked, redwood needles pricking his bare skin, and he talked long to the earth, until the shadows of night began to fall, and he begged the earth to fill his belly with peace. Very faintly, like the thundering of a waterfall miles away, he could almost hear it answer.

Fava nudged her mammoth's small ears with both toes, urging it down through the mountains in the moonlight. They had left the firs early in the evening and traveled now through straggling ponderosa pine, nothing like the lofty redwoods of the south. The mountains had eroded to large rolling hills. Snow lay on the ground two feet deep, and traveling would have been all but impossible if not for the mammoths, who ran quickly, crazed with "ice fever," the fear that came on mammoths when forced north during the snowy season. Ahead of her in the moonlight Hukm warriors armed with twelve-foot clubs rushed over the hills, a blur of white on white snow.

Everything, the wide open sky, the lack of sea air, the army of Hukm—none of it had the taint of old kwea upon it, and Fava felt like a child, free to experience everything new, as if life were a stew cooked with exotic spices, none of which she had ever tasted. Fava found that she enjoyed the ride through the forest with the Hukm, in spite of unpleasantness ahead. Already they had turned west, leaving the hills of the coastal range, heading inland toward Bashevgo, another three weeks away.

Fava worked her legs down under the hair on the

mammoth's neck. She had found in the subzero temperatures that she needed little to keep her warm but a hot mammoth under her legs and a thick red wool cloak she had taken from some Blade Kin slaughtered by the Hukm in a skirmish.

Darrissea sat on the mammoth's back behind Fava atop a load of food, asleep—a trick that Fava did not want to master. Stavan followed along beside, and Fava was happy to see that her friend had found someone to love.

A mammoth hurried up beside Fava, and the driver, a young Hukm girl that Fava recognized as Apple Breath, waved her fingers. Fava was learning the basics of Hukm finger language. It really could be quite odd. The Hukm described humans, Neanderthals, and Mastodon Men as "Meat People," since they ate meat, and any herbivore with antlers was called a "knives-on-head," whether it was a deer, moose, elk, goat, or ox. In some ways their vocabulary was very limited, and the Hukm seemed so nonobservant as to appear retarded. Owls, swallows, eagles, and dragons were all simply "fliers," while tadpoles, salmon, otters, and eels were classified as "swimmers." A duck could be either a flier or a swimmer depending on whether it was in the air or on the water when spotted. On the other hand, the Hukm had names for every bush, weed, or tree, and described each with one of dozens of prefixes to define its taste. The bitter wild garlic was called "weasel-pee garlic," and was easily classified with other plants that Hukm swore tasted of weasel pee. Still, Fava found that she could communicate so long as she kept from discussing herbs. In the thin moonlight Fava had difficulty following Apple Breath's finger movements. "Why angry, Meat Person?"

Fava realized that she'd been smiling. "I no angry," she fingered back. "This Meat Person happy."

"You like Fruit Person?" Apple Breath asked. It was a question she asked a lot, as if convinced that Fava would change her mind and suddenly hate them all.

Fava studied the girl. Apple Breath, like all her kind, seemed a benign, quiet beast-woman, camping without fire, chewing dry squash or sugar cane or rice or any of hundreds of sweet-smelling fermented leaves. And Apple Breath treated her mastodons with more gentility than most human taskmasters would show a Pwi worker. During the days she'd take the mammoths to windswept plateaus to feed, often stroking the mammoths' trunks or giving them special treats.

"I like Fruit People. All Fruit People," Fava fingered back, chopping her hand at the end for emphasis.

"You like eat Fruit People?" Apple Breath asked. She seemed to think that humans and Pwi were predators, and all week she'd pointed out various animals—bobcats, skunks, snow owls, mice—asking which Fava ate. Still Fava could not imagine the Hukm worrying about whether humans might eat her. Fava looked up into Apple Breath's dark brown eyes, saw a sparkle of reflected moonlight, and realized the girl was teasing her.

"No like eat weasel-pee Fruit People," Fava answered.

Apple Breath barked in staccato bursts, Hukm laughter.

Suddenly, from over the ridge ahead, a Hukm let out a howl that cut off abruptly at the end, a signal for the whole caravan to stop while Ironwood Woman and Phylomon went ahead to investigate. Fava stopped, and upon the hill in the pale cinnabar moonlight, a Hukm waved his hands, finger talking. Fava could not make out his message, and Apple Breath repeated it for her.

"Meat People ahead—" Then she used some symbols Fava did not understand.

Fava sat and waited, wondering how big the army was. This far north it could only be an army of Blade Kin. The question was, Would the Hukm attack tonight or be forced to retreat?

As she waited, Phylomon and Ironwood Woman

galloped past on their mastodons, and Fava urged her own mastodon ahead without asking permission.

They crossed one hill, a second, and after nearly an hour came to a bowl-shaped valley where the pines opened into a small meadow. Camped in the snow were probably three thousand people, all Neanderthal households with women and children dressed in furs and occupying half as many tents as they needed. They had trampled and dug the snow out around camp, which seemed strange, since the snow should have provided good insulation, and they had ringed the camp with torches. Within this perimeter the Hukm had frightened the Neanderthal spearsmen witless, and their faces shone pale even in the moonlight. But as Fava rode closer, she saw that the Neanderthals did not have pale faces: They had painted their faces with white skull masks. "Okanjara," she hissed.

When Fava and Phylomon got near, the Okanjara retreated a few steps, staring in wonder at Phylomon. The blue man had taken off his coat and wore only a necklace and a breechcloth, so that his blue skin was naked to the air. Phylomon called, "How does the sky feel this night?"

A white-haired woman answered. "The kwea of our meeting is good, Phylomon Starfarer," she said almost as casually as if they'd exchanged greetings in town. She added darkly, "Considering our many misfortunes, and the strange company you keep."

"The Pwi and the Okanjara have long shared a common enemy with the Hukm," Phylomon said. "We've all battled the Blade Kin together. How can it seem strange to find me riding beside Ironwood Woman?"

"It's strange that you have so many Hukm here in the dead of winter where the Hukm must carry food," the old woman said.

"Just as I find it strange to meet Okanjara east of the Dragon Spine Mountains," Phylomon said. "Does your war against Craal go ill?"

The old Neanderthal woman struggled forward through the deep snow, and Fava saw that she wore black moccasins and leggings with the silver crow of a Spirit Walker. Fava touched her forehead in respect. "Our war goes ill, but it is not Craal we fight," the old woman said. "We have a new enemy, one I do not know how to defend myself from. Have you not seen the snow eels yet?"

"Yes, Mother," Phylomon said. "I've seen gray eels, carried in the beaks of large gray birds."

"No," the old woman said, "the ones we've seen are white and cold as ice. They burrow under loose snow and bite those who dare walk or camp in the open, poisoning them, then they leave. They do not feed on us. They come only to kill."

Phylomon frowned. *It has started,* Fava realized. *The Creators have begun our extermination well before Phylomon has had time to attack.*

"When did you last see one of these eels?" Phylomon asked.

"A week," the woman answered. "They were thick around the Dragon Spine Mountains, and even a few days from there. Still, we watch ourselves. We're going toward Storm Hold, to the protection of the city walls, but the snow delays us. We have seen many Blade Kin coming down out of the north this year, at least three Dragon Riders with full contingents headed south from Bashevgo. It gladdens me that the serpents will be attacking them, instead of us."

Fava considered. Three hundred thousand Blade Kin, poisonous snakes in the snow, all waiting on the road ahead.

"Will we meet the Blade Kin ahead?" Phylomon asked.

"Not many," the old woman said. "The snow is too deep, and most of the Blade Kin passed through before midwinter."

"We've seen many Blade Kin, too," Phylomon said. "In fact, I suspect that Blade Kin from Bashevgo have wiped out Storm Hold, along with all the other eastern cities by now. The Rough has been captured."

Several Okanjara cried in dismay, and one young man shouted, "But where can we retreat? Why do the Creators attack us?"

"There is no retreat," Phylomon answered. "There is no sanctuary in the Rough from the Blade Kin, and if you are correct, then the Creators have already attacked here in the wilderness. They will use their eels to drive us into the cities, where we will think we are protected, and then they will attack our cities.

"As for why they attack us, when the Starfarers gave the Creators charge over the planet, the Starfarers bid them to control the populations of plants and animals. In the west and north, the Slave Lords have overextended. Now the Creators hope to destroy us and repopulate the world with new people."

The woman laughed bitterly. "All our lives we've fought the Slave Lords, and now the Creators will destroy them for us. I only hope I live to celebrate on the Slave Lords' graves."

Phylomon smiled grimly. "So do I."

For the next several hours Phylomon acted as interpreter for the Okanjara and Ironwood Woman. Ironwood Woman wanted the Okanjara to join her attack on Bashevgo, but the Okanjara were leery of Hukm. For centuries the Hukm had frowned down on both humans and Neanderthals. The Hukm could not abide their stench, claiming that both humans and Neanderthals had the "putrid-smelling" flesh of carnivores. Add to that their smoking fires, their habits of peeing on bushes next to their camps and of leaving their feces uncovered —all revolted the Hukm, so that the Hukm had never fought a battle side by side with any other species.

In the end Ironwood Woman got only part of what she wanted. Most of the Okanjara were women and children. Even those who could fight saw little reason to throw their lives away in Bashevgo. Five hundred Okanjara joined their ranks, while the rest continued their trek to Storm Hold. At dawn, as most of the camp packed up tents and began trudging through the deep snow, Fava watched Phylomon's face. The blue-on-blue eyes were empty, and the lines of his face betrayed no emotion as he watched at least six hundred good warriors depart.

"What hope have we of winning?" Fava asked.

"I have hope," Phylomon said. "In Bashevgo, four million slaves hunger for freedom. If they join us, we can beat the Blade Kin. Besides, we now have five hundred trustworthy Okanjara warriors on our side. They may help even the match." He watched the Okanjara and his eyes narrowed, calculating.

"How? They are only five hundred against thousands of Blade Kin."

"We shall see," Phylomon said, yet for the next five days he showed her nothing. The Hukm advanced over the plains and twice came on small bands of people, a brother and sister here, four there.

In one band the humans introduced themselves, and Phylomon questioned two men, "Didn't you once take a woman slave, a Pwi named Thomba?" The men froze momentarily. Phylomon gunned them down and took a long time questioning their companions, who swore they'd met the others only the day before.

Fava was amazed to see so many humans so far north, where the slavers had scoured the land for decades, especially where the land was so inhospitable. At night green dancing lights shone in the north, and the winds driving across the hills were swift and vicious and icy cold. Each time they met a small group, they found them without a home, without even the shelter of a tent. The snow grew deeper, and at last Fava wondered aloud to Phylomon the morning after they came upon a third small camp, another brother and sister.

"Two more humans. What are they doing out here —all in pairs, a man and a woman? They all claim to be trappers or hunters, but where are their traps? Where are their weapons? They do not even look like slavers.

They look like twins. And why do they join us so easily?"

Phylomon didn't answer. They were camped in a ravine, and Phylomon had made a fire to brew tea. The weather was so cold that even the tea could barely keep Fava warm. She huddled in a robe and said, "And have you noticed? Of the six we've brought into camp, none are old or have children. They are all the age of warriors."

"The Rough is not kind to the old or young. I'd be surprised to find many of either," Phylomon said, yet clearly his tone showed that he was worried, too.

"Could they be Blade Kin? Spies of some sort?"

"The Invisible Arm of the Brotherhood?" Phylomon asked. "I suspect. We are closing in on Bashevgo and should reach it within three weeks. I'd expect the Blade Kin to post guards, but . . ."

"But?"

"But normally the guards aren't so far out. They would hide until we pass, then run warn their troops. By coming with us, these six accomplish nothing, unless they hope to sabotage our attack. Yet I don't fear that. It is something else. Something else about them bothers me. . . ."

"What?"

"The fact that they are human at all," Phylomon said. "If I were to post guards so far from Bashevgo, I'd post Neanderthals. They run faster and have better endurance than humans, and would get a message back more quickly."

"Perhaps the Slave Lords fear that Neanderthals would run away?"

"No," Phylomon said. "Two hundred years ago that would have been true. But today many Neanderthal Blade Kin are as faithful as any human. . . ."

"Do you want me to try to infiltrate them? Find out what they are doing?"

Phylomon stirred the fire so that it kicked up some embers, and Fava pulled the cloak around her tighter.

"No. If they are Blade Kin, they would arrange an accident for you. Perhaps only chance has brought them to us."

Throughout the day Fava watched the humans from her camp. They congregated in a small group and sat around a fire talking and laughing among themselves. Stavan went and spoke to them, but moments later, when Darrissea tried to join the group, the six suddenly became quiet. Some turned away, others went off to sleep under their furs. Watching them gave Fava a shiver, and she looked over to Phylomon. The blue man had noticed the odd behavior, too.

Fourteen days after Mahkawn left South Bay, his great iron ships began plowing through the ice at the Straits of Zerai to reach the docks at Bashevgo. For hours they moved at a slow grind, crashing through the ice again and again, the gleaming lights upon the hills beckoning them, until at last he gave up hope of reaching the docks. They turned off the engines, settled for the night, and let the ice freeze around the fleet.

At dawn Mahkawn got out of the ship and walked through a thick fog the last two miles to Bashevgo, over the ice, and entered the city triumphantly. There was no cheering, no crowds, yet Mahkawn felt his victory keenly. In history books children of future generations would read of the Black Cyclops and his conquest of the Rough.

From the basalt walls of the city, Mahkawn climbed atop the gleaming golden laser cannon that sat atop the Wall of Five Hundred Cannons guarding the straits, and as the morning sun touched upon him, he looked down into the white sea of fog and ice and fired the laser blasts that cut the ice, freeing the black ships to enter the harbor.

He rode the Death's Head Train from Bashevgo to Mount Sidon, gazing over the city: From the days of the Starfarers, there were still vast buildings made of exotic material with domes and spires. Three hundred years later captive Neanderthals had crafted monolithic buildings in black stone and then decorated them with horrific statues and columns. Historians called it the "decadent" period of architecture. Mahkawn's private train—the Death's Head Train—was a macabre relic from the decadent period, a giant engine of black iron, and upon its front was a bas relief of a Neanderthal's skull. The train seemed to radiate evil, and no one could mistake it for anything other than the personal transport of the Black Cyclops.

After the thirty-minute ride, Mahkawn went to meet Lord Tantos in his palace chambers. The Lord seemed distracted, yet Tantos spent the day debriefing Mahkawn meticulously, exacting death counts of Blade Kin versus numbers of slaves taken, ammunition spent versus booty captured. Mahkawn delivered the books, listing the names, home cities, and description of each captured slave. All in all, the mission had been a rousing success—sixty-four thousand slaves taken, versus twenty-seven hundred Blade Kin dead. The amount that Lord Tantos feared that he may have "squandered" on weaponry and salaries promised to be more than tripled when booty from the expedition was sold off along with the excess slaves, and of course there was the land. When the Mastodon Arm of the Brotherhood crushed the Hukm in the south, there would be the land. All in all, it was a glorious achievement.

Yet near the end of the debriefing, Tantos took the log of Smilodon Bay and read over the names. "You did not capture the Starfarer?"

"No," Mahkawn said for the third time during that day.

"I would be happier," Tantos said at last, "if you set his dead body before me." The Lord drew back his hood, exposing his own red symbiote. No one knew better than Tantos how hard it was to kill someone so protected. He looked down the book, stuck one red finger on a name, read off Tull's description, height, and weight. "And this Tull Genet. Lord Atherkula informs me that this big Tcho-Pwi killed two of his sorcerers, along with one of our Crimson Knights. He suggests that we make an example of him, let him die in the cage of bones. Has he been put to death yet?"

"No," Mahkawn said, controlling his anger, wondering how Atherkula had sent word so fast. "The death sentence is just, but the young slave is good, strong fighting stock. I wish him to fight in the arena, to earn the privilege of becoming Blade Kin. He also has training as a Spirit Walker. Rather than waste him, I believe he might come to serve in the stead of one of the sorcerers he slew."

"A raw slave, fresh from capture?" Tantos asked. "Dubious. I doubt you could break him. If he fights as well in the arena as he does in the wild, he might well win his life. Yet I suspect that he'll remain Pwi at heart and run off the first chance he gets."

"We have caught him twice. We could catch him again."

"I think," Tantos said, "we should execute him outright."

"Humor me," Mahkawn asked, and Tantos looked at him askance.

"Very well," Tantos said, "I will humor you partway. At the Spring Festival you may let him fight—under one condition: On the morning before the first fight, you will take a hammer and break both of his thumbs."

Mahkawn frowned. "But he will not be able to hold a weapon! He will have no power behind his blows!"

"Tull is a big man, an accomplished fighter. Anyone who can strike through the armor of a Crimson Knight should not be allowed to fight in the arena without a handicap, don't you agree?"

"If you wish, my lord," Mahkawn said, thinking, *Perhaps it would be kinder to execute Tull outright.*

Tantos closed the books. "You did well," he said, "yet I fear it may all be for nothing." Tantos stood and walked to his window, looking to the north. In his shadowed hall the roaring fire highlighted the red hues of his cheeks. "In the past month we have had numerous reports of white snakes in the ice, attacking our citizens. You yourself were attacked by the Creators. We've had to pull our Blade Kin out of the northern reaches of the Rough. In southern Craal, thousands of people are dying by drinking strange parasites carried in the water. We must strike back at the Creators soon."

"I would lead such an attack, my lord," Mahkawn asked, hoping that in this he might be honored a second time.

Tantos continued staring north. "We cannot attack the Creators until we know where to find them. They're sending gray birds to watch our city walls, and I have some of my Blade Kin prepared to follow the birds on hover sleds, like bees to their hive, when they return to the Creators. Within a few weeks we hope to know where to hunt. You will be among the ranks of that attacking force, but I will lead."

"As you please, my lord," Mahkawn answered, dismissed. He left the palace while the sun hung low over the snowfields, and as he watched his hot breath steam from him, Mahkawn thought of dinner. The cold was causing the arthritis in his left shoulder to flare up. A sour mood settled on him.

I've been defeated, he thought. He had hoped that this campaign in the Rough, a campaign he had prepared for over fifteen years, would be his last, but now it seemed the Creators conspired to rob him of his peace and honors. Even Atherkula, with his wagging tongue, had managed to rob him by convincing Lord Tantos to take Tull's life.

Mahkawn thought briefly of Tull, of his little home in Smilodon Bay, the simple pleasures Tull had taken with his wife and child. The fact that Mahkawn had irretrievably stolen that option as a way of life made him feel even more defeated.

He thought of his own favorite, of Pirazha in her

stone house, and the kwea of his time spent with her. It had been months since he had spawned with her, and he thought longingly of her golden eyes, of the orange hair going silver, of the sagging breasts with dark nipples that had suckled his children.

I've been too long at sea, too long without sex, Mahkawn told himself. He went to the Death's Head Train. Right now he needed Pirazha more than food or drink, he needed the sweet perfume of her sweat, the embrace of her arms, the taste of her kisses, the slow ecstasy of ejaculating between her legs. After a moment he convinced himself that he should spawn, but a small voice inside ridiculed him: *She breeds, but gives you only Thralls. Why not find one more worthy? Besides, is it really spawning anymore, now that she is past the age of childbearing?* and Mahkawn answered himself angrily, almost defensively, *No, but I shall spawn with the Thrall anyway. I've earned that much,* and Mahkawn made his way to her home, a defeated man.

The Hukm left the coastal mountains, and for several days they made good time over the Mammoth Run Plateau. The glistening Dragon Spines rose above the plain, seeming to march nearer with every step. Often during the nights, Darrissea would stop in the moonlight and look behind her. The great mammoth herd stretched behind for miles like black pearls on ivory satin. In the mountains she'd never really seen what a huge company they were.

The white snakes never attacked them. Phylomon surmised that the pounding feet of the mammoth herd kept them at bay. During the nights, sometimes, a thousand Hukm at once would take out their giant flutes and play as they traveled. Their melodies seemed to Darrissea to be fluid, quirky—the sounds of windsong and rainsong and women pining for men on a lonely afternoon. The Hukm did not play human music—no vibrant dance tunes, nothing one could sing to. Darrissea at first imagined that each piece was improvised. Yet as she listened, she found that all the Hukm played together, high reedy flutes harmonizing with deep basses. But in her weeks of travel, she never heard the same song twice.

Sometimes when she looked at the Hukm in the early morning, she would see them standing or sitting beneath the trees, hairy giants tending their mammoth herds, and she'd hear the music in her head. And for a moment she could almost imagine what it was like to be a Hukm, a creature of the field, living in isolation, the peacefulness of bluebottle flies buzzing around your head and a few green leaves to chew.

Sometimes they'd come to a frozen river, and the Hukm would break the ice and dive, playing like otters, steam rising from their wide nostrils, and she could hear that in their music, too—joy, celebration.

But in the evenings she would watch the Hukm women practice with their great war staves, whirling the clubs and smashing one another faster than she'd have believed possible for such large beasts. Even in practice they fought like berserkers, often drawing blood and knocking one another into the snow. Yet the Hukm played no war music, nothing with marches or the pounding of blood in it, and Fava sensed that this up-coming battle, these ages spent fighting the Blade Kin, were some alien thing thrust upon them, something they would never really comprehend.

Darrissea had not learned the Hukm finger language, but she spoke with Fava about it one day, and Fava said, "You are right. Even after all these hundreds of years fighting the Blade Kin, the Hukm still do not have a word for *war*."

During the days, Darrissea and Stavan often talked after sword practice or in the evenings. Though she was drawn to him, she felt guilty for it. She'd watch Fava's back during the night as she rode her mammoth and spoke finger language with the Hukm, and knew that Fava felt lonely. There was no one for her to talk to.

The Okanjara were marching somewhere south of the camp, so there were no Neanderthals. Phylomon remained aloof, self-absorbed. And the few odd humans in camp were a little community to themselves, which left only Darrissea and Stavan for Fava to speak with, and Stavan's attempts at conversation with Fava were always half-hearted. He spoke no Pwi, and Fava's English was terrible, deeply nasal in accent with greatly shortened vowels.

After nearly a week, as Darrissea rode next to Fava one night, Fava said simply, "Thank you."

"For what?" Darrissea asked.

"For being my friend. For staying close when I need to talk."

Darrissea found that her throat was tight. "You're welcome."

"Yet I know you would like to spend time with Stavan," Fava said. "Your eyes shine when you are near him. I think you should spend more time with him."

"You wouldn't feel bad?"

"If I am feeling bad, I'll know where to find you."

Darrissea slowed her mammoth until it came even with Stavan's, and felt as if she had just made a great change in her life. That night, when they stopped for a brief rest, Stavan invited her to ride with him for the rest of the night, and he kept his arms around her, warming her back with his body, resting his thinly bearded chin on her shoulder. He snuggled, as if they were longtime lovers. Yet they had spoken little. "Tell me more about yourself," Darrissea asked as they rode. "I don't even know your last name."

"Toucher, I guess."

"You guess?"

"I . . . don't really know. My father had a last name, Toucher. I guess that would be my name."

Darrissea turned her head to the side, looked into his yellow eyes to see if he was telling the truth. He really didn't know his last name, she decided. "Of course Toucher is your last name." Stavan nodded thoughtfully, as if he had just figured something out. "Where are you from?"

"North," Stavan said. "The mountains."

"What? No city?"

"No. We lived in the mountains. My father is a trapper, and an ivory carver."

"And your mother, is she Pwi?" He did not look Pwi, but he acted it, between his openness and his mannerisms.

"No, she's—you ask too many questions."

"I'm sorry," Darrissea said. "I only want to know you. I want to know everything about you."

"I'm hungry for you," he whispered savagely, "that's all you need to know." Though the night was cold, Darrissea began to perspire. She leaned back, kissed him.

Stavan's lips and tongue tasted sweet, sweeter than another man's, almost as if the faint scent of honey lingered there, and his lips felt faintly warm. She kissed him more firmly, twisted in his grasp so that her right breast pressed into his chest, and the next kiss lasted minutes. In all the hundreds of love poems she had written, Darrissea had never envisioned such passion as she felt in that one kiss. All her life she had imagined that when she first made love, she would take hours, that she would use the time to compose a poem even in the act. Yet as she kissed Stavan, feeling his taut body beside her, Darrissea's plans all seemed like romantic nonsense. She knew she would give herself to him in the morning.

Near dawn the Hukm stopped. Fava told Darrissea that the scouts had come upon another caravan of Blade Kin, and Darrissea set camp while the Hukm mounted an attack.

They ate breakfast, and for a while after dawn, Darrissea stood beside the campfire, letting the smoke rise to warm her, feeling it caress her face. Stavan crept up behind, wrapped a wool blanket around her, large enough for the both of them.

"Thank you for keeping me warm last night," Darrissea said, and Stavan whispered in her ear, "I'm hungry for you, now." Darrissea looked around. Most of the Hukm had gone to fight, Fava was washing pans with snow, Phylomon had left with the others. Two hundred yards away the odd humans occupied the only other camp in sight.

"Where?" Darrissea said, her heart hammering, and Stavan pointed up a ravine. "Let's go over the hill. We can be alone."

They walked up the narrow trail, hand in hand, until they found a small cubbyhole wedged between snow-covered rocks. "I—I've never done this before," Darrissea said, as he made the bed.

"That's all right," Stavan answered, and he kissed her, a long slow kiss from lips that tasted sweet. She could feel her skin burning right back to her eyeballs, and she stood, frozen, not wanting to stop. In this one moment, she felt she had touched glory.

Stavan made a bed of his cape, pulled his knife and set it in the snow, its blade naked. Then he began to undress her, and she found the clasp to his belt, opened it. They kissed, undressing slowly, and Darrissea closed her eyes and relished the moment. When they had undressed, Stavan helped lay her down gently.

Footsteps crunched through the snow, coming toward them, and Darrissea imagined Fava searching for them. Stavan stopped kissing her, raised his head cautiously. She kept silent, hoping Fava would go away. The footsteps stopped just outside the circle of rocks, and Darrissea listened for a long moment, hearing nothing, thinking that perhaps the person had departed.

Then someone moved into view—a girl—one of the newcomers to camp, found only three nights earlier, a human named Allon Tech with pale skin and blond hair. She glanced behind guiltily, as if checking the trail, her lips full and puckered, then faced them.

"Oh, you're awake," Allon said.

"Yes," Stavan answered.

Allon averted her eyes as if caught off guard. Darrissea realized she must be a thief, for she'd obviously been checking to see if anyone had seen her approach the rock.

"What do you want?" Stavan asked. Darrissea stirred, moving from beneath him.

"What are you doing?" Allon asked Stavan casually, as if asking whether he had eaten dinner yet.

Stavan said, "What concern is it of yours?"

She stared at him blankly, as if trying to comprehend his words. "I . . . I need," she said to Stavan. "I thought, we might share . . ."

Stavan rolled off Darrissea just a bit, enough to look up at the girl. Allon had a strange blank look in her face, and her eyes did not focus on either of them, as if she looked past them. Darrissea suddenly realized that the girl was insane, possibly dangerous. "Go away," Stavan said. "I have nothing to offer you."

"The others, they want it, too," Allon answered. She made a strange moaning noise, like the whine of a small pup, and moved closer, breathing heavily so that her breasts heaved.

Stavan grabbed his knife, and his muscles tensed. Darrissea could feel his arms, incredibly strong. "Leave. Now!"

"Oh, oh," Allon said. She turned, shot a feral glance over her shoulder. Darrissea crawled free, watched her go.

"What was that all about?" Darrissea asked, heart pounding.

"I swear, I have no idea," Stavan said.

Allon had just crested the hill when Phylomon and Fava appeared, riding a mammoth. Darrissea began pulling her clothes on, then stood as they approached. Stavan remained naked, wrapped in his blanket, scowling at the intrusion.

Phylomon looked down at them, neither approving

nor condemning. "The attack failed. The Blade Kin sounded an alarm, so we lost the element of surprise. However, before their caravan had a chance to retreat, we caught some prisoners—a Dragon Captain and two Smilodon Lancers. I'll question them tonight."

"Good," Darrissea said.

"For now," the Starfarer asked, "Darrissea, I'd like you to come with Fava and me. I have something to show you."

"Now?"

"Yes," Phylomon said. She looked in his eyes, wondered if he asked for her now only because he was jealous. She went to the mammoth, took a running leap, and grabbed on to the hair on its left haunch, then scurried up to the top of the hump on its back and clung to Fava's waist. Phylomon kicked the mammoth's ears, and they headed north, through the camp. Allon was with her odd friends, and all of them were watching Darrissea leave, all six strangers. Darrissea shouted, "Quit staring at me, you mutants, or I'll take my knife and abort your mutant asses!" Yet the strangers watched her.

Phylomon, Fava, and Darrissea rode north at a trot for two hours, to a small frozen lake, and the mammoth waded through a tangle of scrub until Phylomon reached some rocks—four monoliths standing a dozen feet tall. A fifth flat slab covered the others, forming a small enclosure. They dismounted.

"What is this place?" Darrissea asked.

"Upon this slab, eight hundred years ago, we built a pyre for Theron Major. His bones are buried here beneath our feet. I thought we should come and pay homage."

Fava and Darrissea knelt on the soil. Theron Major, the first human Starfarer to begin teaching the Pwi, a man of peace, and the first man gunned down by the Slave Lords. Darrissea wondered if Theron knew that in Smilodon Bay alone, his deeds were so well remembered that a dozen men were named for him.

"Did you know him?" Fava asked.

"Very well," Phylomon answered. "I was young when Theron ran his school in South Bay. We had heard rumors that Starfarers were taking slaves. We came on an expedition from South Bay, flying in hovercrafts. At Bashevgo we found many Pwi taken as slaves to work as farmers, miners, laborers. Theron tried to talk the Starfarers there into setting them free. We thought we'd succeeded, but here the slavers ambushed us and murdered Theron."

"Is this the same path you took to Bashevgo then?" Fava asked.

"Yes," Phylomon whispered. He stepped outside the small structure. Looked up. A Red Drone shone in the sky, palely visible even in daylight, a spear of white. Phylomon muttered, "I seem doomed to travel the same paths, over and over."

"What?" Darrissea asked.

Phylomon said, "That summer I traveled these same plains with Theron, and afterward I learned to hunt slavers in the darkness. Three hundred and sixty years ago, I came here leading Terrazin Dragontamer to our first battle on the north rim of the Mammoth Run Plateau. Now I circle round to Bashevgo again. It feels like some great cosmic chase, an endless battle between enons."

"Enons?" Darrissea asked.

"An old term," Phylomon said. "A concept borrowed from our friends the Eridani." He nodded up into the sky at the Red Drone. "Enons are opposing combatants that can never win, never dominate. You would think that the Eridani, with their communal minds, would have reached some consensus on issues such as justice and mercy, good and evil. But they haven't. They view the universe in terms of competing opposites, called enons. In the physical universe enons are observed in the form of matter and antimatter. Creation and chaos. Enons appear to do battle, but their forces remain equal. That is the way I feel about the

Blade Kin. I and they are enons. I battle them, hack them down. Always they come at me again, as if freshly created only to bloody my sword.

"Anyway," Phylomon added, "to work. For over three hundred years, I have kept some armaments hidden. But now I must unearth them. If I die, you will know what is available to you." Phylomon walked into the brush, set his hand on a huge boulder; then Phylomon had Darrissea and Fava place their hands beside his, and each woman spoke her name. Last of all Phylomon spoke his name.

The boulder collapsed in dust, and a great stone box appeared. The mammoth, only a few yards away, trumpeted, and Darrissea fell back in surprise. Fava felt her own stomach fluttering.

Phylomon spoke to the box in English, saying "Open," and the lid slid away to reveal odd devices—rods, medallions, strange guns. The box emitted a rotten odor, like some long-unused pantry. Fava stepped back a dozen yards, terrified.

For a long time Phylomon studied the great box, and then he pulled out a tiny black cube and swallowed it.

"What is that?" Darrissea asked.

"A weapon that will remain hidden in my stomach until I call upon it," Phylomon said. He pulled out eight white rods and one blue one, like long pipes, and he gave three each to Fava and Darrissea. "These were not made as weapons," he said softly. "Originally, when our forefathers terraformed Anee, it was very unstable. Situated as it is, the largest moon circling a gas giant, it undergoes phenomenal gravitational stress, causing volcanoes and earthquakes and tremendous tides. Those stresses were necessary for the planet to build an atmosphere, but they are also inconvenient. So we used harmonic resonance rods"—he held out the sticks—"to trigger earthquakes and relieve the tectonic plates so we could build our cities." Phylomon looked at the two women and must have realized that they didn't understand. "When we get to Bashevgo, we may need to breach the walls to the city. To do so, you must plant the rods in the wall and twist. Plant all eight white ones first, and the blue one last. Within a few minutes the walls will shatter."

"These start earthquakes?" Fava asked, her eyes wide.

Phylomon nodded. "Bashevgo is fairly stable. I don't know exactly how much damage we could cause there. But in some other cities—down in Greenstone where they are closer to the fault lines—we could level the entire countryside."

Fava set her rods on the ground, gingerly, as if afraid of them.

Phylomon reached into the box, pulled out other objects—five guns, exactly half of those in the box. "So little left," he muttered, and held them out to Fava. She would not touch them.

"Those are evil weapons," Fava said. "They are not friendly to me, I can tell."

"I offer you portable laser cannons, and you decline? What will you do, fight the Blade Kin with spears and swords?"

"If I must," Fava said, but Darrissea took the guns, carrying them like an armload of firewood.

Phylomon studied Fava a moment. "I'm sorry. I didn't mean to frighten you. Perhaps I can find some friendly weapons for you."

He pulled out a shining bow of silver with two knobs on each end. "That looks friendly," Fava said.

"No, we would need an allosaur to use this. It's a tamer, used to control an allosaur. It attaches to the allosaur's brain, and when you speak commands, it translates them into impulses that the allosaur can react upon. When I was young, we used to bring allosaurs over from Hotland to race. The Slave Lords used to have their captains ride them."

He pulled out three pieces of green leather—two

inches wide and a foot long, like pieces of dry jerky. He studied each in turn, peering at them closely.

"What?" Darrissea asked.

"These are the cauls of the symbiotic skins taken from dead Starfarers. Unfortunately, these were not available when my first wife was alive. Only after the Talent War, when the Starfarers died. You see, sometimes a body is so destroyed that even the symbiote cannot regenerate it. Then the caul separates, and the symbiote must wait to reattach to a new host. Would you wear a skin like mine?" Phylomon looked up at Fava and Darrissea, held out the strips of jerky. "You need only cut yourself and place the caul on the cut so it can feed on your blood."

Darrissea's heart pounded. She knew what he was offering—immortality, and his love. His eyes showed pain, loneliness. She had thought she only imagined jealousy in his eyes when he caught her with Stavan. She suddenly saw that the Starfarer must be so alone, living forever in his cage of flesh. In a way, Phylomon did not live, but merely existed.

"No," Fava said, and Darrissea waited, considering. Phylomon's loneliness should not have mattered to her at all, did not really matter much. Darrissea had found Stavan now.

"Wise choice," Phylomon said when she did not reach out to take one, and he smiled down at her, and his cerulean eyes were ancient. "I never would have chosen to live my life either. When I was young, we slipped symbiotes on and off with hardly more effort than you would change your clothes. Unfortunately, these cauls have died over the years and will do no one any good." He crushed the strips of leather in his hand. They crackled and tore like chaff, and he let them float on the wind.

Phylomon searched the remaining pile of odd boxes until his eyes settled on a small bundle of wrapped leather the size of a loaf of bread. He picked it up, as if testing its weight, then looked steadily at Fava.

The leather bundle was crudely tied, as if by a child, and Darrissea could almost imagine that the leather protected some girl's wooden doll.

The Starfarer held it out for Fava. "You wanted a friendly weapon. This is not a weapon, but it is friendly. Unwrap it."

Fava tried to unwrap the bundle, but the leather straps broke easier than they untied. Still the leather smelled sweet, as if it held some treasure. Inside was a small silver flask and a beautiful ivory broach with a leaping sabertooth carved into it.

"You have heard of faders, those of my people who it was said could 'walk invisible.' Would you become one?"

"Would I be invisible?" Fava asked.

"No," Phylomon said. "The fader distorts time. It causes an intense energy field around you, warping time. While others live in our timestream, you can speed up."

"I don't understand," Fava said. "What would happen to me? Would I speed up forever?"

"When you activate the fader, for a brief moment, a few seconds, time would seem to slow around you, and you'd move quickly. The air would seem thick and unyielding, like water. Perhaps this would frighten you, but as long as you move slow and breathe deep, you will be all right. As the rest of the world ages three seconds, you will have about five minutes in which to work. You could retreat from danger or cross a wide field unseen. You can walk so rapidly over water that you will not sink, or you could kill enemies. In these ways Starfarers who wore faders served as spies. I think that since you are both already disguised as Blade Kin, you would make a good fader."

Fava nodded dumbly, and Phylomon opened the silver flask, had her drink the fluid, then fitted the ivory medallion to her cloak. "The fluid from the bottle takes two days to be absorbed by the cells in your body. After that you can activate the fader by pressing the medallion hard between your fingers," Phylomon said. "But remember, the medallion requires a great deal of energy, which it gathers from radiation."

"Light from the sun?"

"No," Phylomon said. "This radiation blows through our world day and night, never slowing as it passes through the planet. Still, the fader must gather energy from these particles, and it takes several hours to recharge. You must use the fader sparingly and rely on your wits."

From the box Phylomon pulled out several large white plates, then took one small black one. "Hover mines," he said, and he pulled his knife, slit open his left arm, then placed the small black hover mine in the incision. The symbiote began healing the incision immediately, concealing the weapon. The women watched in disgust, and Phylomon said, "I carry more weapons than you know. Now that we are going into battle, that is exactly as it should be."

He looked at the box one last time, said, "Close," and the great stone slammed shut. He said, "Conceal," and all around them dust seemed to flow upward, like millions of insects, until it closed around the boulder. When he finished, the great obsidian boulder sat with bits of crimson and yellow lichens on it, a simple boulder except that it was no longer covered with snow.

He sat, showed them how to use the weapons. When he finished, Fava sat perfectly still. "There will be much to remember," she sighed.

"I will make it easier for you," Phylomon said. "In order for your brain to make temporary thoughts into permanent thoughts, it must use electrical energy to change the DNA in your cerebrum. The process takes half an hour. On the trip home, sit for half an hour and think about what I have told you, practice each action in your mind, and if you can manage to concentrate for that half an hour, then even when you are an old, old woman, you will recall all that I have said."

Darrissea did not understand much about electricity or DNA, but she pondered his instructions as they rode home.

When Darrissea returned to camp with Fava and Phylomon at sunset, they found the three Blade Kin prisoners decapitated and hanging by their feet among the barren trees. Phylomon wondered aloud if the Hukm had decided to kill the men, and he checked the scene. There was no blood on the ground, though a bloody cooking pot stood by. Darrissea looked at the gory mess, the footprints in the well-trampled snow. All the footprints under the tree were human—the big toe pointing forward instead of curving in as on the feet of a Neanderthal.

Phylomon spoke to a dozen Hukm who were sleeping in the camp nearby. At last he gazed over to the group of six humans, the outsiders. They were all awake now, but none of them looked his direction. Instead, they stood with shoulders hunched. Phylomon cut the dead men down. He picked up the bloody cooking pot. There were marks in the blood around the rim, the marks of lips.

"Someone drank their blood?" Fava asked.

Phylomon loosened his sword in its sheath, carried the pot back to the six. The sun was falling behind the mountains. Darrissea and Fava each took a gun, followed behind Phylomon.

"What are you?" Phylomon asked the six. None would look at him. "Why did the Creators send you?"

The beautiful blond Allon leapt at him from a sitting position twenty feet away, seeming almost to fly through the air.

Phylomon ducked and slashed above him with his sword, and great gouts of blood poured from her stomach as if from a sack. The other five jumped away, began running.

It all happened so quickly that neither Darrissea nor Fava had time to fire, but Phylomon howled in parody of a Hukm, and within moments the Hukm were rising from camp, leaping over the ground, slapping at the humans with their huge clubs.

The strangers leapt away, sometimes jumping five feet over the head of a charging Hukm, gyrating and twisting in the air to avoid the deadly clubs. One of the strange men landed on the shoulders of a giant Hukm woman nearly ten feet tall. He slapped her temple, tearing open a bloody swathe and snapping her neck. The Hukm around him roared in anger and raced forward, and suddenly, among the snow-covered hills, thousands of Hukm roared in answer and began to converge on the area, loping over the snow between the twisted limbs of scrub oak and juniper. The Hukm caught two strangers quickly and began pummeling their broken bodies with great war clubs. Two others seemed far more interested in escaping than fighting. But Darrissea watched the Hukm converge. The outsiders didn't stand a chance.

Phylomon ran and caught one woman, a nubile young brunette, pinned her to the ground, but the muscles in her arms twisted like steel cables, breaking his grip. Darrissea watched the Starfarer's symbiote release a blinding bolt of electricity, and the girl's muscles spasmed. She jerked forward and lay face down in the snow. Hukm circled the two. The big white females with their pendulous breasts raised their clubs, threatened and growled. Their brown eyes were wide, fierce, excited. Darrissea feared they might leap in and smash Phylomon in their blood lust. But the most shocking thing was not the sound of their roaring that echoed over the hills, or their eyes glazing in their fury. The most fascinating thing to Darrissea was their smiles: The Hukm were smiling as they snarled and stifled the urge to attack.

Phylomon leapt on the downed woman, pinned her tightly.

"Answer me!" Phylomon shouted. "What are you?" He flipped the girl over, and Darrissea saw that her face no longer looked human. Instead, her features were distorted, caved in over her skull. She was still spasming from the shock. She reached up with her nails and slashed Phylomon's back, a blow that shredded his thick leather jerkin. Darrissea was sure the blow would have ripped the kidney from a normal human. The girl's face puffed out again, the hollows on her cheeks and forehead expanding like balloons, and Phylomon pulled his sword, rammed it through her neck, and staggered back, gasping.

Darrissea watched the girl's features deflate, even the pendulous breasts beneath her jacket.

"We remain camped here for the night," Phylomon said, panting. The Hukm brought over the bodies of the other four humans, and hundreds of the Hukm circled them. Phylomon looked up at Darrissea and Fava. "I'm going to dissect them, find out what we're fighting," he said. "It won't be pretty."

Darrissea nodded, walked over the uneven ground back to her camp, which was hidden in a shallow depression surrounded by willows.

The snow was deep here in the depression, and the air seemed somehow cleaner here away from the heavy scent of fur. The Hukm were beginning to quiet. In the distance, miles away, Darrissea could hear the Hukm's questioning roars, almost like the calls of some odd, feral nightbirds preparing to sleep.

Stavan lay there in the snow in the setting sun, curled in his bedroll. Darrissea looked down at him, at his burnished hair, the sleek angles of his face. He breathed erratically, shallowly. She knew he was awake.

"Stavan?" she said, recalling those lips, sweeter than any man's lips had a right to be, the way his muscles had felt like iron cords, the way he had set a naked knife beside their bed earlier in the morning. "Stavan?"

He looked up, smiled at her as if just waking. He stretched his arms wide, displaying his sleek musculature. He was nude within the bedroll. Darrissea's voice sounded faraway even to herself as she asked, "Are you still hungry for me?"

Stavan gazed into the barrel of her gun, and his beautiful golden eyes opened wide. "I'm not like the others," he breathed, "I love you! I really love you! I wouldn't have hurt you—I was just . . ."

"Hungry?" For a long time she stared into his eyes, and the setting sun was so golden that it highlighted each hair on his brow, the golden skin of his face.

He swallowed hard. "I'll go away, leave you and your friends. Tell me the name of a city, someplace where your enemies live, and point the way for me. I can hunt elsewhere."

"Denai," she said, jerking her chin west toward the mountains.

Stavan nodded, began packing his bedroll. Night was falling, and he'd be weeks marching through the snow. She'd seen the hunger in his eyes earlier, knew he couldn't make it without feeding. But he was strong. Darrissea knew she couldn't let him get close. He moved slowly, pulling his bedroll tight, as if pondering the same things. When he turned and leapt at her, Darrissea fired into his throat, knocking him backward, where he sprawled on the ground. There he lay, unnaturally still, not breathing, not moving in the slightest. Darrissea found herself panting, wanting to scream or run, but she forced herself to stay. She stood for an eternity watching his face deflate.

Phylomon lit torches and set them in the snow around him, then took his knife and began dissecting the woman.

He started at the top, skinning its head, simply because he needed a place to start. He found that the fat around the cheeks was only a thin layer, that where the sinus membranes should have been in the cheeks and temple, instead it had narrow tubes and air sacs. Tiny gray pheromone glands were hidden next to the saliva ducts. He discovered the glands only when he touched some of the fluid they exuded and found himself getting an erection.

The creature's brain was smaller than either a human's or a Neanderthal's. After nearly an hour, Phylomon noticed something odd—in the torchlight the brunette's hair changed to a soft red, and the skin faded to a dead white. Phylomon took his torch around to the other corpses, found that they too had all reverted to a similar hue. With the air sacs and color-changing ability, he realized that the creatures were quite adaptable. They could look male or female, possibly even look human or Neanderthal. He considered: They might even be able to doppelganger others, take their place. He went back to the first corpse and cut some more.

At the top of the pharynx, he found a small passage that he imagined would lead to the air sacs, but instead it went down the throat to a second stomach, which was filled with blood. He found the liver to be overlarge, the spleen almost nonexistent. He cracked a femur and found it to be hollow, lacking marrow, like the bones of a bird. He quit dissecting at that point, for he had spent several hours with the creature, and it had grown dark, and he felt uncomfortable slicing it up alone in the night.

Phylomon washed his hands again and again, and could not feel clean. He went and lay in the snow, looking up at the sky, at the thin layer of clouds hiding the Milky Way. One of the Red Drones beat its path across the sky. Until that moment, Phylomon had believed the Creators intended to destroy mankind, wipe them out and start anew. Now he wasn't sure. The Creators were introducing new breeds of predators, new horrors to thin the human population, but it seemed to him that a plague would have worked more thoroughly. Phylomon lay for an hour, replaying memories of his youth from the days when he was still taking seritactates. Phylomon had helped program the predator/prey equations that told the Creators when to introduce new predators into the ecosystems, or when populations of herbivores had overextended enough to endanger the local flora. The crystalline brains of the Creators could only hold so much information, and those brains were crammed with genetic codes, sophisticated equations dealing with allowable flora and fauna populations, and equations dealing with possible solutions.

Beyond this type of information, the Creators were actually quite stupid, and Phylomon wondered: Are the Creators refraining from wiping out mankind with a plague simply because they are too stupid to recognize it as the best alternative, or have they been programmed against it?

After great consideration, Phylomon surmised they had been programmed against it. He had entered many equations in their brains offering solutions on how to deal with higher mammals—such as dire wolves and Mastodon Men—but the solutions all required the Creators to control the mammals using either parasites or other predators. The development team which formed the Creators must have decided that teaching them to use biological warfare techniques would have been impractical in such a complex and fragile ecosystem.

Phylomon found it grimly humorous to realize that the only reason the Creators had not destroyed mankind already was because they weren't designed well enough. *Ah, with a bit more work,* he thought. *What might they accomplish.*

Phylomon considered the blood eaters. They were well-designed. Mankind might flee other predators—might find ways to burrow into the ground or climb trees to escape, but these blood eaters could hunt men in their warrens, in their most desolate and well-protected shelters.

As a Dicton, Phylomon had been born with a genetically created dictionary of the ancient language of the Starfarers—English. He knew all the words in the language, yet he did not use them when speaking to ordinary humans. His descendants, whose blood had mingled with that of the Neanderthals over the centuries, had forgotten so many of the words that some were meaningless. Only those rare throwbacks who happened to be born with the internal dictionary nowadays could communicate on Phylomon's level. Certainly, even if he told Darrissea and Fava and the Hukm what he had found, they would not have understood—a creature that does not create its own blood and therefore must prey on others.

He calculated in his head, knowing that the walls of red blood cells would erode after pounding through the arteries for a few weeks, and suspected that the creatures would have to feed at a minimum of once every three weeks. He imagined how they must be spreading, searching out every city in Craal, trying to infiltrate the communities, waiting until the time was right to attack the cities from within. Phylomon mouthed the word for what the Creators had formed: *vampire*.

Chapter 11
A Cry for Freedom

In his dark cell beneath the earth, Tull was free to remember and dream. The hay on the cold stone floor smelled of dung and urine and mice, reminding him of barns he had cleaned back home. The chittering of mice in the night reminded him of his own childhood, of how Jenks had chained him in his room when Tull threatened to run away, and at times late at night Tull could hear the mice squeaking and scurrying through the kitchen. The food for prisoners here was cold—stiff bread, boiled potatoes left in their own water until it turned almost white as milk—and he remembered milking cows for Hendemon Strong when he was young, the warm milk squirting into a wooden bucket.

For a few moments when they reached Bashevgo, the Blade Kin brought Tull from the depths of the ship into the stunning sunlight, marched him over the frozen ice with the others, shivering for lack of a blanket or coat. Nearby, he'd seen people from town—Theron Scandal the innkeeper, Fava's mother Zhopilla. Tull had heard beneath the ice the groan of the sea serpent, eager to free him, but Tull had warned it, "not yet." There were far too many people around. If the serpent dared break the ice, innocent Pwi would die. Yet the serpent knew it was his last chance. Tull could feel the monster under the water, brooding, and Tull could barely restrain it.

Far too quickly, Tull walked over the ice, and under the archway that led to Bashevgo. Everywhere, curious Thralls lined the streets to watch the last free men of the Rough brought in. The Thralls seemed emotionally confused by the spectacle. Some old Neanderthal women were crying to watch the end of an era die. Other Thralls cheered the Blade Kin guard that marched along.

At last the other Pwi turned up a street, heading uphill toward the Capitol, and three Blade Kin escorted Tull in another direction. He had hoped to be put in a cell with some family or friends—but Tull alone had been brought here, to a cell far beneath the arena.

And here he dreamed, thinking of his last conversation with Mahkawn. What do you want in life? After six weeks he dreamed of Fava's lips, of sleeping with her under the bear skins in his cabin. He had wanted a bigger house, and since he was free to dream, he imagined the house would be larger than the mayor's. He dreamed that he would get free and someday teach Wayan to read, and that they would someday be respected, like some human shipping magnates or gentleman farmers. He dreamed of food—lemons and oranges shipped north in winter, grapes fresh off the vine in fall, wheat bread with leatherwood honey and butter, new clothes.

What do you want in life? Sometimes Tull would look at his thumbs, his clumsy Neanderthal thumbs that would not let him handle small objects with the precision of a human, and he imagined that if he learned enough about human hands, perhaps he could find a doctor who would break the knuckles in Tull's heavy paws and then somehow twist the thumbs and reset them so that they would work like a human's.

Next to Tull was a cell with a strong young Thrall named Khur. He'd been a willing sex slave for a human master, and when she took another human lover, Khur had tossed a spear at his rival, ramming it through the man's leg. "It felt good," Khur said, "just to watch him bleed. I did not want to kill him, only to hurt him."

"I don't see what you accomplished," Tull said one night. "You will probably get killed, and your master will still have her human lover."

"It makes no difference," Khur insisted. "Now she will always know that I loved her, that I was willing to die for her. Every time she tries to make love to another man, she will think of me. I will always be remembered," Khur boasted, thumping his chest and pacing back and forth across his cell.

Tull puzzled. "You will die for someone who doesn't love you? You will make her feel guilty for what she has done to you? It seems a great waste, when you could have found another lover. Tell me, what have you gained?"

"Honor," Khur said, pounding his chest, pulling his shoulders back. He stood behind his bars and grinned. "People will honor and remember me—a mere slave! And I will have revenge. My master will never enjoy sex more than what she had with me!"

Tull looked into Khur's big friendly eyes, his generous smile, and realized that he did not understand Thralls. To Khur, who had nothing, a little bit of honor and respect seemed worth his own death. Tull turned away, thought of things he had lost.

So it was that Atherkula found him dreaming.

The sorcerer came without his robes of office, wearing instead a simple green tunic and red trousers, with a leather long coat thrown over it all. He had come quietly to the cell door and found Tull smiling.

"You are a madman," Atherkula said, "to be smiling down here. As a lunatic you will be worth nothing— fit only for culling."

Tull looked up quizzically, and for a long moment could not place Atherkula.

Atherkula demanded, "Why are you smiling?"

"Have you ever tasted Frog Hollow cheese?" Tull

asked. "The land is cool and foggy down there in the winter—almost a swamp—and many of the trees there have rotted at the core, though they still stand. The folks take those old hollow trees and put bladders of goat's milk in them to age for the winter. The cheese is yellow and creamy, very pungent. You should try it, really."

Atherkula looked at him, and the old man's eyes were filled with curiosity. "You are dreaming of freedom, aren't you? You know, I am the man who took it from you, and I could give it back. Mahkawn wants your ear and would make you a Blade Kin if I permitted it. What would you give me for your freedom?"

Tull looked up, held the old man's eyes.

"I tell you what I want for your freedom," Atherkula said. "Among the Blade Kin, we have an old custom. We pick children who may become Blade Kin, and we give them a pet, and give them time to learn to love that pet. Then we order them to kill it. If they can kill the thing they love, we know they are worthy to become Blade Kin. We know they can be trusted to follow our orders. I tell you this: I will trust you when I see you kill the thing you love. But who? It seems you do not care for your mother or father. So I will make it Fava. We caught her at Muskrat Creek, you know. I slept with her last night. If you killed her in the arena, I would consider you worthy to be Blade Kin."

Tull closed his eyes.

"You're not going to speak to me?" Atherkula asked. "You're not going to speak?"

Tull kept his eyes closed, realizing that if he hoped to make his dreams come true, he'd have to kill. In Bashevgo and in the Rough, he had killed without compunction, but never like this. He imagined his dream house, a great stone house in the woods—cream marble with cedar panels on the interior—and it would sit next to a deep pond where trout would swim and mallards would land at night in autumn. He decided to build it in his mind, design and construct it, and imagined piling stone upon stone upon stone.

The attack on Bashevgo was not like anything Fava would have imagined. She had thought they would storm the city, taking it by force, but that was not the Hukm way, and Phylomon used the Hukm tactics of stealth. He had his Hukm spies spend nine days watching Bashevgo, and often during that time, the days warmed above freezing, rotting the ice out on the sea— their road to Bashevgo.

Phylomon sent an Okanjara to scout the city twice while the Hukm army remained concealed in the hills ninety miles off. Yet Fava knew the attack was nearing, for the Hukm began to wrap their long wooden clubs, strengthening them with bits of leather and then painting them with a thin white paste to camouflage them in the snow.

Phylomon could not pick just any day for an attack. He needed a night of bitter cold during mild tides. With the strong pull of Thor, the tides on Anee often caused variances in sea level of a hundred feet, and the changing water levels would break up the ice near shore. Only when the night promised to be bitter cold and the tides mild could Phylomon launch an assault.

With five days' notice, Phylomon split the army into seven Divisions and set them to attack different targets in the city. Fava had hoped to fight beside the Okanjara, in the company of other Neanderthals, but Phylomon sent them north with their guns to a Blade Kin barracks where a firefight would most likely break out. Phylomon had gone on to lead the attack. Which left Fava and Darrissea alone with the Hukm, prepared to use the harmonic resonators to bring down the south walls of Bashevgo, if necessary. Fava had never imagined the strategic difficulties they would face, trying to attack a city of millions at night, where nearly half the Blade Kin slept among slaves instead of in a barracks.

The night of the proposed attack, the skies were clear and cold, but a fog blew over the ice. Fava and Darrissea stood on a ledge just five miles south of the city, watching the halo of lights above it. Thor had just set, giving the signal to begin the charge. Not till Freya began to rise would they attack. With fog on the ice, only the very top of Bashevgo floated in a sea of clouds. Fava could see the great white capitol dome and some mansions around it, but not the laser turrets on the wall of cannons.

Fava stopped while the Hukm ran down the slope onto the ice, white fur becoming lost in white fog. Fava put on a white head band so the Hukm would know she was not a Blade Kin once they got to the city, then pulled her sword and tested its edge, dropped it back into its sheath. She had honed it often enough. Phylomon had vanished into the fog, leading the charge, and Fava suddenly wished desperately that she could be down there next to the Starfarer.

"What are you waiting for?" Darrissea asked, her voice hard. Fava wondered if fear made her speak so harshly.

"I just realized how I am stupid as a tadpole," Fava answered. "We're really attacking Bashevgo, aren't we?"

"That's why we came," Darrissea answered, with a toughness in her voice that Fava could not match.

Fava looked back. "I guess that's why we are here." Fava willed herself to move forward, but her legs seemed locked, and she trembled. The ice below rumbled with the sound of running feet. "I've always been so *zhefasha*, impulsive like the mountain goat," Fava said. "I jump ahead whenever there is danger so that I won't be left behind."

"You aren't going to Bashevgo because of the danger," Darrissea said. "You are going there because of your husband. That is the deal we made together."

Fava stood a moment, unmoving, and finally the fear tore through her in great waves, and she began

weeping, trying to work it out. Darrissea wrapped her
thin arms around Fava and hugged. "You will be all
right. You have been strong for me when I needed it, so
I will be strong for you now, all right? Together we can
be stronger than any two people alone."

"Tchezza fae, so be it," Fava answered, and Darrissea did not move until Fava stopped weeping. Then
Fava held her hand and whispered, "You are a good
friend. Can I call you *sister*?"

"Yes, I think we should be sisters now," Darrissea
answered. She took Fava's shoulder and whispered,
"Come," then said more softly, "Don't get yourself
killed. Remember, we can find Tull only if we infiltrate
the Blade Kin, not if we fight them outright."

Fava nodded, then rushed down the slope to the
sea. When they reached bottom, Fava could hear the
dull drumming of feet on the ice, and the city was lost in
the fog. Fava watched the back of the Hukm before her,
an indistinct mass, and ran, trying to keep up, but soon
was running blindly in the darkness. A youngster
charged forward to pace beside her, a young Hukm who
barked softly in greeting. Fava could not see, but recognized that it must be Apple Breath.

The Hukm girl gripped Fava's shoulder, guided her
over the ice, and Fava was running blind, placing her
feet with care. Often she'd find sharp edges where the
ice had cracked and refrozen, and she'd fall headlong.
Only Apple Breath's firm grip saved her.

After what seemed hours, the sky began to lighten
above them, and Fava realized they were close to the
city. She could smell wood smoke mingled with the fog,
and dark masses loomed about them. They were standing on the ice between two iron ships.

Apple Breath stopped, and they huddled while
thousands of Hukm rushed from behind, surrounding
them. There had been no cries of warning from the city
walls, and the only sound was the panting breaths of the
Hukm. Fava could not see anything clearly and knew
that the small pale moon Freya had begun to rise only

when the Hukm moved forward noiselessly on their great padded feet.

She waited as Hukm infiltrated the city. Certain youngsters were sent to clear the guards away, but she never heard any sounds of their work.

Suddenly the Hukm began to run stealthily uphill, and Fava rushed up with them, into the gates of the city, holding Darrissea's hand. Apple Breath rushed ahead, eager to begin killing. There were no guards on the wall, no one minding the laser cannons. Here in the fog the guards had never seen the Hukm coming.

Fava and Darrissea crept down the city streets, and everywhere they went, the Hukm flowed ahead, while others raced past them. They saw no Blade Kin or Thralls, absolutely no one. The streets were lined with carts full of goods, and Fava realized she must be in a market sector. It was eerie, running dark narrow streets past buildings where the only light issued from fireplaces behind curtained windows. Among the carts were thousands of places to hide. After seven minutes Fava heard a shot in the distance. It could have been five miles away, at some outpost in the great sprawling city. A moment later she heard another shot, and another. Within three more minutes the crackling of gunfire was rising from the city, yet Fava never saw an enemy.

She ran with Darrissea down a street, and while the crackle of gunfire mingled with screams began to rise, she rounded a corner and came face-to-face with a dozen grim Blade Kin. Her heart stopped.

Four men and a woman had overturned a cart and set it ablaze. At the end of the block seven others were doing likewise. They wore green capes sewn with the golden dragon emblems of Bashevgo. The sergeant saw them, shouted, "Quickly, come in here! Hukm have attacked!"

Fava could not move. She had promised Phylomon to use the fader sparingly, and she had not yet tested the device, but suddenly she knew she could not follow Phylomon's orders. She reached up and squeezed the ivory brooch, and everyone stopped.

She stood a moment studying the sergeant, torch in hand. The flames on the torch writhed slowly, like eelgrass blown by a soft underwater current, and the man did not move. There were sounds, deep popping noises at the edge of hearing, a distant roaring like the sound of the ocean. The air seemed thick when she turned her head, as if she sloshed water, or as if a strong wind blew against her. Fava pulled her knife and rushed forward a few steps, the air beating at her face, and stabbed the sergeant in the throat.

Shoving the knife into him was like stabbing into hard clay, and it took a moment to make a wide cut, then she moved forward and stabbed another and another. By the time she got the sixth throat slit, the Blade Kin must have become aware of her, for at the end of the street, one woman had raised a gun and her mouth was open to shout. Fava rushed forward and felt as if she were moving through water, pressing against some invisible mass.

The hammer was dropping on the gun, but Fava reached the Blade Kin before it fell. Fava slit her throat, recocked the gun, and set its safety before killing the others.

When she finished, she looked at her handiwork. All twelve Blade Kin stood with gashes on their throats, and the first three victims were stumbling.

She waited—suddenly the Blade Kin around her dropped, blood pumping from their necks, one with a cry of warning bubbling hot from her throat.

Darrissea stood, trembling. Gunfire crackled all across the city, and there was a roar of human screams and howls of pain from Hukm, and Fava had no idea whether they were winning or losing, and she thought it was the end of the world.

She looked up to the tops of the hills and saw the white towers around the capitol burning. Laser fire flashed around it. *Phylomon must be there,* she realized, and she ran for the capitol. The sound of gunfire grew frantic, and as clouds of smoke rose, the firelight reflecting off the smoke lit the city in a red haze.

They rushed down a long street and began finding dead Hukm mingled with the corpses of Blade Kin, and everywhere frightened Thralls were streaming out of houses, looking out windows. The street was a battle zone, and one Neanderthal woman rushed to Fava, grabbed her uniform and shouted, "Adja! Please, rescue us!" and Fava tried to push her away, and the woman shouted, "Please, I fear the Hukm!"

Fava stopped dead in her tracks, looked the woman in the face. The terror was genuine, and a slave ran from a building, grabbed the sword from a dead Blade Kin. The slave ran to a Hukm that lay bleeding on the dirty street, and hacked the monster, and that is when Fava knew they would lose. They would not be fighting a few hundred thousand Blade Kin. They would be fighting millions of slaves, terrified of the wild Hukm with their bloody reputation, and the monumental size of Phylomon's error struck her.

"The Hukm—" Darrissea started to explain, but Fava stopped her, pulled her up the street, and found that they were running through avenues littered with corpses, the dark bloody corpses of Blade Kin, the white furry corpses of giant Hukm. As they rushed to the steps of the capitol, they found the huge dome ablaze and the Hukm retreating, fleeing the city for the sheltering darkness.

A great blinding flash erupted in the sky, and the capitol exploded in a mushroom cloud that seemed to go up and up. Fava realized that Phylomon must have decimated the building with one of his hover mines. A moment later, to the north, a second mushroom cloud erupted—the barracks at Badger Hill.

"That's the signal to prepare for retreat," Darrissea whispered. And Fava froze, surprised that Phylomon would recognize that they were losing so quickly. The battle was not fifteen minutes old. Darrissea reached into her pack, removed a white rod, looked up at Fava, holding her harmonic disrupter. "Should we start the earthquake now?"

Fava looked down. "No! Tull and Anorath are here, and my mother! An earthquake could kill them!"

"But Phylomon said—"

"I don't care!" Fava shouted, then looked to see if anyone was watching. "If we do not worry about our own families, what of the Thralls? Think of their children!"

Darrissea stopped, still shaking. The street was choked with bodies of Hukm. "We're losing!" she shouted, and she began to weep.

"Then let's lose with honor," Fava said, and she took Darrissea's harmonic disrupter. "I . . . don't know what's happening. Let's find Phylomon."

They ran up the street toward the capitol, unprepared for the scene that awaited. The great dome had collapsed, and thousands of Blade Kin lay dead before it like blackened flies. Flames licked the sky.

Yet hundreds more Blade Kin swarmed around a pile of bracken in the courtyard. Fava heard gunshots and shouting, and saw a blue flash of lightning from the bracken, and Phylomon stood there alone, sword flashing, among hundreds of Blade Kin, and they were fighting him.

Phylomon pleaded, shouting a cry of "Freedom," but the Blade Kin became like mad wolves who have circled a bear and lost all sense. She watched the Blade Kin shoot Phylomon a dozen times, and his symbiote withstood the bullets. She had no idea whether he could keep it up. The Starfarer's skin had already turned from its normal blue to a pale gray that looked half-dead. He stepped back and blew at his enemies, and a cloud of smoke issued from his mouth. Hundreds of Blade Kin, touched by the cloud, dropped. Fava remembered the black cube he had swallowed days before.

Phylomon hurried into the wake of his cloud, rushed through the shadows. A lone man in red armor leapt in front of Phylomon, and the two struggled for a heartbeat before Phylomon tossed him aside. Guns fired, and the bullets knocked Phylomon to the ground.

Darrissea shouted, "Wait! He came to save you! Stop!"

Phylomon began crawling, and the Blade Kin faded back from the black cloud and fired through it, again and again, until the Starfarer collapsed. Still they fired.

The flames from the capitol leapt into the air, and in the red light Fava squeezed the ivory button to her Fader, hoping it had had time to recharge. Nothing happened. She squeezed it again while the Blade Kin shot Phylomon. She could see now that his blue skin had faded to white, and finally one Blade Kin shouted for his men to stop firing.

An old Blade Kin commander, a man with a black robe and an eye patch, went to the white body of Phylomon, kicked him onto his back. The commander stood looking down for a long time, grinning.

Darrissea began to weep, tried to pull away and rush to Phylomon. Fava grabbed her arm and said, "Listen!" The gunfire had stopped, and they turned and looked over the city. On the hill, their view unobstructed, they could see that everywhere thousands of fires lit the streets and slaves were issuing from hovels, hacking the dead Hukm, leaping for joy and shouting.

"They don't understand," Fava whispered. "They don't understand what we tried to give them. They think they've won. It's the end of the world."

Fava grabbed Darrissea's wrist, and together they faded back into an alley, away from the fires, and held each other.

Tull lay in his cell, not knowing whether it was night or day. He'd wakened to a tremble, thinking a quake had struck, but the trembling ceased. An hour later he heard the guards shouting, jubilant voices, and went to the cell door and looked down the hall.

It was choked with men, armored guards in heavy wool cloaks. They came to his cell in a knot, shouting and talking excitedly, one of them saying, "Careful, careful," and someone else saying, "I have his foot. I have it!" They opened the cell across the narrow hallway from Tull and brought their prisoner.

At first Tull thought it a corpse, for he saw only a long, narrow, ash-gray hand, yet as they turned the corner by his cell, he saw the thin face, the hairless brows, and recognized Phylomon. They dumped the Starfarer in an empty cell, then slammed the door and made it sure with chains.

"Phylomon?" Tull called once the guards left, but the Starfarer did not answer. Tull watched, unsure if Phylomon was breathing or if he only imagined it.

At long last Phylomon moved a single finger. Tull heard the clanging of metal doors, heavy bootsteps, and the hallway filled with people again.

Mahkawn came into view, leading a tall man who wore red robes with a deep hood. Tull somehow hoped that Mahkawn would speak to him, but the Black Cyclops ignored him, and instead they stood looking at Phylomon.

"Are you sure you left him alive?" the man in red asked.

"Yes, My Lord," Mahkawn said. "Barely." Tull could think of only one person who ranked higher than Mahkawn, and he was amazed to see the Slave Lord. Tantos stood tall—almost as tall as Phylomon's seven feet—as if he held the pure blood of the Starfarers of old. Tantos had his back to Tull, so that Tull could not see his face.

"Remove the straw from Phylomon's cell," Tantos said, "so that he does not eat it and receive nourishment. See that he gets no food or drink for one month. At the end of that time, bring his skin to me."

"Yes, My Lord," Mahkawn answered. "If you wish, we can skin him alive for you now. He is very weak."

Tantos leaned forward, wrapped his lean hands

around the bars of Phylomon's cell, and Tull saw that they were red, as dark red as a cardinal. "No. He has done me great harm these past two centuries. I want him to die slowly."

"I could arrange that," Mahkawn said. "A little water would keep him longer."

"No," Tantos said. "I killed his brother by keeping him in a pit for months, without food or drink. The symbiote wrung water from the air, as much as it could. No, Phylomon's symbiote has been his ally these many years, but without food or water, it will be forced to eat him. That torture is more exquisite than anything you could devise."

Tantos turned. Tull saw a brief flash of his face under the deep hood, a crimson face without hair or lashes. The guards came again, chained Phylomon where he lay.

Tull counted the days by the number of meals served, and for the next four days he sat in his cell, and from time to time he would get up and look at Phylomon. The blue man lay on his back, his right hand in the air as if grasping something, his head turned to the left. He did not move in four days outside the shallowest breathing, and sometimes Tull would speak to him in the darkness, try to say something to comfort the dying man. Finally, once when the torches were burned down to stubs and fluttered in their sconces, Phylomon moaned in pain, begging for water.

Khur was sleeping in his cell, so Tull spoke softly. "There is no water," Tull said, and the blue man lay silent for a long time.

"Chaa said you could throw down the Slave Lords," Phylomon told Tull at last. "He said . . . you could destroy them, if you, get free."

Tull went to the bars of his cell and pressed his face tight against them. Phylomon lay in the same position, unmoved, and if Tull hadn't heard the words, he would have sworn that the mound couldn't speak.

"What did he say?" Tull asked.

"Before we captured the serpents, Chaa, told me . . . you would throw down the slave lords." Phylomon's dry lips barely moved. "He told me, I'd die, horribly."

"Is it horrible?" Tull asked.

"I feel the symbiote," Phylomon said at last, "consuming. It has . . . kept me alive—centuries. Now, I keep it alive."

Tull said, "In order to get free, the Blade Kin want me to become like them. They'll put me in the arena, and they want me to fight other innocent men."

"They want you to fight . . . criminals, who deserve to die."

"But some do not," Tull said.

"I have battled . . . a thousand years. Watched, half a million, innocent men—die. Carry on that fight. Their blood, is on your hands. Free yourself."

Tull lay thinking. "I'm afraid," he said at last. "To kill innocent men is . . . Mahkawn knows me. He sees himself in me. It would be too easy to become like him." Phylomon did not answer, and lay as if sleeping. Tull strained against his chains, snapping them at odd angles, trying to find some way to pull them from the ground. But the chains were well anchored, and hours of struggling bought him only bloodied limbs.

Phylomon did not speak for the rest of the day, and on the next, his chest began to heave, and he gasped for air. After a long time he wretched and choked on his vomit, then stopped breathing altogether. Tull called for the guards, told them what had happened, and they brought Tantos and Mahkawn down to witness the death.

Tantos looked at the body for a long time, felt for a pulse, then said, "Leave it, for another three weeks. Do not let it out of its chains."

"But he's dead!" Mahkawn countered. "Smell him. He's beginning to stink."

"Perhaps," Tantos said, leaving.

For the following week Tull worked at his chains

daily. He watched Phylomon's body rot, saw flies enter the mouth and lay their eggs, watched as the belly swelled and maggots erupted through the symbiote. The reek become loathsome beyond belief, as if Phylomon were a dozen corpses, and the guards began to shun Tull's part of the prison, giving him more time to work his chains. Until one night ten Blade Kin dressed in the green cloaks of the city guard came and brought him the news. "You will fight in the arena tomorrow, and if you win, you may give your ear to become one of us." Then they broke both his thumbs with a hammer.

That night, as Tull lay in pain, he dared dream of destroying the nations of Craal and Bashevgo, of killing their armies and tearing down their prisons. He dreamed of Fava beside him.

The predawn fog came thick as a blanket, scented with smoke and blood. Fires still burned across town in the gloam, flickering red. Fava and Darrissea walked the streets, looking among the white-furred corpses. Since the south wall had been best defended, the large females had made up the southern attack force while the smaller male Hukm had gone north. Because of this, Fava and Darrissea found themselves walking the streets looking at the bodies of slaughtered women, thousands upon thousands of them, gray shadows in the early morning. They had never imagined in the darkness that so many Hukm had died in the battle.

They found Ironwood Woman, the great queen of the Hukm, lying on her stomach in a pool of her own blood beside a burning wagon, the great oak-bead necklace identifying her more than the twisted features in her face. Fava and Darrissea used all their strength to turn the queen over.

"She almost made it back to the wilderness," Fava said, nodding toward the gates by the docks south of town. Darrissea began to cry, little coughing spasms that jerked out of her. "Don't do that," Fava warned. "We must act like Blade Kin now."

"What's the purpose?" Darrissea asked. "Everyone is dead. Ironwood Woman. Phylomon. It's been an hour since we've heard a gunshot. The Okanjara must all have been killed. Even if we do find our friends and manage to sneak them out of town, everyone is dead, and we have no place to run."

Fava looked down at the twisted features of Ironwood Woman. "Not me," she said. "I'm not dead. I will never die." She ground her teeth. Thor would be rising soon. Already it was casting a strange orange glow through the fog. A brown deer tick was crawling in the fur by Ironwood Woman's large, too-human ear.

"What are you thinking?" Darrissea said.

Fava got a purposeful expression on her face, and she sat down on her heels, closed Ironwood Woman's eyes. "Phylomon lived for a thousand years and fought the Blade Kin. Even if he is dead, perhaps his skin is not. He has made me a fader and given me some power. What if I were to wear Phylomon's skin? I could fight them forever."

Darrissea looked up into Fava's eyes, held them for a moment. "You would be killed, like Phylomon."

"Still," Fava said, "we must make certain that Phylomon's skin does not fall into the wrong hands."

"You have *owe taxa,* worms in the head," Darrissea said.

"Not worms," Fava said. "Hope." A bell rung to the north of them.

"Where are we going to stay?" Darrissea asked. "Do they have inns here?"

Fava looked up and down the street. "They must, somewhere. We can find one when it gets light." Secretly, Fava wished that one of the Okanjara warriors would come running out of the fog, someone to save her. But the Okanjara were far to the north.

Across the city in the predawn, people began to exit their houses. Fava realized that the bell had been a signal—something to tell common slaves they could come out. Within five minutes the streets filled. Slaves began cleaning, moving dead Hukm into carts without supervision. Many of them carried torches. A hundred Blade Kin marched out of the fog, and the commander looked at Fava's and Darrissea's uniforms, ordered them back to their company, jerking his head north.

North, Fava thought. *Perhaps we can find a band of the Okanjara warriors yet.* The women headed back up through town, walking nearly a mile, and found Blade Kin everywhere forming into groups of hundreds and thousands. Soon the streets were swirling with Blade Kin, alive with the march of feet, the sounds of drums, and all of the warriors were heading south by torchlight to try to overtake the escaping Hukm. The slaves cheered and leaned precariously from their windows, urging them on, waving rags.

The Blade Kin are heroes, Fava realized, and at last a company came by that was uniformed as Fava and Darrissea were. The commander stopped momentarily, studied their faces as if trying to place them. He was an older man, a human with a strong jaw, black pearls for eyes, and graying hair. He wore a silver dragon pin on his cape, and many in his command carried torches to light the way.

He pounded his chest in salute, and the girls saluted back. The streets seemed almost festive now with the roar of applause, the bright Blade Kin uniforms, the drums, the marching feet. The Dragon Captain shouted at the women, his eyes burning with accusation, but the words were carried away by the noise of the streets. Fava leaned forward to hear, and the Dragon Captain pointed to the ground behind him, shouted again.

Darrissea grabbed Fava's arm, frightened, and they fell in line, hurrying downhill. The streets were a fiery river in the fog, dark bodies of Blade Kin in black leather armor and red capes, carrying torches, flowing downhill like a river of lava to the frozen sea. The walls of houses were canyon walls, dark and forbidding, rising on each side.

Fava and Darrissea marched downhill, south, bone weary. Fava had not slept for nearly twenty-four hours, and they were marching, pushed from behind by those Blade Kin who were most eager to fight, and soon it all became a swirling in her mind.

They marched to the sea, and in the foot-deep snow the Blade Kin began to run, a great race to overtake the Hukm. Fava had no choice but to run too. She paced herself, racing beside Darrissea, and soon found that she was gasping for breath, trying to keep up.

She scooped snow to cool her burning tongue, found it odd that she was so hot when they were running through white fog and snow. Everywhere around her was a sea of bodies and torches, and she fought her way for each step, afraid that if she slowed, she would be trampled.

At least we are going the right way, Fava thought. The Hukm had left their mammoths in the hills so they could make a hasty retreat, and now the Blade Kin were rushing headlong toward them. Fava glanced up at the rising moon, turned, and realized Darrissea was falling behind. She ran and grasped the girl's hand.

They rushed across the frozen sea and suddenly turned—on orders—heading east, using the sea as a road, and Fava realized that someone must have spied the Hukm with their herds of mammoths, must have guessed the direction they would flee. They ran for nearly an hour and their feet were a dull roar on the ice. The fog was thick so low, and Fava could see nothing, began to fall behind the faster Blade Kin.

Then she heard a distant rumbling, like the sound of thunder. The ice vibrated under her, but she still ran forward, saw men halting, throwing up their hands in indecision. "They're charging! They're charging!" someone shouted, and then the Blade Kin retreated, racing back through the mist.

The mammoth was upon her before Fava realized

the danger. One moment she was running through the fog, and the next a mammoth charged past her, a great black mountain of flesh with curving ivory tusks, a young Hukm upon its back, urging it forward. Guns began discharging, and Fava was stunned to realize that she was so close to some front, and then another mammoth rushed past her, and another, and another trampled a man beside her, and the thunder of mammoths stampeding over the ice roared in her ears.

They're killing themselves, Fava realized, looking at the young Hukm, *taking the Blade Kin with them rather than surrender.* Fava turned, saw men behind fleeing. She spun again. A dark mammoth bore down on her, twisting its head from side to side, well aware that it was supposed to kill her. The child that drove it aimed for her unerringly, and Fava pressed her ivory button.

The world went still. Darrissea stood only a few feet away, mouth agape. Fava grabbed the girl and rushed forward in a fog that seemed thick as water—pushed Darrissea up on the mammoth's back. Fava climbed up by grabbing the mammoth's long hair. From the mammoth's hump, she looked out over the battlefield and saw torchbearers in the fog, saw mammoths around her. Many did not have riders. The Hukm had left nearly thirty thousand mammoths in the hills south of town. Now all of them seemed to be on the ice. The fader did not give her its full five minutes.

One second Fava stood on the mammoth surveying the battlefield, and the next the mammoth lurched forward and she was clinging for her life as it charged. Darrissea screamed and grabbed Fava, then caught hold of the mammoth. They thundered through the darkness, flakes of snow flying up to slap their faces. The Blade Kin were no match in the snow. They could not run nearly as fast as the mammoths, and Fava's driver cut several of them down before a Blade Kin shot the boy.

Still the war mammoth thundered on. The Hukm had fought Blade Kin for centuries, and the mammoths knew their enemy, stampeded in a frenzy, trampling

Blade Kin, tossing them aside with their great tusks, sometimes grabbing them in their trunks and flipping them back over their shoulders. Fava could only hold on —not guide her mammoth. When its driver dropped from the saddle on the mammoth's neck, the mammoth did not even notice, nor did it notice Fava and Darrissea clinging to its back.

Fava saw a rising shadow before her, the isle of Bashevgo. The rumble of the mammoth's charge was a thunder, and mammoths trumpeted all around, and then she heard cannons firing, saw the flash of lasers through the fog. She could not imagine how the Blade Kin hoped to turn back such a charge.

The ice rumbled under the feet of thirty thousand mammoths, and screams of death and trumpeting filled the air, and then a laser flashed nearby and the air exploded, and her mammoth dropped, hitting icy water. Darrissea screamed, and for a moment Fava dropped beneath the waves, looking up through a clear dark sea at ice lit dimly from above.

The water took Fava's breath, shoved her from the saddle. She kicked twice, brushed the mammoth, and wrapped her hands in the long hair at its neck.

Darrissea thrashed, grabbed frantically at Fava's cloak. She caught a handful of Fava's hair, ripped it. Fava tried to pull her close.

The mammoth bobbed back above the surface, and all around her the mammoths trumpeted and thrashed in the water. Fava grasped the mammoth blindly, Darrissea clinging next to her, splashing toward Bashevgo while her stupid mammoth tried to climb every piece of floating ice. Often the mammoth fell and water swirled around Fava, buoying her, and she looked up at the great hump on the mammoth's back, wondered if she could climb where it would be dry and safer. Darrissea was shouting, holding Fava and shouting, but Fava's hearing had gone numb. Fava looked up and saw the laser flashing, realized that the Blade Kin were carving the ice, sinking both their own men and the Hukm on their war mammoths rather than risk a second attack.

Her mammoth struggled forward, and the cold water rushing around her, the cold air streaming into her lungs, numbed Fava's mind until she no longer felt the cold at all, felt only numbness, a dreamy warmth and desire to sleep.

Darrissea draped her arms around Fava. "Hold on! Hold on!" she said. "We have to get back. You have to find Tull."

The mammoth struggled on, slowing its movements, and she wondered why. She slept for a moment, then woke, found Darrissea cuddling with her, wrapping her robe around them both.

Moments later the mammoth seemed to find solid ice, went rushing up a hill and into the countryside. Fava dimly heard screams, the sound of gunfire, saw the wavering light of the moon rising above the fog, and realized that the mammoth was carrying them through the streets, through canyons where fires gleamed.

Darrissea was whispering to her, telling Fava to move. But she wanted only to sleep, so she unclenched her frozen hands from the mammoth's hair, pushed herself back . . . falling, falling between dark canyons, as if they were her mother's legs and she were a child drifting back into the womb.

Fava woke with a dozen blankets piled over her. She shivered so violently that no part of her body would hold still. Her teeth chattered so hard, she feared they would break, and for a long time she could not recall her name. Someone poured hot tea down her throat, and she choked, yet it felt good. A moment later she begged for more.

"Whose command are you in?" a man asked, and Fava looked up into the eyes of a Neanderthal, a man with such tender blue eyes that when she saw his ear missing, she could not believe he was Blade Kin.

"I . . . I . . . don't know," she answered.

"Do you know your name? Do you know where you are?"

"Ca . . . can't remember. I . . . can't."

"Do not trouble yourself," the man said. "I am a healer. I shall make you whole soon enough."

He placed his hand on her head, touching her temples with his fingers, cupping her jaw with his thumb, and he hummed wordlessly deep in his throat, making a sound that was almost a growl.

Something stirred within her, and Fava suddenly felt warm, as if she were bathed in a heated mist. Over the next few minutes her trembling faded completely so that she felt only warmth, a pleasant sensation not unlike drunkenness that engulfed her as surely as the ocean had engulfed her.

The healer began trembling, and at last he moved his hand away from her head, and he shivered. He studied Fava from the corners of his eyes, trembling, just watching her. *A psychic healer,* she realized, *here among the Blade Kin.* She was too tired to be amazed. As Fava lay still, she could hear the cries of men and women in pain around her, the sounds of a sick house with hundreds of injured.

"What is your name?" the healer asked.

"Fava."

He wrapped a blanket around himself and just sat, watching her. His eyes were deep-set under his brows, so that the blue eyes seemed to glow from within a shadowed cave. "You have a good spirit," he whispered. "Generous, like the winter pear tree." He emphasized the Pwi word for *generous,* Fava.

She nodded, rested her eyes. People cried all around, yet the healer sat next to Fava, unmoving. She looked at the building—large enough so thousands of people lay on the straw-covered floors, and every twenty feet beams of dark wood supported the ceiling. Each beam had an iron peg in it that held a lantern. The injured were spread in great lines, wrapped in bundles.

"Others need help," she said.

"I have touched their spirits, and I know what is in them," he answered. "Aside from the girl who brought you in, let them die."

She looked up at the healer sharply, ready to reprove him, saw that he spoke the truth. Though he professed to be a healer, he would let them die. How long had it been since a healer of his power had walked among the Pwi? Not in many years. Fava felt warm, comfortable, but her head spun, and she closed her eyes, just breathed. The man went to a fire a dozen yards off, then returned and handed her a cup of warm broth.

"Wertha," the healer said in answer to her unspoken question. "My name is Wertha. I may be a healer, but I am not as generous as you. I will not heal those who would destroy my people." He placed his hand on her head and sang in Pwi, using words that she recognized as ancient forms, words that her grandfathers had not spoken for generations. "Still, even here in Bashevgo, you can find some light if you look for it."

"I am not looking for light," Fava said.

"Yet the light is coming. Long ago, a great Spirit Walker named Pwichutwi said,

> *When the mountains walk on water*
> *when the blue undying sun lies broken,*
> *the Mother of Evil a son shall deliver,*
> *And this shall be the Okansharai's token:*
> *Delivered from death in a spray of blood,*
> *Call his name, Generous, and he shall rise,*
> *Light shall drench the earth, as if a flood,*
> *And all shall behold the Okansharai.*"

Fava looked at him sharply. The healer was not young, and he kept his blond hair in small tight braids like a dozen strings that crept down his back. "Who is this Okansharai?" Fava asked. Her heart leapt within her.

"How can you not know who the Okansharai is? Every child of Bashevgo learns the poem at his mother's feet, for this city is the Mother of Evil, and every slave woman hopes that her son will be the Okansharai. You are obviously not of this city, Fava." He leaned forward and whispered, "And if you were Blade Kin, you'd arrest me now, for I have just spoken the forbidden prophecy in your hearing."

Fava lurched back, wondering if this were a trap. "Are you not Blade Kin?" Fava asked. "I could not arrest another Blade Kin for this."

"I must be," Wertha said, "for like you, I am missing an ear. And like you, I wear the uniform of a Blade Kin."

The healer was shivering, hunched with a blanket wrapped about him. He did not look dangerous, though he spoke of dangerous things.

"Who is the Okansharai?"

Wertha said, "The Okansharai, it is said, is the freer of all. He will destroy the nation of Craal and her mother Bashevgo, then free the slaves. Some hold that there will be a great flood before he comes, so that it will appear that the mountains walk on water. Some say that his mother's name will be Fava, and that she will call him from her womb by the power of her own will. I do not profess to understand such things, and the Spirit Walker who foretold this died hundreds of years ago, and he was quite mad.

"Still"—he leaned forward and breathed in her ear —"Phylomon is finally slain. Has not the blue undying sun been broken? And last night I looked from the walls and saw mammoths running over the ice through the fog, and I must wonder: Did not the mountains walk on water, carrying you here, into the city that all Thralls call 'The Mother of Evil'? And is your name not Fava? Perhaps the prophecy is coming to pass, and you shall bear the child that will free us. When I healed you, I touched your womb. You carry a child within you."

"No!" Fava shouted, for she had not known she

was pregnant, and she did not want her child to be born in this city, condemned by some ancient prophecy to live as a warrior in hopes of freeing the world.

"It's true. You carry the child," Wertha said. "He shall bring light to the world."

"You're mad!" Fava countered.

"I know it is true: Last night, I dreamed a dream that reminded me of the prophecy. If not for it, I would never have found you here."

"What dream?" Fava asked.

"I dreamed that a great black crow flew over the land, reciting the words to the prophecy. The crow landed on this building. Now, I've long been a healer, but I would never have come to this building if not for the crow."

"Why not?" Fava asked, and she knew the crow could have only been her father, Chaa. He must have sent the message while on his last Spirit Walk. She breathed deep, trying to stanch the flow of tears that threatened to escape her at the thought. He was watching over her.

"I would not have come here because this is a barn where slavers store fodder for cattle," Wertha explained, and Fava suddenly realized she was lying on a hard floor, thinly covered with hay. At first she'd thought it must just be the way of the slavers, to house their wounded like animals, but now she saw that it was a necessity.

She lay still for a bit. "Will you help me?" Fava asked.

Wertha pulled a knife from a sheath at his waist. Before Fava realized what he was doing, he sliced off his left ear. "I'm yours to command, My Lady," he said, "even to death. Others in this city wait for the light. We will serve you." He lay the severed ear on her lap, a bloody token of his devotion.

"Then help me find my husband, a slave recently captured in Smilodon Bay. His name is Tull Genet. And I have others I am looking for, friends."

"As you command," Wertha said, and he got up, still wrapped in his blanket. "Though I do not know where to look for one slave in so large a city. The ships brought the captives in over a week ago. Tull could be anywhere by now—he could even have been sold into Craal."

Fava lay a moment, wondering, drinking the warm broth. Wertha stood over her, as if afraid to leave. Now that he had found the mother of his savior, he wanted only to be with her. "My husband killed four Blade Kin when they tried to take him. I think they will punish him."

Wertha closed his eyes thoughtfully. "They may send him to the mines. I will begin searching for him at once." Wertha stalked away, his eyes gleaming with the strange compelling light of a fanatic on a mission from god. Fava could not help but think he would get in trouble. If it were against the law to speak the ancient prophecy, then how much more so would it be to declare that the prophecy was coming to pass and to search among the mines for the father of the Okan-sharai.

For several minutes she rested, then realized that she was lying under the blankets in wet clothes. She searched among her belongings, found the packs Phylomon had given them with all nine rods. Yet something was missing: her fader brooch.

She recalled how Darrissea had grabbed for Fava's cape in the water, found the spot where the brooch had ripped free from the red wool. Fava closed her eyes. The brooch was at the bottom of the ocean.

Chapter 12
Decent Execution

Tull emerged from a hole in the ground into a great amphitheater of black stone —ancient, exotic, decadent in design. At each end of the oval were enormous statues of reclining Thrall women, their delicate breasts jutting skyward, bellies swollen as if with child, their twisted faces gazing open-mouthed into heaven. Their long, spread legs formed the oval at the center of the theater. Tull had just walked from a hole at the statue's vagina. Blade Kin in lacquered leather armor with green and crimson robes filled the stands.

Bodies of losers littered the arena sands, which were stained red with dry blood. From the stands Blade Kin shouted, and Tull stood for a moment, looking up at the sky, sniffing the air, feeling empty and dazed. The morning was cold, with a wet wind that smelled of rain. He hadn't seen daylight in weeks, and for some reason his swollen hand felt disconnected from his arm. His stomach knotted with fear. *They will want you to kill.* Tull wondered who it would be, what crime the man had committed.

Flocks of white gulls wheeled above the stadium, and during the lull, several of them dropped, grasping hungrily at animal bones and other tidbits that the Blade Kin tossed into the arena.

An announcer shouted Tull's name, listed his crimes. All morning long Tull had sat below, waiting for his first fight, listening to the cries from the stands. But none of the other warriors could lay claim to having killed so many Blade Kin as Tull, and once the announcer listed Tull's crimes, the Blade Kin rose to their feet in salute and shouted their approval.

On the far side of the arena, from beneath the legs of the great stone mother, came Khur. He strode forward, muscles rippling, flashing his sword overhead.

He saw Tull and faltered, quit smiling a moment, and as the announcer listed Khur's single crime of wounding a human, Tull realized he was being asked to kill a friend. The Blade Kin had matched them because they shared a common wall to their cell.

What do you want of life? Tull asked himself. *What do you want? You can die at his hand and win only death, or you can kill him and win what? Guilt for murdering a fool, win half a life as a Blade Kin?* Yet Phylomon's words rang in his ears, "You must get free!"

Khur advanced on Tull, circling slowly. "You are a worthy adversary," Khur said, feinting a thrust with his sword. Tull leapt back. Khur smiled. "We must give them a good show! They will reward us afterward, should one of us live to become Blade Kin."

Khur leapt in, thrusting. Tull sought to parry, but Khur twisted his blade so that it slashed Tull's chest, then drew the blade back, trying to slice deeper. Tull leapt aside just in time, and Khur grinned ferociously. Tull realized that Khur had tried to cajole him into lowering his guard.

Tull thrust his sword, and Khur deftly parried, slashed up, catching Tull's elbow. "Where did you learn to fight?" Tull asked, and Khur grinned.

"When I was not sleeping with my lady, I guarded her." He leapt forward, slashing and chopping with an agility that astonished Tull; it was all he could do to parry the blows and step back. "I am sorry that in all the days we slept side by side, I forgot to mention this."

Tull stumbled, blocking a blow. Each time he parried, his swollen thumb spasmed in pain. He managed to kick at Khur, forcing him back, but the young Neanderthal slashed at Tull's legs, and Tull tripped. Khur swung viciously; Tull tried to duck beneath the blow and parry simultaneously. The crowd roared in awe, and Tull never knew what hit him. Tull fell on his back, stunned, bleeding from the scalp. Khur stood over him, waving his sword in triumph before dealing the death blow, and the crowd cheered, went silent.

Yet one voice continued shouting: Fava's, "Get up, Tull! Kill him! Get up!"

Khur stepped back, eyes flashing dangerously, and raised his sword, begging the audience for more applause.

Tull twisted his head groggily, saw Fava on the lowest seats, dressed as a Blade Kin. He wanted to go to her, but Fava shouted his name, horror on her face. His mind cleared, suddenly recognizing the danger.

He rolled to his knees, faced Khur, and the young Neanderthal grinned down at him. "So you wish to make a fight of it, my friend?"

In one moment of clarity Tull saw that there was no innocence left in Khur, only madness disguised as innocence. Khur would willingly chop him up. Tull laughed, for it all made sense: The Blade Kin allowed only the most promising criminals into the arenas, and Khur showed promise at becoming Blade Kin. All these men would be like him, morally tainted.

"I'll make a fight of it, if you let me," Tull said. Tull could hardly grip the sword with his broken thumb, so he ripped a strip of cloth from his tunic, then wrapped it around his sword and his hand, giving him some purchase. Khur stepped away, waving his sword at the audience. The Blade Kin howled and applauded the spectacle.

When Tull finished, he held out his sword, circled cautiously, watching Khur's eyes. Khur leapt in with a series of feints, testing Tull, then leapt back. Tull shouted and leapt forward, slicing down with all his might. Khur tried to slap the blade away, parry it, but he did not count on Tull's incredible strength. Khur's sword snapped at the hilt, and Tull's blade pierced Khur's skull, slit him from head to belly, so that blood sprayed across the crowd.

The Blade Kin roared and stomped their feet, screaming in approbation, and Tull raised his bloody sword over his head, walked the ring in a circle, and did not halt when he saw Fava, standing in the crowd next to Darrissea and some strange young man.

In the stands Wertha leaned forward, whispered in Fava's ear.

> *"And this shall be the Okansharai's token:*
> *Delivered from the earth in a spray of blood,*
> *Call his name, Generous, and he shall rise."*

Wertha did not have to recite any more of the prophecy. There was awe in the man's voice, as he suddenly saw that Tull had fulfilled the words—rising from the tunnels under the stadium, spraying the audience with blood once Fava had called his name. Fava watched Tull go underground. When he had first come out, he had looked weak, defeated. Now he was tense, coiled. She had never seen her husband looking so dangerous, never seen that manic gleam in his eyes so close to escaping. When he had paraded past with his bloody sword, she remembered the words that had been spoken of him back in Smilodon Bay: "He has revolution in his eyes." The madness was there, the blood lust, and at that moment he looked like the Blade Kin who howled around her. He'd become a predator, and she was prey. Her skin crawled at the thought of being near so many of them, of having the Blade Kin brush her as they passed.

Weeks spent hunting Tull, and this is what it

brought her, shame. Fava had not imagined such a reunion.

Tull fought three times over the next five hours. As a big Tcho-Pwi, he stood taller than Neanderthals, and he was broader of shoulder and more powerful than any of the humans. He did not finesse his opponents and instead opted for speed and power. He did not give them time to think, but instead charged across the arena sands as soon as they let him out of the gate. He slit two men open with ease, but engaged in a longer fight with the third. In late afternoon Tull began to tire.

In the last fight of the day, fought in the gloom of a setting sun, the final six pairs of combatants all approached one another carefully, calculating. They used longspears for this final round, a weapon Tull did not fancy.

He showed it in the arena, taking the spear and breaking it over his knee. He threw the halves to the ground and beckoned his opponent with open hands, lulling him into a false sense of security.

Tull's opponent was small, a human with speed and deftness, and he attacked too quickly, feinting a lunge. Tull grasped the end of the spear quicker than the little man could believe, ripped it from his hands, and drove the butt end into the man's chest, burying it two feet, then he flipped the little man high into the air, tossing him over the arena walls into the crowd.

The Blade Kin rose to their feet, chanting Tull's name, over and over. Tull marched around the arena twice, then stopped before Fava. He looked up past her head as he took the spear, cut off a tip of his ear, and tossed it into the stands.

Fava thought he had thrown the thing to her, but it landed in the crowd behind. Tull stalked back down to the dungeon looking refreshed, invigorated.

They watched the final two rounds in silence. As the crowd rose to depart, Wertha ventured, "Tomorrow Tull will win a place among the Blade Kin. When all the others lie slain, he will be standing."

"I think Thakunka will best him," a man said from the crowd behind, interrupting their conversation. "Tull has strength and speed, but Thakunka has more skill and versatility." Fava started to rebuke the stranger, but Darrissea took her arm, calming her.

Darrissea looked up, said, "Perhaps this Tull would have more skill and versatility if his thumbs had not been broken before the fight. I'd have liked to have seen him fight without being hampered."

The man grunted, Fava looked up. It was an old Neanderthal with a deep voice, a black cloak and a patch over his eye. Wertha pounded his chest in salute, and Fava followed him uncertainly.

"Omnipotent," Wertha mouthed.

The Black Cyclops waved his hand, muttering for them to be at ease, but Fava could not unbow her neck. She was far too aware that this man was supposed to be her lord, her master, and she feared that he would suspect her, recognize her for a stranger.

"I caught Tull in the Rough," Mahkawn said, "and believe me, too many of my men have seen him fight unhampered. He is a good warrior. As is Thakunka. I will grieve when one of them dies." He pulled something out of his robe, a bit of flesh, and Fava realized that it was part of Tull's ear, the small piece he had tossed into the crowd. Tull had thrown it to the Omnipotent.

"What of Tull's family?" Fava asked. "Has he spoken of it? Does he have younger brothers or sisters of such size and caliber that might be brought into the brotherhood? Perhaps a child that he has sired, even one still waiting in his wife's belly?"

"No," Mahkawn answered, departing through the crowd.

Tantos summoned Mahkawn to his chambers that night, only hours before dawn. Mahkawn had ridden the Death's Head Train and was surprised that at two hours before dawn, Tantos did not sleep. It was sometimes rumored that Tantos never slept, that his symbiote kept him awake for weeks on end.

Whatever the truth, Mahkawn waited in the chambers while Tantos informed him of strange attacks upon Blade Kin in the wilderness, of men and women found bled like cattle within the city.

"The attacks have been stepping up, becoming more common. We have found manlike creatures in the countryside, eaters of blood. We've even brought back the bodies of some. Our surgeons have examined the corpses, hoping to devise tests. The blood eaters can duplicate almost any human or Neanderthal form, but their faces are filled with bladders. If we lance them, they deflate. I have had the secret arm of the brotherhood watching day and night, and we have found that we can usually discover the identity of the blood eaters quickly.

"Still, if we give them time, they will learn, and they could infiltrate every level of our society. Because of this, I have quarantined the city. We know the general direction of where the Creators lie, and I am gathering forces in preparation to attack. We should be able to leave within the next four weeks."

"Very good," Mahkawn said. "How can I serve you?"

Tantos inclined his head, turned to the Blade Kin as if his thoughts had been disrupted. "As I said, I've had my spies working overtime, and we have found something. After defeating the Hukm, we took in numerous Okanjara prisoners north of the city, and some of them have been quite clever at remaining hidden, posing as slaves. Now it has come to my attention that a certain Blade Kin woman has been searching for Tull Genet, sending messengers to the mines. This is the same Tull Genet who fought in the arena today."

"I see. Have you identified her?"

"Yes. One of my men followed her to the arena, where she cheered enthusiastically for the man."

"Have you questioned her?"

"Not yet. She has gathered accomplices around her, and we want to round them all up at once. Indeed, that is why I summoned you tonight. It is reported that you spoke with her today at the arena. What is your involvement with the woman?"

Mahkawn stepped backward, perplexed by the accusation. "I spoke to no one! I sat between two of my Dragon Captains during the entire display."

"You spoke to her shortly afterward, as you were leaving."

Mahkawn suddenly remembered exchanging comments with some man and a couple of women. "Yes, I remember her now. She asked if Tull had mentioned any family, or offspring. I thought she hoped only that his battle prowess had bred true."

"Then she is his family member? Someone who escaped at Smilodon Bay?"

"His wife perhaps," Mahkawn said. "He had a wife, and a small adopted son."

"She shows unusual courage, trying to free him this way. But there is a more important element to the whole thing. It seems that with Phylomon dead, some of the Thralls believe that the time has come at last when the 'undying blue sun is broken.' They believe that Tull is fulfilling Pwichutwi's ancient prophecies of the Okansharai. Even today, when Tull came out of the earth in the arena from between the legs of the Mother of Evil and splashed his audience with blood, some Thralls whispered that he fulfilled the prophecies."

Mahkawn laughed.

"You laugh," Tantos chided, "but the Thralls believe. You broke Tull's thumbs before the duels, but that has not slowed him. Tull must die tonight."

"I do not believe he can win tomorrow," Mahkawn ventured. "His competition is too good, given Tull's incapacity."

"And I believe this has gone too far," Tantos said.

"You will kill him tonight. I want you to drive the sword into him yourself."

"But he has freely given his ear! By all the old laws, he is almost Blade Kin!"

"I will not have Tull glorified by these proceedings!" Tantos shouted, and Mahkawn stepped back. He had never seen the Lord show such wrath. "You will kill him by your own hand tonight! And you will take Atherkula to witness the deed! He has been clamoring for the slave's blood, let him be gratified. As for the wife, I have already sent troops to round up her and her cronies. They have already been taken to the dungeons. She too shall witness the murder. Let her see the end of her Okansharai! You will handle this matter. Handle it!"

Tantos stepped forward, pulled the golden scourge from Mahkawn's belt. "Your softness has displeased me. I shall give my favor to Atherkula now. You are dismissed."

"Yes, My Lord," Mahkawn said. He bowed low, left the room. He stopped outside the door, felt at his belt where the scourge had been. *I have lost his favor. He has a right to be disappointed,* Mahkawn thought, yet he realized that, given time, he could win that favor back. *I should not have let my sympathies for this slave cloud my judgment. I should have never let him live so long.*

Wertha stayed late in the market, buying food for Fava and Darrissea. He was not used to feeding so many, and with little money to pay, he forced himself to shop just before nightfall, so he could bargain cheap for scraps of meat or stale vegetables that might otherwise go to waste. Disguised as a Blade Kin, he need not worry about curfews, and so when the curfew bells tolled, he ran among the stalls, then tossed the cheap goods in a cloth bag and hurried home.

His path took him through the twisting heart of Thrall town, where the poorest of slaves lived above ground in wooden boxes and makeshift tents. These were the old and infirm—men and women whom the Lords were not yet ready to cull—people who worked hard every day in the fields or at the docks or carrying hod at some new factory just to prove their worth to their Slave Lords. A hard day of work bought two feedings of stew, a crust of bread, some wood for the cooking stoves. Some among Thrall-town were so sick that their masters no longer cared to give them proper quarters or food. These lay on pallets in the open, waiting either to recover or to die. None here held any delusions about their own worth.

Wertha passed a pallet where a child lay, a young girl whose legs had been crushed in an accident, and the legs were poorly bandaged. She reached her dirty hands out to him, asked only for water. He stopped, gave her drink and bread from his bag.

A cool wind blew, flapping the ragged tents, blowing smoke from the cooking fires wildly. No one was looking. Wertha could feel the healing power in him strong today, surging like the wind, waiting to be unleashed. He grabbed the girl's feet, pulled the leg bones out straight. The girl did not cry in pain, but clawed, grasping a handful of icy mud from the ground on each side of her pallet.

"Do not worry," Wertha said. "Nothing that I do will hurt you." He touched her legs, felt the pus and swelling beneath the skin, felt the bruises down to the bones. He let the power flow out of him then, a warmth that spread from his fingertips. "Kwitcha, my ally, be near me," Wertha said. "Make your power one with mine." He closed his eyes, felt the cool touch as a spirit filled him, shaking him like a sheet in the wind, but the healing did not come from his hands. Instead, a voice sounded behind him.

"Don't waste your powers tonight," a man said. "Don't be in a hurry to go home. You are being followed." The man was a Pwi, pale orange hair and blue eyes, with a fresh brand on his hand.

"Who are you?" Wertha asked.

"I am Fava's father, Chaa," the Pwi whispered. "I will see you again soon. Watch behind you!" Then Chaa disappeared, walking quickly away through the crates and shacks of Thrall town.

Wertha's spirit ally left him, like a cool breeze that whispered away, and Wertha studied the girl. He touched her only lightly, healing the fevered infection in her legs, leaving the broken bones to mend themselves in time. He fed the girl more from his stores and watered her again, then wandered through Thrall town aimlessly.

Do not be in a hurry to go home, Chaa had said, and at last Wertha moved more cautiously, heading north. Soon after nightfall, the streets came alive with Slave Lords on their way to parties. He skirted a procession where a woman on a hovercraft was dressed like a swan, all white feathers and pearls and silk and glittering. Fifty elegantly clad Neanderthal body guards ran beside her bearing torches, naked swords, and guns. Their eyes glittered dangerously, as if they suspected any straggler on the street to be an assassin from some other family.

Best not to stand in their way, best not to become a target for trouble. Wertha ducked into an alley till the woman passed, then headed back out. As he returned to the street, he glanced behind, noticed a man on the catwalk beside the road. The fellow slipped into a shadow, expertly blended into the night. The Invisible Arm of the Brotherhood.

Wertha crept through the streets and alleys, fled his pursuer when the time was right. When he felt sure he was alone, he headed for home, but stopped several blocks away and climbed to the roof of a building. From there he watched the streets in front of his house, and witnessed the arrest of Fava and Darrissea. When the Blade Kin dragged them off, Wertha followed discreetly.

Mahkawn walked out of Tantos's palace into the night and looked up. All three moons were up; the night sky was bright in spite of the clouds. On such nights Mahkawn often had trouble sleeping. A great-horned owl hooted, hunting over the fields. *Let the mice take care,* Mahkawn thought, recalling lines to an old children's poem.

Mahkawn leaned his head back, breathed deeply the fresh night air. It was just below freezing. Cool, but comfortable. He spread his arms and imagined that they were wings. *The thing I do tonight, it is not evil,* he told himself. *It simply is. The owl and the hawk should not befriend the mouse. Just as I should not have befriended Tull.* Friend. Mahkawn thought about the word for a long time. It had been many years since he had thought of someone as a friend. The Blade Kin were allies, but he did not enjoy their company. Pirazha, now, she was a friend, though he hardly dared admit it.

Still, if I were held captive in some prison in Craal, would Pirazha travel through the wilderness to rescue me? The idea seemed laughable, but for some reason Mahkawn could not put it back on the shelf of his mind. He considered for a long time as he walked to the Death's Head Train, climbed aboard. *I doubt that she would come,* he told himself. *She would resist the impulse, if the idea occurred to her at all. She is, perhaps, too much Blade Kin.*

Once inside, he sat in the dark metal capsule on a plush couch and let the train take him home to Bashevgo. The single lantern in the train swung on its rung in the ceiling, and Mahkawn thought carefully about how he would carry out the murder, planned it in his mind. It would be important to please Tantos and Atherkula, but Mahkawn found that he also wanted to please Tull, give the man death with some dignity. No gory mutilations, no sadistic torture. As for Tull's wife, though she was obviously a Thrall, she deserved some courtesy, too.

When Mahkawn reached the depot, he disembarked, went to the Temple of the Carnadine Sorcerers and woke Atherkula. It was nearly dawn by the time the sorcerer dressed and accompanied him to the arena's dungeon.

In one antechamber before they descended to the cells, Mahkawn and Atherkula found two pasty-faced women, one dark-haired human and one Pwi with a missing ear. Mahkawn almost laughed, for no Blade Kin would have shown such fear. He wondered how they could have fooled anyone.

"You," Mahkawn said nodding at the two, "are Thralls. You shall be branded and put into service." Mahkawn motioned. "Fava, come with me."

She rose from the floor, woodenly, and he took her hand, trying to comfort her. It was a technique that often worked with Thralls. They believed that if you were nice to them, then you would not hurt them later.

"I am pleased to meet you," Mahkawn told her, and Atherkula walked along behind, plodding silently, his black robes swishing. "I admire your courage in coming here, seeking to free Tull."

Mahkawn waited for her to speak, and she muttered something he could not make out, then said, "I . . . fear I do not know what you are talking about."

"You have nothing to fear from me," Mahkawn assured her. "Tull and I have become quite good friends. Close friends. You saw him throw his ear to me in the arena? If he wins his battles this morning, then I will be his commander. Do you understand this tradition among Blade Kin? So you see, you are the wife of a friend."

Fava nodded dumbly, and her jaw trembled.

"Good," Mahkawn said. "I am taking you to see him now. And I will put you under my own special care. You can be a slave in my personal household, if you like. I promise you that. You will be cared for."

Atherkula laughed abruptly, and Mahkawn shot a warning glance back at the sorcerer.

"I understand Tull has a smaller brother that escaped into the forest with you. I trust that the child is well? You have provided for him?" Fava nodded again, her pale green eyes pleading for him to ask no more about the child.

"Hmmm. We must retrieve the child then, bring the boy here where he can be properly cared for. I know that you Pwi, living out in the Rough, think that you have something—freedom. But it really is primitive. Here you will find that our medical facilities, our schools, are much better. If you want to give the child a future, you will help us bring him back here to Bashevgo."

"I have heard of your slave pens and your rapes and your mass graves," Fava said, "but not of your schools or doctors."

Atherkula chuckled openly.

"Well said," Mahkawn answered. "Still, there are benefits here. We will civilize you."

They reached the corner that rounded to Tull's cell and were assaulted by the unholy reek of Phylomon's rotting corpse. Mahkawn, unprepared for it, could hardly make his way forward. Both Fava and Atherkula covered their faces with their robes and walked as if pressing forward through a storm. They found Tull sitting, smiling, but his smile faltered when he saw Fava. The big Tcho-Pwi struggled at his chains.

"Fava," Tull shouted, and she broke then, ran to Tull's cell and stood outside, reaching for him, trying to touch his hand.

Mahkawn turned the key in its lock, opened Tull's door, and Fava ran to him, hugged him, and they were both weeping for joy.

Atherkula bent close to Mahkawn's ear and whispered, "You see how he cuddles with her! He could never have become Blade Kin."

Mahkawn found himself shaking, and he pulled his robe closer around his shoulder. He felt a strong desire to pull his sword and gut Atherkula. Instead, he turned and looked in the cell opposite from Tull's, at the dead body of Phylomon. The right hand, which had been almost pointing into the air, had shriveled, so that bony fingers curled up from it hideously. The stomach was a hole where flies crawled and maggots wandered. Mahkawn felt thankful that he could not see the face.

After several minutes Mahkawn went into the cell, pushed Fava outside, and closed the door so that he stood alone with Tull.

"I'm sorry, Tull," Mahkawn said. "I've been ordered by Lord Tantos to kill you. I had looked forward to . . ." He found his hands shaking, and behind him Fava shrieked and grabbed at the bars. Atherkula caught her from behind.

Tull was chained so that he could move neither left nor right. Mahkawn plunged his long blade under Tull's rib cage, and Tull's eyes bulged and his mouth came open in surprise. "Mahkawn . . . ," he shouted, and blood spurted from his side. "I never dreamed!"

Mahkawn held the sword there for a moment, then stepped in and shoved it up quickly, letting the natural curve of the blade guide it up under the rib cage, piercing the left lung. Blood poured down the runnels of the blade like water from a spout, messing Mahkawn's hand. He withdrew the sword and dropped it aside.

Tull was standing, his face white with terror, panting, and Mahkawn put his arms around him, trying to hold him up. Behind them Fava screamed and beat against the bars like a bird in its cage, and Atherkula held her. Fava's cape ripped free, and Atherkula shouted, "Guards! Guards! Hold the bitch!" spittle flying from his throat. It suddenly seemed strange to hear those human words, so thick and nasal in accent, coming from the throat of a Neanderthal. Mahkawn put his arms around Tull's shoulders, found tears streaming from his eyes.

"Forgive me!" Mahkawn whispered. "Tell me you forgive me! I will promise you anything! I will take Fava and your son and raise them as slaves in my own home!

They will be like children to me! I . . . I . . . my, my—!"

Mahkawn jerked back in surprise. He had almost called Tull his *son*.

Tull had been staring at the hole in his belly, at the blood gushing from it, taking tiny panting breaths. The room shook with Fava's cries, the sound of a madhouse, and Tull raised his eyes. Sweat was glistening on his forehead, and his eyes narrowed, as if he were peering at Mahkawn from a distance. He coughed, and blood came from his mouth.

"Okanjara, I Am Free!" Tull said, "By God's rotting teeth, it's so beautiful!" Then he trembled and sagged. Mahkawn set Tull down gently, held him as he died. And even to Mahkawn, the sound of Fava's shrieking seemed distant.

Tull's breathing stopped and his bladder loosed. His flaming yellow eyes stared open accusingly, so Mahkawn turned Tull's head to the wall and laid him down. Mahkawn took off his cape and used it to clean the blood from his sword. He sheathed the blade, then placed the cape over Tull, covering the body. The guards held Fava, and Mahkawn opened the door to the cell. "Let her in."

Fava rushed to Tull and grabbed his head, holding it and rocking back and forth, and her wails echoed down the stone corridors.

"A decent execution," Atherkula said. "Well handled, I thought."

Chapter 13
Born of the Mother of Evil

Tull had been building his dream house in his imagination before Fava came—stone upon stone—a spiral stair of cream marble, alcoves with tall arching windows to let in the golden light. Vine maples would grow in the alcoves, with gray-green trunks climbing up like snakes, and at the feet of the trees he would place a tiny pool with bushes where golden meadowlarks would sing, enjoying the endless summer of his home.

But then a few mumbled words, Fava hugging him, and Mahkawn standing in the background with Atherkula. Then the sword seemed to fill his belly, a piece of cold steel the only thing that kept him from feeling totally desolate inside, and Tull was looking at his blood flowing down the runnel of the blade, at Mahkawn's sweaty face, listening to his promises. "Forgive me, I will do anything . . ."

Tull beheld his dreams crumble. Heaven warped into the shape of a great hawk with stars in its feathers, black wings swept back, talons exposed, and the night descended.

The only birdsong is the cry of ravens. He coughed blood. Oblivion waited, demanding Tull's acceptance.

No hope goaded him on. No fear held him back. No cares could dissuade him.

And in that moment Tull accepted destruction, and with that acceptance, a great burning heaven flared inside him. *Okanjara!* the words formed naturally on his tongue, like dew on the petals of a mountain orchid, *I am free!*

For one endless moment he stared at perfect freedom. Beyond the Eridani who guarded the stars, beyond the Slave Lords with their armies and chains, beyond all his petty mortal fears and desires. "By God's rotting teeth," Tull said, "it's so beautiful!" and then he trembled, and began his last Spirit Walk.

In a great roaring thunder the world seemed to shatter, and Tull stood upon a plain of crumbled red stone where dim stars glowed in the amber air. Tull lifted away from the crater of cracked red stones he had built for himself and stood outside the clot of his soul, watching the clear thing that had once been his body settle in Mahkawn's arms. Atherkula held Fava, who was gray with grief, and as Tull rose, he could tell that the sorcerer was aware of him. Old Atherkula watched him intently, tracking him with his eyes. The hollow of Atherkula's soul was black, without lightning.

Tull rose from the shallow crater on the barren red plain, looked at Phylomon in his hole. A glowing spirit burned within the rotted flesh, and Tull gazed at it. He had seen opossums lie flat in a field as a child, had picked them up and carried them home for his mother to cook, and all the while that he carried them, the opossum would sit with eyes only partway open, unbreathing, looking so fully dead that Tull could never really be sure whether or not it had died from fright when Tull first touched it.

Around Phylomon's body, around the clear clot of his soul, Tull could discern a thin purple haze—the symbiote. Within the body, Phylomon's spirit still glowed. Phylomon's symbiote must have known the game of opossum, for it played an elaborate version.

The blue man lay among a small circle of broken red stones, with many breaches in the wall of his shelter. Tull picked up a few stones to try to plug the hole, view Phylomon's future. Within each stone he saw the same thing: Phylomon would die when Tantos had him skinned. The symbiote no longer had the strength to protect the Starfarer.

Tull viewed the scene and felt no outrage, no sense of loss. The life Phylomon lived now seemed of no consequence.

Tull drew upward without purpose, like a cinder rising from a fire. Below him on the barren plain, he saw a river, the river of time that Chaa had spoken of.

As before, the Land of Shapes had changed. Tull's spirit eyes seemed to be more open. Or perhaps, Tull realized, he finally saw more clearly because he was now unconnected to his body, free to wander the Land of Shapes as he had before birth. With no more than a thought, a simple desire, Tull stopped the river of time, imagining it was frozen, and with time frozen, he wandered Anee, haphazardly stacking stones around the Slave Lords to see how it could all end. He did not connect the pale lightning of his soul with theirs, did not seek to learn their hearts—merely to watch their end. He built magnificent elaborate structures of the stones, some plain, some exotic, shaping ten thousand futures.

He watched the humans of Anee destroy themselves a thousand times through greed and corruption— Slave Lords assassinating one another in an endless bid for power, till even Tantos would be brought down. He saw the possibilities for suicidal wars between factions of Blade Kin until the land itself became burned and barren. He saw Thralls revolt through a hundred lifetimes, slaughtering all humans in the act, till the planet crawled with Neanderthals who worshiped their own waning psychic powers and lost all semblance of technology. He saw the gentle Hukm rise up in other versions, eradicating mankind, then living peacefully off the land for endless generations.

It became an intellectual exercise, watching powers rise and fall in various combinations. He kept waiting to see if it could succeed in terms he would have considered emotionally valid during life.

He found one branch where, between treachery among Slave Lords and revolts among Neanderthals, a new world order came to pass. The two species bred to the point that they became one—yet they were neither humans nor Pwi. They became dispassionate beyond anything ever dreamed, mating only to produce dull offspring to replace themselves, eating only to fill their bellies. They became living statues that somehow managed to reproduce enough to seem viable.

Tull could not access the minds of the Creators, but he knew that somehow they would enter into the construct.

When Tull had watched the world end ten thousand times, he was still not satisfied. He loosed the river of time, let it thaw and flow again. The lightning of his soul floated over the red rock crags and mountains of Bashevgo, a brilliant golden ball of thistledown for those who had eyes to see. He wound his way through the valleys of cracked rock and over the sifting sands, returning to Fava.

He watched her shriek and wail above his corpse, calling his name, the clot of her soul gray with grief, the color of cobwebs. The clot of his body was clear, as if made from glass. She held his head, rocking back and forth, and Tull decided to try to speak, to connect with his body long enough to tell her not to grieve.

A gray morning rain carried the scent of salt spray and open seas for the first time in months, and out on the frozen ocean around Bashevgo, the morning thundered with the sounds of cracking ice, muted by rain. The slaves and businessmen of Bashevgo did not seem to notice the rain. Wertha paced among them outside the arena, shivering and drenched, an anonymous gray face in the cold morning crowd.

At the arena, the great statues of the Mothers of Evil leaned their heads back, catching the rain in their open mouths. The ancient slave artists who had constructed the statues had formed them so that the rainwater funneled out the women's eyes, as if they cried while giving birth.

Wertha had watched Atherkula and Mahkawn enter the dungeons shortly before dawn, and just as the sun was rising, he saw the sorcerer Atherkula amble out, his black cowl wrapped above him, picking his way through the wet and muddy streets with a smile on his face.

Moments later Fava announced her exit with wails of grief that echoed out from the corridors. The Blade Kin guards unlocked the gate, and two guards exited bearing a pallet with a bleeding man upon it. Wertha saw immediately that it was Tull, stained red from crotch to chin, his body as pale white as the belly of a fish. They had stripped him of his clothes, salvaging them for future use. And it suddenly struck Wertha how like a newborn child he looked, all bruised and covered with blood, pale from its cheesy covering.

Fava was shouting, "Tull, Tull!" beside herself. The crowds on the street barely turned to glance. Mahkawn stalked behind her, one hand clumsily touching her shoulder, unsure how to calm the woman. The guards set the pallet down in the rain as they rested and Mahkawn pulled Fava away from the sight, trying to drag her down the street.

Wertha hurried up toward the guard post, and a Neanderthal grabbed his sleeve, a stranger. The man had orange hair and wore the black cowl of a Blade Kin sorcerer. He emanated power. Wertha looked into deep-set eyes that had lived a thousand lifetimes, and recognized Chaa.

"Will you help me get the body of Tull?" Chaa said. "There is no time to waste, if we are to save him."

"Save him?"

Chaa grabbed Wertha's wrist and drew him toward the guards who rested over the body. Chaa said, "We have been ordered to help you dispose of this corpse."

One of the Blade Kin raised a brow. He was an older human, graying and fat. "You can have my end of the pallet," he said, and trudged back into the shelter under the stadium, fleeing the rain. The second guard, a skinny young boy, said, "Will you take him to the dump?"

Chaa looked up at him. "We've been ordered to take this one to Lord Tantos himself."

The boy nodded and backed away, obviously not eager to attract the attention of the Lord of Retribution. As Wertha leaned down to lift the pallet, he could sense the spirit there, pulsing in that miserable body.

They carried Tull through the cold rain, grunting and slipping over wet, muddy stones. Wertha kept expecting the Blade Kin to come stop them, to question them, until it finally occurred to him that perhaps no one had ever tried to steal a corpse from them before. They rounded a corner, and Chaa stopped, set down his end of the pallet. "Forgive me, Tull," Chaa said, "for this gift you would not take willingly." He opened his shirt and pulled out a thin strip of supple gray-blue leather, then placed it inside the wound in Tull's chest as if it were a compress.

They had to walk for nearly fifteen minutes, and all during that time Wertha looked down on Tull and trembled inside. Chaa finally stopped at a building, took them up to a small room. Chaa sat down exhausted.

Wertha stooped over Tull, touched the body, closed his eyes. He could see the spirit there, a pale fluttering thing, trying to remain connected to the body, inserting its pale fronds, experimenting with fingers, toes. The heart beat, barely; the lungs expanded so slowly that many healers would not have seen it. Yet, by all rights, Tull should be dead.

"What is this?" Wertha asked.

"He is a Spirit Walker," Chaa said, "trying to reconnect to his body. But he cannot do it unless we can heal him."

The healing power was strong in Wertha, billowing like a wind. He had not seriously tested his power in months, and he let his warm hands touch the cold body.

There, in the gut, the sword had entered, pushing aside pale blue intestines rather than piercing them. No food had spilled out of them to foul the abdominal cavity. But in the left lung, the soft pink spongy tissue was severed and clotted with blackish blood, while the sac around the lungs had burst, deflating them.

Wertha's fingers burned at the feel of such damage, eager to heal.

"Wait!" Chaa said. "You cannot do this alone, just as Tull cannot hope to raise himself without your help." Chaa knelt beside Wertha and held his hands.

Together, they closed their eyes, and Wertha unleashed the power, letting the warmth flow free. He could feel energy from Chaa, an unexpected amount of power, coursing through his hands.

"Call upon your ally for us," Chaa said.

Wertha hesitated, and began. "Kwitcha. Kwitcha, my ally, healer of old," Wertha said. "You who once raised the dead at Fox River and taught the mute to sing at Three Still Trees, be with me now."

For a moment Wertha sat and waited for the cool touch of his ally, but it did not come. He opened his eyes, looked at Chaa, but kept his burning hands on Tull.

"My life for his!" Wertha whispered. "My life for his!" Slowly he could feel the clotted blood in Tull's lungs melt as if it were thawing snow. Sweat formed on Wertha's forehead, long cold drops, and he prayed that the lungs would heal. He did nothing but touch, nothing but hold his hands there for long hours. His mind went numb, and eventually he could not feel the damage anymore. It was still there, but all the power had drained from him. Still, Wertha gave what little aid he could.

He smoothed the edges of the ragged flesh in Tull's side, washed and bandaged them. Chaa insisted that he leave the blue leather there. Wertha wrapped the broken joints in the young man's thumbs.

This is not how the Pwi did it in days of old, before they bred with humans, Wertha thought. *This is not how it happened in our lore. The great Talent Warriors of the past. Kwitcha raising the dead.* Chaa stood nearby, unable to channel him power any longer. Wertha rested for an hour, then placed his hands on Tull again, feeling the damage, the fragility within the boy. Yet nothing came out of Wertha's hands.

Wertha must have fallen asleep sometime during the night, for he woke when Chaa was placing a robe over him. "Come, you have done all you can," Chaa said at last.

"I . . . I thought surely Kwitcha would come," Wertha said.

"What, so you could raise the dead and better his reputation?" Chaa said. "No, we are not the Talent Warriors of old. You are not Kwitcha."

"What now?"

"Now," Chaa said. "I will go into the city and take back what is mine. My wife, my children. Fava and Darrissea. In a city so large, they will hardly be missed. Fava and Darrissea left weapons in your house—white rods in sacks. The Blade Kin did not take them, for they did not recognize them as weapons. Can you get them?"

"Yes," Wertha answered.

"Good. I will be back soon. I must prepare to release Phylomon the Starfarer from the dungeon."

"But he is dead. They say his carcass reeks."

"Then he will need a bath after we rescue him. I will see you in the morning. As for Tull, I no longer fear for him. He has the greatest healer alive today to care for him, and he is a Spirit Walker. We can be hard to kill."

Fava's stomach knotted in hunger, but she could not eat, could not drink. The killing grief had taken her since Tull's murder, and after four days she waited for her own death in the luxurious room Mahkawn had given her.

Her single bedroom in the mansion was larger than many homes in Bashevgo, and fine tapestries covered the walls with scenes of peaceful animal herds—mastodons grazing beside woolly mammoths while imperial lions watched from the shade of great trees. Sandalwood burned on the fire, scenting the room, and huge glass windows and a glass door overlooked a wide veranda and the ocean beyond. Freya, one of the smaller moons, hovered over the ocean, a blue globe covered with white swirling clouds. Mahkawn had assigned a matron to care for Fava, an old Pwi woman who sat in a rocking chair in the corner and talked incessantly of the antics of her grandchildren. Fava lay on the red silk sheets of a wide bed. Never had she lived in such luxury, yet she could not enjoy it.

"Please go away," Fava said to the matron, and the chinless old woman nodded, left the room. Fava was gazing out the window when almost immediately she saw a black shadow drop from the roof to the veranda— the shape of a man who ducked into deeper shadows so quickly, she could almost not be sure if she saw it.

Fava went to the window, saw a flash in the darkness along one wall, and a moment later a familiar figure emerged: Chaa stood before the glass door, unbolted it from outside. He wore the red uniform of the palace guard.

Fava rushed through the door, hugged him, and Chaa kissed her forehead. "What is—" she asked, but Chaa covered her lips with his fingers. The night air carried a biting cold, and Fava wore only a thin linen shirt, yet Chaa bolted the glass door from the outside, then pulled her along through the shadows to a rope that dangled from the roof. He picked her up, got her started on the rope. When she reached the roof, Fava found a strange uniform on the ground—black robes with red trim, tall black boots lined with rabbit fur. She pulled the warm clothing on gratefully, and Chaa reached the top of the roof.

He hugged her again, and a bitter wave of grief rose in her, and she began to cry. "Don't worry," Chaa said. "Tull is still alive, barely. I'll take you to him soon, but first we have much work to do. We have others to save this night. Come."

"Wait!" Fava said. "How did you escape? What are you doing?"

"It is not hard to escape from the mines if you know when the guards are going to blink, which paths to take in the darkness," Chaa said. "They don't even know I am gone."

"What of the others? What of Wayan and Darrissea and Mother?" Fava urged.

"Shhh," Chaa whispered. "In time. We can worry about them in time."

They tiptoed across the roof, leapt down to a high wall and into the streets of the city of Bashevgo. Chaa led her boldly, till they reached a doorway that led down under the streets. There he marched her through long tunnels where furnaces boiled water to generate the electricity needed to power Bashevgo's laser cannons.

They passed room after room where naked slaves worked in darkness, tossing logs into huge furnaces, their thin, muscled bodies sweating and starved. In the twisting light they looked like the inhabitants of some hell, and Chaa urged her forward, down hallways clotted with steam pipes.

After twenty minutes they reached a furnace where Chaa stopped, went in and spoke to the Blade Kin on duty. Chaa motioned toward a line of naked slaves against the wall, and the guard nodded, took a blanket from a pile, wrapped it around one of the slaves. In the shadows, Fava could not see who it was.

Chaa came back with Darrissea. Darrissea's face was pale, as if she were in shock, and great drops of sweat rolled down her chin and neck to disappear between her small breasts under the tattered blanket. The Blade Kin had shaved off most of her hair. Darrissea grabbed Fava and sobbed, "They were going to kill me here!"

Fava hugged her back and Chaa hissed, "Not here! Not now!" He took Fava's hand, led them at almost a run down the narrow tunnels until they reached a side opening and a ladder. They climbed up and found themselves outside a stockyard. The air smelled heavily of blood and dung; pigs grunted from pens nearby. Woden had joined Freya in the sky, casting double shadows, and Chaa led the women into a small grain shack. From a bin of oats, he pulled out a backpack and a set of plain street clothes and urged Darrissea to dress.

"We have much to do tonight," Chaa said. "Phylomon remains a prisoner under the arena, and we must rescue him, but we cannot let anyone know that we have taken him."

"But I saw Phylomon!" Fava said. "He's already dead!"

"Not dead," Chaa insisted, "but near death. He is wounded, and his symbiote cannot keep him alive much longer."

Chaa hefted the backpack. "Darrissea, you will remain nearby until we return at dawn."

She nodded, and Chaa led the way to the arena, walked calmly to the guard door, shoved a handful of papers through. "We have business inside. Lord Tantos wants one of his sorcerers to examine the corpse of the Starfarer."

The guard looked at the dragon insignia on Chaa's uniform, saluted, took the papers, and hurried to unlock the gates. Once inside, the guard lit a taper and offered to escort them to the cell, but Chaa brushed the offer aside, saying, "Remain at your post."

They hurried downstairs past row after row of empty cells. Fava recalled a few prisoners being in the cells only days before, but they were all gone; then she remembered the arena games. The prisoners who had survived were freed, which explained the light guard.

Fava smelled Phylomon long before they reached the cell. Someone had covered the body with straw and a blanket, apparently trying to reduce the smell, leaving only Phylomon's right hand and face exposed.

The eye sockets looked skeletal, and as Chaa pulled the blanket off, Fava saw maggots around Phylomon's bloated belly. Fava put her hand up over her nose, unable to withstand the rotting stench, but Chaa opened his pack, took a bottle of wine, and began pouring it down Phylomon's mouth.

The corpse did not move, and Fava wondered if her father had gone mad. Chaa stroked the Starfarer's forehead and said softly, "It is all right. I am a friend. Heal yourself." He spoke as if to a child, and Fava wondered at it, until she realized that Chaa was talking to the symbiote. He reached into his pack, took out a sponge, and poured wine over the sponge, then began dabbing the gray, papery skin. Almost immediately the skin began to change hue to a pale blue.

Chaa kept sponging the corpse for nearly an hour, and Fava watched as the distended belly sank and Phylomon's eyes began to bulge under the lids. The stench lessened. At last Phylomon's eyes fluttered open, and he gazed around with a vacant stare.

Reaching into the pack, Chaa began pulling out food—dried fish, a loaf of bread, apples. Fava fed the Starfarer slowly, while Chaa heaped straw in a pile, laid the blanket over it. Phylomon groaned, flexed his stiff fingers.

"The guard is wondering what takes us so long," Chaa said to Fava. "He will be coming downstairs. Go meet him, tell him your examination is not complete and you need more tapers. Pretend you don't know your way back to the cell, and get him to follow halfway until you 'remember' where to come. By no means are you to bring him back here."

Fava did as he asked. She met the guard halfway

and followed him back up to his guard shack. The fellow went into a side room, bent to pick up a couple of tapers from a stack, and as he did so, Chaa carried Phylomon to the shadowed doorway and stood, holding the Starfarer by the door.

Fava asked the guard to lead her back to the cell and stood aside for him to pass, shielding Chaa in the shadows, then let the guard lead her down. Exactly halfway to the cell, she "remembered" how to get back, and sent the guard away.

Fava sat in Phylomon's cell for several minutes, alone, and worried about how Chaa would get her out. Nearly an hour later Chaa returned, carrying the upper torso of a burned corpse. He laid it in the cell where Phylomon had been, dusted it with flour to color the skin gray, and Fava stared in amazement.

"How did you get back in?" Fava asked. "Where is the Starfarer?"

"I left the gate ajar, then sneaked back in while the guard took a pee. Phylomon is hidden in a wagon out on the street." When Chaa finished with the corpse, he stepped back, gazed at it thoughtfully. "That should fool them for a few days."

Fava stared. The corpse did look amazingly like Phylomon—the same high cheekbones. If the man had ever had hair, it was all burned away now. She didn't dare ask Chaa where he had managed to find the thing.

They left the arena together, and Chaa carried Phylomon back to the stockyards through a maze of winding alleys and narrow streets. A dozen times Blade Kin passed on side alleys—but each time Chaa would stop a moment before, always standing well in the shadows, never to be seen. She listened to him counting under his breath, and every second seemed to be orchestrated, so that at times he would run full-speed ahead, then wait for ten minutes in a shadow until some guard passed. His face was sweaty, twisted in concentration. Obviously he had spirit walked this path many times, practicing his escape. Without knowing the future, he could never have choreographed it. Without him Fava would have been captured a dozen times over. They made it back to the stockyards and met Darrissea, then hurried to a large barn and climbed into a hay loft.

Chaa set Phylomon down, then nearly fell himself from exhaustion. The Starfarer lay askew on the hay, apparently asleep.

The loft was freezing, and its hay smelled moldy. The walls had begun to warp, so that even in the shadows of dawn, Fava could see that the walls were uneven. No one apparently used the barn anymore.

"What do we do now?" Darrissea asked, and the dark-eyed girl sounded frightened. Her brief capture had left her unnerved.

"No one will come to this barn today," Chaa answered. "Tonight I can take you across town to a safe place where Tull and Zhopilla are hidden. Phylomon should be able to walk a little by dusk. Once we are safe, we will need to wait, give Tull and Phylomon some time to heal."

"Then what?" Fava asked.

"I don't know," Chaa said. "In Smilodon Bay the Blade Kin's attack interrupted my Spirit Walk. My vision ends here, tonight. Beyond that, I can only hope and do my best, like any other man."

On the following day, in a small room in a deserted apartment complex, Darrissea tended Phylomon. The blue man would seem to rouse for a moment. He had a look to his eye, a look of fear, of infinite pain, as if he feared Darrissea. But then he closed his eyes and fell away into a deep sleep. From time to time his skin would fade to a papery gray, and he would thrash his arms and mutter, in the throes of evil dreams. Then Darrissea would bathe his skin with wine and water, and it would turn a pale blue and lose its papery dryness for awhile.

Thus, on the following evening, while Fava lay beside Tull who was as still as death, Phylomon's eyes fluttered open and he simply stared at Darrissea for a long time. The pain was still in his eyes, and she wondered what it had been like for the Starfarer to be helpless while his symbiote slowly consumed him.

She fed him tenderly, and he drifted to sleep. When he woke two hours later, he pulled himself up from the floor, moving shakily, and crawled to sit beside the small fire in the fireplace. "How did I get here?"

"Chaa broke into the prison and freed you," Darrissea said. "You nearly died. Chaa managed to save Tull, too. He is still sleeping, trying to recover from his wounds."

The Starfarer gazed around the small room. Tull lay under a pile of mammoth-hair blankets in one corner, with Fava beside him. Chaa roused from his sleep, disturbed by the sound of voices, and sat up, looking at the Starfarer.

Phylomon simply said to Chaa, "Thank you."

"You are welcome, Starfarer," Chaa said.

Phylomon squinted, looked at the rough floor which smelled faintly sour from wood rot. "I lost," Phylomon said. "After a thousand years of fighting the Slave Lords, they have defeated me."

"You cannot rally the Thralls," Chaa agreed. "You are only a relic to them, something left from a forgotten age. They cannot love you as if you were one of their own, and they will not sacrifice for you if they do not love you."

"Then what can we do now?"

"I don't know," Chaa said, and he came and sat beside Phylomon and the fire, his arms wrapped around his knees. "I don't know. I discovered that the Blade Kin would attack while I was on my Spirit Walk, and I immediately began trying to learn how to free us. I was able to bring us here, but now my foresight fails me, and I cannot return to the Land of Shapes. My allies there have turned from me."

"You touched the minds of the Slave Lords?" Phylomon asked.

"Yes," Chaa answered. "That is how I learned

Tantos would attack the Rough. We could not have withstood him."

"So, I have failed," Phylomon said.

"We have both failed," Chaa corrected, fatigue evident in his voice.

"What do you mean?" Darrissea asked. "Do you plan to give up now?" The thought of surrender seemed alien to her.

"No," Phylomon said. "But our attack has left the Blade Kin stronger than before. The Rough is captured; the Hukm armies lie wasted. I can tell by the smell of the air that spring is here. The last Hukm will not be able to cross the sea to attack Bashevgo for another year. Beyond all this, I brought five portable laser cannons into the city—weapons more powerful than any seen here in three hundred years. Now the Blade Kin must have them. We will need to use Fava's fader if we are to steal those weapons back."

"Fava lost the brooch that goes to the fader," Darrissea said.

Phylomon looked at her, resigned, and began to laugh sadly. "Of course," he said. "Of course. And what of you, Chaa? What did you see in our future when you took your Spirit Walk? Have we any hope?"

"The future is dark to me," Chaa said, glancing back at Tull. "Perhaps if I had had a few more days to Spirit Walk. Still, there is Tull. I do not know why the beast approved of him. I did not see what was in his heart. We must decide now whether to let him live. I put the symbiote in his wound."

Phylomon sighed, "I feared you would do that."

"He needed it. I do not think he would have recovered without it."

"Yet if he is a talent warrior," Phylomon said, "as you foresaw, and if he overthrows the Lords of Craal and Bashevgo, he could sit upon the throne for ten thousand years, ruling in tyranny. Once the symbiote reaches maturity and covers his body, he will become nearly invincible. Perhaps we should kill him now, in his sleep."

"I may have erred," Chaa agreed. "Still, he may be our only hope."

Phylomon took Darrissea's hand, held it lightly. It seemed a spontaneous act of affection, and Darrissea wondered at it. She squeezed his hand tight. "This is my world, too," Darrissea said.

"What?" Phylomon asked, as if surprised she had dared speak.

"This is my world, too!" Darrissea said louder, suddenly angered. "And it belongs to Tull and Fava and the Slave Lords as much as it does to you. Who gave you the right to treat us as children? Who gave you the right to decide for us? You two can't even make one simple decision, you are so busy bickering."

"We are older than you," Chaa answered. "We know more about this matter."

Phylomon arched a brow on his hairless face, looked at Darrissea askance. "You are right," Phylomon said. "This is your world, too. You decide for us. What shall be our next step?"

Darrissea sat, looking at him. To her amazement, Phylomon seemed to be totally sincere, and Chaa stared at her patiently, awaiting her orders, and she suddenly realized what it must be like to be Phylomon or Chaa. Everywhere they went, people asked them for counsel, for solutions to problems, as if they knew the answers. And now they were admitting that they had no answers. Both of them feared Tull, and while Darrissea wanted to ridicule their fear as if it had no merit, she had seen Tull fight among the Blade Kin in the arena. He had not merely killed his enemies, he had reveled in their deaths. She recalled his last fight, when he had tossed the dying body of his foe over his head into the crowd, much to the applause of the Blade Kin, then cut off his own ear. What had Tull been telling them? Was he truly Blade Kin? And if he was a talent warrior, and if he overthrew Bashevgo, how could they hope that he would do anything more than take his place upon the throne? She imagined that a thousand years from now her ancestors would serve him, the Blue Lord.

Outside down the hall in the apartment complex, a board creaked. Both Phylomon and Chaa jerked their heads, listening. Darrissea heard another creaking, the sound of a quiet footstep, someone creeping toward the door in the middle of the night.

"Blade Kin?" Phylomon mouthed, and Chaa shrugged his shoulders. The footsteps came nearer, and someone stopped outside the door, snuffling, like a dog trying to catch a scent.

Chaa unsheathed a dagger, and Phylomon picked up a log from beside the fire to use as a club. Darrissea got up softly and went to the door, yanked it open.

A stranger stood there, a young man in his mid-twenties. He was handsome, with perfect skin and a disarming smile. He seemed surprised. Darrissea looked at the young man, instantly knew him for what he was. An oddly sweet scent filled the room.

"I . . . I'm sorry," the young man said. "I did not mean to wake you. I'm new to town, and I was only looking for some place to sleep."

"A strange human," Darrissea said, looking askance at Phylomon. The blue man's skin had already begun darkening in hue, preparing to attack. Chaa and the Starfarer exchanged glances.

"Let him in," Phylomon said with an undertone that chilled Darrissea to the core of her soul. "He can sit next to me. We have ample room for him to sleep here by the fire. Perhaps he could tell us a few tales of his home, of faraway lands and how he came to be in our city."

Darrissea understood. While they sat and argued whether Tull should live or die, the Creators were moving their plots forward. Phylomon wanted to question the monster.

The blood eater stood in the doorway smiling his endearing smile, too naive to understand the dangerous tone in Phylomon's voice. "Thank you, friends," he said. "Thank you!" and as he entered the room, Darrissea took his cloak and set it on the peg beside the door next to where Chaa's Blade Kin uniform hung, then pulled a pistol from Chaa's holster.

"By the way, Darrissea," Phylomon asked. "Did you ever find the rope in the kitchen?"

"No," Darrissea answered, as she stuck the pistol in her belt and went into the kitchen to get Phylomon the rope.

Tull woke in the afternoon, drowsy. Motes of dust floated in the air, lit by the yellow sun. His lips felt parched, thirsty, though his body was cold, and he was deathly tired. It did not bother him. Instead, beneath the nagging pains he felt only ecstasy—the steady sense that he needed nothing. Thirsty, naked, nearly dead. Yet he needed nothing.

Tull lay on the floor. He felt no kwea. No fear, no desire. All such things had burned away. If the Blade Kin were to rush into the room and take him back to die, he'd hardly fight them. *Okanjara,* I am free.

The sense of perfect freedom would not leave, and Tull realized he had no name for this thing he felt. He tried to sit up, eager to explore this strange new companion. But dizziness forced him back down. He turned his head. Across the room Fava slept on the floor in a dark-blue dress. Her hair was braided and slung over one shoulder.

Tull lay watching her, happy to be thirsty and cold, his belly cramped with hunger. He heard footsteps in another room, and Phylomon walked in, dressed in a loose flowing robe.

"How did you get here?" Tull asked.

Phylomon smiled, but there was a look in the Starfarer's eyes that Tull had never seen before, a haunted animal look. "My skin's ability to feign death and make a nuisance of itself thereafter seems to have left you all somewhat astonished. Fava tells me that I smelled worse than a family of skunks in a dogfight. To be honest, I had almost forgotten that my symbiote carried that ability."

Fava woke, stretched, and smiled gently at Tull. "Can I get you anything?"

"Water," Tull said, "and a kiss." She got up, gave him the kiss first, then went into the kitchen. "How long have I slept?" Tull asked.

"Six days," Phylomon answered. "I would appreciate it if you would heal immediately. We need you." The tone of his voice said that he was not joking.

Fava returned bearing a bottle of wine and a goblet. She sat and poured.

"While we were all managing to get captured," Phylomon said, "the Creators have already begun to attack outlying communities around Bashevgo with poisonous snakes and something far more dangerous—beings who look human, but must dine on human blood. I questioned one of these. Darrissea has been out on the streets. Rumor has it that Tantos plans to lead an army to attack the Creators."

"I know. I think we should let him," Tull answered.

"I fear Tantos will not accomplish much," Phylomon said. "He does not know how to battle the Creators. None of us do, but he knows far less about them than I."

"What of the gray birds with their snakes?" Tull asked. "Have they attacked the city?"

"The blood eater we captured said that millions of gray birds hatched in midwinter. It will take time for them to grow and learn to fly, but if they grow as fast as other birds, I suspect they will be ready to attack this summer, when the skies are clear."

Fava helped Tull sit up, poured a sweet red wine down his throat. He lay back afterward, dizzy, and closed his eyes.

"I mean it when I say that I want you to heal soon,"

Phylomon said. "Now that the ice is clearing, we must set sail."

Tull considered. In all his Spirit Walk, he'd never set Phylomon or himself back into the equation. He knew it would change the world, but he did not know precisely how, or how much. If Fava had stayed with Mahkawn, the Omnipotent would have been trying to seduce her by now. So Fava too had moved out of the time line.

Tull considered: evening, six days after the stabbing. At this very moment little Wayan and Vo-olai ran in a swamp down by Smilodon Bay, fleeing Blade Kin who would bring them to Bashevgo. Tantos planned to attack the Creators, and Tull could not guess the outcome. Theron Scandal, the old innkeeper from town, was congratulating himself as he tasted soup in the kitchens of Lady Initha while Slave Lords prepared to party at her house. The people of Smilodon Bay were scattered across Bashevgo. In five days Tantos would think to order Phylomon skinned. Tull realized they would need to get away from the city well before.

Fava lay on the floor next to him, stroking his chest, and Tull gazed at her a moment before drifting back to sleep. A great sense of peace flooded over him. She smiled. "Why do you look so happy?"

"I was just thinking about the end of the world."

Two days later Tull was able to sit up for short periods of time. With a bit of food his energy began to return. Chaa had been gradually filling the apartment with refugees. He rescued all of his children first, then took Zhopilla last. It was a great reunion when he brought her, with Fava and all the children crying, and Zhopilla trying to comfort her little ones.

"Tull will be able to travel soon," Chaa said to them all that night, "and he must get out of the city. I want him to go with Phylomon, to fight the Creators, but though I have tried to walk the future, even I do not know what chance he has of fighting them. Phylomon will need others to help handle the boat. And so we will send Fava and Darrissea. Wertha and I must stay here, for we have work to do."

"I won't be well enough to go," Tull said. "I can't handle the rigging."

"The slavers have small iron boats with huge engines that they use to pull barges from Craal. They are powered with ancient energy cubes made by the Starfarers. Such a boat requires only two people even for long journeys. You must leave, Tull, for you are a Spirit Walker. As your power grows, Atherkula is becoming more and more aware of you. Even now I am shielding you from his eyes, but I cannot do so for much longer. If he finds you, he will kill you."

"Why don't you come with us?" Tull said.

Chaa sat beside Tull, cross-legged. "Wertha and I have much work to do here in Bashevgo. I saw little on my last spirit walk, and I know nothing of the future. But I know some slaves who will die without my help, people who must be freed—somehow."

Chaa looked up at Phylomon. "You say that you do not think Tantos can kill the Creators? What will you need in the way of weapons?"

Phylomon answered, "I am not sure. My ancestors provided the great worms with symbiotes like mine, but theirs are twenty times thicker than anything a small human could wear. Conventional guns could not harm them. Even a laser cannon would not do the job."

"The one symbiote that I saw struck me with lightning. Will a larger symbiote be able to attack more fiercely?" Tull asked.

"Yes," Phylomon answered. "Yet that is not the worst of it. My symbiote has a small, crude brain. But I suspect that the Creators' symbiotes will be far more resourceful, more intelligent, than my small ally. If their symbiotes are even four inches thick, then for a worm sixty feet long and twelve feet in diameter, the symbiote itself will weigh over fifteen tons. My own symbiote is about one-eighth neural material. If this holds true for the Creators, then each of them will be defended by a brain that weighs more than a ton. Our intellect, even boosted by culture and enhanced through drugs, is dwarfed in comparison. I have been thinking, and I believe that the Creators themselves pose little threat, but their symbiotes, I'm sure, will have considered ways to protect themselves."

"Then," Tull asked, "you are telling me that the symbiotes are a completely different threat from the Creators?"

"The Creators are simply biological machines," Phylomon answered, "operating according to instructions given by our ancestors. But their symbiotes are living, learning beings, capable of forming new ideas. I've been considering, and I believe the symbiotes themselves are the cause of our worries, for we never programmed the Creators to form blood eaters or experiment with worms. The symbiotes must be controlling their masters, experimenting."

"But the symbiotes couldn't take complete control of the Creators, could they?" Darrissea asked.

"Yes," Phylomon said quickly. "It happens to me often. When I'm forced to protect myself, the symbiote takes control, coordinates muscle groups, causing me to crush an enemy's esophagus with a palm before I have time to think. Sometimes I become a mere spectator in my own battles. In the same way the Creators' symbiotes will defend themselves—by formulating battle plans, devising tactics, preparing escape routes. For the symbiotes, this is all they think about."

"You don't have any weapons that can kill them, do you?" Darrissea asked.

"I have weapons I can try." He nodded toward two cloth bags in the corner, where white rods spilled onto the floor, and he crossed his arms, resting his left hand on a small bump that protruded from his right arm. "All I need now is a sharp knife."

"A knife, we can provide," Chaa said.

The others went their way and talked for a bit in the kitchen, but Fava came to Tull beside the fire. "How do you feel?"

"I feel pretty good. Weak."

"Your scar looks terrible," Fava said, lightly touching the dressing on his wound.

"My scar?"

"Wertha healed you. He is a great healer. The wound is fully closed, though you have a blue scar there, a wide blue scar."

"I should count myself lucky."

Fava put Tull's hand on her stomach and asked, "What do you feel here?"

"Your belly."

"No," Fava said. "Our child." She grinned down at him, a broad smile on her face. "Wertha says it will be a son."

Tull held his hand there for a long time, wishing he did not hurt so bad, wishing he could do more than merely touch her.

Later that night while the others slept, Chaa came to Tull and woke him. "You are happy now, I see it in your eyes."

"Yes," Tull said. The others were sleeping in the room, Phylomon snoring loudly. Tull glanced at them, noted that Chaa spoke in a hushed voice, his mouth inches from Tull's ear.

"That is because you have found your center and discovered your true name. Lachish Chamepar, Path of the Crushed Heart." Chaa lightly touched Tull on the chest.

"You told me my true name long ago," Tull whispered.

Chaa smiled, his face lit by the fireplace. "Still, you did not understand it. Hearing your true name and knowing it are separate matters. Few men would willingly walk the path of the crushed heart, even if they knew of the peace on the other side."

"I know."

Chaa put his heels up to his buttocks, curled his arms around his knees, and sat with his chin on his knees. "Now that you know your true name, the trick is to remember it, to stay in touch with the center of yourself."

"How do I do that?" Tull asked.

"Each morning, when you awaken, you must sing yourself into existence." Tull looked at him, puzzled, and Chaa continued. "When you rise, you sing your true name, Lachish Chamepar, and focus on the peace at your center. Then, throughout that day, you will always remember who you are."

"I have never heard of this. Do you sing your true name?"

Chaa laughed. "You would be surprised at how many Pwi sing their true names in the morning. We sing softly, in our hearts, to ourselves. We do not tell children of these things that we do—it would only frustrate them. If they have not found their center, then it does them no good to sing their true name.

"Long ago the Pwi sang more. Each day at dawn they would rise and sing the world into being, create the world. That was long ago. We do not do it so much now, but I keep thinking we should start again. When I was young, I tried to get some Pwi to do it with me, but they thought it was stupid. They said 'Look! The sun rises whether we sing of it or not! The trees and hills and grass are here when we waken! Why do you waste our time?' and I could not explain to them very well why this one thing is so much more important than they could imagine."

Tull grinned nervously. Chaa went on: "You see, the world is indeed created new every day, whether we desire it or not. It is shaped by the minds of men, to some small degree, every day. A house is built, a ditch is dug, a war is fought. Change does not just happen. If we leave a pile of dirt, we do not come back and find it fashioned into brick and changed into a house or a salamander or a tree overnight. So we change the world, we shape it, often without thinking.

"That is why we must sing the world into being. We must waken each morning, envision the trees and the wild daisies, and sing the trees and daisies as they should be. We must remember the beauty of the lake, the cry of the loon, and sing these things into being. We must remember the warmth and the majesty of the sun and our campfires and sing them into being. We must see the strength and beauty of ourselves and our friends and sing of them as they should be. Otherwise, all these things will become forgotten, and eventually they will be lost."

"You sound so sure of yourself," Tull said.

"Oh, I am sure," Chaa said. "You have seen the Neanderthals of the Blade Kin. You have seen the arenas of the Slave Lords in Bashevgo. These people have forgotten the world as it should be. They have not sung the world into being for far too long.

"I'm talking to you as if I were a human," Chaa said, and he closed his eyes. "I think I should explain. There is more to this magic than I have said. You have seen Anee, you have seen how the Starfarers formed it. They speak of their technology—of geneticists and DNA—and they think they formed this world. I am happy to let them think so. But that is not how this planet was formed."

"If you don't think the Starfarers created Anee, how did it get here?"

"Oh, the Starfarers made it with their hands, but I will tell you a secret my father told me," Chaa said. "A hundred thousand years ago, on Earth, a shaman of the Pwi met a human. The Pwi woke every day and sang the world into being, and he had few tools, but this human with his clever hands had fashioned many tools—knives, spear points, hide scrapers, bowls, needles. The human did not sing the world into shape with his heart and tongue, he molded it with his hands.

"The Pwi looked down on this human and saw that the human, in his own way, was singing a new world into being, and that his song would conflict with the song of the Pwi. Since the human was weaker, the Pwi could have killed him and ended the conflict, but the Pwi took pity. So many Pwi gathered, and together they sang of two worlds—a world where the humans could create with their hands, and a world where the Pwi would create with their hearts.

"Earth became the home for the humans, and all the Pwi traveled to the Land of Shapes to wait. Now the humans have returned the gift, using their hands to make this world. Anee will be the new home for the Pwi forever. So we must begin again to sing the world into being each morning." Chaa hesitated. "Can you even imagine that this would become a peaceful world?"

"No," Tull said. "I walked the future in the Land of Shapes. I don't see much hope for peace."

"Then you must dream it into being," Chaa answered. "You must dream it into being, and you must become a man of peace yourself. Sing your true name each morning, remember your center, do no harm to others, then sing of the world of peace, as I do each day. If enough people do that, peace will wash through this land like a flood."

Tull reflected on the words and felt guilty for having strayed so far. He recalled walking home in the dark in Smilodon Bay, trying to avoid stepping on a blade of grass or an earthworm. Reverence for life, reverence for the world. That was all Chaa really wanted from him. "I will do it," Tull said.

"Good." Chaa clapped him on the shoulder. "You have come far in a year. Some day, perhaps, you will make a good shaman to the Pwi. Now we must speak of other things: Tantos will have Atherkula hunt Phylomon," Chaa said, "and I do not have the power to fight Atherkula."

"I know," Tull said.

"Yet your spirit eyes are opening. You have seen how the sorcerers of the Blade Kin capture their quarry. They bind us with the shadows of their souls."

"Yes," Tull said.

"That is not how a Spirit Walker connects. We walk in a more peaceful way. To walk the paths of the future for a person, I must first learn him and learn the souls of all those who might connect to that person later. I entwine one strand of lightning from my soul with each of his, then let the tips of those strands dance over the shadows of his soul. Then I step back in time to the moment of that person's birth and relive what he has lived, and I learn him—his thoughts, his loves, his secret fears and ambitions. Only then, when I have lived his life with him, can I move ahead into the future. Yet to do so perfectly, I would have to walk the future of all men, bind myself to all of their loves, all of their fears. No one can do this—even to try drives one to madness."

"Yet," Chaa continued, "to glimpse even part of the future, you must connect with many people—touch thousands at a time."

"How can this happen?" Tull asked.

"You have counted the fronds of lightning in your soul. They number twenty-two. But this is true only when spirits are at rest. A countless number of those lightnings reside within you, hidden beneath the shadow of your soul. When you wake more, you will be able to open yourself, reach out with many tongues of lightning at once, and taste the lives of countless men. This art of connecting, of learning the hearts of men, you are ready to practice."

"I . . . am not well enough," Tull said. And he thought of what it would mean to merge his consciousness with others, to lose himself, his identity. It was frightening, and he focused on that peaceful place in himself where there was no fear. He sang his true name —Path of the Crushed Heart—until peace returned, then reconsidered Chaa's request.

I lost myself once, Tull thought, *when Mahkawn tried to steal my life away. Now Chaa asks me to give it freely.* Tull suddenly realized that Chaa had been waiting for this moment all along, had been waiting for a genuine commitment. Chaa had known that Tull would first have to lose himself before he could learn to give himself. Tull looked into Chaa's narrow face, into his deep eyes, knowing that Chaa had somehow arranged it, had at the very least permitted Tull to taste death.

"I know you are weak, but the moment is coming when you must take your Spirit Walk. Once you learn this art, you will find that in the past you were a child living in a small town, someone who had come to know the meadows and the bushes around his house well, but now you will be stepping into a far larger world, with icefields and jungles and forests that no single man has ever explored. This is what it means to be a Spirit Walker. At this moment you taste freedom, and you think it is ecstasy. Now you will explore the bounds of it. I want you to bring that ecstasy to others, help me give them their freedom. That is what the art of Spirit Walking is for."

Tull closed his eyes, an ancient Pwi sign of acceptance. "When will I be ready to learn?"

Chaa sighed deeply. "Learning to connect is a difficult act. It can be done only when you are at the gates of death."

"I'm not afraid," Tull said.

"I know," Chaa answered. "If you are to connect, it is best to do so with a small child. The weight of a short life is easier to bear."

"Wayan," Tull said. "I want to connect with Wayan."

"He is not good," Chaa answered. "Though he is small, he has endured much."

For a moment, an image flashed in Tull's mind in which he saw Jenks, his father, as if he were a towering giant, shouting as he placed the manacles on Tull's

childish legs. "I lived through as much," Tull answered.
"I too had Jenks for a father."

"Very well."

"When should we do it?"

"Now, if you wish," Chaa said. "There are many
paths to the Land of Shapes, as many ways as there are
to die. I'll take you to the border for only a moment, if
you wish."

Tull nodded. Chaa asked Tull to lay his head on
Chaa's lap, and Tull found that his heart was pounding,
just a bit, with controlled fear. The night seemed deep
and quiet, yet somewhere in the distance a dog howled.
Nearby in the fireplace the pitch in a log popped, and
the log shifted, stirring the coals. Tull lay down, and
Chaa whispered, "Close your eyes. Trust me. I have no
seer's tea to make this easier, so you must not fight me."
Tull nodded, and closed his eyes. He felt Chaa's fingers
steal over his nose and mouth. Tull tried not to fight,
tried not to push Chaa away, but nature took over and
he twisted. Chaa held on, and Tull became dizzy, tried
to shove Chaa's hand away.

"There are as many paths to the Land of Shapes as
there are ways to die," Chaa said. "Do not worry, my
friend." He held tight.

Tull gasped, struggled for air. His lungs were burning, and he kicked wildly, and spun as if he were in a
great whirlwind.

He found himself floating free, the fire of his soul
rushing south over barren lands. He thought of Wayan,
south somewhere, and moved toward the child as if following a distant voice. Tull found Wayan held captive at
Muskrat Creek in the dingy storage cellar of a burned-
out home. Six Blade Kin held Tchavs, Vo-olai, Wayan,
and several others as they waited for a ship to Bashevgo.
Tull floated over their sleeping forms.

The lightning of Wayan's soul flashed in shades of
turquoise as he hovered between fear and despair. Tull
floated nearby and tried to manipulate the lightning of

his own soul, tried to force the pale fronds outward. They would not bend to his will.

Do not force it, Chaa whispered. *Close your eyes. Let your spirit eyes see, let your heart touch him.* Tull relaxed, imagined only that he wanted to touch Wayan, and the pale fronds slithered outward, across the gulf.

The fingers of light brushed Wayan, moved through the clot of his soul, and Tull sensed the boy's uneasy sleep. He imagined caressing Wayan.

Taste him now. Taste his hungers and his passions. The lightning wriggled across the shadow of Wayan's soul, entwined itself around Wayan's own fiery tendrils, and Tull felt images come to mind, brief flashes like snowflakes blurring past his eyes in a blizzard. Blinding images that melded into one another: Jenks was in many of them, a beefy-armed giant more than twice his height. The great roaring man often screamed, sometimes slapped Wayan hard enough to knock him to the floor. There were images of Wayan hiding in thickets and under his bed, brief confused explosions where Jenks would capture him and chain him to his bedpost, memories of nights listening to the whistle of wind or the sound of squirrels scurrying over the roof.

In one particularly strong memory, after Jenks had slapped the boy hard enough to knock him across the room, Wayan's mother had warned Jenks to go easier.

"He's all right," Jenks had answered. "Pwi kids are indestructible. You might as well try to break an anvil with a hammer."

"How many Pwi kids did you try to kill before you figured that out?" his mother had asked, and after that Jenks called Wayan "Stonehead," as if somehow to reinforce in both the child's mind and his mother's that you could beat a Pwi all you want and never really hurt him.

Yet for every memory of violence, Wayan cherished three or four of kindness—being held by his mother and resting his head on her breast, the treats Jenks gave out when feeling guilty for one of his crueler outbursts, playing in the tidal pools down in Smilodon Bay.

And then Tull saw himself through Wayan's eyes, rescuing Wayan from his natural father. Tull was taller and stronger than other men, but Wayan saw him as a giant with rippling muscles, a giant who could protect him from everything. Wayan, at age three, did not conceive of Tull as a mortal. Instead, he was an absolute—a sun that rose every morning, a mountain that never moved. Tull was protector and friend, and Fava was the feeder and the source of all wisdom. Tull found that Wayan's love for Fava was more than a little sexual. The child became aroused by her touch, by the smell of her hair.

And suddenly Tull was being pulled back to his body, over the barren, rock-strewn earth. Tull lay for a long while, reconnecting himself to his own physical shell.

The emotions came, threatening to rend him. The comfort he often took by curling to sleep by the fireplace. The fear of Jenks as a giant—a towering beast with unimaginable intent who dished out pain and favors without reason. The dull ache of teething. The thrill of sleeping with Fava and feeling his small pud swell. The nightmare of listening to squirrels on the roof crack nuts, fearing that they were small monsters cracking bones with their teeth. Dreams of grasshoppers eating his legs. Being captured by Blade Kin in a swamp and carried to a land rumored to be ruled by Adjonai, the God of Fear.

All the horror and hope of Wayan's short life came at once, unmooring Tull, threatening to sweep his sanity into oblivion. The memories seemed to slam against his skull, bursting like brands thrown against a rock wall, and with each small explosion, Tull reeled with the pain, until he slumped on the ground, as if he had been physically battered.

Chaa was there holding Tull, calming him with a touch as if Tull were a child himself. Tull's heart was pounding and his very skin seemed to ache. He wanted to scream the pain out, but Tull found he could only whimper.

"You did well," Chaa said. "You did well. For a few nights you will have horrible dreams. For a few days you will live in pain. But it will pass. You two have become one."

Two days later, in the first shadows of evening, Fava and Darrissea and Chaa prepared to walk Tull down to the docks. Fava's younger sisters clung to her legs, trying to keep Fava from leaving. Zhopilla cast her eyes around as if to keep from having to look at Fava. Outside, the moon Thor was setting with the sun, and a strong gravitational wind hissed through the streets, rattling the walls of the old apartments, seeping through cracks.

Fava went to her mother, held the woman. Zhopilla hugged Fava back, her arms weak, loose. Fava rested her head on her mother's shoulder, smelling the familiar scent of her hair, and said quietly, "The kwea of this day is good, for I am leaving Bashevgo with my husband. Soon, we can all return home."

"I will never see you again," Zhopilla cried. "I feel it. You are going to go to the island of the Creators, and you will all die there. You might not even get free of Bashevgo. What if the Blade Kin catch you trying to steal a boat?"

"You worry too much," Fava whispered.

"That is my duty," Zhopilla said, "to worry for my children when they are too stupid to worry for themselves."

"I am worried, too," Fava admitted. "I will take care of myself."

Zhopilla pushed Fava back at arm's length, held Fava's shoulders, and looked deep into her eyes. "No, you will not take care of yourself," Zhopilla said, as if gauging her. "I have seen you—always giving, always helping others. You will not take care of yourself. You will take care of others."

"Is that so bad?" Fava asked.

Zhopilla reached down, touched Fava's belly. "If you take care of anyone, take care of this one first. You must stay alive, if only for your child."

"I will," Fava said.

Zhopilla nodded sincerely. "You are a woman of the old blood, with a child in your belly. Soon, the child will open, and a spirit must enter it. This is a very important time. Did old Vi teach you how to Summon a spirit?"

"No," Fava whispered. "She did not know I was pregnant yet." The men were stirring by the door, packing up bundles as they prepared to leave.

"That is a shame," Zhopilla said. "As the daughter of a Spirit Walker, you should be able to choose the spirit of your child. When I Summoned you, there were many spirits nearby in the Land of Shapes, anxious to enter your body. But I saw the lightning of your soul, so brilliant beyond all others, and I called to you. I knew you were special.

"When you return, I will teach you the woman's magic, prepare you to Summon a powerful spirit to the body of your child."

Fava nodded and hugged her mother once again while the others stood by the door. She kissed each of her little sisters one last time and smiled at them, hoping to leave them with good kwea, and then Fava, Darrissea, and Chaa made their way down to the docks. Tull was still weak, too weak to make the journey without resting, and had to stop often.

The streets bustled with people, and the docks smelled strongly of fish and seals, for the fleets were beginning to work in the Straits of Zerai.

They found a tugboat at the docks, a newly painted steel vessel with two great turbine engines. It was smaller than they wanted—at only forty feet—yet it served their needs well, for it had a broad hull and a deep keel and would not flip over in a storm, and since the engines were powered by one of the Starfarer's ancient energy cubes, no one would have to feed it fuel.

The harbor master spotted them cleaning the boat, preparing it to sail, and questioned them. Fava told him that they would be hauling a load of fish to Denai in a few days, and only needed to ready the tug for the summer. The harbormaster let them work in peace as they loaded the boat with food and supplies, and a few hours after dark Phylomon used the cover of night to join them, and they set sail into the uncharted waters of the north, where ice floes were so common that only Craal's bravest sailors would go there to hunt giant pliestocene walruses that sometimes weighed as much as a young mammoth.

The ice in the north was thick, still breaking up, and they took four days in a zigzag course, trying to navigate to an island drawn on a crude map—written from memory by the blood-eater. It was little help, but the creature had known the number of days it had sailed and the general direction it had come from.

The northern winds bit down on the small boat, freezing those inside. Brief winter storms buffeted them often, sometimes arriving and passing in minutes. All but Phylomon spent their days huddled in thick blankets.

By day they searched the horizon for signs of an island, and at night let themselves float, keeping their bow to the wind in hopes that they would not be thrown off course. After searching for the island for nearly a week, Phylomon finally admitted that perhaps they had drifted too far off course. "We can be sure only that we are in the right ocean," he said. "We probably passed it in the dark during a squall." The wind had been blowing them west, and he set sail east for two days, then began a zigzag, heading north and south. After a week he imagined they had missed it again, and they began sailing east-west courses, then sailing north a little at a time.

Steadily Tull's health improved, so that he could get

out of bed for an hour at a time. Fava nursed him and
found him to be pliant, undemanding. Though she had
never thought of him as demanding before, she now saw
his behavior as something unnatural. So one day while
Phylomon slept in the hold and Darrissea sat in the
cabin, driving the ship while watching through the glass
windows, Fava asked Tull about the change.

"Okanjara," Tull said, I Am Free. "Every slave who
has escaped Craal or Bashevgo has said those words,
but I feel it. I am free."

"Of course you are free," Fava said. "We've all escaped."

"That's not what I mean," Tull answered. "When
Mahkawn stabbed me, I saw you on the far side of the
room, and I had been thinking of all the things I want in
life, and suddenly I saw everything—my family, my
friends, my dreams—all ripped away, and something
strange happened.

"I realized suddenly that for all my life I'd been
carrying a weight on my shoulders, all these little burdens. I had all these dreams of happiness, and I'd always
thought that if I worked hard enough, they would all
come true. I would get married and father a child and
build my house and make my fortune, and I would
somehow reach this moment when it would all be mine
—everything that I had ever wanted or dreamed of
would be mine, and happiness would be like an apple
plucked fresh from the tree, and it would be mine.

"Instead, when Mahkawn tried to kill me, in that
moment when all my hopes were crushed, nothing mattered anymore. I didn't need the apple. I could already
taste perfect freedom. I still taste it."

Tull stopped talking, took a deep breath. Fava
looked at him, puzzled. "What are you saying? That
hope is evil, or that it doesn't matter? In a world like
ours, what more can we have than hope?"

Tull studied the horizon. "You hope for peace. I
have peace. I think that if you were destroyed, perhaps
you would find it, too. That is all I can say."

"But not everyone can have peace, not when there are Slave Lords and Blade Kin," Fava said, "all trying to take it from us."

"Yes, you can have peace," Tull said. "Inside you. The Blade Kin and Slave Lords cannot steal it away. They search for it too. The Slave Lords *consume*— wealth, land, people—stacking riches upon themselves. They think that if they can gratify themselves enough, then they will attain it. I guess, in my heart, I was a Slave Lord.

"Then there are the Blade Kin—Pwi who imagine that if they can free themselves of kwea, they will find peace. You think that the Blade Kin are purposely cruel, but they do not see themselves so. They have so trained away their own compassion and fear that they cannot be touched. They see themselves as tools, like iron blades, that exist only to bend others to their wills. Perhaps if they were not misled, many of them would also find peace, but they have been fooled by the Slave Lords into believing that they, too, will find happiness through gratification."

"Does this mean that you won't build me that big house you promised?" Fava joked.

Tull laughed. "I wish you would come live naked with me in the forest until you learn that houses do not matter."

"I think you say that only because you want to see me naked," Fava said, and she kissed him.

Tull held her for a long moment, kissing her tenderly. "I mean it. Sometimes, when I am sitting still, I feel inside myself, and I am flying without strain. It's like I am diving through clouds, the wind ripping at me, tasting the snow and rain on my tongue, and I am all alone. Other times I feel as if I were in a forest, when all the trees around me close others out, and in that place I feel perfect contentment. I want to share it with others, but I don't know how. Should I burn their houses and chop off their limbs, then threaten them with death, hoping that when their dreams are destroyed, they will find peace inside? Could such a plan even work? I can't even imagine words to tell you what I feel. And I wonder, if you were destroyed, would you feel it too? Every moment I feel as if I am a redwood, with my branches touching the naked sky, and the sun is rising and I want to sing anthems to all the small creatures on the shadowed ground below me, 'Listen, listen, let us taste the light.' All I can hope is that you can find it. So I ask you, will you come live naked with me in the forest?"

Fava shook her head. "It wouldn't work. Zhofwa has blown her kisses on us. When I am with you, I think I too have found happiness. How could I keep searching for something I already possess?"

Tull looked her in the eyes. "I love you. I've known the taste of that happiness in your arms," he said. "It is the closest thing that comes to what I am talking about. But your peace is not lasting. When you watched Mahkawn stab me, I saw you. You lost all the happiness you thought you had. I wanted to share this feeling with you. I wanted you to relish it as I do. That is why I came back from the Land of Shapes. To tell you. But now I find that there are no words."

The wind blew Tull's dark-red hair in wisps across his face, and Fava thought momentarily of braiding it. She looked down into the cold blue water, felt the salt spray bite her tongue. The wind, the water felt good, but all were colored by kwea, by her fears of the Blade Kin and of the Creators. She touched his hand.

"Don't give up on me," she said seriously. "I want to feel what you feel. I wish I were a Spirit Walker, and could touch you, and taste that freedom. In Bashevgo they say that when the Okansharai comes, he will free us all. So perhaps it can be done."

Tull glanced up at the sky to the north, at dark gray clouds. "Perhaps we should go inside," he said, shivering. "It looks as if we are heading into another storm, and I'm getting tired."

Fava looked up, thought it odd that the storm was not heralded by any stronger winds. Then she saw the island on the horizon, beneath the clouds. "Those are not clouds," she said after a moment, "those are birds!"

Phylomon went above deck and studied the sky, the clouds of birds. For a hundred miles across the island, the skies were black. In his head he quickly calculated—there were not merely millions of them, there were hundreds of millions, more than mankind on Anee could ever hope to fight.

"Have Darrissea idle the engines," Phylomon said. "All of you stay inside. The birds might attack the ship." Fava rushed into the cabin, but Tull stood beside Phylomon a moment.

"Maybe we should shut off the engines," Tull said.

"Why?" Phylomon gave him a sidelong look.

"I hear serpents speaking in the water," Tull answered. "They will be looking for our boat."

Phylomon knew that the sea serpent was Tull's animal guide, but the big Tcho-Pwi looked worried. "Why should we fear these serpents?"

Tull shook his head. "These are not like the serpents at Smilodon Bay. These are . . . strange. Cruel. They will hunt the boat," Tull said with certainty.

Phylomon exhaled a long sigh. "Can you guide us past, get me to the island?"

Tull nodded. "Perhaps." Then he went down into the cabin. Phylomon watched him, worried. The boy was still weak and had been up for hours.

Darrissea came topside, and took Phylomon's hand, just held it. "What are you going to do?" she asked.

Tull reversed the engines, turned the boat away, and headed east of the island, out to sea.

"We'll see if we can reach the island, then decide," Phylomon answered. The young girl looked up at him from dark eyes.

"Can I come with you?"

"I don't believe that will be possible," Phylomon

answered, nodding toward the birds that darkened the sky, but he did not move his hand away. Tull kept on course for several hours, then circled up north and cut the engines. By then he was sweating and breathing shallowly, and Phylomon had to force him to bed.

"Just let the wind blow us toward the island in the dark," Tull whispered in pain. "Don't move around or speak. The serpents won't attack if we remain silent."

Phylomon agreed, and as the sun set behind the island, he let the boat drift. A stiff breeze battered the boat so that waves hit the hull with a ringing sound. Tull seemed agitated.

"Let's go back farther out," Tull whispered. "They'll hear the waves slapping the boat! No, wait— they're too close!" He began muttering to himself, looking to the south and saying, "We are brothers. We are brothers."

He clutched the rail and stared into the water, as if he were in a trance. He carefully walked into the cabin, stood at the throttle, and closed his eyes, sweating, but did not start the engines.

For several minutes he stood there, then shouted, "They've found us!" He gunned the engines, spun the boat. Phylomon held on, looked back. A dozen young serpents surfaced at once, only yards from where they had sat—small serpents, in the fifty-foot range—but still larger than the boat.

Tull kept the boat at full throttle, leaping over the waves, and the serpents followed in their wake, gaining, when all of a sudden, directly behind the boat, a great serpent rose, a huge male with a dorsal fin longer than the boat. He roared and flashed his head in the last rays of sunlight, displaying teeth longer than a man's arm. He came down and grasped a smaller serpent in his jaws, then disappeared under the water, trailing blood.

Phylomon glanced at Tull's pale face. The big Tcho-Pwi kept his hands on the wheel, kept running. Behind, a serpent roared again. Phylomon saw the great one rolling in the water while the others attacked, biting him in several places. The big male threw them off, killed four, but the water around him teemed with small serpents.

Tull held the boat on course for an hour, then headed south, shut off the engines, and slumped at the controls. Darkness had fallen, and the wind had died. They sat quietly, and Tull looked far off.

"Is your serpent dead?" Darrissea asked.

Tull nodded, gazing out to sea. "He couldn't have killed them all. There were too many to fight."

Fava nodded, put her arm around Tull.

"The wind is calmer now," Phylomon said. "We shouldn't have that trouble again." He did not bother to say that if the serpents attacked again, they wouldn't make it away from the island alive. "Once the boat gets close to shore, I may have to jump out and ask you to leave." The others merely nodded. "If we can get ashore safely, I'm not sure it would be wise for you to stay. There may be more blood eaters on the island." Fava shivered, and Phylomon added, "In fact, if you can make it out, I'd prefer that you leave. Give me two weeks, and then come back for me."

Darrissea said, "What if there are eels here, like the blue eel the Creators sent to attack you in Smilodon Bay?"

"Then I will have to avoid them," Phylomon answered.

By midnight the others had all fallen asleep. Phylomon sat with Darrissea for a while, holding her hand. The girl was beautiful in her way, and Phylomon realized he would miss her. The fuel-air bomb he'd hidden in his arm was powerful—too powerful for Phylomon to use at close range. Perhaps if he had a pyroderm for his symbiote, like the one his brother had worn—but Phylomon's symbiote wouldn't be able to withstand such heat, and Phylomon knew he could not count on the harmonic resonators to kill the Creators. He might shake down their mountains, bury them for a while, but they would just dig their way out. No, he needed to use the incendiary bomb first. If he lived, he could try the rods after he'd done as much damage as possible.

Phylomon kissed Darrissea's cheek as she slept. "Find someone good to love," he whispered in her ear. He stroked her face, then got up to leave.

He went on deck and watched the boat wash to shore. There were rocks on shore, rocks enough to tear apart the small boat. Tull, Fava, and Darrissea apparently did not suspect such a thing. Being from the Rough, they'd never sailed in a steel boat, and they must have believed the metal shell gave their vehicle some kind of invulnerability.

Let them sleep, Phylomon thought. *Let them imagine themselves invincible.* Phylomon had a name for those without symbiotes: He called them "temporaries," for their lives came and went like leaves passing in the wind. At times he found them amusing. Sleeping like babies when the boat was about to be dashed apart on the rocks. He stayed at the wheel, ready to start the engines if necessary and back away from shore.

They actually got lucky, and the wind drove them up on a steep but sandy beach. Thor was up, and under the orange light of the massive gas giant, Phylomon could see that the bank was black with sleeping birds.

The blue man packed his weapons into one sack, then slipped out the door of the boat, locked it behind him, and covered the windows with a tarpaulin. The birds would probably not recognize the boat as man-made, but he would not want them to be able to see into the cabin.

Phylomon tied the boat to a large boulder, then slipped off through the darkness, walking among the birds. They were larger than gulls, the size of small eagles with sharp beaks. They often readjusted their wings and pecked at one another in their sleep, and Phylomon found them so numerous that he frequently had to move them aside with his boot so he could place his foot. Yet the birds were unnaturally silent. Gulls or terns or nearly any other type of bird would have emitted cooing noises or an occasional cry, but these were absolutely silent, and from time to time one would flip its neck in its sleep and try to slice Phylomon's impenetrable hide.

He headed for a dark line of trees where the brush was thick and took nearly an hour to cross the three hundred yards of open beach and hit the trees.

The ground under the trees was littered with white bird guano and small animal bones piled many inches deep. It made squishy cracking noises as he walked through it, and as he passed over the miles, he remained constantly amazed to find that it never got any better. Always, above him, the birds sat thick in the trees, so that even under the light of an ample waning moon, he felt as if he were passing under the darkest jungle canopy. As if he had already entered the caves that would lead to the Creators' lair.

Chapter 14
The Sun Lies Broken

At dawn Darrissea woke to the sound of hundreds of clawed feet scrabbling atop the steel boat. She rose, found the windows covered with leather tarps, and walked uneasily about the cabin. She relieved herself in the latrine, then ate a small meal. The fresh water was low, and she drank little, then sat in the shadows, munching thick moist rye crackers from Bashevgo. She tried not to think about the birds on the roof.

She recalled the great blue eel that had come out of the Creators' messenger back in Smilodon Bay, and in her mind's eye she watched it wriggle in the fire, filled with bullets, yet unable to die, and she could not help but wonder if the birds above her might carry such creatures in their stomachs, and if the cabin had any holes to the outside that would allow them access. She tried to look outside, hoping to see through a crack in the tarpaulin.

When Tull rose, Darrissea said, "Do you think any blood eaters are out there?"

"If they were close," Tull answered, "I think Phylomon would have come back to warn us, or he would have pulled the boat under cover to hide it."

Darrissea nodded. For the rest of the morning they spoke seldom. Darrissea's muscles were cramping, and she often stretched or rubbed herself. Her neck and head ached particularly, and by watching others, she saw that they had similar problems.

Several times during the day, they heard sea serpents roar out in the waters, a deep bellowing that had been familiar in Smilodon Bay. Then, the sound had been comforting, but now it filled her with fear.

That evening the whole boat rocked as some huge creature pounced on the deck. Fava grabbed a handrail and righted herself. None of them moved for nearly twenty minutes as they listened to snuffling outside. The beast brushed past a window. A hooked claw ripped the tarpaulin, and they saw a massive black shape, part of a wing.

"Dragon," Tull said, but it was not like the little tyrant birds that protected the forests and hills from pterodactyls back home. This was bigger even than the great horned dragons that rode the thermals out at sea, and Darrissea knew instinctively that it had been engineered by the Creators to hunt humans, that it was sniffing at the doors for them.

A few moments later, after circling the deck, the dragon returned to the cabin door and sat, sniffing and licking at the door, tasting their scent on its tongue.

None of them moved or spoke for nearly an hour, simply hoping the predator would leave, but Darrissea sweated a storm and realized she was only making it worse, filling the cabin with the taste of her fear.

Finally the dragon roared and leapt into the sky. Darrissea heaved a sigh of relief.

"*Adja.* I fear we can't stay here," Fava whispered. "This place has evil kwea."

"I don't think we can leave," Tull said. "I hear serpents patrolling the coast."

"I can't hear them," Darrissea said.

"They talk very deep. You can almost feel the sound trembling through your bones rather than hear it with your ears."

Darrissea listened, shook her head.

"I hear it," Fava answered after a few minutes.

"If they become silent, can we leave?" Darrissea asked.

"If they become silent, it means only that they've quit talking," Tull said.

"Could we outrun them?" Darrissea asked.

"They can call to one another for miles," Tull said, "and they hunt in packs, driving their prey." The serpents they had seen were small, and Darrissea wondered if the metal boat could protect them if a serpent wrapped the boat in its coils.

Fava stared through the small tear in the tarpaulin. "I see more dragons outside, floating on the wind." She exhaled a deep breath. Above they heard the soft scrabbling of bird claws, the scrape of beaks as gray birds settled on the boat again.

They went into a storage room below and locked themselves in. For hours they waited, and Fava pulled off the bandages from Tull's chest to store them. The wound had finally stopped seeping altogether, though the strange blue scar seemed to have grown wider. It was nearly two inches wide and a foot long, and seemed to her to be larger than the original wound. She asked Tull how it felt, and he said the wound felt better. Once he put his tunic on, he let Fava lay her head on his chest and softly sing.

For some reason Darrissea couldn't fathom, she could not help but feel jealous. Darrissea wished Phylomon were near so that she could lay her own head in his lap, feel safe in his arms. She could not help but think about how Phylomon had kissed her last night, when he thought she slept. "Find someone good to love." They were not the words of someone who was dead to love.

Yet she feared he was dead to the world. For the past several days, she'd been thinking about it. If the Creators' symbiotes were so much more powerful than Phylomon's, he would need a powerful weapon to kill them. She knew without his saying that his weapon would kill him, too.

"You know, you once told me that you admired my courage, because I always speak the truth," Darrissea said to Tull. "And I've admired yours, because you are not afraid to live." Tull grunted. "I feel like we are both cowards now. We came to fight the Creators, but we're not fighting. We're letting Phylomon do it. And in Bashevgo, what did we accomplish? Back in Smilodon Bay we promised to destroy the slavers, but we've run from them."

"The slaves don't want to be freed," Fava countered. "You saw how they turned against Phylomon and the Hukm."

Darrissea apologized, "They were only afraid of the Hukm."

Tull said, "You're right, we made a vow, but who do we kill? The Slave Lords? I saw them in Denai—beautiful people who were more interested in parties than in ruling slaves. Most of them don't *run* anything. They're just merchants, buying and selling goods to one another. So shall we kill the Blade Kin? They're apes, beating their chests to seek one another's admiration. You should have seen Mahkawn's eyes as he thrust the sword into me. He called me his 'friend,' and he was being as compassionate as he knew how. So shall we kill the Thralls who continue to serve the Slave Lords and the Blade Kin? Shall we be reduced to eliminating the greatest victims of the state?" Tull said. "In Smilodon Bay the answer seemed easy. Perhaps the Creators are right, and it is time to tear the whole thing down, destroy mankind and start over."

"You don't believe that, do you?" Fava said.

"I don't know what to believe."

"In Bashevgo," Fava said, "Wertha had begun to think that you are the Okansharai, that you could free Bashevgo. He was praying for you."

Tull laughed. "He shouldn't waste his breath."

"We made a covenant," Darrissea said. "You promised to help me."

"I'll do what I can," Tull said. "Once I learn the art

of Spirit Walking, we should be able to help some escape Craal and Bashevgo. But think of it: For every slave we free, a dozen more will be born. In time we could build a nation of free men, but we would never be a match for Craal." Darrissea began to speak, but Tull stopped her with a motion of his hand. "Listen—"

Darrissea heard moaning. She'd have thought it the creaking of timbers in the boat, but this metal ship made no such sounds.

"The serpents are leaving," Tull whispered. "They're angry." He opened the door and ran up into the cabin, then stood hunched, looking out the slit in the tarpaulin. It was far darker than Darrissea had expected, and she realized that her time below had gone fast. Night had fallen. "I see a ship!" Tull said. "Tantos has come to battle the Creators. He is firing his cannons."

Darrissea and Fava rushed up, looked out the slit. Several miles out to sea, the huge metal ship lit the night with cannon fire. A huge battle raged. The Creators' dragons had besieged the ship from above, the great serpents from beneath, yet Tantos had brought the same armored behemoth he'd used to transport slaves from the Rough, and against that ship the Creators' beasts appeared ineffectual. The conventional cannons roared from the decks, while portable laser cannons sliced the air. The gray birds didn't join the attack, did not even seem aware of the roaring cannons in the distance.

"They're getting closer," Darrissea said. "Could they spot us?"

"Not if we leave now," Fava answered. Before Darrissea had time to react, Fava opened the cabin door and stepped outside. For several minutes she made no noise, then the tarp over the front windows opened.

Darrissea went to the window. The shore was black with sleeping birds, as was the deck of the boat. She watched as Fava tied the tarp at the top, then walked slowly to the bow of the ship, tiptoeing between the sleeping birds. Sometimes birds would turn and slash her ankles with their beaks as they slept, and Fava bit her lip and tried not to cry out. She untied the rope that held the boat to shore, and stood up, wobbling. She staggered back to the door, heedless of birds nipping at her ankles. As she stepped in, she was panting, sweating, and she fell to the floor.

Tull grabbed her and hugged her. "You shouldn't have done that."

"Wash my feet!" Fava cried, near hysterics. "They are like ice. I can't feel them!"

Tull ran down, got some water, and Darrissea held Fava. "I . . . I'm sorry," Fava said. "I think I've been poisoned. I had to do it before I had time to think."

Tull rushed back up and began pouring water over Fava's wounds. "They're bleeding well. The poison should come out," he said, and Darrissea looked at them. They were bleeding more than well, they were a mess, slashed half a dozen times each, and Darrissea was amazed that the birds could have done so much damage so casually.

Outside, the booming cannons drew nearer. Fava looked up at Tull, panting. "Get the boat out of here. There's nothing you can do for me."

Her constricted breathing filled the silence of the cabin, and sweat gleamed on her forehead in the pale starlight. Darrissea took the stick, fired the engine, and tried to back the boat away from shore. It wouldn't budge.

"We're too high on the sand," she yelled at Tull. "We need to push off." She looked down at Fava's feet. The girl had not been wearing boots. Darrissea grabbed some cloth, tied it around her own boots, reinforcing the supple leather. The Blade Kin had taken her armor when they captured her, so she had no other protection. She threw on a heavy tunic, grabbed a long-bladed knife. Tull was still on the floor, washing Fava's feet.

"Good luck," Darrissea said, and she rushed up to the cabin door, went out on the deck. She walked slowly in the moonlight, and still the birds ripped at her feet when she tried to nudge them aside.

She used the knife to parry the birds' attacks and made her way to the sand. She leapt down, pushed the boat off. It moved easier than she had thought it would, and soon the boat was bobbing out in the waves. Tull appeared at the window and waved his hand, urgently motioning for her to jump into the water, wade out to the boat.

Darrissea waved good-bye, whispered, "Good luck." She pulled her cloak tight, then slowly began making her way up the beach to the tangled woods to find Phylomon. Tull waited several minutes, then turned on the engines and the boat sped north.

Inland Phylomon found that the birds were not so thick. The brushy hills were full of small rodents, something like pikas that feasted on tall, lush grass that grew even in winter. No snow covered the ground; no chunks of ice even clung to the hills, and so far north, Phylomon recognized such plant growth as virtually impossible until he placed his hand in the soil and felt its warmth, the depth of the humus. He picked up a bit. It radiated warmth.

Bacteria, he realized, generating heat to warm the soil. Around him the lush grass grew so fast that it seemed he could actually watch it grow if he stood long enough. The little pikas ran in herds of thousands, feeding and breeding all through the night. At dawn gray birds swarmed to feed on the rodents, then left after only a few hours. In the course of a day Phylomon watched the survivors bear large litters of twenty or more in the deep grass, saw young feed and reach adulthood by midnight, completing an entire life cycle within hours so that the birds could feed again at dawn.

Walking through the open, Phylomon was an easy target for dragons. Tyrant birds, small and ferocious, came upon him three times, swooping out of the night sky. Each time ozone crackled around Phylomon, and lightning flew from his blue skin to kill the birds. It wasted terrible amounts of energy, weakening his defenses.

In the late night he climbed some foothills and looked down on a small seaport with orchards all about, a town of many thousands, and he grew wary, kept to the rocks. There were no towns this far north, no human or Pwi settlements at least, and Phylomon realized that these must all be blood eaters that the Creators planned to unleash.

The town was not built of simple wood or stone; instead, the houses were octagon enclosures, resembling gray tortoise shells. Phylomon had not seen their like in ages—bioengineered so each house was a living entity, like a coral formation. The blood eaters had no windows to their homes, no chimneys. Phylomon suspected that the beasts needed no heat; warm dirt sufficed. Phylomon hid in the shadow of a rock and watched.

The blood eaters worked in the moonlight, planting and harvesting fields, building ships in the bay. Phylomon could see no young among the blood eaters. Apparently there would be no future generations. Still, if the blood eaters managed to invade the human settlements, they could feed for forty or sixty years. The sheer number of gray birds warned Phylomon that the Creators would try to wipe out mankind in one massive attack. Those who managed to escape would fall prey to the blood eaters; finally, when the last humans and Neanderthals died, the blood eaters themselves would starve.

Even if a few people managed to survive the attack of the birds, Phylomon felt sure that the blood eaters would destroy mankind. In order to save themselves, men would have to shun one another, become solitary animals, suspicious, violent. Children would be teethed on paranoia, nurtured in barbarity, until the fabric of society unraveled. Technology would be forgotten. Any survivors would live a stone-age existence, hunted by the blood eaters.

If I cannot kill the Creators, Phylomon thought, *perhaps I can rescue some small portion of humanity. Hide them in Hotland, on the far side of the world, and return in a few hundred years. Perhaps the Creators are right, and it is time to tear it all down, start over.*

Yet Phylomon could not console himself with such a solution. Too many lives were at stake—lives that, too often, he detested. Phylomon became weary, closed his eyes, and let his mind drift.

From his youth hundreds of years ago, Phylomon replayed memories of things his father had taught him about the Creators. Though Phylomon had helped program the Creators, he had never seen the finished product. He remembered his father, an old man who would no longer wear a symbiote, saying, "They've taken refuge in a cave to the north." Phylomon tried to recall if he'd ever seen a map of the island showing the entrance to the caves. If he had, it had not been in his youth when seritactates enhanced his memory.

Still, he recalled schematics of the Creators from a holo: Heat from their huge bodies generated power to drive their crystalline brains. Platinum neurosynaptic adaptors fed commands from the brain to the biological portion of the giant worms. To facilitate birth through their omniwombs, the Starfarers had built the Creators without skeletons, giving them a strong, flexible pseudoskeleton of cartilage. Then there were the symbiotes.

It would not be well, Phylomon told himself, *to underestimate them.* The symbiotes, most likely, would protect themselves with beasts of their own design. Not for the first time the Starfarer wondered at his own audacity. He could creep through some of the defenses the Creators had set up. The dragons and small birds posed no significant threat. One man could sneak past, while an army would merely attract their attention.

But beyond those, what would the Creators have

prepared? Perhaps it would not be possible for Phylomon even to get close to the Creators. Thinking such
morbid thoughts, Phylomon drifted to sleep while light
clouds blew in, blanketing the fields with snow.

He woke shortly after dawn to a silver sky with
feathered clouds that still smelled of water. The snow
had melted so that the green blades of grass peeking
from the stone around him looked as if they were covered with dew. Below, in town, the blood eaters worked
their fields and orchards. Many were walking a makeshift road beside a river that led through the trees into
the hills.

Phylomon watched a large gray bird with the head
of a woman fly along the rocky ridge where he hid, up
toward a craggy volcano several miles away. When it
neared the base, it dived out of sight.

Phylomon set out immediately, skirting the road,
climbing through rocks. Once he stopped to look down
on a small orchard where blood eaters gathered around
squat green trees and drank from dark-red fruits that
hung like bladders. Even at this distance Phylomon
could discern the red dripping from their faces, like children drinking the juice of watermelons. Phylomon was
grateful that the Creators had given them a source of
blood, for he had imagined herds of humans kept alive
solely to feed the bellies of these monsters. A little farther up the road Phylomon reached a line of trees that
were bone-white, leafless, and smelled of carrion. In all
his thousand years, he had never seen such trees, so he
skirted them, keeping from under their limbs.

Two miles beyond that he came on a second road
that intersected the first. He stopped. Both roads ran
through steep gullies and were deeply rutted—not by
wheels, but by feet. At the juncture of the two canyons
stood a gray tyrannosaur, watching as blood eaters disguised as humans and Neanderthals passed almost at
belly height.

Phylomon pondered the beast for a long time. It
held almost perfectly still, in the way reptiles will, watch-

ing the road with one dark eye. Up ahead the mountains were too steep for Phylomon to climb. He could see no way to move forward without climbing down to the trail. But that meant passing the creature. He waited till the road was clear, then backtracked around a corner and climbed down into the deep, narrow canyon.

Just as his feet hit sand, wings whistled above him as another of the Creators' messengers flew overhead, a large bird with the face of a woman. Though her eyes stared at him as she flew over, Phylomon saw no gleam of recognition in them. Marked with his own blue skin, Phylomon was singular—unlike anything else in the world. He feared that his markings would be known to the beasts formed by the Creators, but at least that one messenger seemed not to recognize him.

He crept up the sandy trail, and as he turned the corner, the tyrannosaurus stepped in front of him, barring his way. The beast did not thrash its tail or lower its head to display its teeth. It did not behave like its wild brothers. Instead, it watched him with cool, intelligent eyes. Phylomon could have killed it, but then he would have had to leave it in the road where it would soon be found. He did not want to alert the Creators.

"Do not detain me, friend," Phylomon said to the beast. "I have business with our masters in the caves."

The tyrannosaurus studied him, and Phylomon walked steadily past, up the winding canyon road. When he had gone only a few hundred yards, the tyrannosaurus roared, a choking noise something like a yelp. Phylomon wondered if the beast was angered. He stood a moment, heard it loping up the canyon behind him.

Phylomon rushed ahead, knowing full well that he could not outrun the monster. He turned a corner, threw himself against a wall, and lay flat between two protruding rocks. The tyrannosaurus yelped again and rushed round the corner, great streams of blood flowing from a gash in its neck. The wounds were whitened, puckered, and smelled of cooking meat, and Phylomon recognized that they could have been formed only one way: The tyrannosaurus had been shot with a laser cannon.

Fear, I taste your fear, his symbiote whispered.

Phylomon answered, "Strengthen me against my enemies, Gireaux, my old friend," and the symbiote hardened. Phylomon felt a slight pressure as his eardrums drew tight, making them more sensitive than normal so he could clearly hear his own heart pounding. His skin felt tight, like leather, so that no blade could pierce it. Even common bullets would turn aside. Yet Phylomon's skin could not protect him from a laser cannon, so over the years he had destroyed nearly every laser on the planet—except the five Tantos had captured at the battle for Bashevgo.

The Starfarer breathed deeply, considering. Had Tantos come to lead the battle himself? Probably. Behind him was a man with a symbiote as powerful in its way as Phylomon's own, and that man bore a weapon that could slice Phylomon open like a razor.

Phylomon sprinted up the road, looking for a place to try to leap up the cliff between the narrow arms of the canyon, looking for an escape route. *This is the kind of place where one would not want to be caught in a flash flood,* he thought absently. He turned a corner and found the tyrannosaurus slashing its tail and thrashing on the ground, blindly biting at the stone walls in its death throes. Phylomon ran at it, stepped on the beast's tail, and leapt. The tyrannosaurus snapped at the empty air beneath him, then Phylomon was past, running toward a cave, an irregular-shaped hole with dried vines clinging around the edges.

Once inside the cool shadows, Phylomon stopped to let his eyes adjust. The air smelled dusty, smoky, and slightly of . . . hot bloody steel. It was an odd fragrance, one Phylomon had not smelled in many centuries, the scent of many symbiotes in the same room. But it was far beneath him.

Down the shaft, echoing laughter sounded, snatches of conversation from some blood eaters. The monsters sounded disarmingly human. Millions of feet had pounded the path as hard as concrete. Far ahead a torch beckoned. Phylomon pulled out his knife and crept down toward it.

He did not have to go far to meet the first of the blood eaters. When he came upon three of them, the last in line turned and sniffed the air, somehow recognizing even in the darkness that Phylomon was a stranger. The creature shouted and leapt at him, a jump of forty feet that made the beast seem to soar. Phylomon slashed the blood eater as it sailed overhead, then brandished the knife at the others.

They stared at him in the shadows, seeing him clearly in the darkness, like cats.

"What are you?" one of the two remaining blood eaters asked, and Phylomon stood, unsure how to answer. "What are you?"

The questioner held a torch and appeared to be a fat dark-haired man with a beard and simple rough clothes. He had a jolly, innocent face, the face of a youthful laborer, the kind of face that Phylomon would naturally be attracted to if he stopped at an inn and were looking for conversation. The other was a younger woman in buckskin pants and a dark tunic, a woman who looked tough and rangy, the kind of woman he would want as a companion if he were hauling supplies through the Rough.

For a moment the illusion that these might be simple humans was so complete that Phylomon stopped, wondering what to answer these new children to Anee. "I am Phylomon, the last Starfarer on this planet."

The woman growled through the back of her throat, sounding like a vicious dog, and she ran at him, then raked him a ferocious blow with a cupped hand, a blow that knocked Phylomon aside as if he'd been hit with a sledge.

Phylomon stopped and held his belly. The woman mistook it as a signal that he was actually wounded, and closed immediately. Phylomon plunged the knife into her throat, severing her head from its body.

The man with the torch stood, watching the whole event, then raised his brows. "We cannot kill you? How queer," he said casually, as if it were a mere observation.

More than anything else, those few words made Phylomon realize that this blood eater was not a human analog in anything more than form.

The blood eater threw back its head and shrieked, a great piercing cry that rang through caves like a war-horn. Phylomon leapt forward and slashed its neck. The cheerful-looking man stood for a moment, smiling, still holding the torch, then crumpled.

From deep in the cave, hundreds of cries issued from answering throats, thundering through the ground. *We are not alone,* Phylomon's symbiote observed. In moments the blood eaters would issue forth, joined by whatever other defenses the Creators had formed.

Tantos cannot be far behind me, Phylomon realized. He snatched up the fallen torch and rushed forward, down the cave. He came to a point where the passage split in two, and above him was a fissure in the rock. Down the dark passages below he heard shouting, so Phylomon tossed the torch, held his bag of harmonic resonators in his teeth, and climbed up the crevice, grabbing at small handholds, until he was dozens of feet above ground. There he waited. Up the passage from which he'd come, the light of the torch still burned. Like a magician who provides his audience something to focus on with one hand while his other performs the trick, Phylomon hoped that the light would distract the blood eaters, divert their attention to the scene ahead.

Within a minute blood eaters began boiling out of the cave, hundreds of them, rushing forward. Phylomon dared not move, but kept himself wedged in the rock.

The blood eaters ran up toward the mouth of the cave, and then screamed as they met Tantos. Phylomon complacently clung to the walls for a long time, listening to death cries, the shrieks of the blood eaters. Hundreds poured past him, and Phylomon was content to listen to the sounds of Tantos's battle. He imagined Tantos, in his red symbiote, the symbiote he had stolen from Phylomon's dead brother, casting flames and hip-deep in bodies with more rushing upon him all the time. The blood eaters would not know that he was virtually impervious to their attacks, but perhaps they would do some good. They might wrestle away his weapon. Most likely they would die in their attempt.

As the cries continued, great spiders began to scurry past Phylomon's hands. They were larger than tarantulas, with thick spines, and huge mandibles. They crawled past and Phylomon imagined how a normal person might fare as they dropped from above to bite their victims.

A few moments later, Tantos walked beneath Phylomon, and the Starfarer wanted to attack. But Tantos was not alone. Twenty elite Crimson Knights followed behind, secure in their nearly impenetrable armor. Two of them carried laser cannons while the rest bore more conventional arms and explosives. They moved warily, watching all around by the light of ancient glow cubes that one man held in his hands. Huge spiders dropped from above but bounced harmlessly off the armor like children's balls.

Tantos has succeeded in replicating the armor of the ancient Crimson Knights, Phylomon realized.

Centuries ago, the Starfarers had made such armor for their law enforcement officers. Once, it had been considered a high honor to be allowed to wear the uniform. The armor itself was made from spun polymers of carbon and cesium which were lighter than Benbow glass, but nearly as tough. The outer shell was not difficult to make, and Phylomon had always suspected that the slavers would someday regain the technology. More important, and more dangerous, were the modulators built into the helmets—for the modulators emitted electromagnetic waves in frequencies that could alter the brain waves of those nearby, sapping the victims of their will. As a weapon, the modulator left the common man vulnerable to the Crimson Knights' every suggestion. And so, among the Starfarers, only the kindest of men, only those proven worthy, had been awarded the honor of becoming Crimson Knights.

For hundreds of years, the slavers had been unable to duplicate the technology found in the remaining dozen suits. But now, Tantos had begun to succeed. Watching these horrors as they snaked through the dark caverns, Phylomon felt repulsed.

Tantos had more knights with him than Phylomon had believed existed in the world, and Phylomon worried. How many more were there? Hundreds? Thousands?

Probably none, Phylomon told himself. *If Tantos had had an army of Crimson Knights, he would have brought them.*

Phylomon let them pass, let them get far down the corridors, then dropped thirty feet, landing as quietly as a spider himself.

He waited, curious. Perhaps Tantos would kill the Creators. Those lasers could cut through Phylomon's thin symbiote, but he was not sure that they would cut through those of the great worms. He followed behind, walking softly, guiding himself only by hand as he touched the walls.

After nearly an hour, he lost the faint reflections of Tantos's lights and found himself stumbling in darkness. The smell of the Creators was getting stronger, and he heard the gurgling roar of a distant underground river, swift and strong.

Water. Yes, his father had once told him something about water. The Creators needed it in great quantities.

Phylomon wore a necklace of ancient glow cubes under his tunic, but found he like the shelter of darkness. He continued guiding himself with his left hand against the wall, and after another two hours realized he had made a mistake—at first while following Tantos, he

had come across a number of dead bodies, but now he
was finding none. Tantos and his men must have turned
another way, and Phylomon had taken a side passage.
But he could smell the Creators ahead, and he could
hear the water.

Phylomon reached a place where the walls suddenly fell away, and he could hear a strong river flowing,
almost deafening in its intensity. The burnt-steel smell
grew powerful, and in the distance a pale ghostly light
emanated from the walls, bioluminescence.

Sharpen my vision, Gireaux, Phylomon whispered to
his symbiote, yet the hazy light did not resolve. The
symbiote was exercising its full powers. Ahead, the walls
and ceiling seemed incredibly high. Phylomon walked
toward the water, found a strong icy river flowing
through the cavern, and bioluminescence from the ceiling made the waters gleam faintly black. Phylomon took
out his glow cubes, pinched one so that the cavern was
lit. Still, he could not see how deep the water was. Phylomon tentatively stepped in, testing the water's depth,
and fell in over his head, found himself tumbling, carried swiftly downstream through a raging torrent until
he splashed over a short waterfall into a deep lake. The
glow cubes sunk into the depths.

Suddenly the bioluminescence became stronger.
He'd found a great dimly lit cavern, like a world full of
starlight, and all around was life: Trees grew in the cavern, massive and hoary, hundreds of feet tall, larger
than redwoods. Yet they twisted up like great elms.

He saw giants under the trees—huge, sedate, misshapen men. Men who could be no less than eighty feet
tall and that could not have weighed less than imperial
mammoths. They were ogres really—broad, squat, nothing human about them except their general form. In the
bioluminescence, their skin looked pale gray, and their
eyes were huge black pools. They squatted, sedately,
and with their long arms plucked giant fruits from the
trees, and the creatures fed more slowly than sloths.

A pale white luminescent moth fluttered overhead,

with a wingspan of perhaps a yard, and lighted among high tree branches. From those branches grotesque birds cooed, larger than dragons. Of the beasts in the cavern, the birds alone consciously made noise.

Phylomon suddenly longed for more noise. The sounds of Tantos and his men doing battle with the Creators would have been comforting, and Phylomon wondered where Tantos was. It had been two hours since he'd lost Tantos's trail. Could he have already found this passage, already done battle with the Creators?

In the water beneath him, a giant fish rubbed Phylomon's leg, a fish so enormous that it could have swallowed him.

All the creatures in this cavern breathed evenly, so that their inhalations and exhalations sighed like a gentle wind.

One of the giant ogres grunted, turned his head toward Phylomon, and under the bioluminescence Phylomon could suddenly see within the trees the pale reflections of dozens of moist eyes, watching him.

It was strange, surreal, for none of the ogres moved except to follow him with their eyes—as if they existed only to sit in silence, enormous and unmoving, to decorate this forest. A deerlike beast stood drinking from the river, perhaps thirty feet at the shoulder.

Phylomon felt small, insignificant, like a child again on the space station orbiting Anee, wheeling among the stars, while around him moved the adults, massive and powerful and ancient and mysterious.

He floated for a while on his back, almost afraid to move. The currents of the small lake carried him farther downstream, until he realized that he was not in a lake at all, merely in a wider, deeper channel. For twenty minutes he floated with the current, through the great unending forest, beneath mushrooms that sprawled above like houses, until at last he stopped, cast upon a dark shore.

Gravel scraped his feet, round and slippery. He splashed out of the water, crawling over clamshells larger than himself. He fell upon a deep bed of moss that grew as high as wheat, and there he lay, unsure what to do.

A worm came to him then, sliding through the semidarkness over the wet moss until it stopped, a hundred yards away, and it breathed upon him, the scent of hot metal. The worm was enormous, forty feet at the shoulder, and only the tip of its head showed. Phylomon could not guess at its length. Its pale green skin was covered with strange bluish bumps, perhaps some form of lichen or colonies of mold.

"What are you doing here, Phylomon Starfarer?" it asked in a mild sonorous voice that whispered through the trees like a morning breeze. In the darkness at this distance, Phylomon could not see a mouth.

Phylomon had not imagined the meeting to be anything like this. He had imagined that the Creators would be together, huddling in one large cave, and that he could use the deadly hover mine concealed in his arm to kill them all at once—or at least kill enough so that they would be diminished, unable to fight the humans effectively. But here was only one Creator in this giant cave, and though the bomb might kill it, the others would live. Phylomon could not kill them all, and he found himself sobbing, choking on his words.

"I followed one called Tantos, who wears a red symbiote, a pyroderm. He came to destroy you. I was curious to see if he could succeed."

"Yes," the Creator said. "He came. He and his men are dead. His machines of death lie broken. We squashed him. You may sniff the remains, if you are . . . curious?"

"No," Phylomon said, certain that the Creator spoke the truth, and he was stunned. *Even at our fiercest, we are insignificant to them,* he realized.

The worm sat unmoving, apparently observing Phylomon for a long time, and Phylomon did not know what to say. In the dim light he could not see if it had eyes, could guess only that it smelled him.

"Which Creator are you?" Phylomon said at last.

"By the Starfarers I was named Seven. By the Pwi I am called Zheforso, Ruler of Mankind—humans, Neanderthals, Hukm, and Mastodon Men."

Phylomon's heart leapt within him as he recalled the giant creatures of the forest, the great ogres that sat like totems. Though the other Creators would lend a hand in destroying mankind, Zheforso was the only one who could rebuild them all again someday. Phylomon's throat swelled. He had so many questions, yet only his fear spoke.

"May I leave?" Phylomon asked.

"If you desire," the worm answered.

"You will not kill me?"

"You may live, for the moment," the worm said, and Phylomon heard a tone in its voice. The creature was obviously not accustomed to speaking to humans—when it spoke, it did not modulate its voice with emotion well—yet Phylomon could detect a certain reverence that the worm might have once accorded his ancestors, but which Phylomon himself felt he no longer deserved.

"Yet you will kill my people?"

"Yes."

"And you will recreate us someday?"

"The populations must be controlled," the worm answered.

Phylomon took one long last look at the grandeur of the cave—the vast trees, the ogres feeding beneath them. *Yes, totems,* he realized, *monuments to Zheforso's power.* Phylomon wished he had time to explore this cave, see what wonders it held.

The Creators are programmed to protect *above all,* Phylomon knew, *and only Zheforso has the power to rebuild mankind. If this one dies, the others will be forced to change their tactics. Their programming will not allow them to exterminate us completely.*

"If you only knew how much I want to return to the stars," Phylomon said, his mouth dry. "I would have left this planet, if I could. We would have taken ourselves away, if not for the Eridani." He pulled out his knife, and with a trembling hand cut into his arm and removed the black hover mine, small compared to other hover mines, yet so much more powerful. The disk was covered with blood, as if it were his own bloody child.

The great worm sniffed and recoiled in fear, its whole mass shuddering. Phylomon saw an opening then, a mouth perhaps a yard wide. Phylomon pushed the detonator and tossed the bloody hover mine toward the worm, hoping to get as close as possible to its head. The mine glided gracefully on its cushion of air as Phylomon grabbed his sack of weapons, leapt for the water.

At the far end of Zheforso's hallway, the giants roared as a brilliant strobe of flames burst through the canopy of trees. Rivers boiled, and great birds larger than dragons dropped from limbs, their feathers streaming flames like meteors. The giants beneath the earth fell more slowly, yet even for them death came swift.

Chapter 15
Spirit Walk

The small boat bounced over the waves at irregular intervals, lying dead in the water. Tull had stopped the engines hours before, and now he held Fava in his arms as the poison wrung sweat from her. Moonlight shone faintly through the one uncovered window, and Fava spoke. "Water."

Tull went to the barrel, pulled on the tap, and found that he had to wait long for the water to come out. He filled the small jug, brought it back to Fava.

"We are going to need more fresh water," he told her. She didn't answer. "I'll have to watch for an ice floe. We have been skirting enough of them. Perhaps we can melt some ice."

Tull gave the water to Fava, then got up. He looked out the single uncovered window. He could see no more birds on the deck, no ice floes; he could see very little at all.

He went outside, closing the door quickly, carefully walked the deck, untying the tarps that covered the windows. They had sailed barely forty miles from shore, and he listened. The voices of serpents spoke underwater nearby.

Closer than he expected. He looked toward the sound. There in the distance, perhaps three miles off, was Tantos's ship, a dark blotch on the silver line where the water met the sky.

Tull ran inside, gunned the engines, and headed due east, giving the little boat full throttle. The boat leapt over the waves, and Tull stood hunched at the controls, watching behind.

After a few minutes he realized he was losing them.

"Good," Tull whispered, but he felt something, a cool touch inside his chest that made his breath come sharp. It could have been only a flashing pain from his wound, but he knew it was more. A fear took him then, something that threatened to ruin the peace that had built up inside them. Atherkula was following on the ship.

He watched for an hour, until the ship dropped below the horizon, then Tull ripped some cloth from his shirt, pointed the boat east, and tied the throttle on full.

Tull went to Fava, held her fevered head in his lap. Sweat dripped from her, making his legs damp, and his back ached. The pain in his chest was sharp and thick, and he tried to sleep.

In his dreams Tull sat at a campfire where blue smoke wreathed up from the wet wood, and around him ancient Pwi danced. Men, women, and children—faces tattooed with whorls and spirals above the brow—sweated and leapt for glee around the fire, joined hand in hand, twisting and singing, while some of the elders only sat around the outskirts of the fire singing or just clapping hands to keep beat with the drummers and the flutists. The smell of baked salmon came strong on the wind, and behind him was a long hogan where a half-wild dire wolf nursed her cubs in the doorway.

In the dream Tull realized that this was something that had happened long ago. Only once in his life had Tull seen one of the old Pwi who had cut his face and rubbed in the ashes needed to make the whorls and spirals. Not in anyone's living memory had the Pwi dwelt in the long hogans with their sod roofs. He listened for the words of the song, but they escaped him, as if the singers were all speaking in some foreign tongue. Yet here and there, he heard snatches of words. *"Tcho-fethwara, Tcho-fethwara,* no darkness, no darkness."

Were they calling for an end to darkness? he wondered, or do they sing of their fears? He watched their faces, and knew they did not sing from fear. He felt the cool wet wind whipping his cheeks, smelled the rain. Out beyond the edge of the campfire, the grass grew short and vibrantly green. Tull was suffused with the sweet sense of belonging, as if the people dancing around him were dear friends. "Come dance with us, and sing the song," a voice whispered, and in the dream he heard a girl say something about grass and sunlight. He listened carefully to the words, realized that the vowels had shifted, but that he knew the words. "The grass will raise its face to the sunlight. The grass will raise its face to the sunlight."

Suddenly Tull understood. Spring was coming, and the ancients wanted him to come join them, wanted him to come help sing the song that would bring springtime.

Tull rose from beside the fire, and the line opened up, and he grasped the hands of an old woman. He looked her in the eye as they leapt and twisted, saw the braided cords of her gray hair, the merry gleam in her eye. "Yes, Spirit Walker," the old woman said, "we must sing in order to bring the sun. Otherwise, spring will never come." Then Tull recognized her. He looked down at her feet, saw her black moccasins with daggers before the silver moon, the Spirit Warrior.

Tull gripped her hand tightly, found himself shouting in her face. "Who are you? Why did you leave me?"

"I am Thunatra, the dream warrior," she said, and she pulled out of his grasp and broke from the line. An old man behind her took Tull's hand, and Tull danced around the fire, straining to see the Spirit Warrior, but she disappeared into the crowd, leaving Tull with only the music of drum and flute, the wild reverie, the sense of companionship and something lost. They danced in

circles, sometimes throwing their hands in the air to
look skyward and spin in time to the music.

Tull listened, learning more and more words to the
song of spring, until at last, dazed and weary, he broke
away and threw himself on the ground, winded. Others
had done the same, and he listened earnestly to one of
them talk, a young man who told of making a great
spear and who spoke eagerly of joining the coming
mammoth hunts. An old woman sat in the darkness,
sewing beads to a dress, while some father spoke to his
girl about the sweet potatoes and onions they would
plant the next day and a harvest to come. Tull just lay
with his head spinning, giddy with a sense of peace and
ease. He looked up in the sky at the bright stars that
seemed to float in the wind. Thor was up, and as Tull
stared, his heart nearly stopped: There were no Red
Drones in the sky.

Tull woke, realized that in the dream there had
been no humans, only Pwi. Thunatra had sent him a
dream of a song that had been sung centuries before he
was born, a song sung before the Starfarers ever went to
war with the Eridani and fell from the sky, bringing
their slavery and their weapons.

As Tull lay beside Fava, he wondered why he had
dreamed this, wondered how the Spirit Warrior sent the
dream. Thunatra the dream warrior had died three hundred years ago, yet somehow she was communicating
with him. A Spirit Walker could learn the spirits of others by touching them with the lightning of his soul. The
sorcerers of the Blade Kin bound others with the shadows of their soul. But the Spirit Warrior was using a
different power, somehow touching Tull in order to *send*
messages.

He pondered the implications, wondered if he
could learn to speak to the spirits of others, as the old
woman did.

After a bit Tull woke from a shallow sleep. Fava's
head had dried, no longer sweating, though a light fever
remained. Tull kissed her forehead, then got up,

checked the window. In the distance he could see the lights from the iron ship. They were gaining on him again. Tull changed course, heading southeast toward Hotland.

Surely they will not chase us so far, Tull thought. *We are nothing to them, only a small boat.* But a voice in his mind said, *You are in one of their small boats, at the isle of the Creators. Curiosity will drive them.* . . . He kept a steady course for several hours, until the sun began to rise golden along the skyline. It would be a clear, beautiful day.

He looked behind. The ship was there on the horizon. His lungs hurt, and Tull could no longer stay sitting. He tied the wheel in place, hunched over it, and slept like one dead.

He woke to a booming sound, hours later.

Fava was on the floor, sweat pouring from her forehead. She crawled up, looked out the window. "The slavers are on us! They've fired over our bow!"

"We'll keep going," Tull said, feeling a great sense of peace. "They don't want to kill us. They want to question us first. They want us alive." He did not know if it was true, did not trust his own words, but he realized with certainty that he would rather die quickly and violently than be taken captive again.

The ship loomed behind, tried to pull alongside for boarding. Tull zagged away from them, abruptly turning due south, and the great ship, unable to match his maneuvers, kept going straight. When they caught up to him a second time nearly an hour later, Tull veered east, and soon sighted land.

The sun was setting when they veered south again, and the great ship lumbered after. They did not have far to go before they spotted the entrance to a small river. The ship fired its cannons, raising flocks of black pteradons that flapped out over the water, their long kite-shaped tails floating behind. Tull veered west, out of cannon range. As the ship tried to turn, he circled them, heading north, hugging the coastline in the darkness, then steered into the river he'd spotted hours earlier.

The passage over the shoals at the mouth of the river was bumpy, and twice the boat hit the sandy bottom as it plunged over breakers. Fava had gone back to sleep, but she stirred and moaned, then lay looking at Tull as they headed upstream.

"Where are we?" she asked.

"Hotland," Tull said.

Worry lines formed above her brow. "What are we doing here?"

"We need fresh water," Tull answered, "and the Blade Kin are still on our trail." After what seemed only a few minutes, the boat scraped bottom, and Tull cut the engines. Outside, small waves lapped the hull, and Tull could hear the forest sounds around them, the chirping whir of frogs in the spring, the honking of a hadrosaur in the distance. Tull had never been this far north in Hotland. He looked out the window.

They were in a forest of twisted red madrone, without leaves, that marched over the hillsides. Down closer to the water was a marsh with trees that looked somewhat like cottonwood. A small sailfin dinosaur chewed water plants in the chill evening air.

"We can't go upstream in the dark," Fava said. "The water is too shallow. We'll end up on a sand bar."

Tull waited, unsure what to say next. "Shall we anchor, or tie up?"

"The Blade Kin have shoreboats," Fava said. "They'll follow us."

"I know," Tull sighed, and he calculated. The shoreboats, with their single masts, would go slower than this boat, but a thermal wind stirred the trees, blowing inland. In two hours, maybe three, the Blade Kin would be on them.

Fava said, "We have to head over the ground."

"And do what, remain trapped here in Hotland for the rest of our lives?" Tull asked, suddenly angry, enraged at the Blade Kin who would not leave him in peace, who for his entire life had somehow managed to leave him not one hour of peace.

Fava stood unsteadily, went to the controls, pulled a cover panel off, and reached in. Inside was a small white cube, like the one Theron Scandal had used to run the freezers back at his inn. "If we take the power cube, maybe they won't take our boat. We can hide, wait until they leave."

Tull acquiesced, for there was nothing else to do. He floated the boat downstream a bit, then gunned the engines to full speed and ran the boat aground in the mire, well offshore, then tied the boat to a fallen tree, just in case rains swelled the river over its present bank. Tull was tired, and his lungs ached, yet he managed to help Fava up into the trees while struggling through the mire carrying two guns and a small pack filled with food. In the darkness they made their way into the hills, twice startling large creatures that looked like giant rats feeding in the underbrush.

Tull's lungs burned and his heart hammered. He felt as if he were making great exertions, but accomplishing little. He ambled like some old man, moving no faster than a walking pace. Fava could manage nothing better. They both knew they would not be able to outdistance the Blade Kin. Their only hope would be to hide.

By sunrise they found themselves in a small brushy thicket. Tull staggered in, covered his tracks behind him, and Fava slumped beside him, gasping for breath. "You've been awake all day and night. I'll take first watch," Fava said.

Tull lay next to her warm body, covered them both with his cloak, kept a gun in his hand. "I love you," he whispered before he fell asleep, and in his dreams, Tull ran.

Tull heard a harsh voice. A foot kicked his ribs. He cried out and clutched Fava, not really awake. The sun was high above them, and the gun had been taken from his hand. Two men in red body armor bent over him, their faces covered with iron masks. A Crimson Knight shouted, kicked, and Tull sucked air painfully.

"Get up, Thrall!" the knight ordered. Tull rolled to his belly, tried to stand. His legs wobbled and his head spun. As he tried to stand, he found blood streaming from his nose and realized they had kicked him in the face.

For some reason he recalled his youth, how his nose would bleed each time he got mad, and he felt inside the warm flow of peace, and Tull laughed. The Crimson Knight struck him in the stomach, pulled him down by the hair, and slapped manacles on Tull's wrist. Tull sat on his knees, unable to breathe, and found that his laughter turned to tears.

They kicked Fava, rousing her until she struggled to her knees. Tull shouted and tried to rise, to strike back, but a Blade Kin held him as the others manacled Fava and chained her to Tull in front.

For the next few hours Tull staggered forward in blind pain as the Crimson Knights beat them and led them down from the hills, and Tull wondered why he had bothered to run. What could it have won? Freedom? He already had that. The Crimson Knights hurried them along with great energy, as if they were a stream rushing down a mountainside, as if they were a force of nature.

At the river at least a hundred Blade Kin camped, tents pitched in a circle. The Crimson Knights threw them to the ground, and Tull lay, gasping, grateful for the rest.

After a few moments, he opened his eyes, saw the hem of a long black robe with red trim. He looked up and met Atherkula's eyes. The old sorcerer seemed bowed by fatigue, his eyes rimmed with red. His jaw was set in anger. "What were you doing at the isle of the Creators?" he asked.

"We went to kill them," Tull said, "just as you did."

"You are stronger than I thought," Atherkula whispered, touching Tull on the chest, looking into him as if in wonder at something he saw beneath the flesh, "if you can raise yourself from the dead. It is a pity that you are not Blade Kin."

"I tried to join once. You wouldn't let me," Tull said.

Atherkula closed his eyes, considered. "Of course you are the ones who stole Phylomon from prison. You left him on the island to fight the Creators?" He opened his eyes and looked at the Blade Kin gathered around. "We'll have to return to the island. Tantos must be warned." Atherkula made a sweeping motion with his hand, and the Blade Kin began tearing down the tents. They dragged Tull and Fava to a shoreboat, threw them in the bottom. One Crimson Knight sat on Tull's chest, as if Tull had been born only for that purpose, to serve as a chair in the bottom of a boat. Tull's lungs ached, and he struggled for each breath.

Fava was moaning behind him as the boat shoved off, and then they were just in the boat, gently rocking, and Tull felt at ease in spite of it all, cradled by the sea. Fava's bare leg nestled warm against him, and he longed to caress her, to turn and kiss her. He reached down and took her hand, and she clenched his, and that was all he needed. He remembered when he was small, how his father Jenks had chained him to the bed in his room, and Tull would fight the chains, ripping the flesh from his ankles and wrists, twice snapping the bones in his own right leg, hoping to escape.

It had accomplished nothing, and now Tull lay feeling warm and fulfilled, accepting. He was drowsy, as if he'd just eaten a large meal and decided to nap on a warm summer day. The sun above him was pleasant, and in his mind he sang the song to the spring.

> *"The grass lifts its face to heaven,*
> *Both mammoth and cottontail bear young,*

I am a chick in a down-feathered nest
Stretching my wings in the sun,

Ice water flows from the mountains,
Young bison kick their feet up for fun,
I soar like the horned-dragons northward
Before the geese bring the sun."

As he recalled the words from his dreams, he thought it
strange. He remembered how his mother had told him
as a child that it was the geese who brought the sun
north in summer, and it was the dragons who chased the
winter away before them. As a child he accepted this as
a reasonable truth. He could never remember having
heard the song, yet its essence had remained among the
Pwi people.

Darrissea dogged Phylomon's trail, treading with stealth
the path that he had forged. During the nights, she
walked only in moonlight, and thus avoided the watchful
eyes of dragons. At dawn, she would conceal herself
beneath rotting foliage, mindful of the hunting birds.
She had no food, dared not light a fire, and so she was
reduced to eating raw the small rodents she found in the
grass.

    All through her travels, a sense of foreboding grew
in her. The land seemed too quiet, dead. She found it
hard to believe that another human could be anywhere
near. At least not a live human.

    She had fallen farther and farther behind the Star-
farer, until at last she found the mouth of the cave outside the city of blood eaters. There, she took a half-
burned taper from the hands of a dead woman who had
been rotting for days. She lit the taper.

    Darrissea followed the trail of corpses downward.
A great battle had been waged. Several times she found
the corpses of Crimson Knights, their weapons crushed
and broken, the armor torn from their bodies. She put

on some scraps of armor, shielding herself. She opened one man's pack, removed some food, and sat to feed on bread and last summer's apples.

When her third taper had nearly burned out, she found what looked like a star glowing on the ground.

It was an ancient glow cube, an artifact of the Starfarers. She squeezed it, and light erupted from her hands so that it shone redly through her fingers.

A dozen yards ahead, she found the body of Tantos himself, smashed on the rocks. The crimson skin of his pyroderm had faded to a dull orange. She reached down to touch the Slave Lord's chest.

With a tearing sound, a scrap of flesh broke away, wrapping itself around her wrist. Darrissea stumbled back in fright as the pyroderm grasped her, then she pulled it off, threw it to the ground. It sat, wriggling, like a tapeworm.

"Come on, little one," Darrissea said, and she picked it up, stuffed it into the pocket of her tunic.

For hours more she wandered, until she found the cavern and held her glow cube aloft. Through all the destruction she had witnessed, nothing prepared her for this: the huge trees burned to rubble, the corpses of giants lying sprawled on the ground, a stream where the fish had boiled from the searing heat.

Darrissea followed the stream until she found the Creator. Perhaps its symbiote still lived, for the thing trembled as if in pain, but the tapering front end of the beast had been blown away. Where its head should have been was only a blackened depression. It stank of soured flesh.

Wandering beside the pool, she found the body of Phylomon. The symbiote that enveloped his hairless corpse was normally a washed cerulean blue—summer sky on the horizon. But he was grayish white now, the gray of paper ashes. The outer peel of his skin had dropped off in flakes, as if he were some ancient fish whose scales, being infested with sea lice, had become discolored and outworn.

Beside the body in the mud lay the ashes of the cloth bag. The nine rods had spilled onto the ground, and Phylomon's dead hand still clung to one.

So the Starfarer failed us, she realized, and wondered why she could not cry. Perhaps she had known he would fail, had been sure that he would be dead ever since finding Tantos. It had all been hopeless from the start. One Creator killed, and no more weapons except the rods. Yet this island was filled with weapons formed by the Creators—blood eaters, the gray birds, a new breed of dragon. Phylomon had not finished the job.

Darrissea reached down for the harmonic resonators, gathered them in her arms like a handful of twigs, and tried to pull the last one free from the Starfarer's outstretched hand. The dead hand held tight, and Darrissea shook the rod.

The hand pulled away with it, and she gasped, stared. It was hollow, like a glove. Darrissea probed the skin with her foot, squashed it, found it was all hollow, and had split down the back. She held her light close to the mud, saw naked footprints coming out of the water, followed them up into the deeply scorched moss.

There, on the ground between two logs, lay a tall naked man with patches of burned skin and short golden hair. She touched his shoulder to see if he were alive, and the man raised up, looked at her with wide brown eyes. "Help!" he said, in Phylomon's voice.

Mahkawn lay in the arms of Pirazha with the sheets twisted around him, wrapped down around his waist so that the smell of sex was muted, and he could see sweet Pirazha's beautiful body. The late morning sun streamed through the window, and already his sons and daughters had run into the streets to play.

He had wakened softly from his dreams, then laid with an empty belly all during the morning, content. Though he had lost Tantos's favor and the right to lead the assault against the Creators, he was taking refuge in other comforts. The smell of cooking fires and breakfasts in other houses made him hungry, and he thought absently of pushing his lover from bed, forcing her to cook him breakfast, when a sturdy fist pounded on the door.

"Enter," he shouted, not willing to get up and answer the door.

A Blade Kin entered, one of his Dragon Captains from the Invisible Arm of the Brotherhood, a human named Bittermon Dent. "Lord Tantos's ship arrived last night, and our presence is requested at his palace immediately."

"Our presence?" Mahkawn asked, for he could think of no reason why Tantos would send for the Dragon Captain. "How did you find me? I told no one I was here."

"You were followed, Omnipotent," Bittermon said.

Mahkawn sighed. Followed. An Omnipotent followed, as if he were a common criminal. He rolled out of bed, pulled on his tunic, robe, and boots, strapped on his sword and eye patch.

When they got outside, the day was bright, clear, with the promise of warmth. In the soil beside Pirazha's doorstep, the first tender leaves of a crocus were beginning to push through the ground.

As they walked to the train depot through the crowded streets, Mahkawn found himself eager for news. "How did the campaign go?" he asked. "Have you any word? Are the Creators dead?"

"No, no word," Bittermon said, looking away.

The Dragon Captain was a damned secretive man, and Mahkawn suddenly resented his game. "You have not even heard a rumor?"

"Very little, Omnipotent."

Rage took Mahkawn, and he grabbed Bittermon's ponytail, spun the ass, threw him to the ground, drawing his sword as he did so. "Answer me, damn you!" Mahkawn shouted, and his Neanderthal blood raged through him. His world went red and his hand trembled on the sword, and everything in him screamed out to kill the man.

Bittermon kept his eyes to the ground. "Forgive me," he said. "The rumors are not good, and I did not want to speak them in public, for fear they are wrong. I beg you, wait until we have reached Tantos's palace."

Mahkawn stood, chest heaving, muscles twitching. He shouted and swung the sword down, turning it at the last moment so that it whizzed over Bittermon's head, slicing off his ponytail. "Damn you, damn you," Mahkawn grunted, and realized he had wronged the man with his impatience. He wiped the hair from the sword blade on his cloak, sheathed the old steel, then turned his back on the man.

He had embarrassed himself, pulling a sword on an inferior in a fit of rage as if he were some old Thrall woman who could not control her emotions. "I—I am sorry," Mahkawn said. "I thought . . . never mind."

They rode the Death's Head Train in silence, Mahkawn embarrassed. *I was caught spawning in the bed of a woman who can no longer breed, and I nearly slew one of my own Dragon Captains. What is wrong with me?* Yet Mahkawn knew what was wrong. He'd seen old Neanderthal Blade Kin do this before, saw the emotionalism surface in them. After a lifetime of fighting it, of denying that it existed, the Thrall in them would arise—often the first sign of senility. *I am but fifty-two,* Mahkawn told himself, *I am but fifty-two,* and already he could see that his life was over.

When they disembarked, Mahkawn was so preoccupied that he let Bittermon lead the way, and the young Dragon Captain took Mahkawn up the long route to the palace, through the Street of the Dissidents, up the long avenue where the skulls of Tantos's old enemies glittered white in the walls on each side of the street, only the holes in their eyes and noses staying in shadow. The scene was supposed to inspire the proper state of humility in those who might come seeking favors or mercy from Lord Tantos, and as Mahkawn walked up the street, a sense of foreboding grew in him. Was it an accident that Bittermon had chosen this route, or had he been commanded?

As they passed the Cage of Bones before the doors that led to the great audience chamber, Mahkawn saw four Blade Kin in the cage, removing the starved corpse of the last dissident to have died there.

Bittermon opened the great iron doors, and they crept into the palace. Braziers of sulfur were burning as always, filling the audience hall with a stench, and at the far end of the hall, in his red robes of state, Tantos stood with his back turned, looking out the window.

Mahkawn cleared his throat, "How went the battle, my lord?"

The robed figure raised a hand, and one of the attendants went into a side chamber, brought out Tull and Fava. They were chained hand and foot, and Mahkawn gaped at Tull as the Blade Kin forced the two to their knees. Both had purpled and swollen faces, for they had been badly beaten, and Fava leaned against Tull for support.

The robed figure turned, and Atherkula stood, wearing the robes of state, the red hood, the heavy belt with the golden scourge tucked in behind it.

So Tantos had died. Mahkawn could not help but think that the outfit looked somehow baggy on the old Neanderthal. He was too short and too broad for the fit, yet Atherkula's eyes were the glittering, unfeeling eyes that Tantos had once had, and his smile, the tight, slightly upturned lips, were very similar. *Ah, he wears the mask of state well,* Mahkawn thought, looking at that cruel smile.

"Come and see what I have found," Atherkula said, and he walked down to the prisoners, stood glowering at them.

"Where is Tantos?" Mahkawn asked.

"The battle went ill for Tantos," the sorcerer said heavily, and waited as if Mahkawn might say something to console him. "The Creators killed Tantos, destroyed his forces. Only one of our Crimson Knights escaped to tell the tale. We will have to mount a larger assault." Atherkula touched the scourge at his belt meaningfully, a tone of boastfulness in his voice. "I will lead Tantos's armies now."

"What?" Mahkawn said. "Tantos may have given you that right. But do you think you could replace him? Have you considered what the other Slave Lords will say? You will start a war! They will want a human in your place!"

"They have no reason to fight me," Atherkula answered. "Tantos gave his scourge for me to wield, and the right of succession falls to me. He has no offspring to claim his throne, and he saw that I would lead well in his stead. We do not need human lords to govern us any longer. The armies of the Blade Kin can govern themselves."

Down at their feet, Tull looked up at Atherkula and laughed, a bitter laugh that touched Mahkawn to the bone. Tull said, "So the slaves will hold the keys to their own shackles? What a prize you have won! You will be able to take Tantos's seat at the next arena games!"

Atherkula pulled the scourge from his belt, raised it threateningly. The golden chains on the scourge glimmered in a ray of sunlight from the high windows, and the sharp flanges at their ends sparkled.

Tull spat on Atherkula's feet.

Atherkula swung the scourge, a whistling blow that struck Tull across the face. The golden chains on the scourge could not tolerate the impact, and half of the balls thumped across the floor. Tull sat for a moment, blood oozing from the cuts on his face, as if he had been clawed by a lion, then he pitched forward, face down.

"You will not mock me," Atherkula said softly. "I will not tolerate it. As the Minister of Retribution, I'll finish the job."

He turned to Mahkawn, eyes flashing. "You were ordered to kill this man, and failed to fulfill that order. As of today, you are no longer Blade Kin. I will find a suitable job for you as a Thrall, gutting fish on the docks. Bittermon Dent will take your office."

Mahkawn bowed his head in submission, dropped to one knee. The first act of a tyrant was always to remove the opposition, and Mahkawn knew he could not withstand the sorcerer. He pulled off his black robe of office and laid it at Atherkula's feet. Bittermon scooped it from the floor and fumbled with the pin, placing it on his own shoulders.

Atherkula continued. "As for you, Tull Genet, you shall die upon the Street of Dissidents, locked within the cage of bones! Guards, take this rabble from me!"

Blade Kin guards ushered forward from their hidden alcoves, pulled Tull and Fava to their feet, and Bittermon placed his hand on Mahkawn's shoulder, lifted him.

Two Blade Kin escorted the old general from the room. Mahkawn was so stunned that he felt as if he were stumbling through a dream world. They took him out into the bright sun, down the Street of the Dissidents to the Death's Head Train. The huge engine sat among the green fields, a monstrosity of black iron with its great Pwi skull on the front.

This is the last time I shall ride this train, he realized, now that he had been stripped of rank. The two guards sat on either side of him, so that he was sandwiched between. Their dark-red wool robes smelled of grease and smoke and nights in the snow, the way that they do at the end of winter, and Mahkawn studied one of them —a young Neanderthal, hardly more than a boy, yet his jaw and neck muscles were so rigid that Mahkawn would have sworn that he could crack his head open on those muscles.

I could fight him, kill him now and try to use my men against Atherkula, Mahkawn realized, yet he felt fatigued, weakened by age. *What would be the purpose? To set myself in Atherkula's place until the human Slave Lords depose me? Shall I take a place in line among the despots who rule?*

The young guard flexed his muscles, and his hand drifted absently to the sword at his side, and with great clarity Mahkawn realized that Atherkula anticipated such a move, and that he would not allow it. These guards would be Mahkawn's assassins. Atherkula planned to kill Mahkawn, just as he would kill Tull, only more quietly.

Mahkawn savored the way Tull had spat on Atherkula. It was admirable. Altogether admirable. Good strong Blade Kin stock. Mahkawn rested his eyes. *My son. I almost called him my son, once. He is better than all the Thralls I have spawned put together.* Mahkawn grinned to himself. He should have understood his own infatuation for the boy long ago. A son. That is what he wanted, a Blade Kin son. *Ayaah, would it not be good,* Mahkawn thought, *if Tull really were the Okansharai.*

He toyed with the idea of using his power to free Tull. He could gather some men and get Tull to a boat, send him back into the Rough so that Atherkula could fret. *The old sorcerer could have me, but not those under my protection.* Mahkawn could barely recall a single instant of the walk back to the train and kept trying to focus, to recall some detail of the trip, but all he could recall was Atherkula's ancient chinless face, the tight cold smile, the piercing blue eyes at once haughty and empty. Mahkawn lay his head back on the crimson silk cushions and closed his eyes, confident that the assassins would strike soon, before the Death's Head Train even reached Bashevgo.

Mahkawn casually moved his hand to the dagger concealed up his left sleeve, then whirled and struck.

Shortly after dawn, Darrissea and Phylomon emerged from the caves and made their way down the mountain. Phylomon wore pants taken from a dead blood eater, carried a bent sword taken from the body of a Blade Kin.

He urged her forward, moving as fast as he was able on wobbly legs, setting white rods in the ground. They reached a fork in the road, and Darrissea ran ahead, but Phylomon shouted, "Not that way—blood eaters!" and urged her to a second path.

After nearly an hour the path opened onto a broad plain, and Phylomon looked off into the distance—clouds were rising around the island, clouds of birds in vast flocks that zagged back and forth wildly. Phylomon stretched, letting the sun play over his naked chest. His skin was paler than Darrissea had imagined, like the flesh of a child. She imagined that perhaps this was the way a god would appear, or perhaps all Starfarers had been beautiful. Yet his face was drawn, haggard. And on his back were nasty red welts.

"Are you going to be all right?" Darrissea asked.

Phylomon nodded. "It will be hard to adjust. I feel . . . drained. The symbiote did all it could to keep me from boiling alive." He shook his head grimly, as if still in pain.

"We can rest here." Phylomon looked weary, as if he would drop, and in the sunlight Darrissea could see the white puckering welts on his back more clearly. The flames had burned right through the symbiote, criss-crossing the Starfarer's back with reddened skin, as if he had suffered under the lash. He stumbled a little, and Darrissea held him. "Come, sit and rest."

"No," Phylomon said, nodding toward the birds. "Something is happening. They're like—starlings—in the fall, nervous, preparing to migrate. Look at them! Every hour we stay gives the Creators more time to launch an attack."

"So you want to hit them first?"

Phylomon nodded. "The caves back there are magma tubes. The mountain was a volcano. The resonators might do some damage here, if we're lucky."

"And if we're not lucky?"

"At the very least, I think I can collapse the caves.

Perhaps the Creators would be crushed. It might only seal the Creators in, until they can dig free."

Darrissea watched the clouds of birds zigzagging across the sky. He was right, something was happening. She could feel it in the air, an electricity that made her skin itch. She imagined trying to go east or west to set the rods—but the birds were so thick. Only to the south was a path open, and it led into the territory of the blood eaters. She turned south, and Phylomon followed her through the rocks, past a forest of sinister trees, white as bone.

They stopped in hills of round rocks and looked down over a city. Among clearings between the single-celled huts, the blood eaters tended their gardens, beautiful pairs of brothers and sisters. But something seemed odd. The beach down in the bay was filled with boats, hundreds of small craft with white sails, and thousands of the blood eaters worked on the beach, fixing masts to the boats, preparing an expedition.

Darrissea looked at Phylomon, at his fair skin. He stood a head taller than the blood eaters. Darrissea said, "How bold are you?"

No mere Blade Kin ushered Tull from the palace. Instead, six Crimson Knights in their red body armor, faces masked with black iron, unchained him from Fava and dragged him outside.

Fava screamed, "Tull," and grabbed his hand, trying to hold him, but a knight stepped on her wrist cruelly while others pulled her back. As they dragged him out the door, she screamed, *"Ay-zhoken-thrall!* You gave me the love that enslaves."

Tull shouted back, *"Ay-zhoken-thrall! Ay-zhoken-Pwirandi!* You gave me the love that enslaves. You gave me love that made me crazy." Her eyes met his, and he tried to bore the knowledge of his love deep inside her.

Outside the sky was clear blue, the day sunny, and they dragged Tull by his feet along a green lawn wet with water from the winter snows. As they dragged, he kept hitting bumps, white rocks in the lawn, but as he passed one, the mud scraped away, and he saw that it was not a rock at all, but a human bone buried under the grass.

They dragged him up a hill, higher and higher, where soon there was no grass at all to hide the hill of bones, and they pulled him into a cage and dropped him, left him in his manacles and irons, slammed the door, then stood outside in a circle, watching.

The cage was too low for Tull to stand straight, so he got up and had to stoop. Dried feces and clumps of dark-brown human hair littered the floor—as if someone had torn out his own hair and left it. The cage was shaped like an inverted bowl, with bars of human and Neanderthal bones painted thickly with some white resin. The bones crossed and recrossed in triangles and squares. The door had no hinges, only three massive iron chains wrapped around it many times, then bound by locks.

Tull pulled some of the bars, hit one with his hand. The paint on the bones somehow made them unnaturally strong, harder than mere cement. He checked the floor. There were no bowls for food or water.

He found he was breathing hard as he realized that they would starve him, so he closed his eyes and leaned his head back, sang his true name, searching for that clear peace inside. It was still there, very deep, but he found it. Yet holding it, trying to retain his calm, became a battle.

He thought of Fava, of her upcoming slavery. She would be aching for him now, mourning, and Tull found it hard to remain calm knowing that.

Downhill, Tull could see the Street of Dissidents with its wall of skulls. Thralls had begun to gather there by the hundreds, lining the streets to gawk. Behind him in the distance, bright-green hayfields alternated in bands with unplanted farmsteads in swaths of brown. Flocks of gulls flew about the fields, following slaves who were hooked to plows. Closer to Tantos's palace, barren oaks covered the hills, and Tull mused, realizing that within a few weeks, the oaks would be green with new leafbuds. The palace itself was beautiful, all gleaming white stone with spires and sweeping arches. Only the ancient Starfarers could have designed such a thing.

The knot of people on the streets grew thicker, and Tull wondered why. It would take him days to die, yet they had all come for a show. He recalled how Etanai had shown a picture of himself in this cage, and how it had affected the Pwi back at Smilodon Bay. It had seemed the ultimate horror, yet Tull did not feel it. Instead, he took refuge in his calm.

Dying here, of lack of water, would be an easy death.

A few moments later, half a dozen Blade Kin came and set a large fire only a dozen feet in front of Tull's cage, then brought out a great black cauldron and a tripod and began cooking what looked like white paint.

Tull compared the paint to the color of the unnaturally white bones in his cage, saw it was the same.

"What are you doing?" he asked the men.

A Blade Kin sergeant with a wolf badge on his leather cuirass looked up from where his men stirred the pot. "We must add bones to your cage."

"My bones?" Tull asked.

"No," the Blade Kin replied. He whispered to an inferior, and the man went to the palace. Moments later he and several others brought Fava, dragging her by the feet, and laid her beside the pot.

Fava stared around with wide eyes, looking to the people on the street below for help, calling out softly.

The Blade Kin worked quickly, pounding deep stakes into the ground, then fastened Fava's manacles and leg irons to the stakes so that she was pinned flat to the ground. Fava was breathing rapidly, sweating and pulling at her manacles, reciting bits of songs and muttering to herself, and then the Blade Kin sergeant pulled his knife and looked down at Fava, and Fava softly sang an old death song,

> *"Heavy loads are made for martyrs,*
> *May the gods grant me something I can bear,*
> *I have seen that the winters are growing harder,*
> *I feel the frostbite burn my hair."*

A second Blade Kin moved close to Fava, ran his fingers under the curve of her breast, and she shouted something, closed her eyes.

"Leave her be!" Tull yelled. The Blade Kin laughed. Two of them took Fava's arm.

The sergeant wiped the blade of the knife, looked up at Tull, and said, "We'll take the right arm first." He knelt on his knees and cut into Fava's wrist, preparing to remove the bones. With three men leaning above Fava, Tull could not see much. He heard more than saw the act, heard a little squirting noise, and specks of blood pumped out, splattering the sergeant's face.

Fava whined pitifully like a child, "God slap you! I swear, I'll destroy Bashevgo!" She muttered the oath that she refused to make back in Smilodon Bay. She grunted and struggled and her chains rattled.

Clearly before his eyes, Tull saw the redwoods back in Smilodon Bay, recalled the young men of town drunk and boasting in their beers of how they would someday destroy Bashevgo. All for nothing. Smilodon Bay now lay in cinders, and all her children were here in chains.

Peace left Tull then, and he was filled with a grief that could not be spoken. He realized that he didn't want to see Fava die. He turned away, and though the skies above were blue, in the north he could see great black clouds on the horizon, hurtling toward them. A storm, he thought. He knelt in dung and bones, holding on to the bars of the cage.

Fava screamed, and Tull looked down at the bones littering the hill. *When I was young, I'd hoped for children at my knee, and here are the bones of someone's children.*

I wanted to be wrapped in the arms of a lover, and now the bones of her arms shall wrap me in this cage. His breath came ragged, and Tull's chest ached. *I no longer fear my own death. Atherkula must know that, so instead he shows me the death of beauty and goodness in the world.*

Tull pulled at the bars, straining to rip them from the cage, yanking at their thinnest places, hoping they would snap, and nothing would yield. He felt the muscles tear in his own arm and thought wildly that if he died first, perhaps the Blade Kin would spare Fava.

Tull screamed and smashed his head against one of the bars. He pulled back, saw his own blood spattered against the supremely white bones, and he slammed his head again and again and again. One of the guards shouted at Tull to stop, and Tull beat his skull against the bones and the guard rushed forward, jabbing with his spear, trying to force Tull away from the bars, and Tull struck his head again and grabbed the spear.

"I swear by my blood to free Bashevgo before I die!" Tull screamed, yanking the spear and slamming the tip into his own belly. He jerked the spear free from the Blade Kin and stabbed himself again and again in the belly.

He suddenly felt lightheaded, and the world began to spin. The Blade Kin managed to grasp the spear, pull it away, and step back in surprise. Tull grabbed the bars of the cage over his head. "I swear," Tull said. He looked down at his belly, at his tunic slit open and the red blood gushing from the blue skin, and around him the skies seemed to dim.

The city became a red plain of stone, and the Blade Kin before him were dark orbs, engaged in eating Fava's tendrils of light. The sun shone as an iridescent lavender flower in the skies, and across the land the spirits of grass and trees shone with a flickering purple.

All around to the south, a spirit city rose—blocks of red stone set against a black sky—the dreams and plans of the millions of Slave Lords and Blade Kin and Thralls. Sinuous towers snaked overhead, joined by tedious causeways, huge and dark and misshapen. The designs of the domes and towers and causeways were overwhelming in their bulkiness, monotonous, as if they were monuments to brutality, built by fools.

Below him, on the Street of Dissidents, the ghoul-ish Thralls appeared as a crowd of green flames over black orbs, scared witless by this spectacle, and all about him Tull could see a thousand hues of green within the clots of the slaves' souls.

The guards that hovered over Fava looked up at Tull, hesitating, and Tull decided to stop them once and for all—immediately the fingers of fire that made up the lightning of his soul leapt out. He recalled how Atherkula had tried to control him, pulling on Tull's own lightning, and Tull ripped through the veneer of darkness over the Blade Kin, then grasped the tendrils of light still hidden within them, pulled them out straight, so that the Blade Kin rose from the ground and hovered in midair, unable to move.

He quickly saw that he was using more than his normal twenty-two fingers of light—everywhere fingers of light erupted from him in a great cloud, such was his wrath—and he clenched the Blade Kin that circled him all at once and snapped off the lightning of their souls—tore into their blackness and shredded it, watched their empty husks, the clot of their bodies, fall to the ground, as insubstantial as dead jellyfish washed up on a beach after a storm.

Tull did not understand what was happening. He had heard how Terrazin Dragontamer had slain entire armies with a thought, and he felt that power within him.

I shall destroy this world, he thought, and he did not feel guilty. Like Terrazin the talent warrior of old, Tull sent tendrils of light from himself, until the black skies of the Land of Shapes filled with light. *Every man, woman, and child,* he told himself—and the tendrils shot across continents as he connected.

Simultaneously, he became a Slave Lord in Craal

raping a servant, a young woman in the wilderness nursing an infant child, Chaa running blindly toward Atherkula's palace, a fisherman falling off a boat, an old woman in her sickbed breathing her last, an infant girl gazing at a newt in a clear pool while filled with a sense of wonder, a human in South Bay savoring a bowl of fresh peas, a young Thrall trying to escape Craal in hip-deep snow over the White Mountains, an infant screaming from the womb, an old Neanderthal with a toothache, a teenage Thrall girl sleeping in the tangled arms of her lover, a human tailor sewing green peacock feathers into a dress of black cotton, an old woman studiously biting her nails, Wayan huddled in a cell in the wilderness, a lone Okanjara warrior tossing a spear at an imperial lion.

Everywhere, everywhere, there were people— sleeping, loving, shitting, breeding, dying, waking to life or love or wonder or their own mortality—too many images to flash before his eyes at once, too many lives to conceive. The light from him filled the Land of Shapes like fire. He took them all, grasped the lightning of their souls and prepared to rend them as Terrazin had, thinking it merciful to send them shrieking into nonexistence.

Phylomon and Darrissea walked through the town of blood eaters in the broad light of day, strolling casually like all the other blood eaters, yet Darrissea could not restrain herself from taking Phylomon's hand. She found her breath coming ragged and knew that her face had gone red. Sooner or later someone would recognize them as imposters.

They ambled down to the beach, mingled with others. Hundreds of boats waited all around, masts rising from the beach like an odd forest. Some blood eaters glanced at them, but none raised a cry. Phylomon led her to a secluded spot, checked the sails on a small boat. Darrissea stroked the cloth, mimicking the sedate actions of a blood eater. Her hands trembled, and she stifled a whimper.

"Take care, be strong," Phylomon whispered, and began pushing the boat down the sand toward the water. Darrissea casually helped, and nearby a man and woman looked at them, obviously distressed.

Simultaneously several things happened: One nearby blood eater, a Neanderthal man with a red face, sniffed the air and turned, looked directly at Phylomon, and said, "Food?"

Above them on the mountain, a sound like blaring horns rang out, and everyone stopped, mesmerized by the noise. It was a call of some kind, a signal that Darrissea felt ringing through her bones, shuddering through her muscles, crying, "Move! Move! Move!"

Around the island, gray birds rose like clouds and began shooting inland toward the volcano, and from three separate fissures, something began oozing from the ground—pale shapes that flowed like milk down the mountainside, the gray worms Phylomon had warned about. She did not need to guess what would happen when the birds reached their worms.

Phylomon shouted, "Run!" and pushed the boat down the beach with his might so that it almost seemed to sing as it scraped over sand.

Darrissea grabbed a gunwale, pulling. The red-faced Neanderthal frowned at them, began loping forward with a questioning look in his eye.

Darrissea's feet hit water, and she pulled the boat out a step, tumbled in. Phylomon gave it a shove from behind, and the blood eater lunged—jumping in the air and arcing forward, crossing two hundred feet of ground in only three leaps. He let out a piercing cry that raised the hair on Darrissea's neck, and all across the city, startled blood eaters responded to the call by racing toward them.

Phylomon tossed the blue rod onto the floor of the boat, drew his bent sword, and prepared to meet the blood eaters. "Now! Drop the rod before we die!"

Darrissea grabbed the rod. The blood eater seemed almost to fly through the air, and Phylomon slashed. Blood sprayed over the boat as the blood eater collided with Phylomon, throwing him overboard into the shallows. The boat was still only a dozen feet from shore, and everywhere the blood eaters rushed toward them.

Darrissea saw that she could not stop them, would not have time to escape. She twisted the two halves of the blue rod, tossed it into the ocean.

Immediately her ears began to ring, a dull throbbing, as if her eardrums itched. She felt as if a great vice had been placed over her head, pressing in. Along the beach the blood eaters faltered, covered their ears, and fell, shrieking in pain.

Phylomon climbed from the water, into the boat, hoisted the sail. When Darrissea could stand the pressure no longer, she covered her own ears with her hands, caved in on herself, yet it did not help. The throbbing seemed to come from inside, penetrating every fiber of her body. The ground began to rumble; trees snapped along the shore; rocks and scree broke from the mountain in walls, and then the earth began to move deep beneath them.

Atherkula had gone a mile from the palace to the temple at lake Trout Swimming Deep to pack his belongings. It was an odd thing to do, but he personally wanted to oversee the transfer of his few possessions to Tantos's old palace. He had three acolytes to help, younger boys who showed little promise as sorcerers. He did not mind using such unworthies as beasts of burden to move his things.

The old sorcerer was bent over his dresser, looking at a turtle-shell comb Chulata had worn in her hair as a child. When Chulata's mother had died, Atherkula had gone to the house the day after to retrieve mementos, and found the comb. He stared at it, wondered now if he could bring himself to part with it or if he should take it.

One of the acolytes passed him, saying, "A storm is coming," and Atherkula looked out the window, north of the temple. Ugly black clouds blew in the distance like a great wall of dust.

Then the cold hit Atherkula, the profound sense of violation, and one of the boys beside him cried out and held his chest. Atherkula turned to look at them, and all three acolytes were breathing deeply in exactly the same rhythm. All three of them held their hands out as if they were clutching something before them, and Atherkula felt his own hands reach out, grasping like claws.

He breathed deeply, found that he breathed in their rhythm—the deep inhalations. Their eyes were fixed, staring ahead.

Atherkula shouted, "No!" Yet the icy touch held him, tried to pull him down into a kneeling position. Atherkula closed his natural eyes and looked upon the world as a sorcerer. A great light was sweeping through the Land of Shapes, and Atherkula shuddered, terrified. He could see tendrils of light, reaching into the globe of darkness at his belly, could feel their elemental tug.

Atherkula clutched his stomach, trying to bat away the light. In all his years of seeking to control others, he'd never seen the like, and then he realized the truth: *Tull is dying, and he has us all in his grasp.*

His acolytes fell to their knees, and all three of them blinked in unison, and Atherkula shouted, "Free yourselves! It is the end of the world!" He could see only one thing to do.

Atherkula pulled his dagger and slashed his own right lung open, hoping that he would have at least a few moments to fight. "Adjonai, my ally, strengthen me!" the old sorcerer groaned, and in that moment he was transported into a world where the soft shush of a wind of light whispered through the land, a place where trees were flickering purple flames and the sun a dazzling flower, and his ally was in reach.

_____

Tull heard Atherkula shout in the Land of Shapes, saw
the shadow of Atherkula's soul rush toward him
through the sinister city, a dancing mote of dust. And
for a moment the tendrils of light Tull used went slack
as he lost his focus. Across the red plains to the north, a
second darkness roared, making the air scream—a
sphere as large as a moon; no light came from it. Tendrils of darkness lashed out from the beast, took the
shadow of Atherkula's soul, and pulled him in. Tendrils
of darkness lashed toward Tull like thick black threads
and touched the shadow of his soul.

Out on the red cracked stones of the Land of
Shapes, dust roiled from the ground, billowing up like
clouds. Tull could feel the beast invading him, revealing
itself. On the barren plains, a giant formed and raised
from the soil, crouching like a cat ready to spring, one
hand in the earth. His heavy chest was powerfully muscled, like the chest of a Neanderthal, yet his skin was
purpled like a vulture's and his clawed hands ended in
buzzard's talons. His great black loincloth hung nearly
to the ground in the ancient style of the Pwi and was
formed from swirling black orbs—the shadows of souls.
A green light glowered from his eyes, and filth flowed
out from his feet like rivers. In his left hand he carried a
wooden warshield covered with rattlesnake skin. The
shield radiated despair. In his right—the hand on the
ground—he held a shimmering silver *kutow* with two
stone ax heads that radiated terror, and circling his
brow was a crown of lightning that wriggled and twisted
as it struggled for release—the lightning of captured
souls.

"I have seen you before," Tull said, "on the border
at the nation of Craal. You could not defeat me then,
yet you imagine yourself to be a god?" Tull's heart
pounded. He had indeed seen the being before, but had
not begun to understand it—thought it only a hallucina-

tion caused by his fear of entering Craal, not the manifestation of a being from the Land of Shapes.

The creature swung the great silver *kutow* of terror, and Tull stood beneath its blow. The stones crashed against him, and he felt no fear, received no damage. "You cannot harm me with that," Tull said softly.

Adjonai hissed, "Behold, the great wheel of evil," then turned the round shield to Tull, holding it forward: It throbbed with power, and the rattlesnake skins seemed to crawl in a circle so that the snakes ate their own tails. Tull watched the diamond patterns of darkness and light, realized then that the snake scales were moving—tiny images moving in the distance. "Behold!"

And suddenly Tull saw the shield for what it was—a globe crawling with people, endless herds milling in circles. It drew him. He floated up toward it, mesmerized, ready to take his place. One scale caught his vision, and as he focused on the black dot, an image flashed in Tull's mind, pulsing, vibrating—a crippled Thrall woman begging for sex from a Blade Kin in hopes that she might be treated to better food, and as he beheld it, he tasted the woman's desperation, felt the tightness in her belly that would make her do anything, anything. The scale next to it showed the Blade Kin using her like an animal so that she hardly dared show her face to others. A third scale showed a child born of the union into such destitution that his mother begged him to steal, and Tull felt the young man's hate for his mother, his sadness at what he was becoming. Upon a fourth scale, the same young man at age twelve earned the right to become Blade Kin by culling his own grandfather, slitting the worthless old man's throat. The boy watched the knife do its work, and felt somehow free, knowing what he had purchased. Upon the next scale, in fear of his own mortality, the young Blade Kin spawned a child named Chulata. Linked to the next scale, Tull saw himself kill the sorceress in desperation at wanting to be free, then saw Atherkula seek to exact revenge, until in despair

Tull beat his own head against the bars in the Cage of Bones.

The scales linked together, one by one, becoming part of the magnificent tapestry that was the shield of despair. Tull could feel the timeless weight of years upon it, the eternal heft of the thing. Tull saw himself from far away, just another piece of color in the endless tapestry, and he floated toward it, drawn.

"I own you," Adjonai whispered. "You will adorn the shield of despair. You will take your place upon the wheel of evil and share in my power."

Adjonai held his shield forward, as if bestowing a gift, and closed his green eyes. Tull floated upward helplessly, to take his place on the shield.

Across the world, tendrils of light connected Tull to sixty million people. People who were loving and living, unaware of the beast, uninvolved in its plans. Tull reached out, touching them all, and the blasting sense of hopelessness diminished.

Adjonai shook the shield, rattling it, and Tull's mind went numb. The shield flashed in the sunlight, beckoning. "I own you. You died in despair."

Tull tried to pull back. Despair struck him like a fist, and he could not resist the force that drew him forward. His mind blacked, as if all the connections had been severed.

Tull tried to seek refuge in his past, tried to recall a soft moment with Fava, hoping that Adjonai would lose his grip. Yet Tull could not bring Fava to mind, and found only blackness.

Instead, almost unbidden, he recalled the dream of his ancestors, the ancient Pwi, singing their song to bring the spring. He was dancing around the campfire with ancient Pwi who leapt in joy and discussed their crops. Hope welled in Tull. He looked across the fire to a young girl who twisted and smiled. The music of pan pipes and drums and flutes sang through his veins, and Tull cried out, "Thunatra! Help me!"

Then, with a shout, an old woman appeared between Tull and Adjonai. Thunatra dream warrior held a sheaf of green wheat in one hand, a blazing taper in the other, and she danced before the shield, singing in the tongue of the ancient Pwi. *"Tcho-fethwara, tcho-fethwara,* The grass lifts its face up to heaven. . . ."

The riveting call of the shield diminished, and for a moment both Tull and Adjonai stared at Thunatra. Adjonai shouted in anger, raised his *kutow* to crush her, and Thunatra cried, "Help! I cannot fight him alone!" Then she resumed her chanting.

Tull raised his voice, sang his true name. "Lachish Chamepar, Lachish Chamepar" he sang lightly, "I am Path of the Crushed Heart. *Tcho-fethwara,* no more darkness."

Tendrils of light blazed from Tull, and the beast staggered back. Tull plunged the lightning of his soul into the dark beast, grappling, searching for something to attack within the icy darkness. The lightning of his soul blazed, and with fingers of light he touched the people of Anee, with fingers of light, he touched the Eridani on their distant star. With fingers of light, he stroked the hearts of the Hukm on the snow-covered plains.

He became a mother suckling her daughter. He became a farmer plowing his black field. He became an old woman stroking the liver-spotted hand of her lover, and he touched Adjonai with those images, funneled them.

Everywhere—Tull clasped the lightning of their souls, entwined them with his own, pulled their tendrils of light, pulled the Eridani and the beast toward him. Thunatra's voice raised in a frenzy of song, climbing in power.

Tull found that his spirit knew what to do: Clasping the world by the lightnings of their souls, he bid them dance over the shadow of his own soul. He forced them to touch him, and with the spirit warrior Thunatra Dream Woman, he sang the new world into being.

———————

After weeks of hiding, the Blade Kin had rousted Vo-olai from the woods and forced her into a muddy pen. She'd been waiting now for days, hoping for a chance to escape, but the Blade Kin had come—dragging her, Wayan, and the others to their ship.

I could run, she thought, but her legs seemed locked, too frightened to run. She couldn't muster the energy, and she resolved to let the slavers carry her to Bashevgo.

Then the strange thing happened. The Blade Kin and all the slaves around her fell to their knees and raised their hands as if clutching something. They breathed together, in unison, and though her heart thumped frantically, Vo-olai could not break away.

Vo-olai beheld a vision: She was in a great dark palace where sconces burned some bitter-smelling yellow powder, and an old Neanderthal stood before her in red robes. She knew his name, Atherkula, and the sorcerer was boasting of his power. He would become a Slave Lord, he said. The Neanderthals no longer needed the humans to keep them in chains. Vo-olai spat on his feet and cursed him, striking an ineffectual blow, knowing she might die for doing so. And the rage she felt at that moment, the unabashed hatred for this man, charged through her veins, making her want to leap up and strike out.

Lord Hamoth and Lady Tenebar had been preparing for a party across town in Denai. Hamoth had spent a happy afternoon in the market, purchasing slaves fresh from the Rough, and he was weary. He let his servants dress him for the party. He would be a cloud, dressed in orchid-colored silks decorated with diamonds and amethyst. His costumer had somehow come upon the most fascinating design for a hat: It was a glow ball, fiercely bright, and it would shine out over a silver brim, as if the sun were just rising above his cloud costume. He held a staff of golden lightning in one hand. Lady Tenebar, on the far side of the room, was dressed in a bird-of-paradise outfit, a charming blue.

They were admiring their outfits when the curious compulsion came upon them to fall to their knees, dropping to the floor. Their rage at Atherkula had barely subsided when a giant appeared: Their father, Jenks Genet, stood a dozen feet tall, with shoulders of iron, shouting and spitting, glaring with dark eyes. "Try to run from me, will you, you little shit! I'll chain you to the wall! Chain you to the wall!" and cold terror bound them in place so that their legs could not move, their tongues could not speak, as Jenks wrapped the cold cutting leg irons on them.

They fought the irons with clumsy, childish hands, bleeding, breaking their legs in the process. At a young age they had learned to fear cold iron.

Scandal the innkeeper from Smilodon Bay writhed on the floor of his lord's house. His belly was full from tasting the many delicacies he had baked during the day, and he'd been contemplating a plump young maid that he hoped to seduce that night. He had just poured icing on the tarts when the visions started. He had barely recuperated from the irons when he found himself in the White Mountains outside Denai.

He walked in the mountains, late summer in the summer night, and the dry forest burned with more than summer heat. In a little hut woven from twigs, sprawled naked on the ground, lay a Dryad—a woman formed by the Creators to maintain the forests. He knew this Dryad's name, Tirilee. At fifteen, her mating frenzy had come upon her. Scandal stroked her shimmering silver hair, and skin as white as aspen bark, mottled with dark spots. In the heat of the forest, Scandal tasted the aphrodisiac perfume of the Dryad's scent blowing upon him, tasted her burning lips. In the moonlight he gazed into the pools of her eyes where he felt sure that the color green had been perfected. His hot organ thrust into her groin, and the Dryad moaned, pulled him in tight. An orgasm burst from him, for she was better than every whore he'd ever dreamed of having. His heart nearly stopped in the frenzy of it. Yet his chest ached. He yearned for more, more, and knew that he could never get enough.

Mahkawn had leapt off the Death's Head Train outside Pirazha's house. He'd been stalking the crowded streets, blood on his dagger, sure that Atherkula's spies would find him, when the compulsion took him to kneel: And on the packed streets before him, ten thousand slaves and Blade Kin and Lords all fell to their knees in unison, reaching out as if to grasp something. Then the visions came, pounding like a flood, over and over.

He'd ejaculated into his pants and began weeping in terror of what the next moment would bring, when he found himself lying in the bottom of a boat with a Crimson Knight sitting astride his chest, using him for a chair. Beside him lay Fava, and he loved her more deeply than he'd ever allowed himself to love anyone else. He loved her more than Pirazha, and as he lay in the boat, he secretly relished the sensual touch of Fava's leg against his as she clasped his hand. The fulfillment, the communion in that single touch from the woman he saw as his other self, warmed him like the rays of the sun. It was not a frantic thing, not an endless longing. He felt only security. True loveliness.

Fava lay on the ground outside the Cage of Bones, the bodies of the Blade Kin sprawled around, overwhelmed by Tull's love for her, awed to think that anyone could desire her so fully, could relish her so completely. She closed her eyes, found that she knew how to send the lightning of her soul across space. She danced over the shadow of Tull's soul, wanting to know all of him.

Across the length and breadth of Craal and Bashevgo, every creature that could call itself human or Neanderthal or Hukm found itself trapped in the Cage of Bones, watching the Blade Kin slit Fava's arm as they prepared to add part of her to the cage.

They slammed their heads into the ground, as if against bars, wishing for death, and one of the Blade Kin lunged at them, bringing his spear within easy reach, providing the means.

Among the stars the Eridani had long forgotten their war with the humans, yet now they felt the alien mind of their enemies touching them, warping them. The billions cried out with one voice, hoping for destruction, and suddenly they were in a prison cell far below the arena at Bashevgo, and their friend Mahkawn stood with his sword, shoving it into their lungs so that they could not breathe. Blood poured down the runnels of the sword, staining the floor's yellow straw red, and the sword filled them with . . .

cold metal. an endless swelling. a feared, longed-for death. an endless swelling. peace swelling inside. an eternal river of light. love.

The island of the Creators thundered and groaned from within as the old volcanic cone blew away. The concussion from the explosion raised mountainous waves that swept over the bow of the boat. Smoke billowed up, a monolithic obsidian plume, blanketing the heavens with ash so that even five miles out to sea, darkness reigned. Lightning flashed at the mountain's crown, and Phylomon forced himself to watch, to take it all in. Rocks the size of a rabbits plummeted from the sky.

Overhead, the gray birds flew into that black wall of
ash, mindlessly obeying the summons they had heard
before the Creators died. The blood eaters floundered
on the beach, stunned by the ultrahigh frequencies of
the harmonic resonators. The worms on the mountain-
sides were crushed in slides, boiled by lava flows.

Phylomon watched, almost unaware of what was
happening, and he could not rise from his knees. Darrissea sat in the bow of the boat, wracking sobs tearing
from her throat, trying to cope with the visions, but as
the last vision ended, Phylomon sat peacefully, savoring
a life that had been far more satisfying than his own.

On the plains south of Bashevgo, Apple Breath rose
from a thin crust of snow. Hundreds of Hukm had wakened from their sleep and lay panting on the ground.
She stared, dazed, to the north, unable to fully comprehend what she had just seen, what she felt, but knew
that her love for and understanding of the Meat People
had deepened.

A warm south wind blew across the plains, thawing
the snow so that here and there, green clumps of sweet
grass rose from the ground. The smell of the rich soil
and sweet grasses made her mouth water, but Apple
Breath sat on her rump in the snow, the wind ruffling
her white fur, and pulled out her great wood flute from
its sack, then began playing a song that spoke of the
peace she felt within.

Tull released the world and the Eridani—let go the
lightning of their souls. He heard them lamenting, felt
their wounds, their strength. Thunatra Dream Woman
still danced in a circle, singing, but a storm seemed to
blow across the Land of Shapes. The wind hammered
the giant, snagging his shield of despair and *kutow* of
terror. Dust blew across the beast's broad back, as if
wind were carving a sand dune, blowing portions of the

creature away. Beneath the unrelenting wind the giant diminished, pared away until only a Pwi boy stood on the plains in the Land of Shapes, frightened, alone.

Tull still caressed the boy with one tendril of light. He looked into the child's green eyes, watched as light erupted from the shadow of the boy's soul. "Don't be afraid. We are brothers, you and I," Tull whispered to Terrazin. The two were connected, and Tull let his love, his peace, flow into the boy. "We are Pwi."

Across the Land of Shapes to the south, the arcane structures of the Blade Kin began to topple, and everywhere over the vast red plain the stones cracked and splintered as a new world of possibilities formed.

The earth shook until the very soil seemed to roar. Tull tried to open his physical eyes, but it was hard. His physical ears could hear a rumbling. The very earth seemed ready to crack open. Across Bashevgo, people screamed. Chaa had unlocked Fava's shackles, and she was rushing toward the cage. Tull felt a great sense of peace wash through him. He drifted upward, looked down at the clot of his soul, at the thin gel lying in the Cage of Bones, hand outstretched. Around the clot of his soul was a thin, shimmering golden haze. Tull watched it a moment, until he understood: a symbiote, struggling vainly to keep his body alive.

He drifted higher toward a sun that beckoned him, a great iridescent purple flower. The fiery spirits of birds shot through the sky as a flock of starlings passed beneath him. Gazing down, he saw the world roaring, the ground buckling as if it were a sea at storm. Sixty million people shouted in pain, trying to cope with the visions. Far below, Fava wept and pulled at the bars of Tull's cage. She grasped his hand, shouting, "Don't die! Don't die! Don't let yourself die!"

Yet Tull was already gone from his body as he considered the request. He looked down on the world of flesh. He'd touched them all, felt their lives, learned to love them. That was all he had come to this world for, and the clot of his soul had begun to turn opaque, the

same red hue as the stones around it. He did not want
to return. As the clot of his soul darkened, it reminded
Tull of a door to a house, closing, shutting off the light
that gleamed from the comfortable fireplace within. It
was a door that would bar him from ever entering again.

Fava was shouting for help, pulling on the chains to the
cage of bones, grasping Tull's hands, pleading with him
not to die. The visions had come to her so quickly, even
now she could not comprehend them all: Her ankles
seemed to ache from the night she/Tull had been sentenced to death in Craal and had been hung from her
feet and whipped. Her lips still burned from the aphrodisiac kisses of a Dryad. She still suffered the shock of
watching her brothers slain in the wilderness, eaten by
Mastodon Men. The joy of her wedding day. Fascination with clocks. The full emotional force of a lifetime
all crashed in a tumult around her, and she knew she
would be days, years recovering.

All across Bashevgo, people were crying out, trying
to cope with the visions, and down on the Street of
Dissidents, the spectators that had come to watch her
execution crawled about on their bellies, blindly. A massive black cloud rose to the north as one of the volcanoes blew, and the earth shook as if Bashevgo might
split apart. Fava could hear buildings toppling in the
city, and some of those who shouted might have been
dying. Fava could not manage better than to crawl to
Tull.

Chaa took the keys from a dead guard, and he
fought to stand upright as he began unlocking the cage.

Fava struggled through her tears to look at Tull's
face, at eyes the color of sun striking dying grass. He
stared up at the sun, blindly, with rivulets of blood still
running down his forehead. His face was pale, skin
bloodless, and he had stopped breathing. Yet beyond
that, Fava felt that he was gone. He had left.

She closed her eyes, panting. A spasm of grief

washed through her, and she did not know if the grief belonged to her or to Tull: Was she grieving for her dead brothers Ayuvah and Little Chaa? Fava's head and body ached, as if someone had pummeled her.

Chaa slipped the chains off the door to the Cage of Bones, threw the door open, and dragged Tull out.

Fava clutched Tull's waist and cried. Chaa said softly, "He is not in there," and pointed to the body. "He is up there!" He nodded up toward the sun. *"Pehethwa,* Fava. Call his name, Generous."

Fava gazed up at Chaa, and a powerful earthquake hit so hard that the hill of bones felt as if it were rolling. Fava had never practiced the women's magic, but she understood: "Summon him, Fava." Tull had made Spirit Walkers of them all. Fava knew how to connect.

And then she felt it in her womb: the first stirring, the first fluttering movements of her child. It was preparing to open, to accept a spirit. Fava heard a building collapse in the distance, and hundreds of people cried out in dismay. She did not turn to look. She closed her eyes, closed her ears, and stilled her breathing. She held Tull's cooling hand. The body was so far gone, she did not know if Tull could ever reenter it.

She sat on the swaying hill, and felt more than saw the Land of Shapes. She could feel Tull, in the distance, drawing away. She sent a single tendril from the lightning of her soul out to him, grasped a single tendril of his lightning, and drew it to her.

"Now you shall Spirit Walk my life," she whispered, and she made the lightning of his soul dance across the small black pit at her center. Tull was not a Pwi, could not feel as deeply as she did. There was more to life than he knew. She considered her wedding day, the lust she had felt in bed with him, the love that had carried her across a continent into the land of Slave Lords, and her spirit whispered to him, "This was meant to be only the beginning of my love for you. . . ."

Epilogue

Mahkawn felt nervous taking his trip down to Smilodon Bay alone the next summer. The serpents had become thick in the sea, and some in the north were larger than serpents of the past and did not willingly let men sail the oceans. Pirazha had warned him against it. Since the white snakes had died off, and the blood eaters had nearly all been captured, she wanted him to go by land, but Mahkawn argued for a trip by water.

"I'm not so afraid of the serpents," Mahkawn said. "I am afraid that the others in Smilodon Bay will not accept me."

Pirazha had smiled and clasped her arms around Mahkawn's thick neck. "We are all Pwi, are we not? You are family. Of course they will accept you!"

Mahkawn nodded, but in his heart he did not feel right. He had killed so many people in Smilodon Bay, and he could not imagine that the townspeople would forgive him. For others, some things seemed so easy: They could touch the peace at the center of themselves and cradle there. Yet it was not so for Mahkawn. Even having learned the Path of the Crushed Heart, he could not always reach that destination. Like many of the former Blade Kin, he now called himself a Pwi, but he did not feel he deserved to be called that by others.

Still, he sailed his small boat down to Smilodon Bay, and as he turned inland at Widow's Rock, in the

screams of gulls and the crashing waves of the breakers
Mahkawn could still hear the tumult of voices as they
had sounded that night, after a whole world took its
Spirit Walk and then tried to cope with the pain and
rage and passion and peace that had all been coiled in
one man.

Mahkawn sailed up the fjord through an avenue of
redwoods that stood tall on each side of the water, and
he felt small and insignificant among them. When he
came to town, it seemed minuscule in comparison to
Bashevgo. In the past year some had built a few rough
houses. Others lived in tents. The large dock was intact,
and a cooking fire rose from a large inn that was still
under construction on the top of the hill.

When his boat came into the harbor, dozens of
people came down to meet him. The thin Neanderthal
Vo-olai came with her husband Anorath and her three
children. Chaa and Zhopilla brought their daughters.
The innkeeper Theron Scandal came down himself and
tried to hawk a dinner and night's lodging. Mahkawn
thanked him and agreed.

Last of all, Phylomon the Starfarer came down
from the human part of town, pale and young, with a
long full beard and cascading hair. He walked with Darrissea, whose belly had swollen with child. Mahkawn
had not seen them in months—not since they had returned to Bashevgo after leveling the island of the Creators. Even then, Mahkawn had not met them formally,
for he had just been one spectator in the cheering
throng.

It was an odd, uncomfortable meeting. They all
knew each other through Tull's eyes, all recalled what
they had been before. In some ways Mahkawn believed
he was not much changed, and felt that he deserved
their scorn. Yet they treated him as a brother, hugging
him, welcoming him, but it was Chaa who said, "You did
not come to see us, did you?"

Then Mahkawn looked away to the hillside where

Tull's lonely house stood, apart from all others. Smoke rose from its fireplace. "No. I came to make what peace I could," he said. He got back into the boat, pulled out two bundles. They held some clothes, some tools, an old bottle of vanilla-water perfume, a brass globe, a sword made of Benbow glass—most of the things he had taken from that house more than a year before.

"Go on up," Chaa said. "You will be welcome."

Mahkawn carried the bundle up to the house. *You thought when you took him captive that someday you might give him back his life,* Mahkawn told himself, *but you will never get free from your debt.* He carried the gifts up through the old dirt road, alongside plots covered with weeds and ashes where houses had been. Yet most gardens had been planted, and the corn and sunflowers were tall and thriving.

Mahkawn called at the door, in the manner of the Pwi, "I am here. Is anyone in?"

Fava answered the door, and her eyes shone to see him as if he were a lost brother. "Come, friend, come!" she spoke in Pwi, and Mahkawn blushed to see her. He recalled what it had been like with her as Tull, sleeping between her legs, the hot passion of nights together, and he felt as if he were some type of voyeur. He could not help but look upon her and think of her as a sweet, capable, enchanting woman, a woman he would want to spend his life with. She was modestly dressed in buck-skins and a green tunic.

"I brought you these things," Mahkawn said.

Fava opened the bundles and looked at them, grew misty-eyed. "Come in," she urged, and Mahkawn entered, clumsy, out of place.

"Scandal invited me to stay at the inn tonight," Mahkawn said. "I look—" He spotted a baby on the floor in the corner, a boy with red hair and fierce blue eyes. The child was bouncing on its stomach. "Yours and Tull's?"

"Yes . . . ," Fava said.

Mahkawn tried to fill the silence. "I look forward to dinner at Scandal's. The kwea. I suppose I should get over there soon."

"Aren't you going to wait for Tull?" Fava asked. "He took Wayan hunting. They should be back soon."

"I . . . I would like to speak to him," Mahkawn answered. "If he is well."

"Please. You must stay, then. He's quite well."

Mahkawn sat and smiled nervously, and they chatted casually about the weather and the crops. Long after nightfall, Tull brought Wayan home. They had bagged only a pair of large grouse for their day of hunting.

Tull seemed genuinely pleased to see Mahkawn. The symbiote Chaa had taken from the worm had grown, covered Tull completely. He stood hairless and blue, not even a thin eyebrow. The pale blue of a robin's egg, as Phylomon had once been. *This is the man I hoped to civilize,* Mahkawn thought.

Tull treated him cordially, even kindly. After an hour talking of inconsequentials, Tull said, "I thank you for bringing our things, yet . . . Why are you really here?"

Mahkawn hung his head in embarrassment. "I am getting married to an old friend. Zhofwa, the goddess of love, has blown her kisses on us, and I hoped that you would . . . stand as witness—where my father would have stood if he were still alive."

For a long moment Tull did not speak, and Mahkawn worried. He suspected that Tull would not understand how important this was to him. He suspected that Tull would not know that even now it was hard for Mahkawn, a past Blade Kin, to give himself to a woman without embarrassment. If Tull had never taught him better, Mahkawn would have died without ever telling a woman that he loved her.

"I would be proud to come to your wedding," Tull said, and Fava hugged Mahkawn.

"Please," Mahkawn said, "I would not make you

come so far. I will bring the wedding here. And if you people don't mind, my wife and children and I would like to stay."

Tull nodded, and they talked long into the night, until both Wayan and the baby passed out asleep on the floor, and Thor rose in the autumn sky wearing its autumn colors of cinnamon and mauve.

Mahkawn rose, preparing to leave, but found himself hesitant, and realized that he hesitated because he felt a deep sadness. Something had changed. Something was lost. Indeed, a whole way of life had been lost. The Slave Lords were gone, and the Blade Kin disbanded. The earthquakes of the previous spring had touched off dozens of volcanoes all along the White Mountains, and many buildings in Bashevgo and Greenstone had fallen. It had taken most of the year for Mahkawn's men to hunt down the last of the blood eaters out in the wilderness. But all in all, people were coping. People could cope. Mahkawn looked at Fava, realized what they had lost.

"What will you two do, when Fava grows old?" He dared not ask the words, What will you do when she dies?

Fava shrugged shyly. "I do not begrudge Tull his symbiote. It is all that let him come back to me in the end. Without it . . ."

Tull wrapped his arm around Fava playfully. "I am not worried," he said, and he flipped up Fava's tunic, exposing her belly. A swathe of crimson flashed in the firelight.

Fava pushed his hand away. "A gift from a friend," she said, obviously shy. Mahkawn felt only happiness for them, no jealousy. He hugged them both, said his goodbyes.

Tull and Fava escorted Mahkawn to the door, and as they stepped out under the stars, they all raised their heads as one. *It is odd,* Mahkawn thought, *how much Tull's mannerisms have become part of us all.* So often now Mahkawn found that even in crowds he would watch people do that, mimic Tull's movements.

Yet they could not help but look up into the night sky, at the endless stars and the empty paths where the Red Drones had once barred their way to the heavens.

Okanjara, Mahkawn thought, *I am free.*

Glossary

Anee—A mineral-poor moon 11,000 miles in diameter that circles a gas giant named *Thor* near a type I star 1950 lightyears from Earth. In the year 2681, the Alliance of Nations began terraforming Anee in order to create a terrestrial zoo—a place where genetic paleontologists could store specimens of animals recreated from the Jurassic, Miocene, and Pliocene Eras. Each of three continents stores representatives from one of the Eras.

Creators—A race of highly intelligent beings, part machine and part biological organism, designed by genetic paleontologists to maintain the ecosystems of Anee. The Creators are living DNA synthesizers. To control animal populations, they frequently design and give birth to predators and parasites. The Creators are strictly programmed to perform their specific jobs. After the death of the Creator named Forester 1, the Creators designed *Dryads* to protect the forests.

Dire Wolves—*Canis Dirus*—A heavy-bodied dark gray wolf common during the Pleistocene, short on cunning but long on tenacity and viciousness.

Dragons—Warm-blooded flying carnivores created by the Starfarers to be an eco-barrier. Each continent has several varieties of dragon in various sizes—from the giant great-horned dragons to the tiny hawk dragon. Each dragon is born with a genetically transmitted memory that encourages it to destroy species that it recognizes as foreign to the environment.

Dryads—A being made by the Creators to maintain forests in Pliocene areas after the Creator Forester One was killed in an earthquake. Dryads are humanoid females with long life spans and strange abilities. The abilities, size, and coloration of the dryad depends upon the type of forest it was created to maintain.

Eco-barriers—Certain animals have the ability to migrate across oceans. For example, many types of semi-aquatic carnivorous dinosaur could easily make such journeys, and the introduction of such animals into an area populated by pleistocene sabertooths could be disastrous, since the sabertooths could not compete with the larger predators. The paleontologists who terraformed Anee recognized the danger such transoceanic migrations could cause. Therefore, they erected a series of "eco-barriers" to prevent migrations. These barriers consist of artificially engineered predators: primarily, the deep-ocean "sea serpent" to patrol the waterways; and various species of "dragon" to patrol the sky. Both the sea serpent and the dragon are ruthless predators without equal in nature.

Eridani—An alien race that went to war with humans in the year 2902. Using small FTL drone warships, the Eridani successfully stopped all extraplanetary travel within a matter of four years.

Hukm—*Homo-gigantis*. A race of large apelike humanoids with long brownish-red or white fur. The Hukm, one of several races of giant hominids once native to Earth, were originally restricted to a small region of Northeast Asia, and the species thrived only for a few thousand years. Fossil evidence indicates that the race probably died out about 396,000 B.C. Extinction appeared to occur due to climatic changes between glacial periods, and may have come about as a result of interspecies warfare accompanied by starvation. When reintroduced into the wild on Anee, the Hukm showed themselves to be highly social vegetarians who quickly domesticated the woolly mammoths.

Kwea—Emotional resonance. Often passionate feelings aroused by memories. Neanderthals have specific words that can refer to hundreds of different kinds of kwea, based upon the types and degrees of emotionality, but these are ignored in translation for simplicity's sake. For a Neanderthal, every object, every experience, every memory carries an emotional weight, a value of kwea. For example, a common knife may be considered sacred or of great value to one individual because of his associated kwea, while for another the same object would seem plain and unimportant.

Mastodon—On Anee, any of eleven species of pachyderm that inhabit woodlands and grasslands in every climatic region.

Mastodon Men—*Homo rex.* A race of carnivorous humanoids of low intelligence, averaging some 8.5 feet in height and weighing 500–600 pounds. Mastodon Man originally inhabited mountainous areas in Asia from 250,000–75,000 B.C. On Earth the Mastodon Man apparently did not compete well with smaller humanoids, but on the fecund world of Anee they quickly gained a strong foothold.

Neanderthal—*Homo neanderthalus* (see also *Pwi, Okanjara,* and *Thrall*). The Neanderthals are a distinct species, similar to modern humans in size and build. Neanderthals tend to be larger and stronger than humans, and have slightly shorter arms and a muscular build. The Neanderthal spine has less curvature, so Neanderthals stand straighter than humans do, and their large toe is curved inward, allowing them to run faster. The Neanderthal's chest cavity is larger than that of a human, and their arms rotate at a greater angle. Their skulls are thicker, hips slightly wider.

Neanderthals have sandy yellow to red hair and green, blue, or yellow-brown eyes. They have heavy supraorbital ridges that give their eyes a deep-set appearance. Their teeth and palate tend to protrude more than that of a human, yet they completely lack a chin.

The hands of a Neanderthal differ in structure from that of a human. The hands of a Neanderthal are larger and stronger than those of a human, with large robust knuckles. The human thumb is tilted at a forty-five degree angle to the fingers so that the tip of the thumb can touch the tip of each individual finger; however, a Neanderthal's thumb is not tilted at an angle to the fingers, and the Neanderthal is therefore far less dexterous than a human.

Differences in the Neanderthal palate, larynx, and sinus cavities do not allow them to vocalize most long vowels or semivowels used by humans. Instead, the Neanderthals shorten long vowels and tend to speak through their noses.

The cerebral cortex of the Neanderthal brain is slightly larger than that of a modern human, and they are fully the intellectual equals of humans. However, the Neanderthal hypothalamus, the area of the brain responsible for processing emotions, is three times as large as that of a human. For this reason Neanderthals tend to lead a very complex emotional life. Because of the way that the Neanderthal brain processes information, memories frequently carry very strong, emotionally-charged ties.

Because Neanderthals feel their emotions more powerfully than humans do, they feel a consuming need to express these emotions. Neanderthal dialects vary by region, but their languages have some similarities. Any noun or verb can be modified by various suffixes to express the Neanderthal's feelings about an object or action. The order of the suffixes always goes:

noun or *verb + emotional indicator + person + emotional degree indicator.*

For example instead of saying "the sky is gray," the Neanderthal might express his feelings about the subject: *szerzhoafava ah femma.* This sentence literally reads "Sky-love-I-generously is gray," and would be translated "The gray sky which I love completely." The first word in the sentence, *szerzhoafava,* is translated below:

	Emotional		**Degree**
Noun Base +	**Indicator**	**+ Person +**	**Indicator**
szer (sky)	zho (love)	a (I)	fava (completely)

The degree indicator is often a noun itself. For example, the word *fava* means "pear tree." On Anee, several varieties of wild pear bear fruit in late Autumn. Neanderthal legends often embellish this, telling of heroes starving in the wilderness who are saved by pear trees that magically blossom and ripen in mid-winter when the tree "sees" the hero coming. Because of this reputation for generosity, *fava* then becomes synonymous with *generous.* When used as an emotional indicator, *fava* means "given with all the heart."

Okanjara—The Free Ones. (Literally, "I am free!") Any Neanderthal who has escaped slavery after a long period of time.

Phylomon—The last living human who was not born on Anee. The last of the Starfarers. A man who, because he still benefits from the technology of the starfarers, has survived for over one thousand years.

Pirate Lords—When an interstellar war between mankind and the Eridani first stranded the genetic paleontologists on Anee, a political argument soon developed over how mankind should treat their creations—specifically the Neanderthals. Certain technicians believed that by conscripting Neanderthals for use as laborers, humans could be left free to build the plasma missiles they hoped could destroy the Eridani warships circling Anee. Others correctly believed the effort would be wasted. Those who favored enslaving the Neanderthal formed an independent colony upon the island of Bashevgo. After two centuries of building, the Lords finally attacked the Eridani drones. The Slave Lords and their colony were nearly decimated in a counterattack, yet the offspring of the Slave Lords of Bashevgo still survive both upon Bashevgo and in the nation of Craal, and the Slave Lords prey upon both the Neanderthal and their human cousins.

Pwi—Neanderthals who have never been enslaved by the Pirate Lords call themselves *Pwi*, the family. By the time that the first humans were forced to move to Anee, the original colony of Neanderthals had covered most of the Eastern half of the continent they called *Calla*, "Homeland," and Neanderthals numbered about two million. Pwi dialects and customs were diverging, and they were on the verge of splintering into several large tribes. But as the Neanderthals found themselves battling a common enemy, they regained a sense of common identity and called themselves only "family."

Red Drones—Orbital warships piloted by artificial intelligences sent by the Eridani to patrol the skies above Anee. Their neutron cannons destroy any mechanical vessel or organic being that climbs over four kilometers into the air. Originally, four warships were stationed over Anee, but two were destroyed by the Pirate Lords.

Sabertooth Lion—*Smilodon fatalis*. A large tawny lion with very long, serrated canines. The sabertooth live in prides in grassy and low, wet areas. Because of poor eyesight and teeth that are not adapted for small prey, the sabertooth primarily hunts large herd animals. Some of its favorite victims are the bison, giant sloth, the giant beaver (a semiaquatic water rat weighing up to 500 pounds), the mastodon, the hippo-like toxodonts, and the giant capybara. The sabertooth was such a successful predator, that when it overpopulated in 8000 B.C., over-predation coupled with climatic instability caused the extinction of over a hundred other species. With its food base destroyed, the sabertooth soon became extinct.

Scimitar Cat—*Homotherium*. A solitary but powerful lion with yellow and brown stripes. Because of its elongated front legs, it runs with a bouncing gait, much like a jackal. The scimitar cat inhabits mountainous areas and hunts large prey by pouncing from a tree or rock. A female scimitar cat will often kill a young mastodon weighing 600 pounds and then drag it two miles so she can feed her cubs.

Sea Serpents—Giant eellike carnivores created by the starfarers to keep animals from migrating across the ocean from one continent to another. Sea serpents can vary their color to conform to background, can grow to a length of 380 feet, and can attack prey in two ways: by swallowing the prey whole, or by strangulation. Thornlike protrusions on the serpent's armored scales tend to slice prey open when the serpent attacks by strangulation.

Young serpents are less than a meter in length when they hatch in the spring. They feed on fish for the first several months, and in their feeding frenzy drive great schools of fish up the rivers. Within six weeks the serpents grow to a length of sixteen feet and head for open waters and larger prey. At the end of their first year, serpents often measure over a hundred feet in length.

Slave Lords—Humans who enslave Neanderthals and other humans. Shortly after the Red Drones forced the human Starfarers into exile on Anee, some of the paleontologists began enslaving Neanderthals for use as miners, field hands, and domestic servants. The human Starfarers believed that if they could concentrate on developing weaponry to fight the Red Drones, they could escape Anee within a few centuries. But when their efforts failed, most of the Starfarers were killed, and much of their technology died with them. The few degenerate descendants of these Starfarers set up the nation of Craal, based upon a slave economy, and became known as the Slave Lords.

Starfarers—The genetic paleontologists and their crew who first began the work of terraforming Anee. By 2816 mankind had been engaged in genetically and mechanically upgrading himself for so long, that the starfarers were, in a sense, no longer human. The Starfarers had hairless bodies of various colors, depending upon the color of the symbiote they chose for their skin; had total recall of all they saw and heard; with mechanical aid could achieve virtual immortality; and the Starfarers had a genetically transmitted "dictionary" that gave all members of their race a knowledge of English and mathematics. When the Eridani destroyed the Starfarer's space station above Anee, the Starfarers lost the technology that would allow them to pass their extended life-span on to their descendants, but some of their genetic upgrades remained.

Tantos—A powerful Slave Lord who rules the island of Bashevgo.

Terrazin Dragontamer—A Neanderthal psychic who used his powers to overthrow the island of Bashevgo.

Thrall—Any Neanderthal or human who is held as a slave. Generally, it refers to anyone who has spent years in slavery. Over generations, the Thralls developed a moral code and a society far different from that of the Pwi. In general, the Pwi consider the Thralls to be untrustworthy and brutal. Many tales tell of Thralls who practice cannibalism or who have become so accustomed to slavery that they themselves engage in it. Thralls who eventually escape their captors call themselves *Okanjara,* the Free Ones.

About the Author

DAVE WOLVERTON was the grand prizewinner of the 1986 Writers of the Future contest sponsored by Bridge Publications. He has worked as a prison guard, missionary, business manager, editor, and technical writer. He is currently at work on his next novel, a *Star Wars*® adventure titled *The Courtship of Princess Leia*, which will be released for Christmas, 1993.

it comes to spinning a yarn that you don't ever want
p reading, there are few better spinners than [Sheri S.
er]."—*The Magazine of Fantasy and Science Fiction*

The Works of
Sheri S. Tepper

❑ **After Long Silence** (26944-5 * $4.95/$5.95 in Canada) "Tepper has a sure hand with romance and self-discovery. She also has the gift of detail, so that she imbues with grand immediacy her world of Jubal and its mountain-sized crystalline Presences."—*Analog*

❑ **The Gate to Women's Country** (28064-3 * $4.99/$5.99 in Canada) "Lively, thought-provoking...[Tepper] takes the mental risks that are the lifeblood of science fiction."—Ursula K. Le Guin, *Los Angeles Times*

❑ **Grass** (28565-3 * $5.99/$6.99 in Canada) "Tepper is a wise and subtle artist. She manages things in Grass with consummate skill that other writers are well-advised not to attempt."
—*The Washington Post Book World*

❑ **Raising the Stones** (41510-9 * $5.99/$6.99 in Canada) "Tepper effectively combines satire...inventive social engineering, strong main characters, and a plot that works on both internal and external levels in what may be her best novel to date."
—*Kirkus Reviews*

❑ **Beauty** (29527-6 * $5.99/$6.99 in Canada) Winner of the 1992 Locus Award. "Rich, multitudinous, witty, metaphysical, continually surprising, *Beauty* is a feast."—*Locus*

❑ **Sideshow** (08130-6 * $21.50/$26.50 in Canada) "An often astonishing work of bold imagination."—*Kirkus Reviews*

Available at your local bookstore or use this page to order.
Send to: Bantam Books, Dept. SF 173
 2451 S. Wolf Road
 Des Plaines, IL 60018
Please send me the items I have checked above. . I am enclosing
$_____ (please add $2.50 to cover postage and handling).
Send check or money order, no cash or C.O.D.'s, please.

Mr./Ms._____

Address_____

City/State_____Zip_____
Please allow four to six weeks for delivery.
Prices and availability subject to change without notice.   SF 173 12/92